I0662367

Marble Creek

Karen Charbonneau

A Ship's Cat Book

Post Falls, ID

shipscatbooks@jrcda.com

Also by Karen Charbonneau

The Wolf's Sun

A Devil Singing Small

Acknowledgment

The author's grateful thanks to:

My husband, Jay Fromkin, and to my friends Cheryl Fleming, Linda Hardy, Jennifer Jefferson, and Marilyn Elliott, who read and critiqued *Marble* Creek. Their thoughtful suggestions allowed me to view it with fresh eyes.

A Ship's Cat Book

Cover design by Donovan Jones

ISBN-10: 0692751114

1. World War I - Pacific Northwest - History - United States - Fiction. 2. Industrial Workers of the World - History - United States - Fiction. 3. Everett Massacre (1916) - History - United States - Fiction. 4. Spokane, Washington - History - United States - Fiction. 5. Butte, Montana - History - United States - Fiction. 6. Marble Creek, Idaho - Logging - History - United States - Fiction.

In memory of Bert and Marie Russell, of Harrison, Idaho. Their self-published oral histories of loggers and pioneers who knew the Marble Creek drainage inspired further research into its history, resulting in this story.

North Idaho and Marble Creek

INTRODUCTION

There were in 1910 in the United States some 10,400,000 unskilled male workers. Of these, some 3,500,000 moved, by discharge or quitting, so regularly from one work town to another that they could be called migratory labor. Because of this unstable migratory existence, the labor class lost the conventional relationship to women and child life, lost its voting franchise, lost its habit of common comfort or dignity, and gradually became consciously a social class with fewer legal or social rights than is conventionally ascribed to Americans. The cost of this experience was aggravated by the ability and habituation of this migratory class to read about and appreciate the higher social and economic life enjoyed by the American middle class.

Carleton Parker, The Casual Laborer and Other Essays

Chapter 1
Marble Creek, Idaho: 1904

Eleven men with troubled minds arrived at dusk in twos and threes in front of Elsie Kirk's empty cabin. Some had walked, some had ridden bareback on work horses. As each man ducked inside, he reflexively jerked off his hat, startled to find the Widow Blake sitting at a table behind a kerosene lamp, her hand wrapped around a single-action Winchester .38-55, butt down on the plank floor. Only Jake Murrell wasn't surprised, having stopped by her claim a few days back to tell her he'd called this meeting.

With each new arrival, bodies shifted inside the one-room cabin. Two homesteaders self-consciously sat on the absent woman's narrow bed. A voice from the doorway suggested they stack rifles in a corner to make more room, but those inside only pulled their weapons closer.

"Mrs. Blake, this doesn't concern you," Bob Smith said.

"'Course it concerns me, Mr. Smith. You're plannin' on stoppin' George Bouley and his pals from jumpin' more claims . . . includin' mine." Once addressed, she had plenty to say. "Since I can't stay on my land in winter, I don't want Bouley goin' to the land office in Coeur d'Alene, sayin' I've been gone more than three months and gettin' my claim cancelled. Bringin' in some lumber company hire to file squatter's rights on my land and slidin' it into the MacLean brothers' pockets." Her accusation drew assenting murmurs. "'Course that's who's behind this. The MacLeans want our timber." Her inflection bordered on the sorrowful, almost as though she personally knew them and was slightly ashamed. "'Course it concerns me. And the law won't do nothin' to help us."

Murrell was seeking consensus and the men's scowls pleased him. A homesteader hunkered in a corner growled, "Wallace is too far away . . . hard to get to."

"Hard to get from there to here," muttered a man perched on the edge of the bed, his rifle jammed between his knees. "Lousy place for a county seat."

The Widow Blake added to their disquiet. "And I can shoot as well as any of you."

Murrell spoke up. "We know there's no law south of Wallace . . . but there is justice. Our justice."

Voice worried, a man interrupted, "Vigilante justice . . . is that what you're saying, Jake?"

"We'll strike before we're struck down," Murrell replied. "Bouley goes after the weakest like a damn coyote . . . women whose husbands are down the Joe or across the lake trying to earn enough to feed their families. Like Mrs. Watson. Everyone knew she was living alone with her kids in the timber. I say George Bouley's jumped his last claim. Who agrees?"

Nate Harkins cleared his throat and spat into a rag produced from a shirt pocket. "I agree. He brags about jumpin' claims . . . heard him myself in a saloon at Ferrell. Carries two guns . . . acts tough."

"Before he hooked up with those MacLeans, he was puttin' up meadow hay at Bond's," said Esau Wright, "and he was a lazy son-of-a . . ." He stopped short, glanced with embarrassment at Mrs. Blake, lamely substituted the word "gun."

Murrell picked up an empty fruit jar. "We want this to end, and we have rifles. We're eleven men here. I aim to put ten white beans and one black bean into this jar. Black bean gets 'er done." The men grunted their assent and Murrell counted out the beans.

Dovey Blake said softly, "Put in eleven white beans, Mr. Murrell."

"All right, Mrs. Blake. You have the same risk as the rest of us. I guess you should share the responsibility."

Her chance of drawing the black bean was as low as anyone else's. With matters going his way, Murrell didn't want to start an argument with her . . . or over her. "Whoever draws the black bean, you'll know who you are. The rest of us don't need to know. I'm gonna douse this lantern . . . open the door there, Esau . . . and then I'll hold the jar up to the window so you can see it. As each of you takes a bean, just walk on out and go home. Keep it to yourself. The rest of us will, too. You all know where Bouley's squatting now . . . and you know what horse he rides and what tote trail he usually takes."

"What about Tyler?" someone asked. "He's just as guilty."

"We'll take care of him later."

Guided by Murrell's voice, repeating, "Here," one by one, each man stepped forward, his rifle butt knocking against floor or table leg, to pluck a bean from the wide-mouthed jar, walk out into the moonlight and return to his cabin.

When only Murrell and the Widow Blake remained, he tipped the jar toward her, saw the faint outline of her hand poking in. She scraped back her chair and stood, hoisting her Winchester as extra cartridges clicked in the pocket of her long wool sweater. The last bean in his hand, Murrell said, "Mrs. Blake, let me light my palouser and I'll see you back to your cabin."

"Thank you, Mr. Murrell, that would be appreciated."

Murrell thumbed a wooden match to light the candle stub in the empty lard can, a hole pried open near the bottom to allow enough dim light to see the trail ahead or to know when he left it. Enough light to see the bean in his hand, which he flicked into the bushes before closing the cabin door.

Dovey Blake lay in the brush above the tote trail she expected George Bouley to ride down, the Winchester loosely propped against a shoulder. Wrapped in a long brown wool coat, she made herself as comfortable as possible on moss and soft rotten wood. Across the trail below, a small pool had been scooped out of a trickling spring. Bouley would likely stop to water his horse, but if he didn't linger, it wouldn't matter. This was no different from hunting deer. You wait. You aim. You shoot. It was her second day subsisting on jugged water and ham biscuits. She ignored ants and beetles, even spiders crawling over and around her. The previous night she'd pulled off five wood ticks.

A prospector plodded down the trail, stopped to water his mule, then went on. A faint movement up the wooded slope behind her sent a painful thrill up her back. She twisted, swinging the rifle barrel toward the sound, but saw nothing. A deer, maybe, or a porcupine. The forest was alive with birds. It was too late in the summer for birdsong; they chattered among themselves, making ready to leave. She'd be leaving, too, in a few months, to spend the winter with Maud in Spokane.

When she grew sleepy she thought of Mrs. Watson. Poor thing didn't know how to use a rifle or a shotgun. What husband would leave his wife alone without showing her how to protect herself?

A horse trotting up the trail raised her on her elbows. She jacked the lever, chambering a cartridge. George Bouley rode into her sights and she forgot to breathe. Hands sweating, she wiped first one and then the other on her coat, keeping the rifle steady. Bouley dismounted beside the spring, his horse side-stepping to guzzle water. She sighted him pissing against a tree and squeezed the trigger. Her shot echoed among the trees and he slowly fell. She chambered another cartridge, but he wasn't pulling himself up; wasn't moving at all.

Blood hammering inside her head was replaced by thudding coming up behind. She swung the Winchester, but it was jerked from her hands.

"Easy!" Jake Murrell went down on one knee, dropped his rifle and raised hers. The horse had shied at the sound of the shot and was stepping on its reins. The Winchester cracked; the gelding threw up its head and toppled. Despite her ears ringing, Dovey heard its heavy thump and last explosive breath. The saddle creaked as it settled.

Murrell held out a hand for cartridges she dug from her coat pocket. Moving through the brush, uphill from Bouley's prone body, he rapidly fired three more shots into it.

When he returned, he said, "Come on, Mrs. Blake . . . I'll see you home."

Ignoring his outstretched hand, she pulled herself to her knees and stood. Bending to pick up her water jug, she retched until her stomach muscles hurt.

The next day Murrell rode up to her cabin and they made careful small talk while he sat astride his horse. "Nice root cellar you've put in." He nodded toward it.

Dovey stepped closer, shading her eyes against the sun. "Nate Bishop dug it out with his big Shire. Got tired of takin' the bag of potatoes to bed with me in the autumn so they wouldn't freeze." She looked away. "How'd you know I had the black bean?" All night she'd tossed and turned over it, using it to divert her thoughts from the Bible's pronouncements on murder.

Looping a leg over the saddle horn, Murrell considered Dovey Blake, her folded arms and haunted brown eyes. Maybe she was a woman with a past, but she kept herself respectable. Her youth was gone, a few graying hairs at her temples. He'd liked her before and the previous day had added high regard. He stuck an index finger inside his lower lip and dug out a wad of chew, flinging it well away from the widow.

"When it got down to just the two of us, Mrs. Blake, I could make out one white bean in the jar, and that's the one I drew." He was quiet and she was quiet. He knew what she was thinking, that they shared a deadly secret. He wouldn't mind if it brought them closer. The few times she'd let down her reserve he'd observed a sad sweetness. Added, "I would've gone there, anyway. I had to make sure . . . didn't matter who got that bean."

Then why in God's heaven didn't you just do it yourself?

* *

Leading a pack string of mules up from the St. Joe River to his fire lookout, Forest Guard Ted Ragsdale found the bodies of a man and his horse. He peered around the dark forest before dismounting to discover the man had been shot in the back at least four times. Recognizing the horse, he figured the man was Bouley, but squatted to make out the face without having to brush away large ants now calling it a meal. After unloading the mules at his fire lookout on Marble Mountain, Ragsdale rode to Ferrell and took a steamboat down the St. Joe River to St. Maries to telegraph the Shoshone County sheriff over the mountains in Wallace.

Deputy Sheriff Gene Elliott was sent to investigate the killing. He rode the Oregon–Washington Railroad from Wallace to its terminal at the sawmill town of Harrison on the eastern shore of Lake Coeur d'Alene; took passage on the steamboat *Idaho* up the lake, into the St. Joe River and up to Ferrell, which was as far as navigation would take him. The last stage of his journey was bareback astride a Forest Service mule, riding up a curving, tree-shadowed tote trail with Ragsdale.

The forest guard was especially whipped up about the horse being shot because it had been a fine animal. Standing well back, he said as much to Elliott, who bent over the corpse, gagging through a bandanna tied around his face while cutting a slug out of the bloated body. The sheriff had ordered him to obtain evidence if he determined death was due to murder rather than misadventure.

Waving off flies, they studied the slug, agreeing it came from a Winchester or a Marlin. Because of the sparse population, Forest Guard Ragsdale was also coroner for the area, so he performed a two-man inquest before they buried Bouley in a shallow grave near where he fell. He'd thoughtfully brought along two shovels. Having shared his theory of why Bouley was killed on the way up, he didn't repeat it. They transferred the dead horse's saddle to the pack mule before using their mounts to drag the horse over Bouley's grave to keep varmints from digging up and eating the deceased. It was too much trouble to bring the corpse out of the mountains. With Ragsdale as his guide, Elliott mounted up to begin his search for the killer. They knocked on a few homesteaders' doors, inviting themselves in to examine weapons hanging on walls or propped in corners.

Ragsdale pointed out the Widow Blake's cabin as they rode past. He escorted Elliott down the tote trail to Ferrell, where the deputy spent the night at its hotel, liking it well-enough, but for the bedbugs, which gave off a musty odor. The next day, scratching bites, he reboarded the steamboat *Idaho*, cruised down the Joe and Lake Coeur d'Alene to Harrison, where he boarded the train back to Wallace to write his report.

Later, someone – maybe the forest guard - carved Bouley's name on a nearby tree. Through the months, and then the years, a dead dog was added to the tale and the number of bullet holes in Bouley's body multiplied. Twenty-five bullets brought him down. Shortly after Bouley was killed, the other claim jumper, Tyler, disappeared. Nearly a year later, a packer found parts of his skeleton a short way off the tote trail, a half-mile from where Bouley was killed. Tyler had family in St. Maries, so his remains were packed out. They didn't weigh much by then, anyway.

* *

The Chicago, Milwaukee and St. Paul Railway was the last of the great railroads to build a transcontinental route to the Pacific. In January 1906 it publicized its intent to cross from Montana into Idaho through the Bitterroot Mountains and along the St. Joe River to St. Maries, then on into Washington State to the coast. Certain interests had known of the chosen route since 1904, when the plan was held close and confidential. When William Ferrell demanded $100,000.00 for railroad rights through his self-named town, the railroad simply bridged the St. Joe a short distance upriver and established a depot directly across from Ferrell, naming it St. Joe City. Most Ferrell residents moved across the river. The Milwaukee began service across the Bitterroots into Idaho in 1909.

The devastating 1910 forest fires destroyed much of the virgin white pine timber in the Idaho Panhandle. One fire swept down the St. Joe River Valley, but bypassed much of the Marble Creek drainage to the south. After salvaging as much burnt timber as they could along the St. Joe drainage, nearly to the Montana line and to the north, the lumber barons turned covetous eyes toward the 80,000 acres of the mostly untouched Marble, vying with one another for logging supremacy there. Some homesteaders sold out to the lumber interests; it was what they'd always intended to do, just wanting to do it in their own time. Others simply sat on what they had, damned if they were going to sell. Dovey Blake was one of these.

Chapter 2
Seattle: Twelve Years Later - October, 1916

Until tonight Robert jamieson had never been shot. Shot at, but never hit. *Run! Get away from the docks! Fuckin' rain . . . fuckin' steep hill. Can they see me?*

He was crouched over a dying Billy Sewell when the bullet smacked into his shoulder. His revolver dropped from a numb hand and he ran like a creased deer. *Fuckin' odds got Billy. Not me.* Rain pelted his face and he snorted wet air, stifling groans that would alert his pursuers.

The jolt of energy that got him away was ebbing. Blood ran into the gloved hand cradling his useless arm as each muffled step failed to raise Seattle's lights above warehouse ridgelines.

Intermittent shouts passed between the shooter and another man. He hadn't shaken them. If he could control his sobbing breath, he might have a chance, but night tarred wood and brick structures squatting one above the other, and every sluggish footfall seemed to drag along a paving brick. He wanted to drop and curl up like a dying dog. *Won't make it to the lights. Gotta find a hole!*

Sensing an open space, he lurched into it - a fuel yard set back from the street. Thrusting his left arm toward the dim wall of a shed, he slammed into something soft . . . someone. They had him!

A woman's gasp, the scent of cheap perfume and exhaled booze. *She'll scream. They'll hear.* Pinning her against the shed with his chest and thigh, Jamieson slapped his bloody gloved hand over her mouth and nose. She struggled, taller and stronger than he could easily handle. He grunted, "Not gonna hurt ya." *Streetwalker? Whore?* He knew whores. "Quiet! They shot me." He pressed his fingers harder against her face. "You scream an' they'll find me."

A sharp pain pierced his thigh and she shoved him away. His wounded shoulder hit the shed and he fell with a groan.

* *

Addie MacLean was lost. Dark alleyways had lured her into a maze of warehouses beyond the ferry docks. Now she turned up a brick-paved street, confident the steep climb would lead her away from the smell of decaying fish and water-slapped wharves, toward city center and the streetcar to her boarding house. Ships' lanterns glimmered out on Puget Sound before another band of rain swept in. A gunshot came from below, near the docks.

Hugging the safety of a brick building, Addie waited. There was a second shot and her heart pounded. Moments passed and then a third shot. Far below a man called out, "This way!" Even closer, uneven padding headed uphill toward her. Wet dancing pumps threatened to leave her barefoot as, grabbing at brickwork, she fled up the incline. Reaching the corner of a building, she turned into an open lot where mud oozed over her ankles. The faint outline of a storage shed drew her until she touched rough wood and smelled sulfur. Coal. Behind her someone squished through mud into the yard. Just before the man careened into her, Addie plucked a hat pin from her tam.

His body crushed her against the wall, a gloved hand gripping her face. Paralyzed with fear, she understood nothing he grunted. When she smelled blood on him, instinct sparked her into action, and she stabbed the hat pin into his leg, while shoving him with all her strength.

He grunted and collapsed in the mud. Hissed, "Get outta here! They'll kill us both!"

Kill? She wanted to rush into the street to escape, but it was too late. A flashlight's halo bobbed into view, sweeping side to side. His earlier words now echoed with meaning. He'd been shot. *They'll find him. They'll kill him. Kill us.* She hesitated, wiped a gloved hand down her dripping face, but then sucked back through the mud and into the street.

"Oh, thank God!" Two dark figures spotlighted her against the brick wall. "I'm so turned around! Do I go uphill to catch the streetcar for Capitol Hill. Or across?"

"What the hell?" Hat brim shadowing his face, a man advanced, breathing heavily. One hand aimed the flashlight, the other a gun.

They'll shoot me! She cowered and twisted away, instinctively covering her breasts with one arm, her face with the other. "Don't shoot me! I just want directions!"

The flashlight dimmed and flickered and the man thumped it against his leg; raised enough beam to outline her again. Keeping his distance, he demanded, "You see a man come through here?"

She pointed past them downhill. "Down there. A man ran down there."

The other asked in an Irish accent, "Which way now ye say?"

The first man spat and growled, "You couldn't see anyone from here."

Breathless, she replied in bursts. "No. Not here. There. I was down there." Her chest thudded. "I was coming uphill. He ran in front of me. Going that way." She waved her arm to the left. *Show I trust them.* "Why are you looking for him . . . officer?" *Blessed Mother, don't let them hurt me.*

"Never ya mind. Just turn around and head uphill."

The second man's voice carried on the wet air. "Sure he's gotten away." He turned around and a few steps later had become a lighted circle bobbing downhill. The first man thumped his fading light again before following.

Cold sweat trickled down Addie's back beneath her corset. She wanted to continue uphill and not return to the wounded man, but she couldn't leave without trying to help him. Acting against instinct, she turned back into the fuel yard. Seeing only the faint white of the shed, she stopped a few feet away and asked in a tremulous whisper, "Are you still here?"

From where he was propped against the doors near the ground, he answered, "Uh-huh."

Wary, she bent only close enough to hear.

In low gasps he told her what he wanted. Asked huskily, "Remember the exchange?"

She repeated the number. "First hotel I find, I telephone. When a man answers, I say, 'Mac needs you.' I tell him where

I am. He comes and then I bring him here. I'll call the police, too."

"No police. Not yet."

Addie hurried uphill, disintegrating shoes splaying her feet. She repeated the exchange with the plea - *Don't die . . . don't die*. A stitch burned in her side as she burst into a mariners' flophouse, the Avon, waking the night clerk. She gasped, "Emergency! Must use your telephone!"

The old salt blinked. The woman wore a cheap coat and knitted tam of a factory or shop girl; wet to the skin, too, with torn and muddy shoes. She'd gotten herself into some trouble. "I gotta place the call. What's the exchange?"

In a shaking voice Addie said the numbers and the old man repeated them to a faceless operator. His hand curled around the candlestick mouthpiece but, in her urgency, she slid gloved fingers around it, dragging it toward her. Reaching for the black horn he held against his ear, she gave him little choice but to release it. "Ah, take it." He leaned folded arms on the hotel desk to listen.

Five repetitive buzzes. On the sixth a sleepy male voice answered, "Pinkerton National Detective Agency. What can I do for you?"

Pinkerton? She took a deep breath. "I have a message. I'm to say Mac needs you. He's been shot."

"Shot?" The voice was instantly alert.

"Yes."

"Is he dying?"

"I don't know. Badly hurt." Now the rest. "He said you're to come and get me and I'll take you to him. I'm at the Avon Hotel."

"And Billy?"

"Who?"

"Never mind. I'm on my way. The Avon?"

"Yes."

The line clicked and, limp with relief, she dropped the receiver into its cradle and stepped sideways to collapse into the nearest armchair. Someone else would be responsible for that man now. A Pinkerton agent? Not the first one she'd encountered recently. Her gloved hands trembled and she felt a stab of pain in a muddy foot. Blood was seeping through the toe of her pump. *When did that happen?*

The Maxwell touring car jolted into the fuel yard, headlights directed at the shed. The wounded man wasn't there. The driver, Agent-in-Charge Philip Ahern, climbed out and pointed his flashlight down a cinder path along one side of the shed, then down the other side. He gingerly stepped through mud to the double doors. The windshield fogged up and Addie rolled down her window to watch Ahern pry open a door.

"It's Phil. You in there, Mac?" There was a muffled response to which Ahern quipped, "I'm going to get my duds filthy, digging you out of there."

Addie drew in her head, relieved Mac was still alive, then stuck it out again, wanting to hear more.

"Got you in the back? Son-of-a-bitch!" He was quiet, listening, then, "They got Billy? Oh, my Lord! Damn them to hell!" He came to her open window. "Lady, I'm going to need help getting him out and into the auto. He's hurt bad."

Ahern shrugged off his overcoat before returning to paw at the coal into which Mac had buried himself. He pulled him through the doorway and Addie helped drag the groaning man to the Maxwell, where Ahern maneuvered him onto the back seat.

"Sure glad you've got some heft to you, lady."

Addie crawled in beside Mac. Ahern knelt on the running board and passed the flashlight to her. She ran the beam over a face and neck smeared with coal dust. He shut his eyes against the light and she lowered it to his chest where a mess of blood and coal dust muddied his dark coat.

Ahern produced a flask and held it to Mac's mouth. He swallowed, coughed and groaned. The agent offered Addie the flask, but she waved it off; he took a long pull before he opened Mac's coat and unbuckled his empty shoulder holster. Carefully unbuttoning his shirt, he pulled it and the undershirt off the wounded shoulder. Addie played the light on the oozing wound. Mac grimaced, his bared teeth contrasting with his blackened face.

"Went straight through, back to front." Ahern pressed the wadded dishtowel he'd used to wipe coal dust from his gloves against the bloody hole. "A little blood sure goes a long way."

"Shut-up, Phil," Mac whispered, pressing fingers and then his hand against the dressing.

"He'll be all right, miss. Sounds like his old self. And you're going to pay to have my auto cleaned, pal, if the agency won't." Ahern buttoned the coat over Mac's shoulder, then climbed in front. Grinding gears, he backed out and turned the car uphill.

Mac slumped against the seat, breathing heavily. Addie worked off the blood-soaked glove and held his sticky left hand. When they reached the lights of Seattle, he whispered, "Tell Phil to take you home first."

"I can get out in town and take the streetcar."

They rolled under a street light. "Not the way you look." He removed his hand to search a pocket inside his coat. "My cousin Maud runs a house. Treats her girls well." He put a card into her hand, the effort costing him a groan. "In case you want to change towns." A few shaky breaths later, he said, "You saved my skin. Thank you. I can help you get off the street." Mumbled, "Always carry her card. If I don't make it, someone will let her know."

Wet and cold, too tired to care that Mac thought she was a whore, Addie gave Ahern her address. She needed sleep and time to sort this out.

Ahern banged on Doc Hayes' door until the aging man came out to help walk Jamieson into his surgery.

Before the morphine took effect, Jamieson told Ahern where to find Sewell's body. Later, when he emerged from a drugged sleep, Ahern was dozing beside his cot. He moved, then groaned, waking his chief, who made him relive his partner's death.

Tongue furry, he slurred, "Lung shot. Lotta blood. Gurglin'. S'all."

"Fuck the bad luck. I goddamn loved Billy Sewell." Ahern scratched his neck and blinked. He unwrapped a piece of chewing gum. "How did those cargo thieves get wise? You two were good at stakeouts. Where did you slip up?"

Drug-hazed, Jamieson mumbled, "Gotta think about it. They knew where we were. Cargo thieves come in packs, so why just two?" Ahern leaned closer, breathing licorice. Jamieson couldn't get beyond those first morphine-thickened thoughts. "Yeah, we should 'ave heard 'em. Must've worn felt soles or gummed shoes." Lay silent. Then, "Gonna sleep now, Phil. Thanks for gettin' me out."

Jamieson came to consciousness with a grief morphine no longer dulled. He'd always looked up to Sewell. The older agent understood that Jamieson's calm and self-control were hard-won. "You won't go through life being lucky, Agent Jamieson," he'd offered years earlier. "Right now, you think the lady is with you, but you're gonna make mistakes. That's a given. Just don't make 'em on the job. Might get yourself killed."

Chapter 3
Seattle, 1916

Monday morning Addie MacLean limped into the casket factory, turned in her time and drew her pay for a week's work. On the train back to Spokane she put her notes in order. Her newspaper series on the hardships of "girls adrift" would expose the abuses of factory owners, who refused to enforce the state's new eight-hour day for women, coercing them to work ten-to-twelve hour shifts before allowing them to leave. Conducting her investigation in the "Queen City" of Seattle only six months after her husband's death posed little risk of scandalizing society matrons back home in Spokane. They wouldn't meet her on the streets of Seattle, note her shabby attire and ask questions.

Needing spice for her articles, she tagged along to observe the factory girls' night out. She should have waited at the dance hall for them, but with Washington State dry nearly a year, a bootlegged bottle of whiskey kept them flirting and dancing with sailors past midnight. She sipped from the bottle, too, and danced the one-step to ragtime with a sailor whose boozy breath caressed her neck.

After passing the sailor on to a girl with glazed eyes and a loose smile, she left. Out in the seedy street men loitered in front of "drug stores," "tobacco shops," and "ice-cream parlors," whose signs saloon keepers had nailed over their doors before reopening. Women called down from open windows, sucked their thumbs and gestured obscenely to potential customers. To avoid walking through a knot of men blocking the boardwalk, Addie angled down a narrow street, intending to turn uptown at the first opportunity. Street lights petered out and rain fell. Pavers became gravel and then mud. Her tam gave little protection and rain dribbled down her face and neck into her shabby coat as she groped her way. Muddied dancing pumps skidded. Jerome had been a protective husband during their short marriage and would have been aghast at her being out alone.

She reached a "proper" street. Uphill promised lights, pedestrian traffic and streetcars. It was a steep climb, but brick-paved. She paused to catch her breath and heard the first shot.

Arriving in Spokane, Addie settled into her large house in Browne's Addition. Now she would buckle down on her series for the *Spokesman-Review*.

*   *

Jamieson took a streetcar near to the address of the woman who saved his life, a boarding house for working girls, but not the type he expected. He hadn't asked her name. Whores never give real names, anyway. He pulled the bell and when the slatternly matron appeared, described her, though not well.

"If you mean Adele Matthews, she skedaddled. Didn't like any job she got for very long. Nice enough, though. Didn't ask for a refund for the rest of the month's rent."

Jamieson didn't cover his disappointment. "Do you know where she went?"

"Over to Spokane, I guess."

Spokane. Maybe she'd use Cousin Maud's card after all. Then the woman volunteered that Adele was from Spokane. "She said she missed her dog."

Chapter 4
Seattle: Late October, 1916

On Jamieson's first day back at the agency, the motherly receptionist clucked at his arm cradled in its sling before she handed him an official-looking envelope. If she steamed it open to read its contents, she did a damn fine job. Tears welled behind her spectacles. "We'll all miss Billy."

"Yes, Miss Turner, we sure will." He walked heavily down the hall into the off-duty agents' office, relieved to be its only occupant.

He read the letter. Was now the time to leave the agency? What would Billy have said? A pair of well-matched scent hounds, for seven years their paths had crossed, re-crossed, and then run together after Sewell got himself transferred from Denver to the Seattle office. Using his seniority, he requested Jamieson for big jobs. They'd rendezvous in a dingy hotel room, the Texan lying back with boots on the counterpane, rolling a cigarette, revealing their orders with, "Just want ya to know I asked for your assist because ya have the right notion on how to do justice to this operation." What he meant was Jamieson had learned his ways.

The letter contained a response to his query about a commission in the United States Army, which had doubled in size after the passage of the National Defense Act of 1916. America would be pulled into the quicksand of war and he'd wanted in on the action. Then he was shot. Rearranging his sling, he leaned back. He was twenty-nine, at the height of his manhood, but couldn't keep his damn eyes open. Tired, weak, unfocused. A memory floated behind closed eyes.

*   *

The Northern Pacific RR Line: July, 1913

In the lighted Fargo freight yard silent men lay under stationary boxcars parallel to the targeted car. Steel wheels squealed as the line of freights began to move. The locomotive's smoke and steam drifted back, fogging the air between hobos and yard bulls farther up the track. There was an eruption of clanging pots and pans swinging from bindles and boots scrabbling on cinders as men converged on the open boxcar.

Jamieson timed his assault on the accelerating car, waiting until a few men crawled safely aboard. A few long strides and he was alongside, tossing in his pack. A man braced in the open doorway reached down, grabbed his outstretched arm and yanked him in. His holstered revolver bruising his ribs, he rolled across uneven flooring and slammed into a bum reeking of bad juice, old shit, and sweat a hundred campfires hadn't smoked away. Those who made it aboard pawed about in the dark for their packs, cursing and rattling utensils. Once they were underway, a hobo slid the door shut. Squatting to absorb the jolt of poorly lubricated wheels, men lighted smokes, but Jamieson hunkered in a corner, waiting. Two miles beyond Fargo the train made a full stop.

The slider rumbled open and a brakeman appeared, one hand holding a lantern, the other brandishing a revolver. Men scooted deeper into corners, cupping cigarettes and cigar stubs, heads flung back against boards.

"Don't make me come in there, boys." He swung a directional lantern, searching the interior, counting bodies. "That'll be a silver dollar from each of you bums or you can hike back to town." Pleadings of "broke" and "down on my luck" agitated the brakey's gun arm. "Everybody out! Get your fuckin' carcasses in line out here!"

Dragging clattering gear they feared losing, men rolled out and lined up. A few tried to diminish themselves behind others.

Wanting a clear view, Jamieson positioned himself center front, pack at his feet. His operation was to observe railroad employees "coining" the ragtag army of men riding the rails. The brakey pocketed his gun and, holding his free hand palm up, moved from man to man, aiming the lantern's beam on one grizzled face after another. Jamieson had only to note the railroad district, location, time and engine number. The NP would identify the brakeman and engineer.

Those the brakey couldn't shake down for a dollar were ordered to produce a pocket knife, even a keepsake. "Empty your pockets."

A youth next to Jamieson groaned, "What am I gonna do?"

Producing two silver dollars, Jamieson offered him a pale disc. "Here's a dollar, bud." His eyes remained on the brakeman.

"I can't take your money, mister." But the lantern approached and he seized the coin. "Pay ya back when I get work. Honest. If I can find ya."

Jamieson muttered, "I'll give you an address. Send it when you can." He wasn't about to reveal where he headquartered and risk a visit.

Men with empty pockets trudged back toward Fargo, a bitten-off prairie moon lighting the tracks. After herding the rest back into the boxcar, the brakey called out, "You boys are good 'til the end of my run. See you at the district line."

Having waited to be pulled in last, Jamieson watched from the open door as the brakeman raised and lowered his lantern, signaling the engineer. He stepped back as the brakey shoved the slider closed and rasped an iron bolt into place, locking them in.

Jamieson hated being locked in. He'd have no chance in hell if the train wrecked and bodies and bindles hurtled into him. *Fuck it.* At least the stinking bum had hoofed it back to Fargo. Pillowing his pack, he hoped the clicking wheels would lull him into sleep, like the two ivory meditation balls Chinamen carried, rotating them. Click. Click. Click. Like the two pleasure balls on a silken cord a Chinese prostitute in Seattle showed him, thrusting them up inside her, squatting on the floor and rocking back and forth.

A voice broke into his reverie. "We won't get shook down when summer wears on." The man was explaining the mysteries of the railroad to the kid. "That's when we head out to the Dakota harvests. They let us get there, all right. It's getting back that's hard. They know we've got dough after the harvest. Always send your dough by registered letter to your folks, kid, before heading home or, sure 'nough, it'll get lifted." This must be the kid's first trip west.

"I don't have folks."

"Wa'll there ya go," another voice piped out of the dark. "Join the One Big Union, kid, so you'll have a place to send it.

They'll take care of it 'till ya git there. I use I.W.W. headquarters in Minneapolis myself."

The routine never changed. The hobo struck a wooden match. "Alright, fellow workers, let me see your little red cards."

Jamieson and others pulled out cards showing they were dues-paying members of the Industrial Workers of the World, every one of them a Wobbly. When a few men, including the kid, couldn't produce a card, the hobo grumbled, "Looks like I got some educatin' to do. You new fellas listen up. The Preamble of the I.W.W. Constitution says the working class and the employing class have nothing in common . . ."

As the train pounded through the night, Jamieson fell into a fitful sleep amid talk about class warfare, low wages and onerous working conditions in the harvest fields, mines and logging camps. Eleven stops between Fargo and where the trainman would release them. Cars being shunted onto side tracks in freight yards awakened them; some men shifted uneasily as yardmen's voices passed outside the locked boxcar. Two sharp whistles, couplings pulling taut down the line, and they were underway again. Seven hours imprisoned with men he couldn't see, other than behind an occasional flared match.

Except for being locked in, he didn't mind tramp work, though sometimes only tolerated it, agreeing with a poetical hobo who called riding the rails the "cruel and lonely distance of America." It beat being at regional headquarters in Seattle, each morning having to greet the large photograph of a short Allen Pinkerton standing beside President Lincoln in a stovepipe hat on a visit to some battlefield.

Tramp work. He learned right away the difference between a tramp and a hobo. Often a con man and thief, the tramp believed the world owed him a living. The hobo believed the world owed him an opportunity and most riders were hobos searching for work. This operation of keeping book on dishonest trainmen along the main line and spurs of the Northern Pacific had been underway for two months. It originated, not with railroad big shots wanting to keep employees honest, but with wheat farmers on NP spurs in Minnesota, the Dakotas and Montana, in need of harvest workers, worried that shakedowns were spooking potential hands, heading them elsewhere for seasonal work.

Arrested twice for vagrancy in small towns, Jamieson had fished out the billfold hanging inside his pants and paid the fines, avoiding thirty days at hard labor. He learned which towns were hostile to hobos and which were indifferent; met some men he sort of liked and a few he wouldn't turn his back on. Had seen a man lose both legs trying to hop a fast-moving freight. Later, he met a "halfy" who lost his legs jumping a train, but still rode the rails, living off begging and fellow hobos. He saw superb wilderness rattling through the Bitterroots into north Idaho. Almost froze when a brakeman tossed him off near Sandpoint one night.

A fellow had to be tough inside and out, as Billy Sewell said. While waiting for a rattler, you couldn't long for velvet seats on passenger trains whistling past. A Pullman car with a bed compartment? Don't even think about it. Like fellow hobos, he wore a union suit under two shirts, two vests, a coat and two pairs of trousers for warmth. When the opportunity arose, he bought a new union suit and threw the smelly one away.

The NP line was too large for one agent to work this operation. Pinkertons from other regions were traveling its rails, unrecognized by one another. It was a hardened man's job. He thought of himself as an experienced detective, adept at handling trouble. Figured he could smell danger in his sleep. A loner now, the easy-going prankster days of college at Michigan were dim memories.

No wife, no sweetheart. There was a whore in Butte at the Irish World, whose company he liked when he passed through, paying twice as much to stay in her bed longer than allowed. She made him laugh with rude stories, salty enough for him to buy her another drink, paying whiskey prices for her colored water. *Here's to the girl with the pretty red shoes. She smokes your cigarettes and drinks your booze. She ain't got no cherry, but that's no sin. 'Cause she's still got the box that the cherry come in.*

She was too good for hard rock miners and dismal Butte, so he gave her Cousin Maud's card. That little redhead was gone next time he came through.

Mostly he studied hobos riding the rails, especially Wobblies, evangelizing idealists believing in every twist of their guts they could change the way men toiled while others reaped. They expected one day to even it out or to get even, and create a workmen's paradise. Incredulous fools wearing blinders.

Sewell had advised him, "You can endure privation and dirt and accustom yourself to the society of Wobblies and hobos. But, Agent Jamieson, you go as a visitor. You don't become one. And don't start lovin' their philosophy of life."

Early next morning the locomotive blew its shrill calliope whistle and slowed for the division stop. The brakeman rumbled open the door. "All out." Heavy-eyed and stiff with cold, they headed toward town in search of food. In the evening they'd trail back to hook up with another freight.

The kid spun around. "Where are we?"

"Mandan," a scrawny man answered. "We was on a slow freight. Still in North Dakota."

Jamieson considered lying over at a cheap hotel to write his report and mail it in, but the kid tagged along, forcing him to stay in character. A Pinkerton let down his guard for no man, woman or kid. It would be easier to buy breakfast for the two of them than to look for a back-door handout.

A second cup of coffee woke up his cold insides. "Call me Mac," he replied when the kid asked his name. He toyed with a plate of flapjacks, pouring on more syrup. "What do they call you?"

"Harvey Johanson." He stuck a strip of bacon in his mouth and offered a greasy hand, larger than expected.

The kid was fourteen, maybe fifteen, pale-eyed, a few blond hairs on his chin. Close to Jamieson's six feet, he was a string-bean with promise if he got enough to eat.

"What's your travelin' moniker?"

"This is my first time."

"And you're goin' it alone?" Kids and railroad fever, wild to see the world on their own hook.

"It was me and Tom. We was sleepin' on top of a freight the first night and when I woke up, he was gone. Went home, I guess."

Likely rolled off in his sleep. Too bad.

"So where're you from?"

He hissed it out like he'd just jumped ship from the old country. "Minnesota." Grinned. A family joke.

Jamieson grinned back. "Minnesota Harv then. Gotta have a moniker."

"Damn right." Stuffed toast into his mouth.

Jamieson pushed his second slice across the table. Harv nodded his thanks, folded it, and shoved it into a pocket. Picked up the wrapped canvas he carried.

"You plan on fishing your way west, Harv?"

"Yah. Someday I'm gonna learn to fly fish. Read about it in a magazine. Guess I'm cheatin' with grasshoppers and worms. Ain't sportin', but I'm too hungry to care right now."

"Important not to starve out here. Being sporting to fish can wait 'til you're a rich man." Another grin from Harv made him feel good. They left the café smiling.

Jamieson bought coffee, bread and sausages to top off his pack. "We'll bedroll on the banks of the Missouri and wait for night. Show you some jungle life." They slept under willows on the river bank near other hobos.

Evening came on and men rose to make a couple of runt fires in a well-established camp run by a jungle cook, who provided all the cooking and eating gear. A man supping there was expected to contribute to the mulligan or explain why he couldn't. Jamieson pulled out ground coffee and part of the string of sausages. As hobos drifted in, limp onions and carrots and a freshly-killed and plucked chicken were tossed into a large pot over a fire. Harv went to try his luck at the river.

Jamieson was passing time with a few recognized faces when a familiar voice called out, "Hey there, Mac!" He started, but caught himself as the new arrival in a tattered coat ambled over. "Didn't I see you last week in Montana, headin' west?"

What name was Billy Sewell using nowadays? "Abilene Ed, you ol' coot. Went back to Minnie for a few days. Didn't get very far west yourself."

"Got myself jugged."

Heads shot up, men asking in unison, "Where was that?"

Sewell pushed back a battered hat, stroked long gray mustaches. "Wasn't for vagrancy." Waved a horny hand. "Got into a fight, so it don't much matter where it was."

Jamieson egged, "Tell us, anyway."

"Nope. Not the town's fault." Cast a glittery eye at Jamieson while pulling tobacco from his bindle and passing it out with that "Billy-be-damned" smile, certain of changing the subject.

Harv strolled into camp with two large walleyes, cleaned and gutted, ready for the pan. Jamieson introduced him. "This fella is Minnesota Harv." Men who traveled in the boxcar with him raised hands in acknowledgement. A few came over to comment on the fish and introduce themselves. Harv's underfed chest swelled at the attention.

Sewell scrutinized him. "You are one long drink of water, son. Oughta go out to Washington and pick them apples. Soon enough, ya won't need a ladder."

Men laughed and Harv flushed. "I aim to be a lumberjack and fish the rivers they float logs down."

A man pushed through bushes and any advice about to be laid on the kid was stillborn. A warning thrill went through Jamieson, his developed instinct for self-preservation. *Watching us from the brush.*

Proffering a half-full bottle of whiskey to the jungle cook, he introduced himself in a flat voice. "They call me Fats." His bulk was deceptive, not fat, but thick; sloping shoulders topped a square-cut chest. Humorless gray eyes studied Harv's fish. Someone asked where he was from and his small, nearly lipless mouth answered, "Chi." To the point, its name unfinished. No one asked where he was heading. A wide short-fingered hand, sporting enlarged scarred knobs for knuckles, accepted a can of stew. Any drunk thinking he'd put down this drifter would wake up in the mud, if at all. A dangerous man. One coat sleeve rested against his ribs a fraction wider than the other. Packing heat. Jamieson pressed his left arm tighter and wrapped a glove around a can of black coffee, surreptitiously eyeing Fats over it as he sipped. Unexpectedly small feet wore well-made boots, not worn out, but purposely scuffed up. A knife sheath was likely fitted inside one. Fats dragged them under a large piece of driftwood he perched on. Nothing got past him. Jamieson stretched his run-down boots toward the fire. His knife rested in a less conspicuous place.

Harv asked no one in particular, "Where do I find work? How far to the logging camps?"

"You come with me," Sewell offered, slapping the kid's skinny back. "I'm headin' west. I'll show you where the work is."

Harv turned to Jamieson. "How do you make your dough, Mac?"

"Oh, this and that. Got my moniker logging on Michigan's Saginaw River when I wasn't much older'n you."

"I'll tell you how," Sewell interrupted with a wicked grin. "He always seems to have the beans, kid. They say he can't be beat in a poker game." In fact, it was what Sewell had encouraged Jamieson to spin out to explain his ready cash.

Jamieson chuckled. "Unlike you, Ed, I don't squander it in every whorehouse along the line. Just a few favorites." He pulled out the worn deck of cards he carried. "Anyone for a game before moving on?"

Fats flexed thick fingers. Others shook their heads. A hobo said, "I'll take you up on that after threshing."

Sewell was at his roguish best. "In that case, I'd bring my own deck if I was you."

A few laughed nervously, but Jamieson grinned and buried the deck in his pack. "You'll not get a fight outta me, Ed. Ain't you heard, the days of the gunmen are over, even down Texas way. Every man jack of 'em has turned to bummin' and ridin' the rails."

Chapter 5
Billings, Montana: June, 1913

Two weeks later Jamieson alighted in Billings to find a telegram waiting from Phil Ahern, ordering him to contact the local NP detective. Outside the depot he dusted his hat by smacking it against a bench while he studied the hot street. Always tricky, contacting a railroad official. Being seen entering the man's office could blow his cover. He turned uptown, away from the yards, keeping to back streets. At a second-rate hotel he'd used before, he shaved off a week's beard and cooled off in a tepid bath. Afterward, he carried a sealed envelope down to the lobby, promising a half-dollar to a boy dawdling at the entrance when he returned with the man for whom the letter was intended.

"The short of it is right here." The railroad dick thumped the ledger he'd carried up the street, suffused neck poking above a cellophane collar, an aging fighting cock ready to let fly. "There's been pilfering from sealed cars in the yards." Why were the Pinkertons so slow to arrive? "I telegraphed two weeks ago." He suspected the NP's own employees. "Goddamn yardmen, when they're making up trains, they shunt a car off to the side, then alert their cronies." Attaching the proper weight for each locomotive to haul gave them access to manifests listing the kinds of goods being carried. "Gotta give perishable cargo movement priority." Non-perishables waited in side-tracked cars, and those were the ones the thieves hit. He was glad the big guns had come. "But you're here to assist, understand? I'm running the show. I just need some backup." He expected the thieves to strike tonight. When the first agent showed up the previous day, the railroad dick had ordered cars shunted to the far end with a false manifest for one: shoes, clothing, silks. A fat car. "Now there're two of you and we can get down to business."

Sewell was the other Pinkerton, of course. Checked into the same hotel, he showed up for supper in a natty suit and shiny boots. They sat at separate tables, but left at the same time to saunter down to the poorly lighted freight yard.

The three detectives hid themselves, eyes fastened on the baited boxcar. It was an unusually hot and sticky night for June, so unlike the dry west. The NP detective whispered that the heat wave had followed days of rain. Moisture rising off the Yellowstone River reminded Jamieson of muggy summers in Michigan. Swatting at unseen mosquitoes, they avoided slapping themselves or scuffing gravel.

It was after midnight when two lanterns dodged among the freight cars, dimly lighting the faces of three men peering at numbers on sealed doors. When they located the fat car, they broke the seal and scraped open the door wide enough to climb inside. Closed it, then rattled it open again, maybe for air.

The detectives observed a lantern moving inside; heard the rusty sound of a pried crate lid, and a muffled exclamation of glee. Someone snarled, "Shut up."

They rushed the car in a noisy scramble over gravel and cinders across ten sets of tracks. Two thieves leaped out, dropped their lanterns and dashed down the tracks. Sewell chased them, the railroad detective at his heels, leaving Jamieson to tackle the man hiding inside the boxcar.

At the NP detective's request he'd left his gun at the hotel. "Headquarters doesn't want bloodshed. It would get in the newspaper. Bad for business if the public discovers how easy it is to rifle these freights." So, no warning shot followed by a command to come out with hoisted hands; no choice but to go unarmed into the dark car after a man with a pry bar.

Propelling himself up and in, he landed in a crouch. Something grazed his head, but not a pry bar. He swung hard and knocked it from the man's hand. What might have been a pistol thudded behind a crate. As they grappled toe to toe, Jamieson realized his opponent outmatched him in weight and strength. They punched and slammed each other against crates in the stifling car until Jamieson grabbed the bib straps of the man's overalls, trying for control. In a dexterous move of sloping shoulders, the man shrugged off the straps, but Jamieson jerked them down, hindering his thick arms, grabbing his shirt. The thief twisted away but, in doing so, tripped himself. Falling backward, his shirt tore away in Jamieson's grip. He landed with a grunt and kicked free of the overalls, snaring Jamieson's feet, bringing him down. Sweat-slicked hands found Jamieson's throat, but a knee to the man's naked groin relaxed his hold. Jamieson jerked free and rolled off.

Regaining their feet, they clenched in the sweltering car, grasping one another, slippery with sweat. They lurched out the open door onto track-bed cinders, the impact jarring loose their clutching hands. Neither man could regain his feet as each pulled the other down. Knuckles smacked flesh. A free hand landed a stunning punch, but failed to connect with a vital spot. Heads glanced off rails, faces dug into cinders. They fought in the dark under the car and out the other side. No words were spoken; only grunts and gasps escaped from abraded bodies.

Sweat-blinded, Jamieson saw only shadowy limbs.

Exhausted, their jabs became harmless. Straining and panting, they lay tangled across a steel track beyond the bait car. Jamieson's senses awoke to pain, the smell of creosote, the taste of blood, and the squealing complaint of rail cars being backed into place, bearing steadily down on them.

The thief grunted, "You first," and attempted to roll Jamieson over him to be the first one crushed.

It came from somewhere, the explosive strength of panic. Grabbing the naked man's thigh to separate himself, Jamieson hooked a fist around an unexpectedly stiff penis. With all of his might, he tried to break it off. His reward was a pop, a roar from deep in the man's throat, and violent kicking. Maintaining his purchase, Jamieson thrust his other hand between the man's thighs and gripped his buttocks. Bracing a boot against a wooden tie, he heaved, throwing his opponent across him.

Jamieson desperately held the thief between the tracks while the man snarled incomprehensible oaths as he struggled to free himself. The cars backed closer, flanged steel wheels ready to carve them out of existence if they moved. The thief butted him between the eyes, knocking him senseless across a rail. Rising above Jamieson, he gasped, "Schweinhund! I'm gonna kill you!"

He had a familiar voice, but what good is possessing a knack for voices when you're a dead man? Amid squealing wheels, cinders crunched nearby and a light shone down.

Sewell pulled the thief to his feet and dragged him from the track, allowing Jamieson to roll off the cross-ties and rail. Freight cars backed past him, but he was too whipped to feel the thrill of a close call as Sewell handcuffed the man called Fats.

"Where're your clothes?" Sewell took a few steps back to shine his flashlight on the man whose hands he'd cuffed over his butt crack.

"Pinkerton," Fats gasped. "You cuffed the wrong man." Cocked a bruised meaty face toward Jamieson. "Cuff him. I caught him stealin' from the car."

"So where're your clothes?" Sewell flashed his light at Jamieson, whose one working eye watched from a face propped on upraised knees. "I know *him*. *He's* the Pinkerton. We're both Pinkertons. Stealin' railroad property naked must be two crimes." Shifting the flashlight to the man's hairy genitals, he exclaimed, "Jesus Christ, what'n hell's wrong with you?" Leaned forward with voyeuristic curiosity. The man's penis resembled an eggplant -- purple, engorged and partly cock-eyed. "You're a goddamn freak!" And then Sewell laughed from deep in his gut while Fats growled, unable to cover himself. Jamieson didn't laugh. He turned his throbbing face away.

Fats cast about for a spot to sit among sparkling cinders. "Check my right boot."

Jamieson cleared his throat to caution, "Check his boots for knives. His gun's somewhere in the car."

Sewell flicked the light on him. "Don't I goddamn know my job?" Addressed Fats. "Sit down!" The man had no choice but to squat and drop awkwardly. "Stick out your right leg. Straight as a horse's dick." Pulling off Fat's boot, he reached inside; pocketed the knife he found before withdrawing a piece of yellow paper. "Whew, you're one smelly bastard."

Fats snarled, "Read who it's from, cocksucker."

Sewell smacked him in the head with the flashlight before peering at the paper. "Looks like a telegram from the Pinkerton National Detective Agency in Chicago." He stopped grinning. "What's your name, other than naked fat man?"

"Frank Gerard. Special operative. Infiltrated this ring and was gonna make an arrest when you barged in on my party.

Find my clothes. Railroad workman's overalls." His eyes were slitted in the flashlight's glare. "You've got the wrong man."

"Let's go get your clothes. I got some thinkin' to do."

Jamieson weakly asked, "Did you get the others?"

"Naw, the NP detective got ahead of me, twisted his goddamn ankle and they gave him the slip. Said thanks for your assistance."

Sewell marched Gerard toward the car. "You'll be pickin' cinders out of your ass for weeks."

*   *

Jamieson rested at Cousin Maud's and wrote his final report on the tramp operation, exposing corrupt NP brakemen and engineers from Minneapolis to Seattle. For a time the routes to fields and orchards would be cleared of dishonest trainmen. There were still good railroad men out there; he was sent through unplucked many times. One brakey even offered him six bits.

After riding out the summer on another railroad assignment, Jamieson returned to division headquarters in Seattle to discover Ahern had hired Fats Gerard as a contract operative for special assignments. "Heard he uses his fists like clubs," his agent-in-charge said. "Take a look at his knuckles when you get a chance. Rival saloons in Chicago pitted their bouncers against one another in bare-knuckle matches. He claims he never lost. He'll come in real handy. Not accusing you of having scruples, Agent Jamieson," he deadpanned, "but he doesn't know what that word means." Everything was a joke with Ahern.

Gerard didn't show that day and Jamieson took on another assignment. Their paths crossed at the agency months later in front of the receptionist's desk. They exchanged withering glances, the incident in the Billings freight yard not forgotten and not forgiven.

*   *

I bolted, Billy, and you weren't dead. You said go. Maybe the lung shot made that sound. I left you to die alone. The third shot. Did you see who it was? Maybe you were already dead and they were making sure. Maybe you weren't. I'm so goddamn sorry.

Chapter 6
November 5, 1916

On a Sunday in early November, the passenger boat *Verona* slipped its bowline at a Seattle pier and steamed north along Puget Sound's coastal route, cutting through choppy waters beneath a wind-swept sky, bound for Everett thirty miles away.

Coal smoke funneled around Jamieson and he turned away, holding his breath until it swirled off to cloak another section of the crowded deck. Two hundred and fifty Wobblies had taken passage. Some sought cover below deck, but most pressed lean chest to muscular back around the pilot house, shifting in unison with the roll of the boat.

A fedora sailed overhead and Jamieson jammed down his wide brim. Freedom of movement restricted, his aversion to being packed into a tight space with other men returned. It was a boxcar on water. He blamed his butterflies-in-the-gut feeling on the boat's vertical pitching, different from the sideways rhythm of trains. Flexing his knees as he had during college summers, riding logs down Michigan rivers, he balanced on the balls of his feet, trying to shed his queasiness. His mission was only to observe I.W.W. activities in Everett, knowing Wobblies take perverse enjoyment from baiting the tiger.

* *

His first day back at the agency after being shot, he maneuvered his slung arm through Ahern's office door to find him cudding a wad of Black Jack chewing gum. "Got some easy work for you till you're fit to go back on the rails."

Easy meant local. Jamieson kicked out a chair and sat down.

"Finding Billy's killer is a Seattle police job. I won't assign you to that, so don't ask. I'm not going to lose two good men." Ahern accompanied this pronouncement with the snapping and cracking of gum, its licorice scent, and his maddening buoyancy. On to new business. "We've been hired to find out the I.W.W.'s plans in support of the shingle weavers' strike in Everett. You've got a Wobbly card. Let me see it."

"I don't carry it on me in this town. The law's picking up Wobblies for every vagrancy infraction on the books, including spitting on the sidewalk." Ahern stopped chewing to listen. "If a cop followed me up here and found that little red card . . ." Jamieson waved his good hand. "Headline . . . 'Pinkerton Agent is Secret Wobbly,' not 'Wobbly is Secret Pinkerton Agent.'"

He didn't mean to convey humor, but Ahern smiled. Snap. Crack. "Long as it's handy. I want you to infiltrate their meetings here. See what they're up to. The client is tired of I.W.W. agitation up in Everett. Shingle weavers struck all summer." He swung his chair a quarter turn, pointed out the window. "Fuck, it's autumn already. The client wants those men back to work. With harvests in, shitloads of Wobblies are highballing it here. Something's in the works and the client wants to be prepared."

"Is the client one mill owner or more?"

"Big bugs. Mill owners and city papas. Could be a large operation before it's done. I pulled in Gerard. He'll come in handy."

Jamieson scowled and stood up. Ahern gripped the edge of his desk. "Agent Jamieson, I don't give a shit how you feel about Fats. You work for the agency and me, and I'm putting who I damn well please on this case." Chomp, chomp, snap, crack.

Jamieson gestured with his untethered hand and left, only to pass Gerard in the hall.

Bumping Jamieson's wounded shoulder, Gerard muttered, "Not sure I can work with a man who abandoned his partner."

"Fuck you," Jamieson snarled. He sprinted down the back stairs to the alley. It took a cup of coffee and a piece of apple pie to calm him down.

Gerard wasn't a real agent, just an operative the agency used for cases a regular agent wouldn't touch, nefarious jobs that broke its own written policies. With most of his own operations outside Seattle, he'd managed to avoid the son-of-a-bitch since their run-in that hot night in the Billings' freight yard in '13.

But his luck ran out on that account, too, back in August when both were assigned to cover the longshoremen's strike on the Seattle waterfront.

"You're both card-carrying members of the American Federation of Labor," Ahern told Jamieson when he objected. "I've got to work with what I've got. You don't have to talk to him. In fact, I order you to stay away from him. Sniff out who's behind the sabotage driving the big wigs crazy. The rough stuff . . . burning warehouses . . . shooting at and beating up scabs . . . that sort of thing. Right up your alley." Ahern tipped up both hands. "Hey! Make me happy."

One night at a longshoremen's meeting Jamieson overheard Gerard's response to a group of strikers complaining they were out of money and couldn't stay out on strike much longer. Gerard slapped his pocket and told the men, "Go out and get it from the scabs like I do."

On a hunch, he began tailing Gerard's activities and discovered he went far beyond the parameters set by the agency. Jamieson saw him approach a union official to ask for $10.00 to buy dynamite so he could blow up a dock he named. He gave a striker a bottle of phosphorous, claiming to have orders from the union to start a fire at Pier 5. Gerard was a provocateur, promoting the very thing they were sent out to uncover.

Jamieson wrote an official complaint and tossed it on Ahern's desk. "Your man Gerard is a powder keg, just waiting for a lighted match to set him off. What he's doing isn't just wrong . . . it's criminal."

Ahern snapped his gum as he read, murmuring, "Agent provocateur . . . not a credit to the agency . . ." He looked up at Jamieson, spouted in French something about every man to his methods. Gerard was Ahern's tool, all right. No wonder he whistled 'There'll Be a Hot Time in the Old Town Tonight' when Gerard appeared in his loud cheap suit for his orders.

Jamieson waited until Sewell swung back into town, found him in his tidy room with a view of ferries plying the sound and spilled out a gutful of resentment. Feet up on a chair, eyelids drooping, Billy listened, occasionally nodding to show he hadn't fallen asleep. He lowered his feet to a worn-out Navajo rug and leaned over to pull out the bureau's bottom drawer. Flipped it over, dumped out its contents, and pulled off an envelope taped to the bottom. "This might come in handy sometime . . . just not now." The envelope contained two photographs, the first one a mug shot taken in Omaha of a younger Frank Gerard under a different name. The other a photograph of a Douglas County, Nebraska, warrant for Gerard's arrest under that other name. Sewell tapped it. "Warrant still outstanding. Keep these safe. Took me some real huntin' to find 'em. When you make an enemy, best to find out all you can about him. What'd I tell you, Agent Jamieson?"

"Always be prepared." A couple of few weeks later, Sewell was dead.

*　　*

His shoulder still painful, but free of its sling, Jamieson observed Gerard at Seattle I.W.W. meetings while they listened to men wanting to set them "straight" about the shingle weavers strike.

Called the City of Smokestacks, Everett was a company town of shingle and lumber mills. Maybe thirty of those mills manufactured cedar shingles. Its workers had been on strike since spring and strikes were always about money. The men wanted wages raised back to what they'd earned before cutbacks to protect company profits during the industrial depression of 1914. When shingle sales decline, prices are knocked down to stay competitive and wages are cut. That's how it works. Workers have to expect it. Save up, the bosses say. With times better now, shingle weavers' wages were back up to pre-1914 par along the northwest coast. Everywhere but in Everett.

Wobblies, always good at firing up the hobo telegraph, had called on men to come to Seattle to support the Everett strikers and, more importantly, the Wobbly cause. They rolled in from all over the west. The I.W.W., that One Big Union, announced it was sending hundreds of Wobblies up to Everett to peaceably assemble. It was the old free speech ploy that in the past had made them the bane of law enforcement and city fathers in the Pacific Northwest.

Here he was on the *Verona*, nearly sea-sick, listening to radical patter, angling for information. Looking the part, he received nods of recognition, not only from men he sat with at meetings, but from Wobs who'd ridden the rails with him.

"Them mill owners brung in scabs. Not a Wobbly 'monst 'em." This from a blue-eyed, ruddy-faced man. "They wouldn't join the union, yah." An assortment of nationalities was on the boat - Swedes, Russians, Irish, and hard-scrabble Americans, the Wobblies' favorite sons. "Scab-herders, that's what they are." His listeners nodded. "That lumber trust gave them goons clubs. Deputized 'em." Jamieson memorized the weather-hardened face doing the educating. That was a Pinkerton agent's job, too.

Another group had other interests. "I rolled in yesterday. No beer nowhere. If all I can get is hooch, it's goodbye uncle. I'll head down to California. What's this state come to?"

Thumping engines drove the boat up the coast as Jamieson squeezed among the men, moving from one group to another.

"Yeah, the I.W.W. opened a hall up in Everett, an' that Sheriff McRae, he tore it up. Beat up good working men when they tried to talk on the street."

A man wearing the ghost of a city suit responded, "He can't do that legally. Free speech is in the Constitution. You bet it is. Street speaking is part of the Constitution."

A youth caught Jamieson's attention. "For a whore, she's a real looker, let me tell you. She's sweet on me." He gauged the speaker's age as eighteen. Grinning, he moved on.

Skin bruised over a closed puffy eye, a scarecrow of a man held a knot of men as audience. "Yeah, I come to Wenatchee for the apples after the wheat harvest outside Great Falls." His was a carnival of a face, purple and green skin covering the eye, red abrasions streaking cheekbones, jaw and neck. "You been there?"

"Great Falls?" asked a shorter man with trousers chewed off at the heels. "Sure, I been there. Prefer the Dakotas for harvests. I winter in Seattle. Work on the NP snow sheds. Never expected to be doin' this."

A cocky-faced newcomer accosted the scarecrow, a callused hand tugging his sleeve. "How'd you get that?" He nearly touched the man's face.

The tired voice must have felt obligated to repeat itself. "See, we had to go up to Everett a few days ago 'cause they kept arrestin' them shingle weaver pickets for nothin'. Beat 'em up. Did it on a trestle over the bay." He pointed at his visage. "They busted my head with brass knuckles and saps. Hit me on my shoulders and hips, too. If I hadn't beat it out a there, they'd a killed me.

"You ever seen what them shingle weavers do ten hours a day?" An anointed Wobbly, he would take the time to educate. "There's this upright saw, see, an' it's slicing through a cedar block sixty times a minute." Brought his hand down again and again. "The shingle weaver, he grabs the shingle off the saw with his left hand and passes it to his right. He's trimmin' up the shingle with his right and throwin' it down a chute to the packer. Now while he's doing this, at the same time he's gettin' another shingle off that saw with the left hand. Sixty times a minute, both hands workin'. Cedar dust so thick ya can't hardly breathe. Can't see, neither. Ya don't wonder they're strikin' for the pay they deserve."

The youngster flexed his fingers. "They lose fingers and hands, don't they? Never catch me workin' there. I'll stick to pickin' apples up here and oranges in California."

Another casualty nudged in, a white plaster taped to his face below a tweed wool cap. Jamieson had chatted him up at a meeting. He went by the moniker "Irish." Seemed every worker with a map of Ireland on his mug was called that. He'd run across a couple of "Spuds" and "Dublin Jacks," but not much else.

Dark eyes smoldered beneath thick brows. He had the look of a man expecting trouble, reinforcing Jamieson's disquiet. His nose, broken more than once, cambered part way down. Not a big man, but his jutting chin might as well have "Hit Me" writ across it. He stood solidly on two feet like a slugger, untroubled by the boat's rocking. A dangerous man in more ways than one. During meetings he focused on the issues, stopping inconsequential yammering with a pointed remark. A self-appointed leader in an organization claiming to have no leaders, he had men at his beck and call. Yeah, he was dangerous. Men were listening to him now.

"'Twas I on that boat, also. McRae's goons beat us to a bloody pulp. Shirts full of sore bones we had." He smiled crookedly, showing chipped teeth. "Sure 'twas great fun." Men around him laughed and others pushed closer. "Should they come for us now, with this boatload of Wobblies we'll hello 'em on with our fists. 'Twill be a regular sluggin' party."

Jamieson grinned with the others. *Give loud service to a cause, you Mick, and you'll have a troop of friends.*

"Any of ye fellow workers have the makin's? 'Tis certain I need a smoke bad."

Jamieson pulled a folded oilcloth from a pocket and withdrew a rolled cigarette. The Irishman tipped his cap. "God bless ye. Mac, is it?" He turned away from the breeze to cup and light it; inhaled slowly. "Have ye come from the harvests?"

"I'm a lumberjack."

"It's I've worked at that meself."

Someone started singing a Wobbly song and talk simmered as others joined in. He could stop listening now. Where was that bastard Gerard? Bumping through the crowd, he spotted him at the back of the boat, hat tugged low, in earnest conversation with a couple of young Wobblies.

Chapter 7

Jamieson pulled an I.W.W. handbill from a pocket and again perused the call for Everett citizens to assemble at the corner of Hewitt and Wetmore Avenues at two o'clock for an open-air meeting. Those Everett lumber barons wanted to know whether the Wobblies intended violence. Well, you don't invite the public to a brawl. He saw no Wobbly carry a club up the ramp and no one was showing off brass knuckles or saps.

His reports had been fastidiously dull. "Free speech" and "free assembly" were terms drummed out at every meeting, but no talk of violence, except from Fats Gerard's nearly lipless mouth. That blowhard had corralled small clusters of Wobblies, taunting, "If you had any guts, you'd take guns up to Everett and clean out those scabs." Eager young Wobblies listened to his fire-breathing talk, but older ones turned away. Gerard flashed Jamieson a belligerent sneer before resuming his harangue. "A few sticks of dynamite would clean out that nest of rattlers at the mills."

Rumor circulated that the Wobblies would "assault" Everett via the Interurban, the train from Seattle to Everett. Jamieson wrote it in his report, but it turned out to be a ploy intended for the Everett authorities and Sheriff McRae. When they gathered at the I.W.W. hall early that morning, they were told to assemble at Colman Dock to board the *Verona*. On his way down to the docks, Jamieson ducked into a "soda fountain" to call Ahern at home about the change in transport, but no one answered.

At dockside milling Wobblies passed word the captain wasn't taking on-board more than two hundred and fifty. Cutting into line near the gangplank to cat calls and jeers, Jamieson waved his I.W.W. card at men turned out in their Sunday best. Arms shot up and little red cards waved back, accompanied by resounding whoops.

Excess Wobblies and other passengers were directed to the *Calista*. From on-board the *Verona* Jamieson spotted Gerard at the bottom of the gangplank, trying to bribe a fresh-faced youth for his space inside the rope. Unsuccessful, he picked up the iron stand and rope with one hand and strong-armed the stubborn young Wobbly out of line with the other, managing to get himself aboard.

When the *Verona* swung up to the Everett city dock, the men were singing "Hold the Fort."

Hold the fort for we are coming,
Union men be strong.
Side by side we battle onward.
Victory will come!

Jamieson had sung it at meetings, but he wasn't singing now. On the dock in front of a large warehouse about a hundred and fifty men held rifles and shotguns, identifying themselves to each other with white bandannas looped around their necks. On a nearby bluff Everett citizens waved hands and handkerchiefs, maybe shouting. But this was no Sunday picnic. More armed men were positioned below the bluff.

The boat bobbed, preparing to dock. Sheriff McRae's corpulence berthed itself center front of his deputized thugs, gun belt almost invisible beneath an unbuttoned coat and enormous gut.

Wobblies were coming on deck from below. A young squirt climbed the flagpole and waved to the crowd. Like holiday excursionists, men crowded the railing facing shore. A deckhand tossed out the bowline and a wharfinger tied it to a dock cleat. Couldn't the Wobs see the danger? The song continued, but less loudly than before.

Sheriff McRae wrestled his holstered gun into view, stepped forward and hiked a beefy arm, palm out. Noonday light glinted off steel barrels. Wobblies nearest the wharf broke off the song, the singing dwindling behind them as at the end of a child's round.

Jamieson caught only McRae's last word, "leader." A Wobbly at the gangplank bellowed, "We're all leaders!"

McRae jerked out his gun and leveled it. "You can't land here!"

Wobblies jostled toward the partially lowered gangplank and a man bellowed back, "The hell we can't!"

Jamieson gripped the railing, squeezing against it to avoid being caught up in the forward surge. This was going to be bad. Gerard was squatting aft, one hand gripping a rail, the other holding an object between thick thighs. His revolver? Their eyes glanced off each other on the rocking boat before a tall Wobbly shouldered Jamieson off-balance.

A bullet fanned Jamieson's neck, ripping into the tall Wobbly's arm, its dark hole an echo of the gunshot behind Jamieson. The Wobbly knocked into men as he fell. The pistol shot was answered by a shotgun blast from the dock, followed by sporadic shooting. Then the men on the dock let loose a full barrage on the men aboard the *Verona*.

Propelled into the deadly world of unintended consequences, Jamieson flung himself to the deck behind a young Wobbly, saving himself, but failing to drag the boy down with him. Fatally wounded, the boy collapsed, surprised eyes on his, a hand slapped against his gashed neck from which blood spurted. It ran down stubby fingers, over a knobby wrist and into a too-short coat sleeve. Temporarily deaf, Jamieson heard no shooting, no moans from the boy. Their looks held until the spurting petered out and the boy's eyes glazed over. Jamieson turned his face away to see wood slivers spitting off bulwarks, men scrambling about, some falling into motionless contorted positions, others writhing. His hearing returned with the zing and whistle of bullets overhead. Pinned down, his clothing sponging up the boy's puddling blood, he had no dark street to run up, no fuel yard to hide in. His holstered revolver was no match against rifles and shotguns.

The youth up the flagpole slid part-way down, flung out his arms and fell to the deck. Men stepped on and tripped over his body as they surged from port to starboard, desperate to distance themselves from the shooters. The *Verona* listed, only the snugged bowline preventing it from capsizing. The railing gave way with a loud crack, followed by shouts and splashing as men fell or jumped into the water, to drown or be shot.

"Jesus Christ!" a man shouted, "They're killing us!"

Jamieson's urge for self-preservation bloomed ugly. Blood ran across the deck, but he resisted gravity's starboard pull by clinging to the boy's dead weight. Nearby, a human eyeball, ripped from its socket, lay impaled on a sliver of wood. This vision would return in a midnight sweat months later. He shifted his chin and shut his eyes, opening them on a huddled wounded man.

"Sweet Lord," the man moaned.

Screams came from the dock as sporadic gunfire continued, the boat's up-tilted deck hiding any view of the chaos. *Sons-a-bitches shooting each other.*

The *Verona* righted herself and Jamieson bellied along the deck, desperate to get below and away from whistling lead ripping wood. Shoving past a body, he rode its life's blood to bullet-shattered stairs where, lizard-like, he crawled to the lower deck and into a tangled heap of men. Clawing through squirming bodies, he kicked free and dragged himself to a bulkhead; slumped against it to catch his breath. Gaining his feet, he pulled out his revolver and stumbled along the passageway to the engine room.

He wasn't needed. Wobbly Jim Billings held a Colt revolver to the engineer's head, cuffing him across the engine room to the controls. "Goddamn coward! Get those engines going!" Billings saw Jamieson hanging onto the hatchway. "Hey, fella, you hit?" His gun-hand wavered as though he would come to his aid.

Jamieson croaked, "I'm all right." The engines turned over, vibrating the entire boat. He couldn't stop himself. "Get us out of here! Men are dying up there."

The propeller churned, lacking direction. Then the *Verona* slowly backed away from the dock. The bowline held for a moment, then snapped, and she was nearly free of the deadly ambush. Volleys of rifle fire followed them. Far from shore, Jamieson went on deck and witnessed a shot shatter a man's leg. During their retreat, they met the steamer *Calista*. The *Verona's* captain, who'd hidden behind his safe during the violence, snatched up a megaphone. "For God's sake, don't land! They'll kill you! We have dead and wounded on board!" The *Calista* turned around and followed the *Verona* the two-and-a-half hours back to Seattle.

While the wounded were being attended, Jamieson and Billings threw their revolvers overboard. Gerard, Irish and a few Wobblies followed suit. A sourness pervaded the atmosphere on-board. The I.W.W. men understood what awaited them at the Seattle docks. When Jamieson touched the back of his head, his fingers came away bloody. He traced a fore-finger tenderly across the short furrow on his skull, studied the bloody finger, then looked about for his hat.

The Irishman approached with a bottle of whiskey and a bloodied linen towel. "Christ! Twice dead ye should be, covered in all that gore."

Jamieson shook his head, fingering blood-matted hair. "Just grazed my head."

"Bend down an' I'll clean that wound."

Wanting no part of the blood-soaked towel, Jamieson pulled a handkerchief from a coat pocket, but it was bloody, too. He refolded it, searching for a white spot; held out a corner. "Pour some here." The whiskey trickled from the bottle and he inhaled its fumes before raising the cloth to his head. "Though I'd rather be drinking it. Shit!" Alcohol burned into his wound as he dabbed at it. Irish appeared unscathed, even the old bandage on his face remained white. "Looks like the luck o' the Irish was with you."

"Christ help us! There's no luck to the Irish. We fight for every cryin' need under God's heaven."

"Like us Wobblies." He stuffed his handkerchief into a blood-soaked pants pocket.

"Like us Wobblies. Sure we're a woeful lot this time, but we'll make 'em smell hell for what they did back there." Accepting the rolled cigarette Jamieson pulled from his fold of oilcloth, the Irishman lit it with a trembling hand.

The police were *en force* at the docks to meet the boats. Four bodies were removed to the morgue, thirty-one wounded taken to the hospital. The rest, nearly three hundred from both boats, were marched to the city jail.

Chapter 8
Seattle: November, 1916

Jamieson hated being locked in a cell with nineteen other men as much as being on that crowded coffin boat. Outdoor men all, they squatted on concrete, cigarette smoke settling low. Two enamel chamber pots, lids chipped and rusting, occupied a fetid corner, cramping the cell's space because no one would hunker close. And yet, having experienced primal fear, they stunk with a rank acrid odor sweated through their clothing. Mixed with the stench of other men's blood, their reek would cling until they were allowed to wash their clothes and soap themselves.

A few Wobs stared with fixed eyes, reliving what they witnessed like men tonguing toothaches in the night. A few hugged themselves, grieving dead comrades, not wanting to break down when toughness was expected.

Some found solace in familiar patter. "If they don't release us soon, we'll run outta makin's."

"Goddamn cold in here, ain't it? Ya suppose it's raining outside?" The mutterings of sleep-starved, anxious men.

When a jailer eyeballed them through the steel door's barred window they punched up their bravado, making cracks about being free speech prisoners, or they sang.

Why don't you work like other folks do?
How the hell can I work when there's no work to do?
Hallelujah, I'm a bum,
Hallelujah, bum again,
Hallelujah, give us a handout
To revive us again.

Anticipating the bucket of watery stew, they passed around a basin of scummy water and a sour rag.

"Hard bread's better for this slop, anyway. Reminds me of the time I was in jail in . . ."

A young Wobbly thrust his head between upraised knees and wept, a half-smoked cigarette drooping from long sensitive fingers. An older man rose, picked up two plates of stew and scuffed over to squat beside the youth, resting a thin hand on quaking shoulders. "Hell, son, that was the worst you'll ever see. It's over now." The boy wiped his eyes and nose on his coat sleeve, accepted the tin plate and sopped up his stew with a chunk of bread.

Jamieson's operation was over, but having played a Wobbly for years, not even the crowded conditions would move him to tell his jailers he was a Pinkerton detective. Always stay in character, Sewell had cautioned or, sure enough, you'll run into somebody, someday, who knows who you are; your operation and maybe your life will be over. He had little choice but to wait with the others. But, goddamn it, he wanted out. What was Ahern doing about him? And where was Fats Gerard?

The police waited a few days before removing the men from the cell, one at a time. A few who'd participated in the Spokane free-speech fight of 1909 tried to prepare the younger ones for what might be waiting, describing how the police doused them with buckets of cold water and beat them with rubber hoses.

When Jamieson's turn came, guards took him down a dim hallway and stood him in front of a darkened cell, a flashlight's beam illuminating his face. Two fingers slid out of a narrow slot below the barred window and flicked from side to side, waving him on. It had to be Gerard selecting out the "leaders" from the *Verona*.

More than a week after his arrest, Jamieson walked out of the Seattle jail, blinked up into a cold morning rain, and raised his collar. Still filthy and stinking, he ducked his head and scuttled down back alleys, an outcast from society. He slipped up the back stairs of his boarding house and commandeered the one bathroom; shaved off a quarter-inch of beard and immersed himself in a tub of hot water, scrubbing off the blood of dead men.

His filthy rags wadded under an arm, he left through the kitchen, surprising his landlady, and buried the stinking bundle in an ash can. Hunting out back issues of Seattle newspapers in trash bins, he thumbed through them at a nickel-a-plate café while bolting down his first decent meal since before he boarded the *Verona*.

Two deputies had been killed on the Everett docks. The *Seattle Daily Times* should have reported they were shot by their cohorts, but it claimed Wobblies shot them from the *Verona*. Seventy-four men from the boat were charged with first degree murder, thirty-eight with unlawful assembly. Five men from the *Verona* were dead. Six men, whose names were on the *Verona* manifest, went into the water and remained unaccounted for. He recognized the name of a man he'd ridden boxcars with, Swede Carl. It was rumored fishermen had seen wrapped bodies dropped far out in the sound at night. The Socialist newspaper, *Northwest Worker*, called the episode what it was, The Everett Massacre.

An hour later, raw from lack of sleep, off-kilter and unable to suppress his anger, he hunched over a mug of black coffee in Ahern's office. "Nine days. Why the hell did you let me rot in jail nine days? I ate pig swill. Twenty men in my cell. I slept sitting against a wall on a freezing concrete floor with one crummy blanket."

Ahern smiled tentatively. "That bad, huh? I knew you wouldn't want to break your cover, Rob. Best thing in the long run." Now the pay-off. "You're in thick with the I.W.W. Our head office in Chicago has big plans for you. Stick with this and you'll end up heading a regional office." He searched Jamieson's bloodshot eyes; getting no reaction, the corners of his smile lowered. A father offering his child a present, he proffered the little blue package. "You want some Black Jack?"

"No, I don't want your goddamn chewing gum." He let Ahern have it. "It was your boy, Gerard, who started the shooting."

An old hand when a poker face was required, Ahern leaned in with casual interest. "Did you see him shoot?"

"I saw enough." *You son-of-a-bitch, you're going to protect that scum.* "He was behind me at the railing with a revolver in his fist. When I turned to the prow, a shot fired behind me. Jesus Christ, Phil! It went past my ear and hit the man in front of me. That son-of-a-bitch tried to back-shoot me!"

Straightening, his agent-in-charge assumed a thoughtful expression. "You think he tried to kill you, Rob?"

"Yes, Phil, that's exactly what I think. Our bad blood goes back a few years."

"Billy Sewell mentioned something about that." Uninterested in the distant past, he asked, "What'd you do when you heard the shot?"

"What'd I do? All hell broke loose. Those thugs on the dock started mowing down men. Gerard's was the only shot fired from the boat. Most Wobblies were unarmed. No heavy weapons on the boat, just a few revolvers. Those so-called deputies killed and wounded? They fuckin' shot each other. And Gerard started it."

"Well, if you didn't actually see him shoot, that's speculation on your part. Gerard wrote up his report. Said the first shot came from in front of him and he described the man as an Irishman."

"An Irishman? Bullshit! I tried to telephone you that morning about the change from train to boat, but no one answered your goddamn telephone. Did Gerard get hold of you, and did you telephone Everett to tell them we were coming up by boat instead of the Interurban?"

"I never talked to Gerard before the boat sailed."

Jamieson's eyes bored into Ahern's. "Then it was Gerard who telephoned the authorities in Everett. He was late for the boat, nearly the last man to board. You tell me, Phil. Is Frank Gerard working for the Pinkerton National Detective Agency or directly for the Everett mill owners? Was he following your orders or somebody else's?"

"That's an interesting question." Chewing slowly. "I don't have the answer."

Jamieson stood, sloshing coffee on his clean suit and the floor. With built-up venom, he leaned over the desk and thrust a finger into Ahern's chest. "You've got yourself an agent provocateur and his name is Frank Gerard."

"Now, Rob . . ." But Jamieson was striding toward the door. Ahern jumped up. "Where are you going?"

He swung around. "I'm going to find that son-of-bitch and beat the truth out of him. And then I'm going to the prosecutor to tell him about the dirty side of the Pinkerton National

Detective Agency and its complicity with Sheriff McCrea that Sunday at Everett."

"Agent Jamieson, hold your ground!" Ahern rushed the door, bracing a hand against it as Jamieson wrenched it open. "Let's be reasonable, all right? Are you with me here?" He managed to close the door. "First, you're in no condition to take on Gerard." He ignored Jamieson's angry face. "Second, you are still in the employ of the Pinkerton National Detective Agency and, as such, must obey the rules of its employment. Third," this said with relief, "you won't find Gerard in Seattle." Ahern stepped back to rest a hand on Jamieson's shoulder as though the gesture would take them back to an earlier, mutually-trusting time. "He's gone. Picked up his pay a couple of days ago. No forwarding address."

Jamieson pushed off Ahern's hand. The agency habitually told its stoolies to get lost when they got themselves in too deep, putting the agency's reputation at risk. Fighting a sweeping weariness, he steadied himself against the door, knowing he didn't have a line on Gerard.

Ahern's tone softened. "Get yourself some sleep, Rob. Write your report, with incriminating statements made by those I. W. W. Give us some names. You'll have to testify at the trial, but I expect they'll try the whole bunch together. One appearance from you, that's all. But you won't be the only agent testifying. Not Fats. Not after what you said." The smooth compromise. "I had a third agent on the boat. Came up from Frisco. Reese. Remember him? Got on a soapbox in Everett the week before and said some incendiary stuff, but the Wobblies pulled him down. His talk was too strong for them."

Jamieson should have known. Bringing in operatives from other regions was an agency strongpoint.

"Got winged in the hand and wrote his report in the hospital. So, the two of you testify the first shot came from the boat. And it did, didn't it. That should satisfy our clients in Everett." Ahern went to his desk and returned with a big cigar. Insisted on lighting it for Jamieson. "Go get some sleep."

Once outside, a sense of betrayal replaced his anger. He'd been hoodwinked by his own kind. Billy Sewell, always long on advice, had warned him to play the game straight. How could he play it straight when the agency he worked for was crooked as a rat's hind leg? A block away he saw his reflection in a shop window - a prison pallor in a cheap suit, complacently puffing a cigar. Not a man at all. The agency had regressed to the days when it allied itself with the big men under the wide blue sky. Mine owners then, lumber barons now, determined to crush workers' attempts to improve their lives. He tossed the cigar in the gutter.

Jamieson never wrote his report. He telegrammed in his resignation, then wired the War Department, accepting an officer's commission in the U. S. Army Signal Corps. He wrote to the Snohomish County prosecutor in Everett, explaining why he was on the *Verona* and what he witnessed, adding that he'd resigned from the Pinkerton agency and was going into the Army. He could hear the prosecutor's response. *That'll keep him out of the way.*

The Wobblies had a hard road ahead in their fight for equal justice under the law. His letter wouldn't make a lick of difference for the men who'd been on the *Verona,* but it was the best amend he could contrive. A fragment of a poem drummed in his head. Kipling, maybe. *Something lost . . . go and find it.* He'd lost his self-respect. Maybe the Army would help him get it back.

Chapter 9
Snohomish County Jail, Everett, Washington:
November, 1916 – May, 1917

Malachi "Irish" O'Neill shuffled along with thirty-six shackled prisoners, the second contingent of seventy-four Wobblies secretly transferred from Seattle to the Snohomish County Jail, charged with conspiracy to commit premeditated murder.

Jaysus! 'Twas the sheriff and his thugs caused the trouble, shootin' one another in crossfire. Divil take 'em.

Processed and shoved into a cell holding three Wobs, he greeted, "God save all here." There being no cots, he dropped his issued blanket on the floor. Four to a cell, ten cells to each of two tanks, one unit above the other with steel floors, walls and doors. *And weren't the Snohomish County authorities clever, charging only those it could accommodate in its new jail, kindly leaving a few spaces for the locals.* He bummed a cigarette off a cellmate and squatted against a wall to study them through a wisp of smoke. Decided they'd give him no trouble.

A long road from Ireland to here. Violent times forced him from home in '09. His uncle's parting words smarted still. *Don't be comin' back 'til times are better, Mally, or certain the English will hang ye. Ye're wild and thoughtless a lad altogether. Come the day ye'll know better, Ireland will need ye to fight with the sense God give ye, so it will. Now be handin' us that gun, boyo. Sure 'twill get ye hanged in America as much as here.* He spent a summer with a cousin and her family on a wheat farm in the Washington Palouse, then seven years with a loose leg, moving about the country. Loved the America he saw from boxcars chattering over prairie, desert and mountains, though sometimes he hated it. Now, for instance. Passionately believed in the I.W.W.'s fight for better conditions and pay for workers.

He knew keeping a man's spirits lifted was the key to staying sane in jail. "We'll be organizin' as we were taught," he told his cellmates, and word passed from cell to cell until seventy-three Wobblies understood what they must do, if not for themselves then for the others.

Through dull winter days they awaited contact from attorneys O'Neill assured them the I.W.W. would hire. When slumgullion was bad and morning mush fouled with mold and maggots, he ordered them not to eat it, but to sing all night. Nourishment enough. "Exercisin' our right to free speech in jail, fellow workers."

He was twenty-eight and had lived close quarters with lumberjacks in a stench of unwashed bodies and sweat-stiffened clothes. He would tolerate the Everett jail. Except for dank cold cells, bad scran for food and lack of liberty, it was much the same.

When he was singled out as leader of the hunger strike, guards removed him from his cell to be isolated in the "black hole" for independent thinkers. He wished then to be back in Ireland with all its troubles.

Unable to see his hands before his face, he couldn't tell night from day. In a silence reserved for the dead, he wanted the crash of thunder and skirl of wind to lull him to sleep. It was so quiet, he worried the jail had been emptied and he abandoned. He sang songs and recited poetry, remembered paragraphs of memorized Latin the Christian Brothers had forced into his young head. Was it to keep madness in abeyance they'd had in mind?

He conjured pleasant smells – clover after rain; peat smoke coiling from a chimney; fresh cut pine; newly printed newspapers and open books; soap – how dear now; and the aroma of freshly baked bread. Tasted tears, but made no sound. He wouldn't alert those feckin' guards that he was close to breaking. *Stop thinking, boyo. Sing out yer heart. Not a melancholy tune of Ireland, but a strident Wobbly song for strength.*

> *Arise, ye prisoners of starvation!*
> *Fight for your own emancipation;*
> *Arise, ye slaves of every nation*
> *In One Union grand. . .*

It echoed nicely, his baritone.

Released from solitary confinement, he was welcomed back by prisoners who'd kept faith and continued the strike until given food a shade better than vile mush. "'Tis well ye've done, men. An elegant day ye've given me." They passed his words through the cellblocks.

December became January, 1917. Beyond the barred window the sky appeared as in his childhood when mist mixed with drizzle and his mother sang to the spinning wheel, sometimes telling tales handed down from the famine years, but mostly dinning prayers into his ears as he sat on the creepie before the fire.

Denied letters and printed materials, the Wobblies speculated on the world outside while rummaging for fleas, cracking them between nicotine-stained nails. They begged the guards to let them boil their striped uniforms in the laundry to rid themselves of vermin, but were refused.

In the lower tank, one blanket per man, prisoners huddled together, sleepless on steel floors in unheated cells, pushed beyond their mettle. O'Neill demanded mattresses and blankets in their name. "The nights are fierce cold on the floor." He was told their own defense fund would have to pay for supplies.

He passed an order, ciphered as a quote from Virgil. "'If I cannot bend the powers above, I will rouse hell.' Prepare, fellow workers, to cause a ruction." Whispered from cell to cell, bit by bit they reduced it to, "Give 'em hell!"

Beating on steel walls and floors with whatever they tore loose, they yelled, stamped, and beat out tattoos on bars with shoes. Crowds of citizens gathered outside open cell windows. There were setbacks. "We'll be redoubling our efforts in the mornin'. Obtaining justice takes time." Finally, the county delivered ticks and more blankets.

A holy joy filled O'Neill when he discovered attorney Fred H. Moore had come from Los Angeles to take on their defense. Moore represented him in Spokane during the free speech trials of 1909-10, and got him and his fellow defendants off. George F. Vanderveer, a former prosecutor for Seattle's King County, now took up the cudgel. Four more attorneys joined their defense team, including a woman lawyer from Missouri. O'Neill met with Moore, and afterward passed word they were in good hands. Their attorneys had been granted a change of venue. The trial would be held in Seattle, not in Everett.

On March 5, 1917, fifty-three-year-old Thomas Tracy was sent to Seattle for trial. The State of Washington intended to try them one by one. Allowed newspapers, they read that Tracy was charged with first degree murder. Not that he killed Deputy Jefferson Beard on November 5, 1916, in Everett, but aided, incited and encouraged some unknown person to kill Beard. It was the charge each would face if Tracy was convicted.

O'Neill muttered, "Sure we're goin' to law against the divil at the court house in hell."

A youth in O'Neill's cell read aloud to a cellmate who couldn't, "And the prisoners in the Everett jail are being held in . . . commun . . . i . . . cado. What the hell does that mean?"

The cellmate offered, "Means we have to share what we have with each other like in a community. An' I could use some brown mule. Anyone got a chaw?"

The I.W.W. was on trial. It wasn't Snohomish County or the State of Washington against Tom Tracy, but the men of capital against the men of labor. Did labor have the right to organize, to peaceably assemble, to speak freely, and to advocate a change in existing social arrangements?

On May 5, a jury of five men and seven women retired to deliberate. They deliberated for twenty-two hours. A friendly guard whispered that he heard some jurors refused to compromise on lesser-included charges. O'Neill waited through a sleepless night.

The verdict came in. "Thomas Tracy Not Guilty! I.W.W. Not Guilty!" Or so O'Neill imagined newsboys shouting as they waited to be set free. Their guards taunted that there'd be another trial for one of them. They were released two days later and all headed for Seattle and the I.W.W. hall.

A mulligan stew simmered on the hall's cookstove and men lined up for their first meal outside a jail in six months. Red Doran, an I.W.W. organizer, greeted each former prisoner with a slap on the back and a proffered basket of chunks of fresh bread. He waited for them to dish up and find seats before mounting the podium to announce, "The U.S. has been at war with Germany for the best part of a month. Where the hell have you Wobs been?" Spoons poised, pallid men stopped chewing. A few chuckled, and then a gust of rusty laughter erupted in the hall. They were free. He grinned, "The word from Chicago is organize!"

Heads shook in disbelief while mopping up gravy with last bites of bread. Others nodded at Doran. Most chewed and swallowed without expression Those who had been first in line lowered empty bowls to the floor, lit cigarettes they were given, and listened.

"We want the eight-hour day in lumber," Doran continued, "not just here on the coast, but throughout the northwest. Better pay, better grub and better camp conditions. We'll grab those lumber tycoons by their hairy nuts and yank 'em to their knees." He jerked down his fist for emphasis.

O'Neill swallowed a gob of fatty meat and called out, "'Tis well I love that American tongue!" Glee surged through him. The I.W.W. had saved his skin again and he resolved to give loud service to its cause. With the others he received his compensation of $10.00 for what he'd endured. His orders were to head for northern Idaho and the logging camps. He was provided the rigging - blank membership cards and $150.00 worth of dues stamps. Time to organize, increase membership and begin the big strike. And it would be big.

Chapter 10
Summer, 1917

The lumber strike spread from western Montana, across Idaho and Washington to Puget Sound. In the Idaho panhandle O'Neill had good days and bad. Hiking into a logging camp, he'd tell the first Wobbly he met to call the men out on strike. The lumberjacks threw down axes and saws and walked out of the woods. He and other organizers did the same at sawmills along rivers and on the shores of Lake Coeur d'Alene. When he observed camps were guarded, he waited until midnight, then sneaked into bunk houses to roust men from hard bunks. They woke up the payroll clerk to demand their wages.

"Yeah, ya goddamn ink-slinger, make 'er out."

They emptied camp at first light and headed for Spokane. The lumbermen expected the jacks to squander their paltry pay in a few days and wander back in, but with liquor prohibition in Washington State, there wasn't much to throw their money at. Authorities estimated 50,000 lumberjacks were loosed on cities and towns. Unemployed men were dangerous men and town fathers erected bullpens in Ellensburg, Yakima, Moscow, and other towns, filled them with arrested lumberjacks, all suspected of being Wobblies, and governors detailed state militia to guard them.

Not all laborers heeded the strike. The MacLean Lumber Company sawmill at St. Maries operated with only one shift, its whistle shrieking every morning at six. O'Neill organized the strikers and brought in fifty Wobblies to camp outside its gates, formed into a picket line to harass workers who wouldn't quit.

Idaho's Governor Moses Alexander, making whistle stops throughout the state's strike region, scheduled a stop at St. Maries. His special train announced its arrival a mile away, whistle blowing, bell clanging, a banner of black smoke waving into the blue sky.

The governor and his entourage approached along a dusty road, led by Alonzo MacLean, the mill owner. MacLean wore a suit, his high laced boots, tucked-in pants and plaid shirt laid aside for the occasion. The previous day O'Neill had spotted MacLean through his open office door, tearing off his hat while coming down with the "Wobbly horrors" when a few more men struck and walked out. Governor Alexander strode alongside MacLean in an expensive suit and hat, followed by his group, some in uniform.

Seeing the mayor and city council, boot-lickers all, tagging along, O'Neill called out, "Here comes the governor. Ye'll be givin' him respect, fellow workers," adding under his breath, "though they be at their old tricks."

Working the crooked picket line, Governor Alexander offered his hand to each man, some having to pull theirs from pockets to shake it.

MacLean, flint-eyed with blue veins prominent on his fists, strode past, refusing to acknowledge men he once considered, if not family, at least loyal familiars. The company guards' platform had been moved outside the gate and MacLean and the governor mounted it. The mill owner stood with arms tightly folded, glaring over the heads of the men gathered below.

Clean-shaven below tired dark eyes, the balding governor removed his hat and spoke in a thin but determined voice with a hint of a German accent. It was all that was German about him. "Now, you men, your country needs you to go back to work. You're not doing your bit for the war effort, slacking off on the job."

O'Neill stood with fists in pockets. *Son-of-a-bitch rascal, thinking he's squireen of us all.*

Alexander spread the eagle's wings and unsheathed its talons, speaking of patriotism and the workers' duty to help defeat Germany. He had his spiel down pat, having made the circuit of struck sawmills on Idaho's numerous rivers and lakes, but knowing better than to trek into empty logging camps.

Guts twisted with resentment, O'Neill watched the governor, who had pushed a syndicalism law through the state legislature, directed at the Industrial Workers of the World. The strikers weren't all Wobblies, just sympathetic to I.W.W. aims. The new treason law, though, frightened the mill workers. Unlike rough and tumble lumberjacks, sawmill employees were mostly family men.

"America can't build ships and airplanes to fight this war if you men refuse to cut trees and saw logs." After more patter, he finished with, "Your country is depending on you."

MacLean's office men, St. Maries' town fathers and the governor's entourage clapped and cheered. MacLean loosed folded arms to join in. The strikers had listened quietly, even respectfully. Alexander stepped down and shook more hands. And that was that. He and his followers raised dust returning to his train.

The men in front of the gate were talking among themselves when Sheriff Buck Roland and his deputized citizens moved in to arrest the Wobbly leaders. O'Neill didn't resist, but it didn't save him from a punch to the face after being handcuffed. Guns were held on the strikers as O'Neill and two others were led away. He called out to a Wobbly, "Jimmy, ye best be gettin' us a lawyer."

Cheekbone throbbing, O'Neill demanded as he entered the basement jail beneath the county courthouse, "Ye'll be tellin' me what we're arrested for, Sheriff."

"You'll find out, you dumb bog jumper. We're gonna stop you foreign riff-raff coming here, stirring up good folk."

A deputy unlocked their cuffs and shoved the three into a musty cell. The heavy wood door slammed shut with a whoosh of stale air; a key turned in the solid lock. As is always the first act of a man in an unfamiliar cell, O'Neill moved to the high barred window. It faced an alley.

Big Lafe hitched up his pants and readjusted his suspenders. Bruises spotted his hands and face from a run-in with company men a week earlier at a remote logging camp. "They're gonna give us a beatin'."

From where he squatted, rolling a cigarette, Gold Tooth Horace nodded, licked brown paper and twisted it. "They'll wait till dark, then kick the shit out of us." He spoke calmly, but made no eye contact.

"Self-preservation, fellow workers." O'Neill removed a pocket knife from inside a pant leg. "What are we havin'?" Big Lafe parleyed up a small knife and a spoon. O'Neill stuck the knives in the lock. "They'll not be openin' this door from outside. 'Twill give us time while hopin' and prayin' for the lawyer to show up to make certain we get a square deal." His jauntiness offered little comfort to his experienced fellow workers.

A couple of jailers returned to jab the iron key into the lock hole. Unsuccessful, they went for the sheriff to make things right. He slid open the cubby-hole through which food was passed and stuck his face up to the slot. "What's the matter, boys? You're interfering with my duties." Then snarled, "Open the damn door!"

O'Neill stepped up. "Sure we don't want ye breakin' the law, takin' us out an' givin' us a beatin'. If ye don't mind, we'll wait for our lawyer. He'll be along in the mornin'."

The sheriff reached in with a blackjack and swung it at him, but O'Neill sidestepped the blow and seized his arm; smacked it against the edge of the cubby and jerked the sap from his hand.

Roland reared back and the wrong end of a revolver pointed at O'Neill. "I'm gonna shoot you, ya goddamn flannel mouth."

"Ye haven't the guts." The Irishman shrugged off Big Lafe's restraining hands and stepped in front of the gun.

On the other side a jailer remonstrated with the sheriff and it was withdrawn. The sheriff gave a muffled order and a spray of cold water doused O'Neill. He grabbed up a dirty glass from the window ledge and hurled it at the cubby-hole, where it shattered, piercing the hand holding the nozzle and the face behind it. There was a yelp and the hose disappeared.

"Open this door or somebody's gonna get hurt."

"Let ye come in here, Sheriff, and it'll be ye with a clout aside yer head." O'Neill smacked the blackjack against the wall as a reminder of who possessed it.

Around midnight their jailers returned with a file and drove it into the lock, intent on pushing out the knives. That failed, but the three men realized how determined the sheriff was when a few heavy strokes of a sledge hammer on a cold chisel punched out the door's lock. It swung open, but the sheriff stood back and out of reach as three shotguns were aimed at the prisoners.

The deputies hustled them outside and into an automobile, then drove them over a rutted trail through timber. They dragged O'Neill out and, while two men held him, two others took turns punching him in his stomach and chest. Unable to breathe, he began to lose consciousness. They dropped him to his knees and a kick to the jaw knocked him out. Gold Tooth Horace and Big Lafe later agreed he was punched about forty times. They got off easier. The thugs were tired when they finished with O'Neill.

"Compliments of the Home Guard," their tormentors said. "Don't forget to take your friend with you."

O'Neill regained consciousness in agony, thinking two devils held him. "Sweet Jaysus! Let me go. I'll die here. No need to carry me down to hell first." Only he said it in Gaelic and his fellow Wobblies limped on, dragging him between them.

Chapter 11
The Idaho Panhandle: August, 1917

"I'm still not optimistic, MacLean," John Holbrook said. The banker handed back the field glasses and folded his arms on the upper deck railing of the steamboat *Georgie Oakes*. Linen jacket unbuttoned, his ample paunch protruded beneath the railing's top rung. He'd glassed the eastern shore of Lake Coeur d'Alene and the blackened ruin of the mill town of Harrison, most of its sawmills burned in July. That single conflagration had so drastically reduced white pine being lumbered in the region, Alonzo MacLean now had the opportunity to dominate the region's industry if he could expand his mill operations at St. Maries. Which was why he had made the banker a virtual prisoner on the boat.

Holbrook asked. "Did the Wobblies start the fire?"

"Nope. Passing locomotive." MacLean wore the same suit in which he'd greeted Governor Alexander the previous month. Pale blue eyes glinted above graying sandy mustaches.

Chewing an unlit cigar, Holbrook tilted his Panama against the sun and peered across sparkling water to distant green-black mountains of prime timber. "We've settled down labor strikes in Everett and along the coast for the long loggers. But you short loggers are still having trouble here in Idaho. It would be a big investment in something we're not sure of . . . expanding your sawmill, Shay engine and flatbeds for your logging operation. High risk. Not a good idea."

MacLean held in contempt paper-collar stiffs with ideas contrary to his, but this big fish hadn't come from Seattle overnight by train to say no to "the possibilities." He just wanted convincing.

"By gad, it's a good risk, Mr. Holbrook." The lumberman gripped the railing, imagining the banker's girth stuffed with gold and bank notes. The man was heavily invested in sawmills in western Washington and Oregon, where long loggers were cutting spruce under government contract for military cantonments, wooden boats and airplanes. Holbrook admitted he'd never been to Idaho, except to cross the panhandle by train. It wasn't on his financial map.

"My men at the St. Maries mill, they're family men. They don't want more trouble. We've run those I.W.W. agitators out of there."

MacLean was out of his element. His brother, Jerome, God rest him, had handled the cravat-and-diamond-stickpin side of the business, stirring men's blood with a desire to be part of the future of Inland Empire timber. His own talent was in felling and lumbering it, and in controlling rough men. He never thought Jerome, five years younger, would die first, leaving his young widow Addie, now part-owner, as someone he'd have to provide for. Having cut a deal with the captain of the semi-retired lake steamer, now hauling only freight across the 22-mile-long Lake Coeur d'Alene and up the St. Joe River to St. Maries and St. Joe City, he was giving Holbrook an exclusive cruise. Its purpose was to set in motion his long chance.

The man accompanying Holbrook leaned against the railing within earshot. The three men turned to watch a wood-burning tugboat with a barge of fuel wood pass in the near distance. It was hauling two booms of logs a mile long toward a mill in Coeur d'Alene. This working lake was one giant millpond, its sandy shores littered with escaped logs and piled high with shrugged-off bark.

MacLean dangled the bait before the banker's bulging eyes. "I guarantee twelve percent on your investment of upgrading our mill. You know the government's gotta have enormous amounts of white pine for this war and we've got access to prime timber along those mountain drainages. Most of it on MacLean land. We're gettin' a thousand feet of lumber per tree . . . four sixteen-foot logs each. Big trees. And there are millions of feet of timber on government land right next door. The Forest Service already signed a contract with us to cut their white pine."

Holbrook mouthed his cigar, watching the tug's brail of logs.

What would Jerome have done now? "I know you're invested mostly in Sitka spruce on the coast, but the government wants white pine for boxes, military cantonments, and it's the only wood used for airplane struts and wing beams. With cables, steam donkeys and short tracks, we can take it from the Marble Creek drainage, drive it down the creek to the St. Joe River, and float it down to our mill at St. Maries. Lumber it and send it out on Milwaukee Road tracks. No extra cost of barging it across the lake." He jerked his thumb back at the tug and its logs. "We need a second production saw mill to keep up with business."

The lake breeze ruffled Holbrook's jacket and he rebuttoned it. "Lucky for you when the Milwaukee came through in '09."

"Heaven sent. You believe in divine providence, Mr. Holbrook?" MacLean didn't wait for an answer. "The bottom line is profit." He let it sink in before repeating, "Profit." The breeze tossed the word into Holbrook's face along with a lick of spittle.

The banker pulled out a large white handkerchief and dabbed at his cheek, while his man moved up the railing to better catch their words. Refolding it, he asked in a clipped voice, "So what's your plan to stop strikes, slow-downs and sabotage in your woods?" The lumbermen's catch-phrase, rapped out like a fist on a tabletop – *strikes-slow-downs-and-sabotage* - the profit-killer. "If the troubles start up again this winter while you're cutting, or next spring to disrupt your river drive, you'll lose another year's income. I read my accountant's report after he saw your books." Added, not unkindly, "You've had a tough year. If I invest in your mill . . . I say if . . . I sure as hell don't want to lose my investment. You can't guarantee control over those lumberjacks." Emphasized each word, "They don't have families."

Lumbermen didn't want men with families in the woods, only transients who would work for low wages in vermin-infested camps. It didn't matter they worked only long enough to get a wad to blow on liquor, gambling and whores, because there was always a glut of lumberjacks coming and going. But with loggers in uniform now, that labor surplus had disappeared. The dearth of men had transformed the lumber strike into a critical threat.

MacLean had his fish on the line now. Just had to set the hook. Waggled a knotty finger. "I know what's needed. I'm gonna reduce the jacks' workin' day from ten hours to eight." He laid his plan before the banker like a potlatch. "A shorter work day was what them Wobblies had the men strikin' for. They'll work twice as hard out of gratitude. Hell, loggin's no picnic."

Holbrook's face suffused and he jerked the cigar from his mouth, twitching it in MacLean's face. "Good God, man! You can't do that!" Hauled himself a step closer. "We're fighting to keep the ten-hour day on the coast."

MacLean leaned toward the shorter man and his thrusting cigar; had it been alight, it would have singed his tweeds. "I don't give a damn what's happenin' on the coast. I gotta get out the lumber."

But Holbrook wasn't finished. "We're all members of the Lumberman's Protective League and its entire purpose is to hold the working day to ten hours. If I invest and you cut hours, we'll both be fined. My partners, too. The best clubs in Seattle and Portland will blacklist us." Popped the cigar back in his mouth. "And that's bad for business."

"It's only a five hundred dollar fine per member, and we're talking about tens of thousands in profits here." MacLean swept an arm toward the nearing mountains. "I gotta stop the Wobbly influence on my jacks. When they get the notion, they can tie up a job tighter 'n a cow's ass in fly time. Shortening their hours will calm 'em down. If your lumberin' friends weren't so goddamn greedy, they'd do the same on the coast, an' them I.W.W. agitators would head down the road an' leave us timber men alone."

Holbrook stepped back. "Out in Seattle we're pressuring the government to declare the I.W.W. public enemies. Seal all the boxcars so they can't beat their way for free. Build more internment camps and send those damn foreigners back to where they came from. That's the ticket, not giving into demands like shorter hours and beds with springs."

MacLean saw a chink in the banker's argument. "Deport foreigners? With able-bodied Americans in uniform, foreigners are most of my labor force. It would empty the logging camps. Can't saw trees with one-armed men. How about we hire women?" Not getting an appreciative snort, he pressed on. "With my government contracts and your investment in the mill and new railroad stock, the government will rain down profits on you and your friends." He'd wound down, so he pointed ahead. " Look out there. We've entered the Joe."

Chapter 12

A freight train's whistle echoed off mountains jumbled into the distance. A sweet sound. The locomotive and boxcars snaked across the river's drawbridge and into the forest, its diminishing rumble trailing behind. Approaching the drawbridge, the *Georgie Oakes* gave three long whistles. The span moved slowly on its axle, then stopped parallel to the bank, allowing the boat to proceed upriver.

Holbrook looked at his gold watch.

MacLean pulled out his silver flask. "Another fifteen miles or so to St. Maries. We'll have lunch at the mill. Are you a drinkin' man, Mr. Holbrook?" His plan to convey Holbrook to St. Maries on the *Georgie Oakes* rather than by train overland was intended to give the man time to think with nowhere to run. Liquor would help with that.

When they were young, Alonzo and Jerome MacLean worked for other men, skidding out logs with horses in winter, building small sawmills for two-and-a-half dollars a day. Then their lodestar shone down. A big mine in the Coeur d'Alenes figured to be the only bidder at a nearby government sale of mining and stull timber needed to shore up tunnels passing farther into the mountain. The MacLean brothers bid higher than the going rate of $4.03 per thousand feet and won. A chancy and dangerous scheme if the mine owners had decided to knock their heads together, but the mine manager cut a deal to get the needed timber. The brothers made a profit without sawing a tree. After that success they bought and sold contracts for timber and land; built their own sawmill; harvested and sawed their own timber. Ten years later, at the turn of the century, a land grab began. Big companies shouldered in from the Middle West – Weyerhaeuser, Rutledge, Blackwell, Herrick. But the MacLean brothers developed some cunning in that game, too. Time and youth sure passed quickly. Now, MacLean just wanted to be rich.

The steamboat blew its haunting whistle over St. Maries and docked.

The MacLean sawmill buzzed with machinery, men and horses, operating at full output, the way MacLean wanted it.

The mill owner's boat-deck shamble became the easy swing of a lumberjack as he showed off his mill. Holbrook followed, picking his way through bark and duff, inspecting decked logs waiting for the saw. The planing mill filled the air with its shrill whine as MacLean pointed out the mechanical conveyor on a large planked area, crisscrossed with tracks, moving green lumber from the saws to be graded and sorted to size. Narrow-gauge cars hauled the lumber to a thirty-acre yard, where Holbrook wandered between sixteen-foot high stacks of drying wood, and peered up steel tracks connecting the mill with the Milwaukee Road main line.

MacLean pointed out the site he intended for the second and larger sawmill, to be backed by Holbrook or by another. *Take it or leave it, you son of a goat, making me beg.* He produced a map and a couple of photographs of giant trees fronted by diminutive lumberjacks. "I'll show you where we're gonna cut. Thirty-eight miles up the Milwaukee tracks and then twenty miles south up into the mountains."

His cigar ghosting MacLean's finger tracing on the map, Holbrook listened to his plan to lay short tracks into a large stand of white pine. The banker juicily rolled the cigar between his lips. "All right, MacLean. You've convinced me. I'll talk to my partners about financing new equipment for a mill and rail stock. One condition, though."

Face flushed with success, he asked, "What's that, Mr. Holbrook?"

"My man, Frank Gerard, here . . . he'll be checking on your progress."

Son-of-a-bitch had always meant to sign on. "You mean he'll be spying on me."

"Think of him as your fix-it man. He'll come in handy with those damn Wobblies. Used to be a Pinkerton."

MacLean looked him over. A beef of a man. With those scarred knuckles, he must have been a pug in saloons, strong enough to heave rowdies out the door, if he didn't smash them to a pulp first.

Chapter 13
Spokane, Washington: August 19, 1917

"Damaging facts. I came to America to tell its citizens the damaging facts about British occupation of my beloved Ireland." Mrs. Sheehy-Skeffington spoke with the soft lilt of an educated Irish woman. Still dressed in mourning, although her husband had been dead more than a year, within the hour, in this small city, unknown to her until recently, she would speak about his illegal execution by a British officer. Seated across from the young woman interviewing her for the local newspaper, she was trying to convey once again the urgency of what had become her life's work. "Ireland has friends here in Spokane, I'm certain."

Addie MacLean stopped jotting on her notepad. She'd asked an insipid question and it had been answered. Why had Mrs. Sheehy-Skeffington come to America?

The widow of Francis Sheehy-Skeffington, arrested and executed in Dublin without trial during the Easter Rising of 1916, Hanna Sheehy-Skeffington had traveled America for eight months, seeking support for Irish independence while detailing her martyred husband's death, the British cover-up, and other horrors of Britain's military occupation of Ireland. She cautioned, "Ye won't be making a sob story of my situation?" Not a woman to suffer fools gladly, dark eyes flashed behind her spectacles. "It's that I'm seldom interviewed by lady reporters."

"I would never write a sob story on so serious a matter." Addie withdrew newspaper clippings from her handbag. "Perhaps these articles on women's working conditions in Seattle factories will inform you of my style."

Mrs. Sheehy-Skeffington lifted a hand as though to wave them away, then adjusted her spectacles and ran a finger down the first column. A few paragraphs down, it paused and she read, a smile softening pinched features. She looked up. "Besides being an activist for the working woman, are ye also a suffragist, Mrs. MacLean?"

"I am, Mrs. Sheehy-Skeffington. I read about your work in Ireland to win the vote for women and that you spent time in prison for your convictions."

With new interest, Hanna Sheehy-Skeffington asked, "Ye won't be offended if I say you have an Irish look to you, Mrs. MacLean?"

"My mother followed her brothers from County Cork to America when she was fifteen." She'd wanted to reveal this, to identify with this woman, who herself was born in County Cork.

"And who is her family?"

"I doubt you know them. Poor tillers of the fields. The name is O'Neill."

"Sure it's a large clan, but I've known some O'Neills . . . a fine patriotic people."

"What do you want the people of Spokane to know about your work? May I call it a crusade?" Addie intensified her note-taking as the woman revealed her hopes for Ireland.

She accompanied Mrs. Sheehy-Skeffington and an escort provided by the Ancient Order of Hibernians to the Red Men's Hall. It should have been a quiet Sunday evening, but streets flowed with people, not everyone gathering to hear about Ireland's troubles. Soldiers with rifles stood at corners, small knots of working men watching them. More I.W.W. trouble, it seemed.

The hall, which seated four hundred, was filling. Mrs. Sheehy-Skeffington went backstage and Addie seated herself on the aisle in the second row. Despite open windows and whirring ceiling fans, heat lingered in the high-ceiling auditorium. She fingered and lifted coiled hair. Having crossed the bar of social grace by rearranging it in public, she waved a palm-leaf fan she'd found on her chair. Other women were doing the same, while men mopped their faces with handkerchiefs. After greeting acquaintances, new arrivals turned toward the stage and the green, white and orange Irish Republican flag suspended from the lectern.

*   *

The previous day, Malachi O'Neill had hitched a ride on a freight to Spokane to meet with James Rowan, secretary of the I.W.W. for the Inland Empire, to recount his observations of the big strike, from the Coeur d'Alenes, through the St. Joe River Valley, and down into the Clearwater. Wobblies and lumberjacks continued to be arrested and thrown into bullpens guarded by Idaho state militia, initially sent to guard Milwaukee Road tunnels and trestles from German saboteurs. Troops bivouacked at the St. Maries fairgrounds had thrown up a barbwire stockade, which Sheriff Roland was filling.

"Christ!" O'Neill exclaimed, "a man's only got to have an I.W.W. pamphlet on him to be charged with sabotage." Strikers were returning to mills and logging camps. "'Tis unlikely we can hold out much longer."

Rowan took notes and asked a few questions. "Same situation here in Washington. Come to the hall tomorrow and I'll have new orders. They roughed you up, I heard."

O'Neill grinned ruefully. "Sure they did me no good. Divil take 'em."

After his meeting, he went to a mercantile and outfitted himself, got a free shave and haircut at the local barber college, and paid for a bath.

A stroke of luck kept O'Neill in bed until noon at the "louse-oreum" where he was staying. Morning sun shining through the open window was a drowsy opiate and, when he opened an eye to the narrow room, he recalled he wasn't in a cell, but in a pigeonhole from which he could fly at will. He slipped back into unthreatened sleep. Damaged teeth at the back of his jaw pulsed dully, but his healing ribs announced themselves only when he jerked in dreaming.

He was eating steak, onions and potatoes at the O.K. Café when he looked out its window to see soldiers marching past. *Jaysus, what now?* He dropped three bits on the table and left to stand with gawkers witnessing the United States Army raid the I.W.W. hall in the middle of a block on Main.

Forty armed soldiers covered the building's front and rear entrances before bursting in. A short time later twenty men with hands raised stumbled into the street at bayonet point. Soldiers positioned at street corners blew whistles, directing traffic away while allowing an Army truck to drive up. Soldiers carried out boxes of I.W.W. literature to shove into its back end.

"Feckin' bastards!" Probably enrollment records, too. O'Neill thrust his fists into trouser pockets when an Army sergeant rattled a chain through the hall's double door handles and padlocked it.

Christ in heaven! Rowan had his own expense notes. He headed toward the I.W.W. office across from Union Station and was a block away when Rowan and two others emerged at bayonet point, hands elevated. They were fast-stepped to join the other Wobblies, then all were paraded under guard down Front Street, across the Monroe Street Bridge and uphill to the fortress-like courthouse and jail.

O'Neill joined a small group following at a distance, but soldiers stopped them from crossing the bridge. *Feckin' government and its toady army grinding up the I.W.W. like so much wheat. Make yerself scarce boyo or ye'll be doin' another stint in jail, so ye will.*

He should catch an out-bound back to the mountains of Idaho, but he had a yen to hear that Irish lady, whose pacifist husband was executed at Portobello Barracks by the English during the Easter Rising. He scrambled down a steep bank to the river's edge to sit on a rock and wait for evening. Rumbling trains billowing smoke and steam arrived and departed on overhead trestles spanning the river. Steel wheels screeched, bells clanged, damnable whistles shrieked, and a sulfurous stench of burning coal floated down.

With the I.W.W. in disarray and its leaders arrested across the country, O'Neill was losing his moral compass. He couldn't do much out there alone. *Ye loon fanatic, will ye blind yerself to the facts?* The I.W.W. was crumbling, its destruction managed by the United States government, and his belief and hope was disintegrating with it. What was left? Nothing.

Near eight o'clock, in low spirits, he joined the throng entering the Red Men's Hall and found a seat opposite the young woman he'd seen enter with the severely-dressed lady he pegged as the Widow Sheehy-Skeffington.

He studied her and her crown of blooming hair. She was lovelier than he remembered. As men rose to offer seats to ladies and join those standing along the walls, she turned to glimpse last minute arrivals and met his eyes. He smiled. She turned away toward the stage, fanned herself, then looked over at him again. He grinned and nodded. She tipped her chin, though not with the recognition he expected. Had he changed so much? He ran his tongue over the broken edges of his front teeth.

Applause claimed his attention as Hanna Sheehy-Skeffington was introduced by Father Brogan, the Jesuit president of Gonzaga University. The audience laughed when she addressed not only those on stage, but "the weary spies who have been following me across America, reporting the content of my lectures back to England." Her rich Irish voice swelled and soared, filling O'Neill with wordless yearning. As she recounted the killing of her husband by an English officer the day following his arrest on a Dublin street and the horrors inflicted by British soldiers upon Irish heads, his blood heated. Wouldn't he always be treated as a foreigner in this country? He ached to be home again. Memories of Ireland mingled with memories of Addie as she was when he came green to America.

Mrs. Sheehy-Skeffington possessed her audience. "The American press hesitates to use the word 'murder' in reference to my husband's death. A British tribunal and the House of Commons found Captain Bowen-Colthurst guilty of murder, but insane . . . which he is not." She directed herself to Addie in the second row. "I see no reason why they should hesitate to use the word "murder" in their newspapers."

O'Neill saw their exchange. When he and Addie were younger, being near her in the same room had made him ill with youthful lust, forcing him to hide in the horse stalls to give himself relief and risk being crushed or kicked to death. Her family's wheat farm stretched in unrelenting golden swells from the farm house and barns, no craggy hills to duck behind for solitude.

"My husband believed all violence wrong, but as a nationalist he supported Ireland's right to self-determination. He said he would die for his cause, not kill for it. And die he did. I believe a war for national freedom must be evaluated differently." Her voice carried over the ceiling fans' hum. The audience leaned forward, hanging on those words – *a war for national freedom.* "While all war must end if civilization is to reign supreme, nevertheless, there may be times when armed aggression ought to be met with armed defense."

Amid clapping and whistles a man shouted, "We'll pay England back!"

She motioned for quiet. "Irishmen now face conscription or famine, death by starvation or death in the trenches." There were boos and hisses for the English.

Addie turned toward O'Neill with recognition and concern. Her eyes were like the bluets of Ireland. He winked at her.

"There are one hundred fifty thousand British soldiers occupying my small island. Ireland is looking to the United States to help free it from British tyranny when the European war ends." Men cheered loudly and ladies clapped. She spoke at length about what she hoped would be America's role in helping Ireland gain independence from Great Britain, concluding, "Each uprising marks a milestone on the road to Ireland's liberty. An Irish Republic may be a dream, but it is the dreamer who passes on the torch of liberty in each generation."

The crowd rose, filling the auditorium with support for this woman and her country. It was their homeland, too, be their connection so far back.

O'Neill appeared at Addie's side. "Did yer mither come from Ireland?"

"That she did." She rose to greet him with joy and censure. "Mally O'Neill, where have you been these last eight years? Mama thought you went back to Ireland or died. She grieved and you never wrote." Kissed him on the cheek with sisterly affection.

"I'd 'ave known ye anywhere, Addie, so I would. Ye've become a fine-lookin' woman. Sure there's girl enough in ye still."

Raising her voice above the hubbub of people going up to shake Mrs. Sheehy-Skeffington's hand, she asked, "Why didn't you come back to the farm? There was a place for you."

"Why didn't I come back? Sure there was ramblin' in me. I come up to Spokane to see the sights and got mixed up in the free speech jailings. Ye mind that, don't ye? In '09?" Addie nodded, searching his face, making him self-conscious of his bent nose and jagged teeth. A hard-looking man now, nothing was left of the fresh-faced youth her family had taken in.

"Been doin' I.W.W. work. Sure ye can tell I'm a rabble-rouser." Did she see nothing of the high-spirited boy who kissed her well and good after she put up her hair at seventeen?

She told him of her widowhood.

"Ah, Addie, 'tis a shame for a fine woman to be alone."

She changed the subject. "I heard your meeting hall was wrecked and soldiers are hunting down Wobblies." She rested a hand on his arm. "Come home with me." He felt her touch almost to his heart. "You can stay until it's safe."

"Ah, Addie, ye'll be takin' me to meet the neighbors so they won't be blatherin' about us."

"Ah, no," falling into his rhythm. "They'll not say a word. You're my kin." But he shook his head. "I'll give you my address and telephone exchange, should you change your mind." She picked up the tablet from her chair.

"What's this? I saw ye with herself outside."

"I'm covering her appearance for the *Spokesman-Review*. I sometimes write for it."

"Ah, 'tis a journalist ye are. A workin' woman."

The crowd was thinning. O'Neill pocketed the folded paper and nodded toward the stage. "Since ye know the lady, would ye introduce one of her countrymen?"

"You're better than a countryman, Mally. She's from County Cork. You're one of her county-men."

"Is she now? We should make haste then."

Addie introduced O'Neill as her Irish cousin.

"Twice removed," he corrected as he took Hanna Sheehy-Skeffington's extended hand, giving his best crooked smile. "I'm from yer own rebel county of Cork, madam. Sent to America to save me neck and keep' me outta more trouble. 'Til I'm needed, me uncle said, but sure he's forgot I'm here."

A smile. An appraisal. "And what have ye been doing in America, Mr. O'Neill?"

"Organizin' men who work, madam. Men without voices. Sure ye'll have heard of the Wobblies?" Interest transformed the woman's face and she nodded, encouraging him to tell more. "I've been shot at and jailed, and lately beaten so bad, I thought the dark angel alighted at me feet." When both women's faces puckered in sympathy, he waved a hand dismissively. "'Tis romantic livin' in a dangerous country such as America." His eyes crinkled. "A great preparation for returnin' home." In his animation to charm Mrs. Sheehy-Skeffington, the ghost of the youth who'd made Addie's heart flutter appeared.

"We've need of Irish patriots here in America, Mr. O'Neill, should ye still consider yerself one."

"I am, 'til the dust stops me ears. Yer words awoke the old longin'." He carried his hand to his heart. "*Éirinn go Brách.*"

Mrs. Sheehy-Skeffington repeated the patriotic phrase. More than words passed between them -- the camaraderie of the Irish discovering one another a long way from home -- and something indefinable.

She asked quietly, "Ye be used to danger then?"

He returned her scrutiny with a highly-charged regard. "I am that, madam."

"Since the Easter Rising chapters of the Friends of Irish Freedom have formed in major American cities. We have a power of men ye're after knowing." A decisive glint came into her eyes, and then she turned to address Addie. "Ye've been very kind, Mrs. MacLean, and I trust yer discretion. But the rest of the evening will not be for newspaper coverage. I have some men I want Mr. O'Neill to meet. I hope ye'll be understanding."

Her abrupt dismissal mystified Addie, but she replied graciously, "I have a story to write for the morning paper." They shook hands.

She grasped O'Neill's hands. "Don't be a stranger, Mally. Please."

Giving her a jaunty smile, he lifted her hand to his cheek. "I'll stay in touch now, Addie." But already she felt him distancing himself, imbued with Mrs. Sheehy-Skeffington's zealousness. "Ah, I forgot to ask, do ye have wee childers about yer home?"

She shook her head, bade them farewell, and left for the nearby *Spokesman-Review* building, her piece already writing itself in her mind. She was certain her editor would consider it a front page "must."

The next morning when Addie carried the newspaper into her study and unfolded it, the front page held nothing about Mrs. Sheehy-Skeffington. The headline read: *U.S. Guardsmen Land Rowan and 26 Other I.W.W. in Spokane County Jail.* Her account of the lecture was on page three. Its small headline, *Free Belgium, Then Ireland* was not her header. Her piece was edited by half, parts of the story dramatically changed. Mrs. Sheehy-Skeffington's husband was identified as a member of Sinn Fein. He'd been a pacifist and was never a member. She'd decided the facts proved he was murdered, but that word was changed to "executed," as though he'd been tried by a jury and found guilty. Should she be surprised? Her editor, George Dobbs, was a transplanted Englishman.

Her weekly advice column was printed in its small entirety.

Mrs. Vandervort's Helpful Hints

To bake potatoes successfully, first boil them in salted water for ten minutes before placing them in a hot oven.

Apply kerosene to window screens to keep off mosquitoes. Fly paper should hang in every room and outside near open windows. Flies carry germs and germs will make us ill . . ..

Chapter 14
Butte, Montana: Late August, 1917

"So, you were sent from Spokane?" Timothy Sullivan set a mug of beer before O'Neill in a back room of Finlander Hall, a haven for Butte's radical elements. Settling himself into a chair that threatened to splinter beneath his weight, he peered at the I.W.W. card O'Neill proffered. "Christ, man, we don't need a labor agitator. Buried one a couple of weeks ago. You probably knew him." Sullivan's broad face wore an earnest expression. "We've got five thousand riled miners on strike an' we're tryin' to keep a lid on 'em. Two hundred federal troops are out there patrollin' the streets, waitin' for somethin' bad to happen. We sure as hell don't want another agitator."

O'Neill listened patiently. "I've done me share of organizin' for workingmen's rights, 'tis true. But I'm here for a different cause, that of the auld dirt." Until he heard the lady from Ireland, his homeland had lain quiescent in his mind. "Mrs. Sheehy-Skeffington sent me. She says, 'Ye'll find friends with plans to help Ireland in her fight for independence. Offer yer services.'" O'Neill flicked the red card. 'Tis but to show ye me credentials." He withdrew a folded paper, tapped a finger on it and handed it to Sullivan, who pushed it over to James Treanor.

Ah, the man in charge. Treanor scanned the schoolmarm's script. She'd written, *You may trust the bearer. He comes from Cork. Hanna Sheehy-Skeffington.*

"Met Mrs. Sheehy-Skeffington, did ye." Treanor had a Dublin lilt. "Where and when?"

"Spokane, three days ago."

The other Sullivan, Brian, shifted his wide-shouldered miner's body. The two Sullivans must be brothers, but Butte was full of Sullivans; his new landlady was a Sullivan. "Being I.W.W. and sayin' you've organized . . . did you know Frank Little that we buried?"

O'Neill crossed himself. "May he rest in peace. I knew the man. First time I met him was at the Spokane free speech trials of '09. Heard ye give him a grand funeral."

Tim Sullivan broke in. "Three thousand mourners marched. Red sashes worn for him, green for us. Red carnations. Did right by the man. The ones who lynched him dragged him behind an auto and tore off his kneecaps. Beat the shit out of him before they hanged him from the trestle."

Blood pulsed through O'Neill's neck. "Soldiers were they?" Mother in Heaven, he hated soldiers. He hadn't much liked that sour wee man with a bum leg and blind eye, but Little had been a fearless hell-raiser and given great incendiary speeches. The man lacked humor, but had been a fanatical Wobbly.

"The newspapers said 'twas soldiers," Treanor interjected, "but likely not. Pinkertons 'tis thought or maybe toughs from Anaconda. Frank Little said at a strike meetin' that the strike won't work without violence against the company. What he said next stuck in me head. 'What if our soldiers sent to fight the Germans laid down their arms and declared they were gonna conduct a peaceful war.' Christ! I'm thinkin', Ireland's been danderin' down that road . . . conductin' a peaceful war. What's been done since the Easter Rising? Not so feckin' much."

Brian Sullivan interrupted, "Ah, James, don't go blamin' Ireland. She's on her knees. Tried to get German guns, didn't she, but the war got in the way. If Germany wins, it'll come to her aid . . ."

"Shut up, Brian," Tim Sullivan cautioned. "You've no call to say that. We're all loyal Americans here. Tell Mr. O'Neill you were but coddin' him."

Brian Sullivan's face twisted, the way a younger brother's might. "I'm a loyal American since the age of four." Glowered at his brother. "Tim here was two when we came over." O'Neill reconsidered their relationship. "I didn't mean I hope Germany beats America. I hope it beats the shit out of bloody England is all."

Treanor said, "Seems we're damned whichever way. First we protested the American draft here in Butte and made the fur fly." O'Neill sat back for a recital of ill-will. "The idea of fightin' for England that riveted chains of slavery 'round Ireland makes ye dog-sick. You're a Wobbly and a Corkonian, O'Neill. I'm a Dubliner meself, but me mither was a Connor from Cork. Lots of Butte Irish from Cork. Irishmen of the proper kind. So we'll say here and now, we believe we can trust ye."

"Why I've come," O'Neill said, "is to help Ireland shake off the English yoke. 'Tis equal whether I do it here or bring meself back to Cork."

These men weren't members of the Friends for Irish Freedom, whose goal was to convince America to recognize an independent Ireland. Mrs. Sheehy-Skeffington had used that group's name in front of Addie as a ruse. What she had in mind were these members of the Pearse-Connolly Club for Irish Independence, named for two Irishmen killed in the Easter Rising. It had a more dangerous agenda, its leaders here in Butte coming from its Wobbly faction. But did their heads hold anything beyond dogma and twinkling eyes? An Irishman will talk a man under the table before getting down to business. "So can ye use me?"

Treanor nodded to Tim Sullivan, who explained, "Ireland needs a new source of guns and we think we've found it." Sullivan spoke of the Canadian Ross rifles, how the mud in France jammed their firing mechanisms and their loose collars allowed bayonets to fall out during charges across no man's land. "The Canadian soldiers threw them away and took Enfields off dead Brits. But they're a good long-range rifle, sniper accurate. If you can see your target up to a mile away, you can hit it. The New York Guard is negotiatin' with the Canadian government to buy surplus Rosses for trainin'. A man in that guard told a Pearce-Connolly member in New York City, who sent word here. Ya catch my drift, O'Neill?"

"Mind, I'll be up an' gone if ye tell me ye're plannin' to steal 'em from the New York Guard."

Sullivan shook his head. "There's no shippin' guns to Ireland from the east coast with the ports being watched. Every boat is searched twice, the Americans lookin' for German spies, the British huntin' for contraband shipped to Ireland. The Royal Navy is boardin' ships soon as they enter international waters. If Canada has surplus guns for the New York Guard, we're bettin' it'll have surplus to sell the Montana Guard. We've got friends in the guard here willin' to make up purchase orders. We'll bring the guns down from Canada legal like, but they won't be goin' to the guard armory in Helena. We'll bring 'em here, then transport 'em to the West Coast and a boat."

"Yer plan then, 'tis not a hedge up to the sky?" With the right Irishmen in the Montana Guard, the right Irishmen along a railroad line and a friendly boat captain, enough money could put their plan in play. He reversed his chair, sitting astride it with arms folded on its top rail. Drained his beer before asking, "Do ye have the funds?"

Treanor nodded. "Funds will be comin' from New York and Boston. The Irish organizations there can't wipe their arses without an English spy handin' 'em the paper. They're lookin' toward Butte, the biggest Irish town west of New York. Money's been promised for guns and bullets. Payoffs, too. Enough fall money to square a railroad route to the West Coast."

"So, ye've a plan to get 'em to the coast." O'Neill's heart sank when the big Sullivan faces went blank and Treanor's turned grim. It would all come to nothing.

"We're workin' on that," Treanor said. "'Tis a fresh idea, this Ross rifle, but we're dealin' with the big strike here in Butte. Would ye be knowin' the lay of the land from here to the coast?"

O'Neill's hopes rose again. "The railroad lines for certain."

"Are ye agreein' it can be done?"

There was no plan, just a clutch of glinty-eyed men, drinking beer and daydreaming. "Leave me to think on it. What about bringin' the arms down from Canada to Butte?"

"Be leavin' that to us, O'Neill. We're on firmer ground there." More beer was poured and Tim Sullivan toasted, "To the harp of Ireland. May it never lack for a string as long as there's a gut in an Englishman." It had a satisfying ring.

Chapter 15

The streets of Butte were thick alive with miners out on strike and armed soldiers in twos and threes watching them. O'Neill knew Butte, had even worked down in the Mountain Con Mine for a week. The city was a delight after dark, but a horror in the morning when daylight revealed a smoky gray cityscape where nothing green grew. That evening he walked down to the flats and away from the "Richest Hill on Earth." It was odd, the absence of mining noises - the hoistings, the distant roar of ore being dumped from skips into huge bins, the ore train careening down through town. Men had struck the smelters out on the flats, too, and no fog of sulfurous smoke blew through Butte. Stars peppered a clear black sky. He reached a comfort point and turned around. On the Hill behind the city incandescent searchlights positioned at mines swept over miners' homes clinging to gulches and hillsides, streams of light crossing beams from searchlights out on the flats and at the tailings dump. Those powerful rays symbolized the class warfare in which he'd skirmished for years. Mine owners who sucked workingmen dry, forcing them to strike for better pay and working conditions for their survival, now watched them day and night. Miners were picketing outside mine gates around the clock, shifts relieved at dusk and dawn. They descended the Hill, stopping off for a mug of hot coffee or a beer before going to desolate little homes and sad families. At dawn mine guards relaxed trigger fingers and searchlights darkened until nightfall. A strike normally filled him with volatile enthusiasm, making him eager to join the melee. But not now. He strolled back to his room.

As he considered how to get rifles and ammunition from Butte to the West Coast without discovery, he always returned to using the Milwaukee Road over the Bitterroots, through the St. Joe Valley, then up to the dreaded rail yards of Spokane. That major division point bristled with Army troops systematically searching freights for illegal booze. If they made it through Spokane, it should be a smooth ride to Ellensburg and then to the port of Tacoma.

The next morning he set out his plan. "Have ye friends workin' the Milwaukee to help us here in Butte?"

"We do," Treanor answered.

"Then the plan I'll be recommendin' is this."

They listened and Treanor said, "We'll want to test it out on a small cache of guns we've collected. If they get to Tacoma, they can be hidden until the big shipment goes out."

"Sensible," O'Neill agreed. "Ye'll be wantin' me to contact some trainmen along the way first, I suppose."

A few days later Tim Sullivan produced a list of railroad crews on a scheduled run to Tacoma. "When you locate 'em, say we'll be havin' a small run of guns comin' through. Be sure they aren't hesitant. When you return, we'll send out the guns."

O'Neill memorized the list, lit a match to it, and then whispered the names. Treanor nodded in approval. "We wondered how you'd handle that, O'Neill. A practical thinker."

"Only experienced."

Ten days later he was back, his contacts made.

"Come along with us now," Tim Sullivan said. "We want you to meet someone." They took him down Wyoming Street to St. Mary's church, built a decade earlier, but already taking on Butte's grayness. "This is the miners' church and you're goin' to meet the miners' priest. A member of Pearse-Connolly himself, and with us heart and soul. He comes from Limerick."

They found the priest in the vestry. As he shook O'Neill's hand, Father Michael Hannan's deep-set eyes appeared to search his soul for past transgressions. A fit figure of a man with bushy eyebrows, a straight nose and jutting chin, but for his receding hair with its accompanying high forehead, he resembled the man O'Neill might have been in a few years, if not for the beatings he'd endured.

Tim Sullivan said, "As we told you, Father, this is the man Mrs. Sheehy-Skeffington sent."

Father Hannan took in his rough edges. "Where ye from?"

"Cork, Father. Eight years since I come to America."

"What have ye been doing with yerself?"

"I. W.W. organizin'. Some lumberjackin'."

"Good. That's good."

"Show him where we're hidin' the guns, Father."

"Now, Brian, what did I tell ye."

Tim Sullivan grasped his brother by the back of his collar, and Brian answered sheepishly, "How many men does it take to keep a secret?"

"Behind the altar, I suspect," O'Neill said.

"Too easy." Father Hannan led them into the church, genuflected before the altar and blessed himself, the men doing the same. O'Neill glanced about. Besides the plaster statues of Mary and Joseph, there was St. Patrick, or maybe it was Saint Finbar, the patron of Cork, where so many hard rock miners came from. A female saint could be Mary Magdalene, appropriate enough for Butte.

Before opening the pine door at the center of the confessional, Father Hannan ordered, "Be lockin' the doors, Tim. No need shoutin' it out." A piece of old carpet lay beneath a padded stool. Like a kid unearthing treasure, Brian Sullivan removed the stool and lifted the carpet to pry up a floorboard with his jackknife.

Father Hannan handed O'Neill a flashlight. Angling it between the joists, he illuminated a canvas bundle. "Enough for a huntin' party, I see."

"Oh, there'll be more," Brian said. "The School of Mines hasn't missed these. Old Springfields mostly."

The priest added, "And all blessed that they fire proper."

Brian grinned. "Father's more the Irish patriot than any of us. Goes out on maneuvers with the Irish Volunteers. Missed his calling. Should be back in Ireland raisin' hell against the English."

"Sure Butte needs missionary priests as much as Ireland needs patriots," Hannan replied. "Me bones will be carried back to Limerick when I die. 'Tis enough for me." He stamped the floorboard back into place, returned the rug and stool, and closed the confessional door. "Love of Ireland and loyalty to America are not incompatible, Malachi." It was strange hearing his Christian name. "We can work both sides of the seam an' not betray one nor t'other." He tapped a finger on O'Neill's chest. "I'll be hearin' confession tonight at seven. Sure ye'll be wantin' a clean conscience for this work."

Chapter 16

O'Neill and the Sullivans met with the chosen Butte yardmen to set the plan. The Springfields would be loaded into a Milwaukee Road boxcar billed as containing scrap iron consigned to Tacoma.

When the mixed train of freight and two passenger cars pulled out of Butte in late morning, O'Neill climbed onto the front of the designated boxcar to ride the buffers undetected. After drawing a dark bandanna over most of his face to protect it from grit, he thrust his hands into gauntlet gloves. He was comfortable holding grab irons on the swaying freight. Hadn't he done this for years? Brian Sullivan rode inside a passenger car.

The train sped along without a hitch, hour after hour. Deer Lodge, Drummond, Missoula. It headed into the Bitterroots and across the Montana-Idaho line. O'Neill exulted in this new calling of transporting arms for Ireland. When it slowed for a stop, passing under a bridge or approaching railroad yards, he hopped off and trotted behind the depot, working blood into stiffened limbs. As the train started up with its devil shriek and locomotion, he climbed back on. Fellow hobos and yard bulls left him alone.

Couplers strained and clacked as the train looped around mountains; steel wheels ground against steel rails in long shrill screams as it descended. Wind rushed past him. Straight tracks became scarcer, curves tighter and more frequent. With little time to relax his hold as cars leaned first one way and then the other in rapid succession, his arms grew weary. The train roared across a long trestle and he grew light-headed peering into the deep shadowed canyon. Mountainsides of skeletal burnt timber still reeked seven years after the 1910 inferno. The train approached the long tunnel he disliked; plunged into its dark throat, its engine roaring and pounding in a deafening din through two black miles beneath a mountain. *Blessed be this electrified engine with no black smoke smotherin' me.* O'Neill dipped his head inside his raised coat collar while groundwater showered from above. The train thrummed under its trolley lines over trestles and through tunnels, then into Idaho's St. Joe

Valley. At Avery, the division point hugging the St. Joe River in a narrow canyon, its electric engine was exchanged for a coal-fired locomotive.

O'Neill climbed down, stiff-legged it into a twenty-four-hour beanery, pulled off his gloves and bolted down some chili, passing the hot bowl from one cramped hand to the other.

It was nighttime now and smooth-going until the train slowed for St. Joe City. The lighted board outside the depot showed the freight was barely ahead of the *Columbian*, the Milwaukee Road's passenger train from Chicago. The freight pulled onto a siding and waited for the *Columbian* to rumble by. Another interminable wait and the *Olympian*, the express train of the line that stopped only at sizable towns, rushed past heading east. The locomotive crept back onto the main track, reaching St. Maries around 10 p.m., then chattered into Washington State. O'Neill clung to the ladder and gazed at the Milky Way between puffs of black smoke from the fireman's stoking the big engine. At the brightly-lighted Spokane yards, the train sat unsearched, and O'Neill used what guile remained in his tired body to plod across tracks and squeeze between boxcars to avoid yard bulls.

Just before sunrise events in Ellensburg fouled the plan. The train entered the freight yard and O'Neill hopped down to await a crew change. Movement around the boxcar alerted him and, as he watched from a distance, yardmen uncoupled and disengaged the car from the consist, maneuvering it from the main line to a repair track. While O'Neill hunkered near the setout, the train continued toward the coast with Sullivan on-board.

Jaysus! What in hell? Had someone in Butte tipped off the feds? Warned the railroad? Hungry and tired, he squatted among weeds, watching for activity around the boxcar. The rattling ride had awakened the throbbing in his jaw, a remnant of his beating at St. Maries. Trains puffed through the yards, going west and east, but the orphaned freight car sat alone. The eastern sky was lightening across Washington's flatland when O'Neill located a café on a nearby dusty street. When he returned to the yards, a workman was repairing a broken drawbar at the end of the car. A second workman broke the car's seal, rumbled open the door, and pulled himself inside; clambered over bailed paper camouflaging the canvas-wrapped guns. *God and His saints, don't let 'em get suspicious.*

A train steaming through the yards covered the crunch of gravel and cinders. When he looked up, it was to see a yard bull standing over him, a club in one hand, a revolver in the other.

"Hold it right there, you goddamn bum! Lemme see your classification card for the draft."

Tempted to bite him in the leg and run, O'Neill instead stood up. "Sure yer honor, we Irish are draft free at present."

"Then you'd better have an alien registration card."

"'Tis in me shoe." He was made to sit and pull it off to retrieve the card. The bull seized it.

"What kind of a spud name is Mal-a-chee? Registered in St. Maries, huh? Whaddaya do for a living?"

"Lumberjack."

"Like hell you are. Now the other shoe."

That was where he kept his I.W.W. card. One shoe away from arrest, he curled his toes to make it appear difficult to remove, stalling for time.

The bull pushed the club into his shoulder. "Hurry up."

"Ye'll be havin' me barefoot, yer honor."

From the boxcar's open door the workman gave a shrill whistle and waved.

The bull yelled, "I'm fuckin' busy."

"Hey! There's guns in here!"

The man dropped O'Neill's card and lumbered across the tracks. The Irishman picked up his registration card and slipped on his shoe, then bolted down the tracks to find cover behind some empty boxcars. He fast walked along a line of gondolas and angled off into a field; followed a ditch until he passed behind the freight depot. Should he lay low and wait out the day for the safety of darkness or chance making a break for an east-bounder and Butte? *Holy Mary, Mother of God, help this poor sinner . . .*

Chapter 17
Spruce Production Division, U.S. Army Signal Corps
Portland, Oregon: November, 1917

Hung-over from an all-night poker game on the train, he saluted his new commanding officer, announcing in a ragged voice, "First Lieutenant Robert Jamieson reporting for duty, sir." He'd expected to be sent to France, not back to the Pacific Northwest.

He'd met Colonel Brice Disque in Washington, D.C., the previous June and the colonel, awaiting an overseas command for himself, had intimated a future assignment for Jamieson under him with duty in aerial reconnaissance. Instead, Jamieson had been given a desk job and Disque had taken command of the newly formed Spruce Production Division of the United States Army Signal Corps to produce lumber for boats and airplanes. The colonel requested Jamieson's transfer to his command, all right, right here on the 5th floor of the Yeon Building in Portland, Oregon.

Sitting ramrod straight behind his desk, exuding a scent of heavy starch and hair pomade that made Jamieson's whiskey-soaked stomach churn, Disque scrutinized him.

The colonel was already impacting the lumber industry in the Pacific Northwest. Thousands of soldiers had been diverted from embarkation to France to barracks in nearby Vancouver, Washington, to cut spruce. The Army had assumed control over lumber production and the men who produced it. "He came to see and stayed to saw" was making the rounds.

A day late because his west-bound train was side-tracked by east-bound troop trains heading for embarkation, Jamieson wandered through the Portland headquarters filled with khaki-clad "sprucers" appearing, if not indispensable, at least busy.

The colonel's eyes flicked over his rumpled uniform and haggard, but clean-shaven face. "Difficult journey, Lieutenant?"

The all-nighter in a smoker had reddened his eyes and graveled his voice. Jamieson cleared his throat. "No, sir. Not until my gear was stolen, sir." He'd borrowed a razor after a fruitless search for his kit.

The colonel's voice was dry and humorless. "I'm giving a little orientation to these new officers, Lieutenant. Good of you to attend. Take a seat."

Jamieson sized up the command hierarchy in the room. Ranged claustrophobically on chairs and the two windowsills, or standing with folded arms, were ten Military Intelligence Division second lieutenants, shavetails newly graduated from Officers Training School at The Presidio in San Francisco. Clear-eyed faces stared at him, but only the three senior officers rated Jamieson's consideration. Major George Gund, the division intelligence officer, whom he'd also met, sat on Disque's right; next to him was an Army captain, name unknown.

At a nod from Gund, a junior officer vacated the chair next to the captain, which Jamieson took, keeping his jaw squared and his back straight, careful not to allow exhaustion and a throbbing head to bend his spine. He resisted the urge to rub his burning eyes.

Imperious and saturnine, Disque began his intelligence briefing. "As you know, gentlemen, you are being assigned to various districts in Oregon and Washington where the Sitka spruce is being logged for aircraft and ships. One or two of you will be going into north Idaho." Like Julius Caesar, Disque had divided his Gaul into three parts. "They're logging white pine in Idaho, needed for supply crates and especially for airplane struts and wing beams. An airplane can't fly without them."

Ten earnest-faced second lieutenants glanced at Major Gund, seeking clues on how to react to the colonel's pronouncements. Gund, a former university professor, sat impassive, eyes inscrutable behind round spectacles. The unknown captain, pale-eyed above a blond mustache, looked smugly omniscient.

"Our mission is to increase spruce production from three million board feet per month to ten million. And that means now." Disque held each man's gaze for a moment. "Not next year, not next month. Now." He paused for emphasis. "In October not more than half the spruce shipped out was good enough for airplane manufacture." Long of face, hair graying beneath slick pomade, he was the unsmiling executive of a large company. "Our orders are to make certain the lumber industry operates smoothly, giving us what we need, when we need it."

Major Gund nodded, aped by ten second lieutenants; the blond captain sat impassive. Jamieson squinted, taking in Disque's words. What the hell did this have to do with him?

"It's why we've formed a division of soldiers, who were experienced lumberjacks and sawmill workers in civilian life. They won't replace loyal civilian loggers and lumbermen, but will supplement labor needed to increase production if we are to win this war." Again his eyes traveled the room. "And we will win this war."

Then he evinced a controlled enthusiasm. "The Army has formed a new labor union, not just of laborers, but of everyone - owners, managers, lumberjacks and sawmill workers. It's called the Loyal Legion of Loggers and Lumbermen . . . 4L for short. You will assist in organizing this new union in logging camps and at sawmills. You will appeal to the patriotism and good sense of civilian workers in every logging camp you visit. Another so-called union in the woods is composed of anarchists." With disdain he said its name. "The Industrial Workers of the World. The Wobblies." Another pause. "They are a menace, threatening slowdowns and strikes to disrupt the war effort. Our new union will counter their influence."

Gund and the officers adopted the colonel's visage of resolve while Disque directed a gaze, opaque as a Pinkerton detective's, at Jamieson.

The I.W.W.? Was that why he was here?

"There were strikes in the lumber industry last summer that slowed and halted production. You men may have been too busy in other walks of life to notice." His words brought self-conscious grins. "I reviewed the demands of legitimate strikers and we've ordered better living conditions in logging camps. And we will institute the eight-hour day they demanded. It will go into effect in the new year."

If Disque's concessions to lumberjacks and mill workers had been reported in newspapers back east, Jamieson had missed it. The turmoil in the woods had paid off, but only because the federal government needed lumber.

"These improvements in lumberjacks' working conditions will remove legitimate excuses for strikes." There were nods from young men with no notion of what the fuss had been about.

Disque collected his thoughts. "You'll recall what Theodore Roosevelt said about immigrants who cling to their un-American goals and character because only part of them has come to our country. He called it hyphenism." The young officers, in knickers when TR was president, nodded knowingly. "But he also said they are no longer German-American or Irish-American when the whole man comes over to our ways with his heart and thoughts. The hyphen drops of its own weight and he is a true American." He warmed to his subject. "Most of the men in logging camps and sawmills are true Americans. Remember that. But . . ." He held up an imperious long-fingered hand. ". . I'm sending you out to look for those un-Americans working against the war effort, using labor conditions as a pretense." As eyes locked on his, ardent faces realized here was their true mission, to search out the unpatriotic. "Are they intent on helping Germany? Are they Irish and more anti-British than pro-American?" In a clipped voice he ticked off, finger-by-finger, "We will eliminate sedition, sabotage and unrest in the camps." He leaned forward. "Your mission, in addition to organizing our new labor union, is to gather intelligence on possible saboteurs. If the Army can ferret out the real culprits behind the troubles in the woods, we will help bring the war to a close that much sooner, and it will be worth our efforts." Disque stood with a crackle of starched shirt. The sitting officers jumped to their feet and came to attention; those standing had only to stiffen.

Jamieson rose with the others. The Army believed the I.W.W. was the culprit behind the troubles in the woods, not worker dissatisfaction. It was going to be another Wobbly hunt. The same old game of fox and geese, but this time the fox wasn't a city or a state, but the United States Army.

The colonel shook hands with each lieutenant, then addressed Jamieson, "You will remain with Major Gund and Captain Dengel, Lieutenant."

Chapter 18

The shavetails filed out and Disque reseated himself. "Rearrange your chairs in front of my desk." He removed a folder from a drawer and viewed its top sheet. Jamieson blinked at his own typed name affixed to a tab. "Lieutenant Jamieson, Major Gund met you back in Washington while he was assisting in developing secret surveillance programs. Captain Dengel here is an experienced intelligence officer, having served with General Pershing on the Mexican border." Disque handed the folder to Dengel. "Please begin, Captain."

Dengel twitched his lips, blond mustache rearranging itself like a woolly caterpillar. "Lieutenant, we're familiar with your background as a Pinkerton detective." He gave Jamieson an approving half-smile.

"Yes, sir." He'd been extensively interviewed when he entered the Intelligence Service. Notes were taken.

"You worked as a lumberjack in Michigan during your college years."

"Yes, sir." If he'd omitted that information, he'd be on a ship now, headed for Europe. You had to have second sight in this man's army.

"You personally knew members of the I.W.W."

"While working the railroad lines."

"And recently?"

No doubt that information lay just below Dengel's eyes. "I infiltrated I.W.W. meetings in Seattle last autumn during labor troubles in Everett to observe whether they planned violence."

Dengel didn't ask for elaboration. "You were jailed with a group of Wobblies arrested on the *Verona*."

"Yes, sir, but they were never convicted of a crime."

Gund interrupted. "One was tried, but found not guilty. Snohomish County declined to pursue cases against the other seventy-three."

"Yes, sir." No arguing with Gund's facts.

Disque interjected, "Lieutenant, did you break your cover as a member of the I.W.W.?"

And gotten himself beaten or killed? Billy Sewell taught him better. "No sir, not with the Wobblies. I did write a letter to the prosecuting attorney for Snohomish County, informing him of my observations during the shootings at the Everett wharf."

Disque addressed Gund. "See if that letter still exists and have it pulled from the prosecutor's file."

Dengel's flaxen mustache compressed above pursed lips. "Lieutenant, we're trying to locate an I.W.W. agitator arrested after the Everett fiasco." He passed a photograph to Jamieson. "Do you recognize this man?"

Christ! Would he be ordered to identify Wobblies for the Army to arrest?

The mug shot resembled any number of undernourished men living the hard life, but his skills of observation hadn't deserted him. Intense black eyes, defiant features, nose slightly angled. The photographer's flash lamp washed out any detail of the defining bridge and he couldn't tell whether it dipped in the middle.

"Could be a man called Irish, who was on the *Verona*. Wobblies all use monikers. You almost never learn a surname."

"His name is Malachi O'Neill." Disque fastened piercing eyes on Jamieson. "Lieutenant, I'm assigning you to Captain Dengel's region, eastern Washington, northern Idaho, and western Montana. He's headquartered in Spokane."

Jamieson's heart thumped with disappointment. When fortune played her little trick of having him reassigned to the Pacific Northwest, he went out and got drunk . . . and hadn't been completely sober since. But this assignment? The real work of spy-hunting and foiling sabotage was in western Washington and Oregon where Sitka spruce was being cut. What had he done to deserve this? An experienced detective – ex-detective – he was being sent to where they were cutting white pine for boxes and a couple of airplane parts. War was hell all right. It took a real effort to maintain a poker face.

Dengel frowned, maybe reading his mind. He'd heard Dengel's name and about his methods of interrogating Mexicans on the border. "Lieutenant, you're not being assigned to organize the Loyal Legion of Loggers and Lumbermen over in my region, but to . . . "

Disque broke in. "The 4L, Captain. Remember to call it that. It sounds better."

"Yes, sir." Dengel bent over the folder and Jamieson detected a smirk. In control again, he continued, "Because you're experienced, your mission is more critical . . ." Corrected himself, ". . is as critical to your government as organizing the 4L."

"Yes, sir." The Army would never organize lumberjacks into a neat union package. They existed to resist conformity. Let others try to work some Army magic. Anything else had to be more important.

Disque interrupted again. "There'll be no paperwork with this mission. Major Gund? Captain Dengel?"

"Correct, sir." Gund was brisk. "No record of this meeting or future meetings."

What the hell was he being pulled into? Assassination?

"Then we'll sit in a circle so we won't be overheard." Disque rose and the men rearranged their chairs.

The colonel sat directly across from Jamieson, their knees nearly touching. God, he must reek of stale smoke and booze. But as Gund and Dengel talked in low voices and Jamieson listened, self-consciousness faded. This briefing wasn't about I.W.W. agitation in logging camps in north Idaho. And it wasn't about elusive rumors of German spies bent on sabotage. Gund was briefing him on the Irish Question. He knew shit about relations between Ireland and Great Britain.

It took Gund but a few minutes to bring Anglo-Irish politics onto American soil, summarizing the background of every Irish-American organization whose goal was to assist Ireland in gaining independence from Great Britain, America's great ally. Gund was in his professorial element. "And you can count on Germany's financial backing of every Irish society in this country. Let me give you an example of the fanaticism of those Irish miners in Butte. Some years back they took advantage of the federal government's program to sell surplus rifles to gun clubs. Under the guise of the Robert Emmet Literary Association, they acquired Springfields, using them to form Company A of the Irish Volunteers of America, preparing themselves for eventual repatriation to fight for an Irish republic. I wouldn't be surprised if some of the guns found in that freight car in Ellensburg originated with that group."

When Gund and Dengel finally wound down, Colonel Disque picked up the threads, snugging them together in conclusion. "So, a boxcar originating in Butte, Montana, carrying guns . . . an Irishman discovered near the damaged boxcar at Ellensburg . . . and a railroad detective recalling the name on his alien registration card as maybe Malarchy McNeal, a lumberjack registered in St. Maries, Idaho. He said the man looked and smelled I. W.W. Military intelligence showed him every mug shot it found of an I.W.W. Irishman, and he recognized Malachi O'Neill's photo. A source in Butte identified O'Neill as having been there shortly before those guns were shipped out. And we picked up rumors, which lead us to believe a movement is underway to arm Ireland. That Irish faction in Butte . . . you ever do any work on those men, Lieutenant? I know the mining interests busted the union in '14. Were you involved with infiltrating the union there?"

"No, sir. Railroads were my specialty. I would have had to work in the mines to be able to infiltrate a miners' union." He didn't add that the Pinkertons used stool pigeons, paying them to turn on their own kind.

Disque nodded. "After those guns were discovered in Ellensburg, O'Neill couldn't be located. Now he's resurfaced, lumberjacking near St. Maries, Idaho. We want you to find him, befriend him, discover what he knows. We aren't one hundred percent certain he was connected with that boxcar carrying weapons. Maybe he was only transiting through. But if he is involved, he'll know who's behind the gunrunning out of Butte. We need names. We've got Military Intelligence officers working on this in Montana, but those Butte Irish are a tight-lipped bunch. All of them radicals."

"Yes, sir." Gritty from lack of sleep, Jamieson mentally sorted related intelligence to analyze later.

Disque added, "You won't be in uniform, Lieutenant, and your identity will be secret. It's a dangerous mission, especially if you go to Butte. Leave us a description of prominent marks on your body, including fillings and missing teeth." Satisfied with having made his point, the colonel sat back.

Dengel wasn't finished, though. "I have some intelligence work in Spokane I want you to attend to first . . . we'll get to know each other." Jamieson's glazed attention rested on Dengel's twitching mustache as he detailed the assignment. Goddamn! He needed sleep. Like a Victrola, he rewound his brain, reset the needle to the beginning of the captain's statement, heard it repeat in his head while catching up. Dengel stood. "I've got a train to catch. Report to me in Spokane in two days."

After he left, Disque waved Jamieson back into his chair. "Captain Dengel is your contact in Spokane and he may think you're under his authority, but you answer to me, and I answer to Washington. This mission has priority. As explained earlier, another uprising in Ireland will distract Great Britain from the war in Europe, pressuring it to deploy men from the western front to Ireland, and leaving the Americans to do the fighting. It could initiate a string of events ending with our losing the war." For a moment he appeared burdened with unshared knowledge. "Any questions, Lieutenant?"

"No, sir." Tired, Jamieson gave a chip-on-the-shoulder response. "I know what's required in undercover work."

"We know you do, Lieutenant. It's why I hand-picked you for this assignment." Disque escorted Jamieson to the door, followed by Gund. They shook his hand. "Do your country proud, Lieutenant. And get your uniform cleaned and pressed. You're still an officer."

Withdrawing a bag of Bull Durham from his pocket as the two retreated back into Disque's war room, Jamieson overheard Gund say, "Disreputable enough for you, sir?" and Disque's reply as the door clicked shut. "He'll do."

He strolled through the office full of Army clerks, but out in the hallway, cigarette stuck to his dry lower lip, he wanted to punch a fist through a wall. "Fuck!" He'd be doing the same kind of infiltration work as before. The only difference -- the stakes were higher.

Chapter 19
Spokane: November, 1917

Cotton soaked in weak carbolic acid and packed against raw nerves no longer relieved O'Neill's throbbing back teeth, souvenirs of Sheriff Roland's thug kicking him in the jaw. He demanded his pay from the logging camp where he'd been lying low and on a bitterly cold day hopped a freight for Spokane. He'd accost the I.W.W. attorney there for some crisis funds and have a dentist pull those teeth, or put him out of his misery.

His jaw pounded to the train's thrumming. The cold numbed his face, but barely reduced the pain. After crawling from the boxcar, careful not to jar his teeth, he trudged the few blocks to the Lindelle Building on Riverside. The pulsing ache confused him and at the third floor he turned right, passing frosted glass doors until he stopped at one partially open. Inside a soldier in profile sat at a desk, earphones bracketing his head. His military uniform stopped O'Neill short. Like the English army in Cork, the American army was an occupying force in Spokane's heart. He stepped back and looked up. Above the door a thick black wire snaked from the transom, at which point it was painted white to match the wall it ran along toward the stairwell, then up and over. Holding his upturned jaw, O'Neill followed the wire down the hall to where it disappeared through another high transom and into the office of the I.W.W. attorney. *Saint Patrick, ye great Mick, 'tis grateful I am ye steered me the wrong way.*

The lawyer recognized him and, cocking his head, correctly interpreted the mumbled request for funds. He took O'Neill into his office and squatted to open the small safe. "Keep taking those beatings and your mouth will look like a piano keyboard with missing ivories."

O'Neill grunted and pocketed the funds, then held up a calloused hand. Seizing the fountain pen, he bent to write on a tablet. Blood rushed to his head, making it beat like a tom-tom. Lifting a finger to his lips, he passed the tablet, pointing to the black microphone unobtrusively positioned on ceiling molding in a dim corner.

Flummoxed, the lawyer read the note and stared up at the microphone behind his desk. "What is it?"

O'Neill beckoned him. They traversed the hall and he shoved open the door to expose a soldier with pad and pencil hovering over a listening device. An officer bent over the desk, a headset cupping his ears.

Across the room, back turned, a second officer stood silhouetted against a window. He swung around and exclaimed, "Captain Dengel!" The officer at the desk jerked off his earphones, straightened and glared at the intruders.

The I.W.W. lawyer roared, "Are you listening in on my conversations? Fuck you bastards and your shoddy government tricks."

The backlit officer barked, "Get the hell out of here!" The one called Dengel slammed the door, smacking the attorney's raised hand. Someone threw a bolt inside.

"I should have stuck my foot in the door," the lawyer raged, heading back down the hall. "I'm going to cut that wire." He stood fuming outside his office. "Damn martial law! No wonder the Army's been arresting Wobs as soon as they mount a soapbox." He anguished, "Jesus Christ! I wondered why the Army knew our every move. I thought a Wobbly had been turned." Fisting his hand into a gun, he pointed his forefinger at his temple and pulled the imaginary trigger. "It was me all along, ratting out the workers."

O'Neill entered the Peerless Dentists office, whose newspaper advertisement promised painless extractions for fifty cents each. When the dentist explained the painless part was using ether to put O'Neill to sleep during extractions, the Irishman shook his head and mumbled, "Get on with it then." He couldn't trust anybody, anytime, anywhere.

After the two broken teeth at the back of his lower jaw were extracted, the hammering pain became a steady ache he could deal with once he got his hands on some whiskey.

The dentist exhibited the last piece of bloody molar. "If you don't stop brawling and losing teeth, your face will cave in like a rotten potato."

Had this man slurred his race and should he upend him into the trash to join his teeth? But the dentist stood grinning in his blood-spattered smock. Codding him then. Most likely he said the same to all men of the proletariat. O'Neill took the proffered prescription for a pint of whiskey to succor his fresh wounds.

"Use it to rinse out the sockets, then let them clot so you won't bleed into your pillow tonight."

The pharmacy lay handy. He entered, making pained noises, exposing the bloody cotton in his cheek.

The pharmacist accepted the prescription and two dollars. Produced a pint of banned liquor. "Sign here. Medicinal purposes only."

"Sure ye're right altogether," O'Neill mumbled through the wadding.

Settled into a friendly flophouse, he took a swig of palliative spirits, swilled and swallowed. Not the first time whiskey mixed with blood found its way down his throat. Sipping carefully, he floated down the comeback trail on a lumpy mattress. Before the whiskey numbed his brain, he had a few moments of broken thought about the listening device. That officer at the window had a familiar voice. Was it possible he'd had a run-in with him before? *Jaysus!* He knew many men, but none with the arrogant balls to become an Army officer. Had he been an overbearing sheriff's deputy or even a pompous sheriff? Not likely. *Blagards* and *bowsies*. That voice, though, alarmed, but quick-witted enough to get them out the door. By leaving the door ajar, those Army apes had made a complete *butthoon* of it, but not before they'd piled more shite onto the damage already inflicted on the I.W.W. The wankers!

O'Neill rose late, peered into the mirror at his swollen jaw sporting a large bruise, but was satisfied there was little pain. The day was too cold to idle along Trent Avenue, so he took himself to the Union Gospel Mission, seeking the company of lumberjacks. He feigned attention to a couple of sermons and was given soup, a hunk of bread, and a passable cup of coffee, which he dined on while catching up with the latest indignities being done to the Wobblies.

In the lead-colored evening O'Neill pulled his cap low, thrust hands into his coat pockets, and trudged through swirling grit and dried manure to his room. After a slug of whiskey, he went out to locate the back stairs leading up to a heatless room in which the Wobblies were holding a meeting. The I.W.W. hall was still under Army padlock.

At the end of the meeting the I.W.W. secretary announced, "I know you lumberjacks are flush from fighting forest fires this past summer. Dig deep, fellow workers, for our brothers being framed and jailed out there. Our lawyers have to eat and buy train tickets to travel from courthouse to courthouse."

Cigar boxes were passed around and men unbuttoned coats and fished in pockets. Dimes plinked, quarters chunked and an occasional silver dollar thudded. Tossing in two dollars, O'Neill said from the good side of his mouth, "Sure 'twas I on that feckin' *Verona*."

He and a few others sauntered over to the Pantages for a vaudeville show. Chester's Posing Dogs made them laugh, but Morris Golden, the Yiddle with the Fiddle, caused O'Neill to tear up during an Irish air.

The next morning he climbed into a boxcar and headed for Butte to see how the plans for the munitions were progressing. Despite the fiasco in the Ellensburg train yards, if it was the last thing he did, he'd see this scheme through for Ireland.

Chapter 20
Butte, Montana: November, 1917

"Now who did ye say is makin' arrangements for the purchase of guns and ammunition from the Canadians?"

"We didn't say, O'Neill." Treanor handed him a cigarette and offered a light. "We said we have a man. He's in Butte now. 'Twas him approached us with the plan about the guns. Said it worked bootleggin' booze down from Canada and figured he could make it work with arms. We asked him why he thought we'd be interested in buyin' arms. He said he did a stint as a railroad detective and kept his ear to the rails."

"Had ye been interested afore yer man come along?"

Treanor blew smoke toward the ceiling. "Sure we'd never heard of the Ross rifle. Are ye thinkin' him a plant sent by the American government?"

"'Tis a growin' thought."

"I'm thinkin' not. We won't be bringin' the guns across the border in secret as he suggested, but legal like. 'Tis grand to be part of the Montana State Guard. On paper, anyways."

O'Neill felt a wave of nausea when the Sullivans escorted Fats Gerard into Finlander Hall. He composed himself before rising to greet him. As always, Gerard looked a right chancer. A man who'd shoot another in the back for certain. How had he gained the miners' trust? He'd briefly trusted Gerard himself for a few foolhardy days and rued it whenever he recalled the shooting on the Seattle wharf. *Jaysus!* Desperate for a black angel they were and here he was.

Gerard spotted him, blinked and then barked in recognition. "I knew you over in Seattle."

A long-lost pal, was he?

Gerard turned to Treanor and the Sullivans. "We was on the *Verona* together. You can trust him." With big-hearted friendliness, he pumped O'Neill's hand. "Good to see ya again, Irish. That Seattle jail sure was a shit hole, wasn't it?" He moved to the table and thudded down a valise, from which he withdrew a fistful of what appeared to be sheathed long knives. He slid a bayonet from a scabbard. "Carried these down from Canada. Bayonets for Ross rifles. Sort of a good will gesture from my man up there makin' the wheels turn for ya." He handed them out.

O'Neill grew edgy hearing Treanor treat Fats like a co-conspirator, revealing O'Neill's part in the plan and that he'd positioned himself in Idaho.

"That so? How're ya keepin' yourself from being picked up as a vagrant over there?"

"Lumberjackin'." O'Neill made a show of examining the bayonet he held.

"That's good. I got ties with the MacLean Lumber Company there. I'm supposed to be the gun if the I.W.W. starts trouble again. Ain't that a hoot." He made sure Treanor and the Sullivans understood the joke. "If ya hook up with MacLean, we can stay in touch. Ya might need me as a go-between with our friends here in Butte. MacLean's camp is on Marble Creek east of St. Maries. Know where it is?" He had the cold look of a snake above his lipless smile.

"I know where 'tis." O'Neill gave them all a crooked grin.

Later, O'Neill asked Treanor, "Yer man, Gerard, is it trustin' him ye be?"

"Ah, sure, we don't trust him, O'Neill. The Sullivans will go with him to Canada to see the guns come across the border proper like. He's no government agent. Just out for himself. Be gettin' a big commission if he delivers the goods. The Canadians don't want their guns shipped to Ireland, so if they suspect somethin', they'll not be allowin' 'em to leave Canada. For sure they're wantin' the money, thinkin' they're unloadin' worthless weapons on unsuspectin' Americans."

Chapter 21

O'Neill and Gerard met late that night at the Board of Trade, a bar fronted by a cigar store, with a gambling joint in back. They bought boilermakers and sat in a dark corner.

"So, what's all this, Fats? Ye're a gun runner now?"

"I'm branchin' out." He slugged down the shot of whiskey and started on the beer. "Gotta hustle to keep ahead, Irish. Gotta keep rubberin' an' thinkin', an' I know how. Find out what people want and get it for 'em. Long as they pony up the plunkers." He ordered another whiskey.

"Sure if anyone can, Fats, 'tis yerself." He'd humor the bastard. Gerard was a braggart, but also clever and vicious. He added with an admiring purr, "Never knew a man with more ideas for the business." Downed his whiskey, but sipped his beer, knowing he was drinking with the devil. *Don't lose yer head, boyo. A year ago too much poteen lost ye the good sense ye had.* "So, yer task is to buy Canadian Ross guns an' bring 'em 'cross the border to Butte."

"An' yours is to take 'em to the West Coast." He gave O'Neill an expressionless look. "If ya don't queer this, we can make it work big time. Those Micks think if they give ya enough fall money, you can square the entire railroad line. What I'm thinkin' is only the Butte an' Tacoma train crews need to be paid off, not the ones in-between. You 'n me, we split the rest."

"Ah, Fats, sure these Butte miners aren't soft-headed. Are ye thinkin' they're so trustin' as to give me lots of boodle raised from hard-workin' Irishmen?"

Gerard shrugged. "You work on that part. What they don't know, they ain't worrin' about. What I got in mind for them Canadian rifles is a fella in California, who supplied guns to Pancho Villa. We'll make ourselves a pile of jack sellin' him those guns." He looked at O'Neill through narrow silver eyes. "Thievin's more natural than honesty. You with me there, Irish?"

"'Tis sometimes easier."

"An' killin' a man ain't bad, ya know, not like the law makes it out to be. It's the extreme edge of man's instinct for self-preservation. I read that in a book. Instinct for self-preservation. I got plenty of that."

"The manly arts, ye'd be callin' 'em." O'Neill's shoulders tightened. His body was a feckin' weather vane. Fats would try to make him his pawn again.

"Yeah, man stuff. The male in us. Like back in Seattle. It could a been them or us that night on the wharf."

Piece of shite. I'm not yer dead horse to beat on, wonderin' if I can be trusted. "So, what's this ye're sayin', Fats?"

Gerard leaned in, shot out a blunt hand and captured O'Neill's wrist. The Irishman saved his glass of beer with his free hand. "I'm sayin' I'll put your lights out if I catch ya rattin' me to your Mick friends."

"An' what would I be tellin' 'em, Fats?" He pried off Gerard's thick fingers. "Are ye thinkin' they love Pinkertons? They'd cheer ye through the streets of Butte did they know ye killed one."

"What makes ya think they was Pinkertons?"

"Now there I can't be certain. Maybe I read it in a newspaper."

Gerard squinted in the smoky room. "It wasn't in no newspaper. Thought ya hated Pinkertons, too."

"That I do, Fats." Keeping his hands visible, O'Neill flattened them on the table.

Gerard emptied his glass and wiped foam from his gash of a mouth. "It was a Pinkerton on the *Verona* put ya away all those months."

O'Neill nodded. "'Tis always a Pinkerton."

"Yeah, but it was the same Pinkerton that got away that night in Seattle. Ain't that a hoot."

"How are ye comin' by knowin' that, Fats?"

Gerard blinked, then folded his arms. "I hear things, same as you."

O'Neill let the subject slide. He was a witness to the killing, but was implicated, too. He might have to kill Gerard someday, but not before the guns came down from Canada. He finished his beer.

"I hear ya thinkin', ya damn bog crawler."

O'Neill smiled. Fats wasn't fey.

Gerard shoved back his chair. "What say we go get some pussy."

O'Neill stood up. "Only if it's Irish. 'Tis bad I'm wanting to plow Irish soil. Red-haired if I can find it."

"Let me tell you about a whore I had on a train a while back."

Chapter 22
Spokane: Early December, 1917

Riverside and Main was a hubbub of streetcar bells, clacking steel wheels, and auto horns blaring at pedestrians making haphazard crossings. Warding off a bullying wind, Addie flattened the folder she carried against her flaring coat. As she reached for the bronze door handle at the *Spokesman-Review* building a policeman's shrill whistle distracted her. Avoiding the opening door, she stepped aside, but not before a uniformed arm knocked the folder from her gloved hand. Typed copy scattered and a whirlwind of dead leaves and grit threatened to skitter the papers into the busy street. The soldier, an officer, squatted to scoop them up; reassembled the three pages before slipping them back into the folder and rising.

"So sorry. Clumsy of me." Touched the brim of his campaign hat.

Her eyes moved from the folder in his gloved hand to his face and the disarming smile spreading across even features. A certain look in his eyes would make some women drop their own, then raise them for more. Some other women.

"I intended to open the door for you, but look what I've done." He was tall but, for a woman, so was she. Hesitant, he asked, "Mrs. Vandervort?"

Clever man, he'd read her byline, her pseudonym at the top of page one. "No. Well, yes," she amended, meeting his eyes. "It's all right. Nothing blew away." His firm chin and straight nose were vaguely familiar. She always considered a man's nose, being just below his eyes, and she invariably looked straight into a man's eyes. *A woman should do that to assist her intuition in reading a man's mind,* she'd written in her column. Addie took in his measure, allowed herself a faint smile, but invited no further acquaintance. She held out a hand for her folder. Slow to release it, he made no move to open the door. His hand on its handle prevented her from opening it.

"Lieutenant Robert Jamieson, ma'am," his eyes questioning. "Have I had the pleasure of meeting you, perhaps before you married?"

Had they met before? The oldest trick in the book. *Oh, soldier boy, really.* "I don't believe so, Lieutenant." His voice had a familiar timbre, but the impression faded before she could capture it.

"We'd remember, wouldn't we?" That engaging smile again. "If we'd met before?"

Brash. She'd have remembered *that*. He lacked the polish of the officers she entertained at Red Cross socials, men with well-bred manners. He might be an officer, but not exactly a gentleman. The war commingled all sorts.

She took her folder. "Yes, we'd have remembered. Good day."

He opened the door and touched the round brim of his khaki hat. She took a dozen steps before her nemesis, curiosity, urged her to glance back. At the elevator she pushed the button and turned slightly. He was still watching her as he held the door for those passing through. A uniformed operator opened the elevator door and she entered, preparing herself for the appointment with her editor.

*   *

"I may not be a virgin, Mr. Dodds, but I *am* chaste." What he'd just said set her teeth on edge.

George Dodds, editor of the *Spokesman-Review*, made a flurried attempt to extricate himself. "Mrs. MacLean, I intended no slur upon your character." English accent broadening, "Come now, you know me better than that. Your husband was my friend."

"*Have* I misunderstood?" It was the right tone for her indignation. "Did you not say I was the type of woman who would be comfortable in a house of ill repute?"

"Please." He opened his cigarette box, realized a cigarette lay half-smoked in his ashtray, and closed it.

She pressed her advantage. "Last year you said you were pleased with my series on Seattle factory girls not getting a square deal from employers, despite the new eight-hour-day law for women."

"Indeed, I was." He appeared relieved to change the subject. "Very Nellie Bly." Smiled in his patronizing manner.

She'd told him months before that Bly's writing thirty years earlier about working women's hardships in an eastern box factory alerted her to an ongoing need to report on women's working conditions.

He spoke carefully, "But this subject you want to pursue now, the causes of prostitution . . ."

"A serious story a woman journalist can investigate successfully." Addie viewed herself as a journalist now, not just a columnist.

"We're a newspaper, not a muckraking magazine like *McClure's*." He wagged a nicotine-stained finger. "What if you don't find that women become prostitutes for reasons other than lacking a firm grounding in morality? Will you invent reasons?"

"I will not." Was he accusing her of stooping to the worst kind of yellow journalism?

Dodds appeared to relax. "No, of course you won't. So you might be wasting your time." She held her tongue while he took a deep draught from his cigarette. "I agree some things need a woman's touch. It's why *Mrs. Vandervort's Helpful Hints* is so popular." He smiled, his eyes behind his spectacles squinting into two horizontal lines.

"I believe, Mr. Dodds, that economic necessity . . . not being able to afford proper food and heat while working low-paying jobs . . . especially the girl adrift and on her own . . . leads many to prostitution." Now the *coup de grace*. "Shouldn't the most prominent newspaper in the region investigate the social welfare of its citizens? You called yourself a progressive. I heard you." At her own dinner table when she and Jerome entertained.

Dodds snuffed out his cigarette and folded his hands. "How do you intend to accomplish your investigation? What I tried to say is you would *not* be comfortable in a house of ill repute, for you *are* a lady."

It was not what he said when she submitted the idea. He'd been huffy and sarcastic, affronted by her rejection of his proposal of a series on sightseeing train trips.

"I'm good at disguises. If I can find a position as a cook, will you publish my investigation?"

"If you gain a cook's position at a local parlor, and discover anything other than what the doves eat," allowing himself a thin smile, "I will read what you write, and I will decide whether to publish it."

She smiled and rose.

"Addie?" He came around his desk to see her out. "You'll be careful?" His breath was acrid with smoke.

She laid a gloved hand on his arm. "Yes, of course I'll be careful."

She'd been employed as the receptionist at the newspaper when she looked up one day to see the man who would become her husband. Tall and broad-shouldered, a fine figure of a middle-aged man with a silver mustache and thick silver hair, he said, "I don't have an appointment, miss, but please inform George Dodds that Jerome MacLean wishes to take him to supper. I promise to bring him back so he can put this newspaper to bed, or does he wake it up?" He grinned like Teddy Roosevelt. The next afternoon he returned. "Miss," he said. "Miss Adelaide Hardwick. I'm in need of a secretary at my lumber business and your editor has recommended you. Won't you do me the honor of having lunch with me tomorrow so I can tell you about my business and what your duties will be?" She'd sat stunned. "I will double the pay you make here." He grinned. "You do type and take dictation, don't you?" Adding, "Not important. I'll teach you myself if needs be."

At home in Browne's Addition, Addie held a cup of afternoon tea as her mastiff Titus settled next to her with a thud that shook the floor. Near her typewriting machine lay her handbag, and in it was the blood-spattered card the wounded Pinkerton agent had pushed into her hand the year before. She hoped it would give her entry to the "House of Maud" as she called the high-class parlor she'd located a few miles east of her own home. Titus lifted his head; a large dollop of drool hung from loose jowls. Snatching up her napkin, Addie expertly caught it.

"You really should be an outdoor dog." She stroked his massive wrinkled head. "We still miss him, don't we?"

Like unbidden guests, troubled thoughts about the night Jerome died lingered in the room, her deathbed promise still unfulfilled.   Beyond the window great sweeps of cloud alternated sunlight with shadow. The sun lighted the stained glass window with a burst of golden glory, giving apples, pears and grapes jeweled life; moments later they became opaque and somber. If only she'd had a child to care for. She pondered the changing light patterns.   They would replicate through a lifetime of seasons, while she sat alone with her sorrow like a lonely lodger holding a scrapbook of memories.

Chapter 23
An Earlier Time: April, 1916

Addie preceded the young mastiff through tall double doors into the study. Seeing the uniformed nurse, stiffly starched in white from wimple to shoes, the dog froze on the threshold and searched the room. Mrs. Schultz removed the tray of uneaten invalid food and gave the mastiff a wide berth on her way out.

Addie rumbled the doors together, polished surfaces reflecting the coal fire across the room. The study's lighting was discreetly shaded because Jerome wished it so. Books shelved floor to ceiling receded into indistinct colors, their purpose of giving identity to their owner nearly done.

With effort, Jerome commanded, "Lock the doors." Sunken eyes watched Addie press a slippered foot on brass latches where the doors met, slotting them into the floor.

Feigning a mischievous smile, she withdrew from a pocket a King of the World Cuban cigar and a silver hip flask, two items Mrs. Schultz banned from the sick room.

A few weeks earlier, unable to climb the stairs, Jerome had been moved into his study. For a time he managed a chair, the dog's head resting on his knee, but no longer.

His ancient mother, Matilda, who herself refused to die, journeyed from across the street with the assistance of Jerome's brother, Alonzo. She sat beside her son a few minutes, reminded him he was in her prayers, and then left. Back in her own house, she refused to return, sending word she wanted to remember him as he'd been, not as he was now.

Addie pulled the miniature brass lumberjack from another pocket, raised the tiny ax, and chopped off the tip of Jerome's smoke. His unnaturally bright eyes followed this ritual that had replaced others in their short life together.

When Jerome broke the news he had cancer, she'd sat stunned and silent and he raised his voice, fear pouring out. "Ain't ya gonna cry for me, Addie, goddammit!"

The tumor grew remorselessly until Jerome needed injections of morphine every four hours. And he itched. "Worse than any logging camp." Addie soothed his skin with witch hazel. "I'll take fleas and bedbugs any day to this." He'd given a gritty snort, drawing a wan smile from his young wife.

She wet his mouth with a sip of whiskey, then lit his cigar and touched it to cracked lips. He took a puff before motioning it away, and she sank into her chair beside his bed.

He muttered, "Gotta tell you something. Can't think straight after morphine." His voice was diminished, rougher and thinner. "A confession." His fleshless bristled chin jutted.

"If it doesn't concern me, dear, you needn't tell me." Their home and social life was her realm, the lumber partnership with Alonzo his. She knew a smattering about the business from her time as Jerome's secretary.

"This *will* concern you."

The skeletal hand she held saddened her. She remembered his hands on the reins of a span of horses trailing giant logs during a visit to a MacLean logging camp. He'd acted like a love-sick boy, wanting to show off how he'd logged when young.

"I was married."

Yes, and lived in this house with Gladys until she died. Then he said the unexpected. "To Mary Smith over in Idaho . . .1886 . . . thirty years ago. Played her a foul trick. Sham marriage. Mother told her."

Addie's heart thumped. "You were married before Gladys?"

A nod only, his strength spent.

The coal fire lisped and slumped. Titus rose, rearranged himself, and thudded down. Jerome retreated into the speech pattern of his youth. "Didn't know it was Ma run her off. Thought she bolted. Didn't want me no more." He drew a painful breath. "When Ma told me what she done, I figured to make it right someday. But I never went lookin' for her." She listened, searching the ghostly face. "She was gonna have my child." Addie stiffened. "Don't want ya hurt when the will's read. Half goes to you. Half to my child if found within two years of my passing." This last effort drained him. He lifted her hand as though to kiss it, but the distance was too great.

Her surge of resentment surprised her. She always thought Jerome was hers alone. "You never tried to find this child?"

"Hired detectives a few months back. Nothing. Papers in the desk. Money for hunt in an account. Find him, Addie . . . for me."

Him? She tasted vinegar at the back of her throat. But her husband was dying and she must be his obedient wife. "Yes, I'll find him for you."

"Still love me, Addie?"

"Of course I do," stroking his hand. Even bewildered, she excused him. "You made a mistake and I'll try to set it right."

"Lie beside me tonight after the nurse pokes me."

She nodded and removed her hand. His lips beneath his mustache had once been fine, chiseled like his chin and jaw. She bent to kiss him, ignoring his cracked lips and fetid breath. As he wasted away, so did she, her robust youth vanished into his illness, her body picked over by the crows of heartache.

She unlocked the doors and Mrs. Schultz entered, sniffing at smoke and whiskey fumes before attending to the drawing of morphine into a large hypodermic needle.

"Nurse . . ." Jerome's voice was weak as old smoke. "Please fill a second syringe. Put it here on the table." He still expected to be obeyed. "Mrs. MacLean will spend the night. She'll poke me if I need it." He wheezed, "Make yourself comfortable. Pot of coffee. Cake. Mrs. MacLean will find you if you're needed."

The nurse gave a satisfied grunt, pulled up Jerome's long night shirt, revealing a withered thigh, and gave the injection.

After Mrs. Schultz left, he gasped, "Want you naked beside me while I still know it's you."

Addie undressed and slid between the sheets, wary of jostling him. She was accustomed to cigar and whiskey aromas, but the sourness of his decay sorrowed and repulsed her.

"Not like that," his voice slower. "Your back to me. Head on my shoulder. We'll sleep."

Lying stiff and uncomfortable, she stretched out to encounter his cold feet and sharp toenails. Jerked up her knees. When had she last trimmed them?

He mumbled, "When you remarry . . ."

"Don't." She pressed her face into his nightshirt sleeve. "Please, Jerome. Don't."

"Want you to marry a man . . . loves you as much as I do."
He gave a low painless snort. Knowing the morphine was
working for him, she relaxed.

"Sleep, Addie."

"Mmm-mm." She would rest the few hours before he
needed another injection. She let go, drifting into the deep
sleep of a tired little animal.

During the night Titus whined and Addie broke through the
surface of consciousness. Jerome lay quiet next to her.
Without moving, she muttered to the dog. The mastiff clicked
around the bed to flop down near her.

Addie didn't wake again until Titus scrabbled noisily to his
feet at Mrs. Schultz' exclamation. "Ach mein Gott!" Her
Germanic voice was high in outrage. "Vat haf you done!"

Jerome's cold hand lay beneath Addie. She pulled her hair
out from under his rigid arm and pushed herself up. She'd seen
death before – a younger brother had died of whooping cough.
But the sight of Jerome horrified her. Jaw open, his eyes were
half-closed and lightless. His face resembled waxed parchment,
a description she'd read in a novel, recalled in this awful
moment.

"Oh, no." The syringe protruded from his nightshirt, the
unseen needle plunged into his chest, his fingers splayed beside
it. A sheen of peppery-smelling sweat rose on Addie's naked
body as she stood to confront the nurse.

Mrs. Schultz gave only the appearance of a white marble
statue of Mercy. "Vat do I tell his old modder and brodder ven
dey ask how Mr. MacLean died? Tell me dat, lady." Flung up
her hands in anguish. "And Herr Doctor?"

"The family won't ask you, Mrs. Schultz. They will ask
me."

He'd planned his death. Later, upstairs, she fell on their bed
and pushed her face into a pillow. "Oh, Jerome, what will I do
with the rest of my life? I wanted to spend it with you." Time
would never heal her loss.

Chapter 24
May, 1916

If dressing in black and wearing a veil was intended to protect a grieving woman from prying eyes, it was having the opposite effect as Addie climbed the stairs of an office building in downtown Spokane and entered the Pinkerton National Detective Agency.

She lifted the black silk veil's weighted velvet band and drew it over her tricorn. "I read your reports, Mr. Gascom. But there's a matter I don't understand." Jerome had kept more than one secret from her, forcing her to seek illumination from this oily-mannered stranger in a seedy office. "Did Mr. MacLean engage you to find two women?"

"That's right, Mrs. MacLean, he hired us to locate Mary Smith and Violet MacLean, Mr. MacLean's sister."

She glimpsed a photograph in the open folder and reached for it. "May I see that?"

"Be my guest." Gascom pushed it across the desk.

The old tintype showed two boys and a girl perched in a wicker chair covered with a buffalo robe, the young Jerome and the older Alonzo staring and unsmiling. The girl, the eldest, appeared to be about ten years old.

"I read the information my late husband provided you. Violet MacLean was a school teacher, who disappeared the same time as Mary Smith. What else did he tell you?"

"It's rather delicate, Mrs. MacLean."

"Since I'm now paying for the search, I think you should tell me."

The detective thumbed through the file, refreshing his memory. "Mr. MacLean told me Mary Smith had been a prostitute before they married." He looked up to gauge her reaction.

She realized later she'd felt shame at that moment, the past tainting not only Jerome's reputation, but hers, also, if only in the detective's eyes. "And Violet MacLean?"

"He told me his sister was a fallen woman."

She braced against the chair back, her corset's steel stays digging into her spine. "Have you found any trace of them?"

"Not yet."

She could stop the search for a child that might not exist, and for two women Jerome must have disdained until his last illness. But she didn't. "I'll follow my husband's last wishes. Continue with your search for Mary Smith and her child for two years from the date of Mr. MacLean's passing. My husband gave me no directive about Violet MacLean."

Gascom cleared his throat. "Mr. MacLean felt if one were found, she would know where the other was."

"I see. Then continue to search for both women." Curious, she asked, "What does your search entail?"

"We have our methods." The Pinkerton snapped shut the folder. How had she dared to ask "The Eye that Never Sleeps" that question.

The following day the MacLeans gathered in Jerome's study for the reading of his will. The Persian carpet had been re-laid, its reds and blues brightening the room; the desk was re-situated with its view of the fireplace, the wall of books and the tall windows; a faint scent of cigar smoke clung to velvet draperies. The study appeared as before, but it wasn't, of course; the ghost whose room it had been was now banished by the living coming through the double doors.

Jerome's attorney, Angus Humphries, presided solemnly behind the desk as Addie seated herself and Titus flopped at her feet. Her life, out of kilter these past months, was leveling. She'd resumed writing her column for the *Spokesman-Review*'s society page. Today, though, she was tense, threading her fingers together, feeling displaced as Jerome's relic and rightful heir.

Her brother-in-law, Alonzo, sat beside her, his hat gripped between his knees. They hadn't told his mother, Matilda, that Jerome committed suicide. Matilda MacLean, a shrunken figure in rusty weeds resurrected from an attic trunk, stiffly lowered herself into Jerome's leather chair by the window and propped her feet on a hassock. Informed she wasn't a beneficiary, she nevertheless insisted on being present.

After enumerating small bequests, Humphries read, "I am married to Adelaide Hardwick MacLean and am without issue of her. I acknowledge that I entered a common law marriage with Mary Smith in 1885 and may have had issue by her." Receiving no reaction from the widow or her brother-in-law, he continued, "To Adelaide, my wife, I leave my house, its contents, and its property. Half of my monies and investments I leave to Adelaide. Half of my interest in the MacLean Lumber Company I leave to Adelaide, with the understanding the business will continue to be managed by my brother and partner, Alonzo G. MacLean, and that Adelaide shall take no active part in its business without his approval. The books will be made available to her and her agents."

Alonzo stroked his gray-flecked rusty mustaches, then hunched forward over his hat.

"The other half of my monies and investments, and my remaining half-interest in the MacLean Lumber Company, I leave to any issue of Mary Smith and myself, with the stipulation that such issue has presented himself or herself to Mr. Angus Humphries or his successor within two years of my death and has been accepted by him as my issue and heir. Should this deadline pass without any such issue presenting himself or herself, then the remainder of my estate shall pass to my wife, Adelaide, to be used as she deems appropriate, whether she has remarried or not."

The attorney was refolding the will when Addie announced, "Mr. Humphries, I wish to sell the house. The furnishings will have to be evaluated, I suppose."

"Well, I never," Matilda exclaimed. "My son's not cold in his grave and she's displenishing his estate." She'd lost her son and the past was being thrust into the present without her approval.

"Ma!" Alonzo chided.

"When my son's last will and testament becomes public, there will be a scandal."

Mr. Humphries cleared his throat. "The contents of the will won't be made public, Mrs. MacLean. That would cause putative heirs to jump through the hedges . . . as it were."

Addie turned to face her mother-in-law. "Mother MacLean, before he died, I promised Jerome I would continue the search for his child . . . if there is one."

The old woman's eyes blazed through folds and wrinkles. "Any child Mary Smith birthed was not Jerome's. She was shanty Irish. You didn't do your duty, either. My son's line stops with him."

"Ma!" Alonzo bleated.

It wasn't the first time the old woman had tried to wound her for having a mother that came from Ireland. She was never at a loss to comment on "the savage Irish." Addie shifted her gaze to Matilda's unusually large, claw-like hands, fastening on the one with the recessed knuckle above the middle finger. A person at first might not notice it, but once seen, the observer's eyes would return to it, trying to puzzle out its cause. Addie always wondered whether it was acquired at birth or in a barroom brawl.

Humphries intoned, "If there's no further business, I'll take my leave."

"I will go home now, Alonzo." His mother tapped her ebony stick. "I no longer feel welcome here." She raised a black handkerchief to her mouth. "I miss my son. He was so good to me."

Addie said, "Before you go, Mother MacLean . . . has your daughter Violet contacted you since she disappeared? Jerome wanted to find her, also."

Matilda clutched her flat chest. "How dare you! Mr. Humphries, if Alonzo won't take me home, you must."

A short time later Addie faced her brother-in-law. Alonzo's features were gullied, weathered by mountain winters and sun and wind year round. In an ill-fitting suit, mustaches tobacco-stained, he was a woodsman on a trip to town. Jerome had devoted his business sense to making deals over brandy and cigars. Alonzo, the hands-on-man and trouble-shooter, managed the day-to-day business.

"Addie, I want to set ya straight on the business."

Jerome had told her, "You can trust Alonzo. He might cheat a little, but he won't steal from you."

"Alonzo, I know most of the holdings are in Idaho and the mountains are steep and difficult. You're logging white pine, right?"

"Mostly."

"Before we married, when I worked in the office, the company was putting a lot of money into getting to the timber with a Shay engine, tracks and steam donkeys. It hasn't paid off yet, has it?"

He shook his head. "No profit in '14. Not much better in '15. The entire lumber market was depressed along with the country. Most of our savings went into buyin' more timber. Jerome was optimistic, ya know. Business is bound to get better with that war in Europe. It's our timber interests west of the Cascades keeps us in the money. We're not loggin' there, but we've got interest from notes and investments in other men's lumber concerns. Railroad stock, too. Jerome believed the white pine in Idaho was worth the capital investment. Hard as the devil to get out, but I'll see it through. Don't want ya worryin' none."

"I have faith in you, Alonzo, but I want an appointment to look at the books, please."

Frosty blue eyes above runneled cheeks contrasted with his reddish mustaches. "Yeah, but right now I gotta get back to Idaho. The drive's underway down the Marble. Got to get them logs to the mill." He peered at her, their knees almost touching. "Your mill, too, I guess. But say, Addie, if ya wanna sell your interest, I might could scrape together the money."

His offer surprised her. "I don't want to think about it yet." She changed the subject. "Tell me about Mary Smith. Did you know her?"

He straightened. "'Course I knew her. Some. If Jerome couldn't find her, you won't either. Most likely she went back to where she come from. Probably long dead."

"Where did she come from?"

"Iowa, I think."

"How did they meet?"

"Well now, let me think. She'd been workin' her way west in railroad camps as the NP laid tracks across Montana. I suppose they met when we was sellin' lumber 'n ties to the railroad as it come into Thompson Falls, then over the line into Idaho. He saw a lot of her. Later she worked out of a tent in the Murray gold camp."

"Because she was a prostitute."

He flushed and stood up, rotating his hat brim with knotty fingers. "Ya wouldn't have called it a whorehouse 'cause it was canvas. I suppose Mary Smith wasn't her real name, either." He creased the crown of his hat as she sat with hands stiffly folded. Maybe he saw the strain on her face. "Oh, my gosh, Addie, let it be. If he wanted to find her after she run off, he'd 'ave done so. But he didn't. He decided he made a bad bargain. We was gettin' somewhere an' makin' big plans. Wasn't till he was about gone from this world that his conscience smote him." He ran a hand over his face. "I shouldn't be talkin' about my brother now that he can't defend himself."

"Oh," was her response. This was about a woman she wished she'd never heard of and a husband with a now-questionable character. What next? "Tell me about your sister, Violet."

"Not much to tell. She was teaching school and fell in love with a mining engineer. Nice fella. He was killed in a mine collapse."

"And?"

He cleared his throat. "And they started a family before they got around to the nuptials. Violet, she lost her teaching position when it become obvious. And Ma wouldn't let her come home." His hat revolved again. "I felt real bad for Violet, but we never went against Ma."

"So they were two expectant mothers on their own without any family support."

"Yeah, that's about right." He focused on a spot in the ceiling. "Felt real bad about it. Still do."

Surely the story didn't end there. "Never to be heard from again?"

Alonzo reshaped his hat, preparing to put it on. "Yup." What wasn't he telling her?

Clock chimes struck in the hall. "I'll see myself out." He opened the double doors, paused on the threshold and then swung around. "It's not as important to everybody as ya might think, Addie. Some people don't want to be found. And things have a way of takin' care of themselves. Or maybe someone else takes care of 'em." And then he disappeared down the hall.

Titus dropped his heavy head on her lap and she stared at the soft hair between his floppy ears.

*   *

Mrs. Vandervort's Helpful Hints

The *Spokesman-Review* is pleased to announce Mrs. Vandervort has returned to Spokane after a regrettable absence and resumes her column with this issue.

It is nearly time to "do up" your sheer summer gowns, ladies. Remove all ribbon or velvet garniture. To retain delicate coloring, do not use soap or hot water. In a small tub put enough warm water to cover the items and add a half-pint of gasoline per gallon of water. Submerge the goods and with your hands, squeeze and press until all the soil is removed. Rinse in several clear waters before rinsing in water tinged with wash blue. Run through a wringer. Mix two tablespoons of cold water starch in a quart of lukewarm water and dip your gowns and filmy shirtwaists in this. Press out as much moisture as possible and roll in a large clean cloth. Let lie one hour, then press with hot irons until dry. Your sheer wash goods will look as crisp and clean as when new.

Chapter 25
Spokane: December, 1917

At one in the morning the Northern Pacific out of Portland crawled into Spokane on the tail end of a blizzard, hours behind schedule, its way through high drifts opened by a slow, but efficient, rotary snowplow engine. Relieved to finally arrive, Jamieson pulled on his overcoat and wedged his head into his campaign hat. He tightened the chin strap before shouldering his duffel, but his precaution was unnecessary; the wind was reduced to a murmur.

No taxis or jitneys waited curbside; no night-owl streetcar clanged along the street. A half-block away a solitary wagon and team made a ghostly passage beneath a snow-shrouded street light, wagon creaking and harness jangling, but hooves and iron-strapped wheels eerily muffled. Leaving behind passengers' rough exclamations of disgust and higher shrills of alarm that followed him into the snow, he trudged toward the South Hill and Cousin Maud's. Breaking trail up a steep street, often slipping, he appreciated his knee-high boots, but wished for snowshoes.

Stars glittered in the sky, lighting his way through luminous drifts unsullied by coal smoke. The blizzard had disrupted electricity. Streetlights and porch lights were out, but dark half-circles where snow had melted at chimney bases told of banked furnaces keeping families warm. Someday he would have a home and family. Someday after the war.

At the top of the hill he turned east. Houses became intermittent, separated by empty lots and young pine. As he trudged along, he brooded over Major Gund's recent briefing and its unsettling final exchange.

"I was in Seattle and met with your old boss, Ahern. He said when you worked the rails, you were a natural bum, but you weren't a natural detective."

He flushed. His parting with Ahern on bad terms had apparently followed him, but he gave Gund look for look.

The major would nitpick the details. "Let me rephrase that. Actually, he said you weren't a natural Pinkerton Agency detective. You acquired a conscience after that Everett fiasco and he said he was glad to see you go."

And I was glad to go. Jamieson imagined Ahern's smirk as he cracked his Black Jack while shattering his reputation. He replied evenly, "And you reported this meeting to Colonel Disque."

"I did. He said to keep you on the case." Then as an afterthought, "Ahern did say one thing in your favor. He said you're lucky."

He didn't feel lucky. But it was good to be off the train, breathing fresh air, his body in motion. He'd avoided going to Maud's the past few weeks while in Spokane. The Army had put all whorehouses off-limits to soldiers and he couldn't be seen entering or leaving it in uniform, but he'd soon be shedding the khaki.

At the the back door of the large three-story house, he searched for the key inside his coat. With this blizzard, no customers and no lights, the entire house should be asleep. He quietly entered and located a kerosene lamp atop a cupboard in the pantry. Lighting it, he savored its warmth before shortening the flame and replacing the chimney.

On past winter homecomings he'd found Dovey in the kitchen, pretending to be tidying up. He didn't telegraph his arrival this time, but now wished he had. He missed her welcome.

He was hunched over bread and preserves when the swinging door squeaked and a white-haired black man shoved through a shotgun's double barrels, aimed at his chest. The man lowered it with a gusty sigh and broke it open. "Robert, you gave me a scare. We didn't expect you."

"Mr. Moses, you wouldn't shoot one of Uncle Sammie's boys, would you?" He took another bite, asking through a full mouth, "Did I wake you?" A widower, the man slept in a small room behind the kitchen. He was bartender, doorman, butler, and handyman. Jamieson had known him his entire life.

"No, I had to get up to stoke the furnace. When the girls get cold, they come tapping on my door, offering bribes for whiskey to warm themselves. Can't be havin' that." He retreated with the shotgun and returned with a lantern.

Jamieson picked up his lamp and they clasped each other's shoulder as they passed. "You get yourself a good sleep, Lieutenant."

Out in the hall, about to mount the back stairs, he heard, "Meant to tell you . . ." But the door swung shut with a loud screech and his immediate objective was bed. It could wait until noon.

The moment he entered his third-floor room, he felt a prickly sensation of not being alone. A woman's clothes were neatly folded over his chair, the woman curled in his bed. So Maud was using his room for trade. He felt tired resentment but, more than that, just damn tired.

He set the lamp on a stand and sat on the bed, making the springs squeak. "Move over, sister. Robbie's home and wants to sleep in his own bed." He jounced the bedsprings and the woman sat up, pulling the covers against her breasts like a surprised actress in a ten-minute cinema reel. She rolled out the opposite side, then turned to face him in a crouch, alarmed and ready to defend herself, a long burnished braid dangling over a shoulder. Her two-piece wool union suit covered a generously curved body. Snatching up a red kimono, she backed into a corner table, upsetting a framed photograph of Teddy Roosevelt and knocking some books to the floor. Her head grazed a pair of dangling boxing gloves. Sidestepping them, she hissed, "You get out of here or I'll scream."

The red kimono belonged in the house, but his sleep-starved mind knew she didn't. For one thing, her face was unpainted. The girls wore make-up even to sleep, emerging for late morning baths as tousled Theda Baras, with kohl-stained eyelids and rouged cheeks. She was no whore.

"Come on, miss, I'm not looking for a trick. This is my bed and I need sleep." The urge was strong to follow the pull of gravity and nestle his face into a pillow.

"I mean it! Get off that bed!" The room was cold and she hugged herself.

Even tired, he retained the habit of questioning everything he observed. If she wasn't a whore, but the help, why wasn't she wearing a practical nightgown? He stood. "Where the hell am I going to sleep?"

"Anywhere but here." Seeing him in retreat, she added, "I did my bit for the war effort. I'm not sharing my bed with a soldier."

He snatched up the nearer pillow and took the lamp, dragging his duffel without a backward glance. As he crossed the hall to the storage room, he heard a chair jammed under the doorknob.

Opening the creaking door, he hoisted the lamp. Somewhere under cast-off furniture and other debris was a cot. He uncovered the thin mattress, then found bundled in a corner a velvet drape of uncertain color he could use as a blanket. He removed his boots, but donned his overcoat, crawled under the heavy drape and blew out the lamp. The woman had scented the pillow with a whiff of vanilla, into which he buried his face and fell asleep.

He awoke a few hours later to muted sunlight filtering through a dusty window. Untangling himself, he sat up, elbows on knees. A memory crawled out to sit beside him. Was it in Wallace? Early memories were of sweet-smelling women covering his face with tickling kisses. But this memory was of another big snow. He knelt in a box sled, his cousin Thea kneeling behind him, small hands clutching his shoulders as a long-skirted woman pulled them along, the sled bumping over frozen horse apples that hurt his knees. He was happy. Then some boys threw snowballs, hitting him in the face. Did he cry, cringing in the box? Did she shout at the boys before squatting in the snow to hold him? She smelled of bacon and cologne. "Be brave, Robbie! They can't hurt us!" Thea was bawling. Did Dovey cry, too?

Chapter 26

Jamieson crossed the hall and tapped on his bedroom door. Finding the room empty, he pulled civilian clothes from his wardrobe and changed, then shaved with icy water from the wash bowl. He made a stop at the second-floor bathroom, enjoying the scent of milled French soap, before passing closed bedroom doors to descend the ornately carved front staircase.

Stale cigar smoke and an aroma of spilled whiskey lingered in the hall. Canadian Club smuggled over the border had found its way to Maud's. No homemade hooch from the woods for her. Muted sounds came from the kitchen at the rear of the house, but he paused outside Maud's suite of rooms near the elegant entry where she and Mr. Moses monitored who came and went and how long they stayed. He knocked.

A woman with bright blue eyes and lightly rouged lips on an aging face opened the door, exclaiming, "Robbie! Mr. Moses said you came through that awful blizzard." She had a long face, dour until she smiled. "Wasn't it awful? No one came last night." She laughed softly, eyes alight. "We'll all go broke, I swear."

"Hello, Maud." He embraced her in what she called his "big bear hug."

"I wanted to see you in uniform," she pouted. "I'm sure you look splendid in it."

He smiled. "I look swell in it." Observed, "You bobbed your hair. You look splendid, too."

Smiling widely, she lifted fingers to her hair, lowered them to cover her mouth, but not before he saw with a nip of sadness she was missing a tooth in back, one of her chompers.

"And who's sleeping in my bed?"

"Where did you sleep?" She gestured toward the horse hair-stuffed sofa he always avoided. "You could have slept here."

"I slept in the storage room and it was darn cold."

"Did you recognize our new cook? She couldn't leave because of the snow." Then she admonished, "We didn't know you were coming, dear."

"I expected to get in earlier." Now he gave out just enough information to satisfy her. "I'll be heading over to Idaho to infiltrate some logging camps. Keep an eye out for Wobblies stirring up trouble or sabotage." He allowed her the time to absorb this high intrigue. "Might even catch a German spy."

She sat down with a thump. "Times are serious, aren't they?"

He changed the subject. "So, you have a new cook. Isn't Dovey cooking this winter?"

"As much as she can, limping about like a preacher's mare and happy to have the help. She's awfully pleased to have you back under her wing. You'll have breakfast in here so we can visit. We've something to ask you."

Dovey and Maud – his two mothers - one to discipline, the other to give unconditional love. After Maud took him back to Michigan to boarding school when he was eleven, Dovey parted company with her and filed on a homestead near Marble Creek. He spent his later summers with Dovey, learning to shoot and hunt.

Having abandoned feminine vanity at the outset of homesteading, Dovey wound her gray hair into a bun at the nape of her weathered neck. Each autumn before deep snow she farmed out her horse and milk cow, boarded the passenger train *Columbian* at Marble Creek Station, and left the Idaho mountains for the comforts of central heating and indoor plumbing. She presided in Maud's kitchen and maintained a semblance of control over the girls until spring when she returned to her cabin.

"Mrs. Matthews . . ." Maud prompted Dovey. "Robbie didn't recognize her last night when he found her in his room."

He eyed Dovey over his coffee cup.

She folded work-worn hands. "The Widow Matthews. She's one of yours, Robbie."

"I don't think so." Some time had passed since he'd handed out a card. Nothing was familiar about the woman and he'd seen most of her. Then he experienced an inner start of surprise. "What's her first name?" He knew who she was.

"She says it's Adele," Dovey answered. "That card had dried blood on it. She the woman who saved your life in Seattle? You told us to expect her, but she never showed up. Maud and me, we've been surmisin' and bidin' our time, waitin' for you."

"She must be. That was her name, Adele Matthews." He was finally going to meet her properly.

"That's what we concluded," Maud interjected. "All she said was Mac gave her the card in Seattle and she was looking for honest work as a cook."

Dovey countered, "She really said, 'Not that other kind of work.' She's a good cook. We just wanted to hear it from you."

"It was dark and raining, and I . . . "

Dovey squeezed his arm. "Don't go telling us that part again, Robbie. It sets us worryin'. Don't it, sister?"

Maud answered solemnly. "Yes, it does, sister."

Chapter 27

Jamieson pushed the kitchen's swinging door inward. Freshly oiled, the coiled spring overhead made a soft *spru-u-ng*. Draped in a long white apron, the young woman shoved a pan of biscuits into the oven before turning. The previous night's encounter lay between them, but a rainy night in Seattle connected them. What he missed before, he saw now - large blue eyes ringed in gray beneath a dark golden pile of thick hair. He stood in stunned silence. Who was this woman? Why was she here, of all places? He'd expected to meet the factory girl who saved his life, but facing him was the woman he encountered in front of the *Spokesman-Review* building a couple of weeks earlier, the well-dressed Mrs. Vandervort.

"Robert Jamieson, ma'am. I believe we've met."

His eyes explored her face as she answered drily with a hint of humor, "We'd remember, wouldn't we, Lieutenant?" Facing him as poised as a kitchen goddess, she took in his civilian clothes, seemingly unsurprised that the man whose life she saved was the clumsy officer in front of the newspaper building. "I hope my being given your room didn't inconvenience you. I'm Adele Matthews."

How could this woman cooking at Maud's be Mrs. Vandervort and Adele Matthews both? What the hell was going on?

Dovey limped into the kitchen to demand, "Well, is she?" Maud, too, had pushed open the kitchen door. Mr. Moses peered over her shoulder.

"Am I what?" The Widow Matthews straightened under their scrutiny.

Jamieson's eyes held the woman's, sharing one secret while revealing another. "Mrs. Matthews, are you the woman who saved my life in Seattle last year?"

"Well, Lieutenant Jamieson, that depends. Are you Mac the Pinkerton agent?"

"I was."

"And are you Robbie the girls have mentioned and in whose room I slept?"

"Yes, but you knew that."

"A man of distinct parts." Was the slight curve of her lips a smile? "Then I suppose I'm the woman you collided with in Seattle. Did I save your life?"

"You know you did." He brushed past Dovey. Whoever she was, she had spunk. Billy Sewell once mused that when a man saves your life, you owe him the same favor some time; but when a woman saves it, it's somehow bigger, more courageous, a debt never fully repaid. "Thank you again." He added, "By custom I'm in your debt until I can return the favor."

Her eyes snapped with humor, but she replied seriously, "I hope I'll never be in a situation where you'll find it necessary."

Come on, lady, give me a smile. Some impulse made him want to throw her off-balance to watch her reaction. "I heard you left your factory job in Seattle because you missed your dog." Her eyes widened at this gleaned tidbit. Given time, he'd read her like a book. He wouldn't bring up Mrs. Vandervort now, not with Dovey and the others present . . . not until he figured her out. The girls would be coming down soon, anyway. "How is your dog?"

"Titus is fine, Lieutenant. Friends are caring for him while I'm working."

"Please call me Rob." He smiled. *I'm as friendly as a puppy*, he hoped it said.

"Not Robbie then?"

He flushed, though he couldn't have said why. "My family call me Robbie . . ." He turned to look at the two older women and old man watching them.

"I don't no more," Mr. Moses offered. "I call him Robert . . . that's a man's name."

"You may call me Addie," she said. "All of you. It's what my family call me."

That afternoon, in uniform again, a mug of coffee between his hands in a café across from the *Spokesman-Review* building, Jamieson formulated a plan. If his suspicions about Adele Matthews were correct, the woman's timing was damn inconvenient. He had only a couple of days before he had to locate that Irish Wobbly, O'Neill. From the telephone box inside the café he placed a call to the newspaper and asked for its editor, George Dodds, only to be told he was out of the office. He dropped a dime for the waitress, picked up a leather satchel and headed across the street.

The receptionist, a pretty brunette, smiled broadly at the Army officer.

"Is Mr. Dodds in?" He leaned toward her, suggesting he found her attractive.

"I'm so sorry. He hasn't arrived yet."

He feigned disappointment, but then brightened. "That shouldn't be a problem." Pulling a manila envelope from his satchel, he said, "This information is for Mrs. Vandervort." Was he on the right track? "If the lady is in, may I see her?"

"She isn't here, but I'll make sure she gets it." The girl reached for the envelope, which he held back.

"She needs it *toute de suite*. That's what your editor told me on the telephone. If you can give me her address, I'll take it to her now. She must be waiting for it." The girl looked doubtful. "And by the way," again dipping into the satchel, producing a tin box of chocolates lithographed with purple violets and pink roses, "I think you'll enjoy these more than that lady." He placed it in front of her with an ingratiating smile.

"Oh." She blushed furiously. "Why, thank you. What a surprise."

Because he was nice looking when his hair was clipped and combed, and because he wore their country's uniform, he expected she would view him as chivalrous. "What does Mrs. Vandervort go by?" Resting his hands on her desk, he made her the center of his world.

"Her real name?" He nodded. "Mrs. Adelaide MacLean. I'll have to look up her address." She pulled out a drawer, glanced up to take in his smile. But he had stopped smiling.

"What's her husband's name?" A demand, not a request.

"Jerome MacLean . . . but he's dead." She jotted down the address and handed it to him, adding, "He owned a lumber company. Left her very well situated, I heard."

A streetcar ride later he sauntered down a snow-cleared sidewalk past a large Queen Anne dominating a corner lot. Around the block and down the alley, he scouted the back with its carriage house, a room above for a driver. A Shetland-pony-sized mastiff spotted him and rushed the fence, barking ferociously. Not a dog he'd have wanted to meet while working the rails. He'd envisioned a lap dog, undersized and over-named. A well-off widow with a large house, who wrote a household-hints column, was now cooking at Maud's. There was a disconnect here that thoroughly engaged his detective's instincts.

Back downtown, he reentered the "tall building," as the eight-story *Spokesman-Review* edifice was called, and descended to the newspaper's morgue. With martial law still enforced in Spokane, his uniform carried authority. He told the clerk, "I want to see all clippings and photos you have on the MacLeans of MacLean's Lumber."

Ten minutes later he opened the brown accordion file and pulled the reading lamp chain. The top clipping was an obituary. *Jerome MacLean Called by Death. Died April 25, 1916, aged 51. Survived by his widow, Mrs. Adelaide MacLean.* He thumbed through the clippings - society blurbs, announcements of lumber contracts, mentions of the brother, Alonzo MacLean, and a thick folder containing *Mrs. Vandervort's Helpful Hints.*

Then he found what he sought, a photograph of Adelaide MacLean in her wedding gown. The date was August 10, 1913. She'd been lovely – still was. He *had* met her before -- twice, it turned out. She'd been the girl with the parasol watching the parade a week before her wedding. What an absurd joke that he kept running into her.

Why had a socialite who wrote advice for housewives been on a dark street in Seattle? Why was she playing at being a cook at Cousin Maud's? What was her game? Who else was playing? He smoothed out a narrow packet of clippings, long columns folded tightly upon themselves. Some words in the first column rose off the newsprint. "Seattle" and "factory girls" and "girls adrift." No byline, but *A. MacLean* was penciled at the top. Wanting to get inside Adelaide MacLean's mind, he read.

Since the passage of the eight-hour day for women and children in Washington State, some have wondered whether factory and other types of employers have adhered to the law. In an effort to discover the conditions of 'girls adrift,' those young women who flock to the big city to make a living, this correspondent presented herself as a factory girl in Seattle, rented a room at a working girls' boarding house and sought employment. . . .

He sat back. *Aren't you the mistress of disguise. And you're at it again.* He picked up the next installment. She found a position at a box factory, working there a week.

At the factory where I gained employment, in a loft at the top of a tall office building, dark and poorly ventilated, there was only one toilet for both sexes, dirty and without heat. It was my experience that this type of factory, unclean and with no consideration for its employees, ignored other regulations, such as the eight-hour day. I found this to be the case.

A week later, employed at a casket factory, she wrote of working conditions even more reprehensible, and he was getting a glimmer of why Adelaide MacLean, aka Adele Matthews, was cooking at a house of prostitution. And he didn't like it one bit. He skipped to the end of her series.

In closing, I must warn of the danger of walking alone in the city at night. This correspondent turned down a wrong street and witnessed a violent crime, very nearly becoming a victim herself.

Jamieson analyzed his intelligence and concluded that Adelaide MacLean had the mind of a reporter and the bones of an activist. If the *Spokesman-Review* was preparing a crusade to shut down houses of prostitution, she must be gathering information to expose Maud's livelihood. His gratitude for her saving his life was wearing thin.

Chapter 28

So, Adelaide MacLean was the girl at the parade. Independence Day, 1913 - a week after he and Fats Gerard got into that imbroglio in Billings at the end of the big NP operation.

*   *

July 4, 1913

He rolled into Spokane mid-morning, tossed out his pack and joined men scattering across tracks that split the heart of the city. Once beyond the reach of yard bulls, he dusted off his dirty ill-fitting suit and smacked his slouch hat against the side of a building. He reset it at a jaunty angle, exposing dusty hair and a sweat band stain across his forehead. He was in need of a shave. After taking a whiff of himself, he knew he'd have to go in through Maud's back door.

American flags decorated shop windows. *Whaddayaknow, Independence Day.* He'd start it with eggs, bacon and black coffee at a café he liked on skid road. He could almost smell the grease.

An hour later he left the hash house feeling a new man. Sauntering along, no longer needing eyes in the back of his head, he breathed the fresh air he'd longed for in the cramped boxcar.   Hearing a distant band marching down Riverside Avenue, he turned up a block to weave among watching flag-wavers. He positioned himself behind a young woman in a turned-up straw hat, who flourished a white silk parasol in time to the music, her other hand fluttering a small American flag. The parasol didn't block his view, but its undulation was giving him a headache. He tapped her shoulder.

The girl swung around, her gaze centered on his grimy collarless open shirt and dirty neck. Blue-gray eyes moved over his unshaven face. She was rather tall for a woman, but was what Billy called "a looker and a two-time winner." Golden hair peeped from under the straw hat. He flushed and doffed his misshapen fedora.

"Miss, I beg your pardon . . . your parasol." He expected her to step back in disgust from the lout he resembled.

"My parasol?" Her bell-like voice sounded unthreatened by his appearance.

"It's blocking my view." Talking faster, "If you allow me to hold it for you, I'll keep the sun off your face and be able to see the parade, too."

"Oh." She swept those glorious eyes from his unkempt hair down to his dusty boots.

"I won't steal it, miss. I just want to see." He flashed a smile that had made him ace high with the girls in college. "Everyone loves a parade."

She smiled back. "Parades are fun, aren't they?" Handing him her parasol, she turned back toward the street.

He held it over her head, maneuvering himself to give her a sidelong glance while they watched some fine horses and carriages clatter down the avenue. Her white linen hobble skirt closely fit wide hips and a nipped-in waist, its matching jacket buttoned below her breasts, which looked to be as fine as her eyes. Long white silk gloves hid the possibility of a wedding band. He was so taken with her, if she'd been a whore, he'd have said to hell with the parade and followed her to her bed.

The girl gestured toward an approaching carriage decked with flowers above a large blue banner identifying the mayor and his wife. "I know them," meeting his friendly eyes. "They're very nice."

Who gave a damn about those old farts when this luscious girl was within sniffing range? "They must be if you think so." Felt stupid, a hayseed off the farm.

A military band followed a half-block away, playing "Stars and Stripes Forever." "Here comes the Army band from Fort Wright.".

"Do you know them, too?" He could have kicked himself, hearing the double *intendre*. Even worse, he saw it was composed of Negro soldiers. "I'm new in town."

She stopped waving her small flag. "Yes, I can tell," but didn't look at him.

The band passed and she asked, "Are you on your way to the wheat harvests?" Then, "No, it's too early for that, isn't it?

My father owns a wheat farm down on the Palouse." She resumed her flag waving, her color heightened.

A middle-aged businessman in an expensive summer suit and homburg materialized at Jamieson's shoulder. They were about the same height. The older man dismissed him with a look and Jamieson's hand curled into a fist.

"Adelaide, I've been looking for you." His possessive tone turned her toward the intruder.

A boxcar mate sidled up on Jamieson's other side. "Hey, Mac, I found a saloon where beer is five cents an' all ya can eat. Come on."

Retrieving her parasol, she hooked her arm into her companion's and walked away without a backward glance.

"Aw, hell," he muttered, turning to follow his fellow hobo.

Chapter 29

Jamieson entered Maud's through the back door, doffed his campaign hat and stamped his boots, determined to confront Adelaide MacLean. Dovey appeared in the pantry, holding high a kerosene lamp and waving a flannel rag.

"Either pull off those boots, Robbie, or wipe 'em down. Don't go puddlin' up the house."

While he wiped his boots, the electricity came back on, the light bulb overhead humming, then flickering, emitting a dim glow before brightening.

"Finally," Dovey said, but waited a moment before blowing out her lamp. "Supper's 'bout ready. Go wash up."

"Yes, ma'am." Whereas Maud treated him with the respect his manhood deserved, Dovey acted like he was still a boy in need of her guidance. He bent to hug her.

For a moment she laid her graying head against his heart. "I'm so glad you're here, Robbie," then gently pushed herself away. "Go on now."

Jamieson nearly collided with Addie, who was removing a pan of sliced potatoes with melted cheese from the oven.

"Sorry, ma'am." Stepped back to allow her room. "You shouldn't attempt to leave tonight. It's dangerously slick out there." And then he lied. "The streetcar tracks haven't been cleared within a mile of here." When she nodded, he said, "You're welcome to my room as long as needed."

"Thank you."

Wanting to see her blue eyes again, he asked, "Will you be dining with us?"

She shook her head, indicated the table in the middle of the kitchen. "I eat in here. There isn't much elbow room and the girls are more themselves when I'm not around." She blinked three times. Clearly she'd said something she regretted. Two blinks were natural, but three showed a weak hand in poker. "What I mean is I leave the door open so I can hear if they need anything." She busied herself slicing a loaf of bread.

The girls are more themselves when I'm not around. Eavesdropping. He swung open the door and glanced back over his shoulder. Their looks splintered against each other. He nodded and she turned away. Dovey was watching them from the pantry doorway.

He wore his uniform at supper for Maud and the girls. Afterward, he changed and descended the back stairs to quietly enter the kitchen. A large kettle simmered on the cookstove; its hissing and the woman's clatter of washing up covered any sound he made.

He caught glimpses of bared arms below rolled sleeves. Her hair, piled and pinned in a dozen places, had flattened and slipped; a small strand corkscrewed down, touching the nape of her neck. When she removed those hairpins later, her hair would cascade over her shoulders and down her back, and then she would braid it into a practical plait because she slept alone. She was humming a wordless tune and he folded his arms, shifting his scrutiny to her low voice. Adelaide MacLean filled his sight and hearing and, despite his suspicions, her nearness pleased him.

Reaching for a linen towel, she saw him and stepped back in surprise. "Edna didn't make it in last night. She won't come tonight, either, if the streetcars aren't running." Edna, Mr. Moses' niece, came in the evening and worked through the night.

"Mind if I sit down?"

"Of course not. Would you like a cup of tea?"

Did she really think it was why he was here in the kitchen? "Thank you. A cup of tea would be welcome."

"Would you like me to bring it to the parlor?"

He shook his head. "Maud's gentlemen callers have nothing to do with me. I have a room here and that's all." It sounded like a repudiation and he stopped. "I grew up with Maud and Dovey and Mr. Moses until I was eleven." Self-conscious, he stopped again. What the hell was he doing, talking about himself? This was about her. Why was she here?

He breathed in her scent of vanilla as he passed, pulled out a chair at the table and sat. Seeking a distraction, he lifted a corner of the oilcloth covering the old poker table to reveal a slot above a money drawer. "I used to stuff things in here when I was a kid." Traced a finger over its worn edges. "It was used for late night poker games."

"Really." She hefted the kettle and scalded the teapot, then emptied it into her dishwater. "What did you put in there?" Measured in tea leaves and filled the pot.

He waited until she carried it to the table, then raised his eyes. "My secrets."

For a pregnant moment their looks held. She asked, "Milk, cream or sugar? No ice delivery today, but we made hard snowballs for the icebox, so nothing soured."

"I'll take it barefoot," provoking a raised eyebrow. "Black is fine."

"Another piece of pie? I made three."

Her offer evoked boyish enthusiasm. "That would be swell."

She served him the pie and poured his tea. Setting it at his elbow, she returned to stand over the teapot across the table.

"Aren't you having a cup?" He wanted her to sit, but not so he could admire her.

"My mother comes from Ireland, and she says, 'Steep it thick enough to trot a mouse across.'" He chuckled. She poured a large splash of milk in her cup before adding tea and then she sat across from him.

If suspicions weren't gnawing his thoughts, he'd like nothing better than to sit quietly with her. But it wasn't going to happen. "You could have used an Irish brogue when you came here. They wouldn't have been the wiser."

"Sure I could'a and what if me tongue got twisted like a skein a yarn? I'll just be havin' me cupan tae, thankee kindly." He gave an appreciative bark, but she didn't smile, only pressed her lips together.

"Does that explain your actions in Seattle? The Irish will jump into a fray, but seldom out of one." He meant it as a compliment.

"I was frightened. I'd rather not talk about it."

It was time for him to get to the heart of this. "Why weren't you surprised to see me this morning? Did you already know we met downtown last month?"

"Ah, that." She poked fingers into her piled hair, lifting it slightly. "Your photograph is in Dovey's room and in Maud's suite. When I saw it, I recognized the officer in front of the newspaper building and put two and two together. Maud was Mac's kin, so any photograph would have to be of him. Robbie as they call you here." She tried to draw him off from that incident. "So, when you were eleven?"

"When I was eleven I was taken back to Michigan to boarding school. I didn't see Maud or Dovey again for a few years. When I did, Maud had moved here from Wallace and Dovey had taken up a homestead down in Idaho."

"Near Marble Creek. She's told me stories."

"What do you think of Dovey?"

"I think she's wonderful. My mother . . ." Her eyes fixed on the hand wrapped around his teacup, its handle too small for his fingers. ". . would enjoy knowing her." As though she'd run out of breath, she silently stared.

His hand wasn't grotesque. A knuckle knocked back an inch was misaligned with the others. He wasn't fingerless, for God's sake. Her stare made him feel like a freak. Two could play at this. "Would you like some bear grease for those chapped hands?"

Her eyelashes flickered. "What?"

"Bear grease. I have some in my duffel. I waterproof my boots with it. Your hands aren't used to hard work."

"No, thank you. Bear grease smells like bear." She was still fixated on his hand.

He spread it on the table. *Take a good look, lady.* Leaning toward it as a child might, her features changed like summer weather. "Did you damage it in a fight?"

Making a fist, he studied the recessed knuckle. "I was born with it. Maybe they should have drowned me. What do you think?"

She raised her eyes to his. "That they should have drowned you?"

"You know that expression . . . deformity of the body stunts a man's character."

"No, I never heard that. But your hand does remind me of someone."

He held up what she found so fascinating, palm raised toward her. "Hold it right there." This was about her and the damage she planned to rain down on those closest to him.

Chapter 30

"Time for you to tell me who you really are." He wanted to discover her game, not hear her thoughts about his anatomy. "Lady, you've told so many lies, you make the girls in this house look like amateurs. Mrs. Vandervort. Adele Matthews. Or whoever you are."

Her chin snapped up, eyes alert. He didn't expect a confession that she was spying on Maud's for her newspaper and she didn't disappoint. Drawing a loose curl over a shoulder, she murmured, "You tell me, you're the detective."

"And a darn good one. I know your real name. I know you write for the newspaper. I read your articles, so I know why you were in Seattle."

Two spots of color bloomed on her cheeks, but her eyes didn't waver from his. "You should be glad I was in Seattle."

"I am. You bet I am. So, knowing you were in Seattle to write about female factory workers, what I want to know is why are you here? To expose Maud?"

"What do you think?"

"I think you're like some 'Creepin' Jesus' mission woman exploring a den of iniquity. I think you and the *Spokesman-Review* are about to launch a crusade to close down Spokane's parlors . . . Mrs. Adelaide MacLean."

It pleased him to have rattled her but good this time, not only with her real name, but with his accusation. Her cheeks flamed and her lips parted. She bit down on each word. "That is not true, Lieutenant Jamieson. My editor did not send me. It was my idea." Voice rising, "And I got the idea because you forced that card on me, the one covered in your blood. You want to know why I came here?"

He sat back with folded arms. "Yeah. Let's hear it."

"I planned to investigate whether the girls were here by choice or by coercion. Maybe even by force."

He leaned in. "If you fell for that white slavery bunk like the rest of the so-called righteous, you've come to the wrong house. They're working women and they're here by choice. Sales girls who happen to own the goods they're peddling."

She pushed up her cuffs, then pulled them down, conceding, "You're right. They aren't forced to stay here. But maybe something bad happened to send them down the road they're on."

He countered, "They went down that road to make good money. They like money. It buys them pretty things, stuff they couldn't afford if they worked in a factory or haberdashery."

"Exactly."

"Exactly what?"

"Economics is the reason they're here." She said it so adamantly, he listened. "When I did my investigation in Seattle on factory girls, I realized that with the low pay they make, they have a hard time supporting themselves. They barely can afford food and rent, much less clothing and recreation. When working girls run out of moral choices, some turn to immoral ones." Her eyes were alight with conviction. "Then they're stuck." She pointed toward the ceiling and, above it, the second floor bedrooms. Folded her hands. "I want to write a newspaper series on bad choices women make from economic necessity. Maybe it *is* a crusade I'm on to convince employers to give women a livable wage."

Relief swept over him. If she were telling the truth and the newspaper didn't plan a crusade to shut down trade, Maud and the girls were safe. For now, anyway. He was about to burst her altruistic bubble, though. He knew whores.

"I bet you think these women were once like you and your lady friends. If my bluntness offends your delicate sensibilities, I apologize, but they never were like you. They're different. These women -- not just here, but in every town -- they don't think they'll lead this kind of life for long. Just until they save enough to open a shop or a café. But stuff happens and most have trouble getting out of the life. Pimps and booze and drugs. It's why Maud is so strict. You won't see her girls sneaking out to consort with lovers or to get drugs. And the booze is for the customer. Maud considers herself as a sort of reformer. She makes them save part of their earnings so they can go ligit if they want to."

"I see," sounding skeptical. He suspected she was picturing Maud in her severe black silk, pearl bobs in her ears. "Has Maud had successes?"

"Some. But you could say the girls working here are hand-picked. They have talent and brains. If you think it doesn't take talent to be a high-paid prostitute, you're wrong. They're not run-of-the-mill. They're firsts at twice the price."

Now she swooped in. "I think you contradicted yourself, Lieutenant. You seem to be saying that prostitutes are born, not made. Yet you claim the girls here are the *crème de la crème* of the *demimonde*, and will get out of the business when they save enough."

She had spunk. He might help her get her story. "You don't know how a high-class house operates, do you? You've eavesdropped on the girls and probably peeked down the second floor hallway." She blinked. He thumbed over his shoulder. "You never saw what goes on in the large parlor, did you? I bet you've used your imagination, though."

She blushed and her fingers caught up that strand of hair again. "I leave before any men come, after I prepare their late supper."

"The gentlemen as Maud insists they be called, are arriving right now." He'd heard a few automobiles backfiring and distant voices in the front hall. "You could take in a couple of bottles of whiskey to Mr. Moses. He's tending bar. Get yourself a good look."

"I can't risk going into the parlor. I know older businessmen come here and I might be seen by my late husband's acquaintances. I only want to understand the circumstances that brought the girls into this kind of life."

"As I said earlier, Mrs. MacLean, you won't find a slippery slope turning a nice young thing into a fallen woman. The story you think you'll write won't jibe with the actual events in the girls' lives." He saw her resistance. "Let's get back to the parlor. Want me to describe what's going on in there?"

Addie pushed back her chair and stood, surprising him. "I guess you don't."

"I'll fetch my tablet. You won't mind if I take notes?" From a high shelf she drew a small tablet and pencil from behind a large faded cookery book. Reseating herself, she flipped a few pages, then expectantly looked at him.

"In the corner is a round table where the gentlemen play poker. The game runs all evening. Hands folding, newcomers sitting in, Maud often dealing." Speeding up, like a station agent calling out a train schedule, he continued, "Gentlemen drink, they smoke, they talk to one another, but preferably to the girls. The girls dance with them." She jotted squiggles in shorthand. "The girls want to make money. The dances are quick, the drinks short. The girls get part of the cost of each drink sold."

Hand raised, she halted him, penciling in words. Jamieson took a last bite of pie. She nodded, he swallowed and continued. "A girl makes most of her money upstairs. Twenty minutes. She sets a timer. Afterward she cleans up, dresses and sees the gentleman to the door. Goes back in the parlor and spends a few minutes socializing. Dances with her new gentleman. The juicy waltz they call it. Takes him upstairs. $20.00 for twenty minutes, $10.00 for the booze. As much as a logger makes in a month. The logger doesn't come here, though. His boss the lumber baron does."

"I thought they sometimes stay with one man all night."

"They'll do that if he pays for the entire night, but these men have homes to return to. They tell their wives they went to their club. It is a gentleman's club of sorts. A man will tarry for a couple of hours before choosing a girl. He likes the drinking, the conversation with other businessmen, the card playing and the flirting. He gets a sympathetic listener in the girl and enjoys anticipating what will happen upstairs. Am I making you blush again?"

"I was married, Lieutenant. I'm just not used to hearing about it from a man not my husband."

He was enjoying himself. "I'm just your source."

She didn't meet his eyes. "I want my story sympathetic, but not a sob story. If I find economic circumstance brought them here, I will write that. And, of course, I'll never mention names. Not Maud's or any of the girls."

"Maud doesn't want publicity. She pays off the police, the mayor's office and city council." He was surprised he'd committed himself to helping her. "Keep these parameters - no names, address, or description of the house, and no physical description of the girls." She nodded. He sensed eagerness beneath her serious demeanor. "You don't have to sneak around, eavesdropping, pretending you're a cook." Then amended, "You're a fine cook. They'll talk to you, but don't count on their being honest. They like their made-up lives."

If her lips didn't smile, at least her eyes did. "Would Cousin Maud mind?"

Good question. He hoped Maud wouldn't be sour grapes about this. "Why don't you ask her?"

"She's rather formidable. I'm afraid she'll terminate my employment and I won't get any story."

"I think she'll allow this one favor." Any reserve toward her evaporated. "Shall I ask her?"

A slight hesitation, "Will you do that for me?"

"I will." He thought she might really smile now. Her lips pursed, and she was about to say something when the kitchen door swung inward.

Katie, one of Maud's top girls, was still in the throes of a foxtrot, sliding over the threshold in Cuban heels. She stopped short and released the door. "Gee, am I interruptin' somethin'?" Blurted, "Guess who's here? The chief of police. Come for Maud's Christmas present. A bottle of whiskey and me." Hand on her thigh, she twitched her hips like a Vaudeville performer. "Wish he wasn't such a jellyroll." Her mascaraed eyes and bright dolly smile were all for Jamieson. *I'd rather it was you*, it said. She held up a brass key. "Mr. Moses wants a couple of bottles from the cellar."

"I'll get them." He stood and reached for the key, but Katie danced away, hiding it behind her. He didn't pursue her, just held out a hand. She shrugged and placed it on his palm, drawing her fingertips down his fingers.

Addie studied Katie as her sulky eyes followed Jamieson into the pantry. She wore an extravagant dress of red crepe, its beaded girdle pulled through an enameled slide in front, the long fringed ends dangling to the hem. A jeweled hair piece sparkled in her wavy red bob. The dress swished, outlining her thighs. "One of my old honeys gave me a little bottle of brandy, so I don't care a cent about anything right now." Raising a tinted and buffed fingernail to red lips, "Don't you tell. Hid it under my mattress."

"Lucky girl. If someone gave me some brandy, I'd make a soused dessert I think you'd like. But it's hard to get now, so I suppose cooking with it would be a waste."

"You can say that again." Katie looked at Addie as though seeing her for the first time. "I heard you saved Robbie's life. Thought it was some down-at-the-heels hooker, who had to work in a factory to make ends meet." She didn't wait for an explanation. "Watch those angel wings, they're gonna get burnt. Robbie is a dangerous man. He sent me here, ya know. Seduced and jilted, that's little ol' me. But I get no sympathy. He's a grand ol' lady-killer, wanting every woman he sees." She held out bare arms, pirouetting as though on stage, warbling softly,

I want you when I'm bright and cheery,
Need you when I'm sad and weary,
Always be near me, dearie,
For I want you all the while.

Wobbled to a stop, blinking Addie into focus. "I've got plans, though."

Jamieson handed Katie the whiskey and key.

"Thanks, sweetie. I told her."

"Told her what?" He observed an angry flush around Addie's eyes.

"I told her you sent me here. Gave me that card. That was all right, wasn't it, Robbie? You must've given her a card, too."

"Yeah, that's all right, kitten. Let me get the door for you."

"See," she tossed over her shoulder. "He calls me kitten. I'm just his little stray cat."

"Have you been drinking?"

"Just a little holiday brandy. I'll bring some up later."

"No. Share it with the girls. They're unwilling teetotalers."

"Okey-doke."

He followed her down the hall to open the parlor doors. When he returned, Adelaide MacLean was gone, leaving tea cups and the pie plate on the table. That was quick. *What the hell had Katie said to her?*

While he stood in the middle of the kitchen, Edna stomped through the back door into the pantry and thumped down on the bench. "Well, Mrs. Blake," she called through the door, "that streetcar finally got me here." She came into the kitchen wearing a long black skirt and a middy with white cuffs and collar, tying on her head a piece of stiff white ruche, prepared to answer the front door and straighten the parlor in the presence of the gentlemen. She once told him she viewed herself as an extra on the stage of naughty nightlife. Seeing Jamieson, she exclaimed, "Robbie, where'd you come from? Good to see you. Month of Sundays since you were here." She surveyed the kitchen. "Someone's being doin' my chores."

"Mrs. Matthews is here. Snowed in. She's using my room. I'm in storage across the hall."

"That's good to know. The bed-hoppin' 'round here gets a body confused." She smiled sweetly, a reminder she had one up on him. The year before, she'd discovered Katie asleep with him in his bed. Maud forbade his consorting with her girls.

Chapter 31

He wouldn't have trouble falling asleep, despite the sounds from the floor below – the opening and closing of bedroom doors, the laughter of satisfied men and cunning women echoing up the back stairs. The door across the hall remained closed, not a sound coming from Adelaide MacLean. He thought about the woman in his bed with a mixture of suspicion and desire. After Sewell's death, whores hadn't eased his discontent for more than twenty minutes. He'd given it the old college try, finishing the evening satiated, but not satisfied. They gave what they promised during dancing and drinking, but it wasn't enough now.

He awoke, startled and on guard, staring into the darkness. Katie whispered from near the doorway. "Robbie, you awake?"

"I am now." She'd crept up the stairs without a light, green cat eyes in the night.

"Would you like some brandy?"

"No." Mumbled, "Is everyone gone?"

She stubbed her toes on his boots and cursed softly. Then a plaintive, "Where are you?"

"Here, but Katie . . ."

She plopped on the cot. "Does your bow-wow need a kitten?" Her suggestive velvet voice was like no other.

"Ah, Katie." What was a fellow to do?

"My Lord, it smells like mouse in here." Then she got down to basics. "I'm clean, Robbie. I've douched and taken a bath. I know you like me clean. Please rub my back. It's so sore. Then I'll be able to sleep." She raised her bottom and lifted the covers, letting in a draft.

His union suit protected him from the cold, but would be little protection from her. He rubbed the silk of her flimsy kimono between his fingers. It was still damp from her bath. A gentleman shouldn't turn away a woman who comes to him in the night, and he didn't want to. They knew each other pretty damn well and that was good enough. Spooning her back to his chest, he drew the covers over her. She turned on her stomach and he pressed the hollow above her hips, moving his hand while she muttered directions.

"There. That feels so good."

He rested his chin on her silky head smelling of cigar smoke and the expensive perfume with which she doused herself. Not bad if you favored cigars.

Almost purring, "This is so nice. Sometimes I get the blues, but being with you perks me up. I don't have to pretend with you."

He caressed her neck and she turned toward him.

*   *

When Katie first laid eyes on Robbie at the Irish World in Butte a few years earlier, she wet ruby lips and smiled when his roving eyes settled on her. He guided her to the bar, had a few drinks and paid for her amber-colored water. She lolled toward him, using her eyes to flirt and promise. His remained wary, watching the crowded room. Then he let it slip he was a wanted man. She'd been on the line only a short time, not long enough to size men up, and she believed him. Oh, brother, did she believe him.

It was early and he was her first customer. Upstairs he undressed her himself. He came in on the train, he said. Which one, she asked, leaning back on her elbows as he unhooked her garters. All trains come through Butte, she added. He rolled down her silk stockings, slid his fingers up her calves and thighs like a man studying the points on a mare. It didn't matter which train, he said, pulling her to her feet, unsnapping her tight corset, which left pink marks on her smooth white body. I'm here now. The way he touched her, she'd honeyed right up for him. He was bathed and smelled nice, tousled dark hair free of pomade that would grease the pillowcase. She felt a thrill when he thrust into her. She expected him to finish quickly. Men who were large often did, saying she was a tight fuck. But this stranger from God-knew-where took his time. She found her own pleasure with a gusty moan, which wasn't good for the long evening ahead. She'd be dried out, unable to cream up. A girl could get rubbed raw, liking sex too much. Keeping a bit of cum inside to stay slick wasn't the same. If she didn't douche, the next customer might not notice. But there'd been that mine manager, a hoity-toity Englishman, who found a curly black hair wrapped around his cock when he pulled out. "Where in bloody hell did this come from?" Did he think she was saving herself for him? Having a red muff, she couldn't claim it. He growled about it coming off some swarthy miner, but the bastard knew hard rock miners couldn't afford the Irish World. "You Irish slut. You insist on disinfecting my manhood before we fuck, but won't clean yourself, bloody *shant* cunt!" He'd scared her, but she'd wanted to scream into his drink-blotched face, "I'm American-born, you jack-off feckin' Brit!" *Damn the English, anyway.*

Maud's was a notch up, the customers older, classier. They fucked like gentlemen should.

A month later Robbie gave her Cousin Maud's card, saying she was too good for a town that couldn't grow trees and flowers. She lay in his arms, wishing he'd paid for the entire night. She didn't tell him Butte was the only town she'd ever known, just wet her lips and smiled. He said he bet she wasn't saving a dime, what with paying rent and fees, and buying expensive gowns and fancy goods drummers tempted the girls with. She didn't deny it. Already hundreds of dollars in debt to the madam, she'd landed in luxury she never dreamed possible. He said Maud would make her save in case she wanted out of the life in a few years. "You think you'll never be thirty. . ." She pouted coyly. ". . but you've seen those poor souls in the cribs in Pleasant Alley. They started in high class parlors and now they live in squalor, doing it for a lousy dollar just to eat." She rose and stepped behind a screen to douche and dress for her next customer. When she emerged, Robbie was gone. He was calling himself Mac then.

The next morning while the other girls slept, she put on her two best gowns, one over the other, and stole a coat from a larger girl; found five gold eagles in its pocket. She added her share of the past evening's take and skittered down the back stairs; hurried through Pleasant Alley past a row of brick cribs behind which haggard women peered through narrow windows, still hoping for trade. She caught the next passenger train heading west, debarked in Spokane and changed her name to Katie.

Robbie kept a third floor room at Maud's, but seldom stopped by. She thought they'd become lovers. Wasn't she the silly twat. When he did visit, she and the other girls were off-limits to him – Maud's orders. Katie obeyed house rules. She was prompt to meals, saw the doctor for a clean bill of health twice a month, and dressed for the evening by seven. But a girl deserved a private life, too, didn't she?

*   *

Lying beside him, Katie put the tip of her finger on his palm, giving him a butterfly's touch that made his pulse leap in his wrist. Not yet. He shifted his groin away from her hip and closed his hand over hers, stilling her finger. His carnal itch for her was less passionate than in earlier years, but his body habitually betrayed half-cocked resolves made out of respect for Maud's house rules. He wanted to pull her beneath him now, imagining that flash of devilment in her eyes as on the night he met her. *Here's to the girl in the red shoes.*

How much could he trust her? He kissed her forehead. "You'll never mention to anyone that I'm in the Army. Without knowing it, you could put me in danger."

"Oh, Robbie," she whispered, "I'd never do anything to hurt you. Remember how I tried to get you to tell me about yourself in Butte, and the more you drank, the quieter you got? I don't even know what you did before you became a soldier. I asked Dovey, but she says it's nobody's business."

That old wariness crawled in between them. "It doesn't matter now. There are men out there who likely would kill me if they knew my past."

She breathed into his neck. "I swear I'll never tell anyone anything about you." Now she had something to tell him. "In the past four years I've saved enough money to set up my own house."

She'd been a skinny kid when he met her, but old enough to be doing what she did, he supposed. Now she was filled out, more woman than girl. "You don't intend to compete with Maud, do you? She doesn't take kindly to one of her girls doing that."

Katie threw a leg over his thigh. "Nope. I'm goin' down the trail pointing south. St. Maries or St. Joe City. I hear those lumberjacks come out of the woods twice a year and throw their money away. I'll hire a couple of girls and hold out my apron for their silver and gold." That husky laugh. "And after I make a pile, I'm gonna open a restaurant." She put her palm against his cheek. "And I'm gonna go to confession and attend Mass again. Begin a new life." She nibbled his ear.

"Mmm-mm." He slipped a hand beneath her kimono, wanting her now. "A good Irish girl."

"I'm ready for you, Robbie." She undid a couple of buttons in his union suit, reached in and pulled out his stiff willy.

He opened her kimono, keeping the covers over them. She spread her legs and guided him to their meeting place.

Later, when they separated, Katie hunted for the bottle of brandy. "Want a drink before I go?"

He tipped back a couple of swallows.

"Not too much." She took it back. "I've got plans for the rest." She shuffled barefoot toward the door. "Did you know we had a listener? We put on a good show, didn't we?"

At the moment he didn't care.

Chapter 32

In the morning, Addie was gone.

"It's her day off," Dovey explained. "Edna made it in, so Mrs. Matthews felt she could make it home. She'll be back tomorrow." Searched his face. "Unless you chased her off."

"Now, why would you say that?" He cast about for sign she hadn't cleared out, pointed at the large purple cookbook. "Is that book hers or does it belong here?"

"Hers. I never felt the need for instruction. She does make some fancy dishes from it, though."

He pulled down the faded purple tome. The tablet and pencil she'd kept behind it were gone. He thumped it on the table and read aloud, "The White House Cook Book." Flipped though some pages. "Squirrel soup."

Dovey was frying bacon. "Made that plenty of times when I was a girl."

"You're supposed to pop them into cold water, not boiling water."

"It don't matter."

"Let them simmer all day."

"Depends on how hungry you are."

"You can add corn, Irish potatoes, tomatoes, lima beans."

"Anything handy. Prefer barley myself."

"Strain the soup through a coarse colander when the meat has boiled to shreds, so as to get rid of the squirrels' troublesome little bones." He grinned, catching Dovey's eye when she set his plate of bacon within reach.

She snorted. "Troublesome little bones. Good for picking your teeth." Patted his shoulder before limping back to the stove.

"Remember that time I brought you a squirrel? My first kill. How old was I?"

"It wasn't your first kill. It was still alive. You had it by the tail, running and screaming."

"It was biting me."

She broke eggs into sizzling bacon grease. "Then you should've dropped it. Lucky for you I still had the butcher knife when I ran out. Cut its throat for you."

"You fried it."

"And you wouldn't eat it. You were five." Muttered into the eggs, "Where did the years go?"

When they conversed, he was almost that boy again, entertaining her while she waited on him. Now he'd tell her why Mrs. Matthews was at Maud's. It would tickle her funny bone for damn sure. "You read the *Spokesman-Review*, don't you?"

"When I can put my feet up."

"You ever read that column, *Mrs. Vandervort's Helpful Hints*?"

"When did you become interested in women's doings? Cookery books . . . ladies' columns."

He threw an elbow over the back of the chair, turning to watch her reaction. "Mrs. Matthews is the woman who writes that column."

A drawn out, "No-o-o. She tell you that?" Dovey scooped his eggs onto a plate.

"She didn't tell me. I moused around yesterday and discovered it for myself." He tapped his chest with the fork handle before shoveling into his eggs. "Detective. Remember?" Dovey sat across from him. "Last evening I confronted her and she admitted it. She writes for the newspaper and it's why she's here."

Dovey seemed disappointed. "I thought she came here because of you. Wasn't she looking for you?"

"Don't go playing matchmaker. I've got war work to do."

"I like those blue eyes of hers. And she has a sweet smile."

"Yeah. Well she doesn't smile at me. Nice hair, though." *And high breasts, a slim waist and damn fine hips.* "Do you want to hear the rest?" Dovey nodded, propping up her chin. "She was in Seattle the night I was shot because she was reporting on the lousy conditions factory girls work under over there. She wrote about it for the newspaper. Now she wants to write about the girls here."

"Our girls? Is she a pestiferous snooper?" A favorite expression.

"She's not out to shut down the parlor, but she believes women choose this life because of hard knocks and poverty.

She thinks if employers paid women more, fewer girls would become prostitutes."

Dovey perked up. "Is that what she thinks?"

"I told her they like the money."

"Is that what you think, Robbie? Don't get grease on that book." She picked it up with a clean tea towel and moved it. "Want more coffee?"

"I'll get it." He scraped back his chair.

"Well, it's all water under the bridge, isn't it?"

"How's that?" He lifted the large enamel coffee pot.

"Why girls choose this way of life . . . and once they're in it. . ." She stopped. "So, her name's Adele Vandervort, not Matthews?"

Should I do this to her, knowing what she's been through? He sat down. "Nope, neither one is her real name. Now don't go falling out of your chair. She's Jerome MacLean's widow, Adelaide MacLean." Dovey looked like she'd bitten into a sour pickle. He couldn't pass up adding, "Small world, isn't it?"

She pressed knuckles against her bib apron between her breasts. "Oh, my goodness. Isn't this a coincidence." She sat thinking while he watched her. "It's just like Charles Dickens put in his stories."

He offered her the benefit of his college education with a course in logic. "It was coincidence she was on that street in Seattle and saved my life." Drank some coffee. "Coming here was not coincidence."

Dovey stood up. "I have to tell Maud."

He stuffed more egg into his mouth. "Wait 'til I finish eating and I'll come with you." Swallowed. "I want to ask if she'll allow the girls to be interviewed. I told Mrs. MacLean I'd help get her story. I owe her that."

Dovey pulled off her apron. "Not now. Finish your breakfast. I want to talk to Maud alone." She pushed open the door with such force, it whooshed when it swung shut.

That afternoon Jamieson visited a rag shop where he'd previously bought old clothes. It was run by a Russian Jew, a friend to the Wobblies. Under the counter were I.W.W. pamphlets with large letters spelling out SABOTAGE and showing the worker's sabot, a wooden shoe; others depicted an arched, hissing black cat.

A running joke among hobos was that Abe greeted springtime visitors with, *"Shana Haba B'yerushalayim . . . Next year in Jerusalem."* Or maybe he said it when the customer left. He never said it to Jamieson, who admired how the Russian hid his knowledge when police or third-degree detectives came sniffing around, giving out nothing more than a shrug and a foolish grin. He told Abe he needed lumberjack clothes and the ragman exclaimed, "Next year I open real men's clothing store. Top of line. Maybe you have good money from woods. You come back and I outfit you." He was nearing fifty and had served twenty years in the Russian army, though not by choice. The last time Jamieson saw Abe, he was still relating how he danced when he read the Czar had been overthrown in March.

Jamieson chose two worn plaid wool shirts; two pairs of denim pants cut off below the knee and rubbed so often with paraffin for waterproofing, they could stand on their own -- tin pants, lumberjacks called them; and a heavy black and white plaid mackinaw coat, probably harboring lice in its seams. The wool socks had holes at the heels, but he pulled on two pair to try on some broken-in caulked boots. None fit. The Russian watched, shaking his head.

"Mac, I find you good boots. How much you pay?"

"How much is this pair?"

"Them shoes ten dollars."

"I'll pay fifteen if they fit."

"Up your foot," Abe ordered. When he complied, the man placed his hand against his sole. "Be back soon . . . clickety-clack." He disappeared into a back room and returned with a pair of nearly new caulked boots, the metal spikes long and sharp. "You try."

After paying, Jamieson stuffed his gear into a canvas Duluth haversack that cost more than the clothes. Leaning on an elbow, he rolled and lit a cigarette. "Say, Abe, remember last month I came in and asked about that fella, Irish O'Neill, and you said you knew him, but hadn't seen him?"

"Sure . . . sure. I gonna tell you he here now. Say he gonna to Idaho woods soon. I tell him you look for him. He say he at mission now that Wobbly hall closed."

"Thanks. Much obliged." Drew on his cigarette, tipping up his face to exhale blue smoke. "Another thing. You know how the fellow workers wonder every year if you're gonna take a trip to Jerusalem? There's fighting there now. Guess you won't want to go any time soon."

"Ah, Jerusalem . . . it here." Pointed at his head. "Spokane my Jerusalem now, because next year a clothing store for real men. Spats, ties, shirts, collars, suits, hats."

Jamieson pointed at the haversack full of lumberjack clothes. "Real men, Abe."

"Ah, you right. Clothing store not for real men. For gentlemen. You come."

Chapter 33

The following morning Jamieson was soaking his lumberjack clothes and haversack in the second floor bathtub, hoping to drown whatever might be crawling around in his new clothes. New to him, anyway.

Mr. Moses hollered up the back stairs, "Robert, git down here! We need you!"

Imagining Dovey had sliced her hand with a butcher knife, he thundered down the stairs, only to find her loading the double-barreled shotgun. A delivery man was leaving by the back door.

"Sam says a pack of dogs is heading this way and it's time for Mrs. Matthews to get off the streetcar. We'll go meet her." She glanced down at his shoes. "No time to put on boots, Robbie. Just don't slip and shoot me."

Mr. Moses pushed the Winchester into his hands. It was the rifle he'd left with them when he entered the Army. "I loaded it."

Jamieson and Dovey headed downhill toward the streetcar stop, passing houses with livestock in back - milk cows, goats, chickens -- their barnyard odors would draw those dogs this way.

From a block away he spotted Addie. She was backed against a wrought iron fence, facing downhill. Did she see the pack? The street leveled where she stood before dipping down another steep hill. He couldn't see the dogs, but heard their bays and cries. How would she handle danger? Then he remembered Seattle.

Out-of-breath, but keeping up with him in crusted snow, Dovey gasped, "Why don't she get behind that fence?"

"Gate's padlocked." He wasted his breath with a curse when he slipped in the snow, but held the Winchester high. Dovey drew ahead of him.

The dogs crested the hill at a lope, snarling and yipping, snapping as they careened into one another. They'd already tasted blood - chickens or pigs or goats. Another flock of chickens would do, or any living creature along their passage.

The dogs paused to mill across the street from Addie, brought up short by her shouting and waving. Dovey braced herself, hoisted her shotgun, and fired off a barrel. Dogs yelped and spun; some retreated downhill. The rest, heads down, glared at the two women. Dovey let go the other barrel, scattering all but one, a large brindled mongrel with a huge head and old fight scars. Ignoring Dovey, it stalked Addie, planting itself between her and Jamieson's rifle sight.

Jamieson dropped to one knee and aimed. Addie was staring down the dog, maybe talking to it, while raising her handbag. It didn't make for much of a weapon.

Dovey yelled, "Robbie! Down on your stomach like I taught ya!"

He fell forward, stretched out and lined up the rear and front sights. The dog hunched, hind legs braced. No thoughts came to his mind, only images of the snarling dog and its beating heart. He rolled, hoping for a cleaner target. Off eye closed, hands steady, deep breath partly released, he squeezed the trigger. The rifle cracked. The mongrel jerked up and dropped, a dead heap at Addie's feet. Jamieson exhaled.

Addie squinted at the dead dog through a wisp of blue smoke rising from the burnt hole in her handbag. Her gloved hand gripped the snub-nosed revolver inside. *Never take your eyes off what you're aiming at,* Jerome had commanded. *And for Christ's sake, don't blink.* She blinked now. Up the street Jamieson still lay in the snow, dark head bowed over his rifle. Dovey limped toward her, shotgun in the crook of her arm. Addie's bullet was embedded in the dog's head, but blood ran from its chest behind a front leg. She withdrew the revolver from her bag, instinctively pointing it again at the dog, whose heart's blood was reddening street ice. Its tongue lolled over curled black lips and bared fangs. She moved shakily along the fence, taking shuddering breaths of cold air. *Don't cry. Don't let him see you cry.*

Dovey propped the shotgun against the fence and threw her arms around the taller woman, ignoring the revolver in her hand. "Oh, Mrs. Matthews," she huffed, "I thought we lost you!"

"You saved my life, Mrs. Blake. Thank you for coming with that shotgun."

"Pshaw!" She stepped back. "It was Robbie saved your life."

Your Robbie could have killed me.

"I taught Robbie to shoot. Appeared the Army tried to unteach him, kneeling down like that. But I never doubted he'd kill that dog. Just worried the bullet might go through it and hit you. Thank God, it didn't."

Yes, thank God.

Chest and legs covered with snow like a boy back from sledding, Jamieson approached the dog. He stood studying it, then skewed his eyes toward hers. She raised the revolver and twitched her wrist. Seeing his surprise, a giddiness swelled in her chest, threatening to erupt into wild laughter. Her hand trembled and she dropped the gun into the handbag. She didn't need him to save her life. She could take care of herself.

Chapter 34

On almost every operation he'd worked with Billy Sewell, the older agent gave him the same advice. Work with what's handy and hope for the best. Schemes miscarry; chance will foil your strategy. But you make do. Above all, you think on your feet and keep your identity secret.

At the Union Gospel Mission, O'Neill's thick black brows stood out at the back of the room. Arms folded over a tweed cap resting on his chest, he appeared to be nodding off during an earnest sermon by a young preacher in a too-large suit. Missions all smelled the same -- unbathed men, cigarette smoke, bubbling beans and onions, and burnt coffee. So, here was the Irishman the Ellensburg yard bull recognized in a mug shot, but was he really involved in the Butte gunrunning scheme? That was what he had to discover.

They began a friendly sparring over bowls of chili. Why was Mac looking him up? *We were on the Verona together, remember?* How long was he in Seattle's rat hole? *I was sprung with some others after nine days.* What had he been doing since? *This an' that.* How did he plan to spend the winter? *With Wobs bein' arrested right and left, thought I'd head for the woods and lay low.* What was his skill? *Sawyer. You, too? Could you use a partner on the saw?*

Jamieson had misgivings O'Neill was already partnered on the cross-cut and he was right to have them. Krause. Harry Krause. When Krause came in for a meal, he vaguely recalled the young man with the German accent from the *Verona.* An Austrian, he seemed likable enough. Nevertheless, Jamieson made plans to get rid of him and let it slip he'd been drafted, but Army life hadn't meshed with his I.W.W. philosophy.

"Sure ye're not the first deserter I'm knowing," O'Neill offered with approval.

Krause, cheeks rosy as Winesaps from the frosty air outside, had better things on his mind. "Yah, me now, I have me a winter bride. She nice whore. Let me stay all winter. Good protection, she say. Maybe I stay longer an' not go to woods with you, Irish. Stay warm."

"Harry, me boyo, a sportin' woman she is, an enchantress with the wiles of a kitten but the morals of a cat altogether. And yerself, handsome when cleaned up and in a natty suit, so ye are. But do ye think ye should stay here? Any man without a job is called an idler and a vagrant. They'll round ye up in a divil's flash of the tail. Especially ye bein' one of them they's fightin' in Europe."

"Yah, but I register as alien enemy. Follow law. All set." Young and confident, he nevertheless agreed to meet them in two days to head for the woods.

It was all the time Jamieson needed.

Chapter 35

Addie was interviewing Inga at the dining room table. A beautiful flaxen-haired Norwegian, when she smiled, dimples appeared in pale cheeks beside a wide, lightly rouged mouth. "We say, 'Pittsburgh is hell with lid off.' I was factory girl two years, but not work good on sore feet. Little work in Pittsburgh for sitting girl." She was physically unmarked by sin. "I am more happy working on back. There, I say it. Why lie?"

Dovey told the girls Maud was allowing interviews. "You don't have to talk to Mrs. Matthews if you don't want to, but if you do talk to her, don't go tellin' tall tales about how you got into the business. Tell her the truth."

"Ya, many times I don't like what I do." Perhaps she was asking not to be judged. "But I pay the bills and I am safe here. An' maybe I find husband. Who knows?"

Low voiced and charming, it was obvious what Maud's patrons found attractive. Addie jotted a few notes. "Why did you leave Pittsburgh?"

"In Pittsburgh, how to say . . . everything going to dogs. The house I work in not good place. The mattress go down in middle. The men don't mind, but sometime I feel like I'm not breathe, like I'm gonna die." More to the point, "And rent cost too much." Smoothed one hand over the other. "I go to Chicago. A little better. No, not better."

According to a study Addie read, there were only two types of prostitute. The first was a girl so passive, non-resistant and somewhat feeble-minded, she would yield to anyone's suggestion. The second was a girl with no self-control over her natural impulses, including an overwhelming urge for the sexual act. Which was Inga? "How long were you in Chicago?"

"A year. Too many men bilk me and they stink like slaughter yard. Their hands dirty and blood under nails. I go to work in better parlor in Chicago, but still not happy. Madam take most my pay. Robbie come, but he say his name Mac. He smell good, just out of bath like clean baby. He is gentle. I fall in love." A low laugh. "No, but almost. He give me Maud's card, tell me come to Spokane. 'Where is this Spokane?' I say.

He show me on railroad map he have in pocket. 'Here,' he say. 'My cousin Maud, she be good to you. Nice gentlemen. Whiskey drinkers, not cheap beer.' He tell me Maud help me to keep money in bank. Someday I stop this if I want. Is for me to decide. So, I come." She smiled at Addie, spreading her beautiful hands. "I must be somewhere? Why not here."

Two more girls allowed themselves to be interviewed. None claimed to have been duped into prostitution.

Addie asked only once, and it was of the worldly New Yorker, Stella. Had she known of any girl held against her will in a brothel?

Stella turned sparkling dark eyes on Addie. "You mean a girl traveling alone and as she's sitting on the toilet at a train station, someone in the next stall leans down and sticks a hypodermic needle into her leg. The syringe is full of dope and the next thing she knows, she's tied to a bed and a brute of a man has torn off her clothes and is having a heck of a good time on her. Is that what you're asking?"

Wishing she hadn't, Addie nodded.

Stella grinned. "I've never known anyone that happened to, but I love reading about it in magazines."

Katie was the last to be interviewed. She wore a goblin green kimono accentuating her red hair. Between the two women lay Addie's having been an involuntary witness to an act of love-making behind a thin wall, but she was determined not to allow it to interfere with the story she wanted. Still, she wondered if Jamieson really was responsible for Katie's becoming a prostitute?

The redhead sat down. "I've got the rag on, so I won't be workin' tonight. Take your time, dearie." She crossed her knees and kicked a feathered mule against a table leg a few times. "Fire away."

Squaring her shoulders, Addie asked, "Where are you from?"

"Come on, sister, ask me a hard one. I'm Butte Irish." Green eyes glinted, small heart-shaped mouth twisted. "Now you're gonna ask what I did before. I was a bucket girl. I stuffed pasties and made sandwiches for miners' lunch buckets at a big boarding house called the Ship. Next question. Oh, don't bother. You want to know why I chose this life."

"Did you choose it?" Addie stopped writing. She would remember every word Katie said.

"Before I tell you that . . . you ever been to Butte?"

Addie shook her head.

"If you'd been to Butte, you wouldn't have to ask what got me into the life. You know what we're called in Butte? The devil's playthings. Not just us whores. Everybody." Her eyes and voice turned brittle. "I grew up in Dublin Gulch and I wouldn't wish that on a dog." She paused to light a cigarette. Inhaled deeply. "Don't get me wrong. I'm proud of my Irish kin workin' those killin' mines. When they aren't workin', they're happy-go-lucky. Jolly Irishmen, you'd call 'em. Not the women, though. They're old even when they're young." With rapid-fire commentary, Katie took control of the interview and Addie let her. "My mam, this is how she said it. 'Butte womens, sure ta poor tings 'er borne eart'ward wit' chillens.' My da drank up the money he earned in the mines and my mam joined him. You know what we call that in Butte? Lookin' for miserable happiness, and it killed 'em. You think me being a prostitute is sad? Well, do you, Mrs. Matthews?" Her scorn was palpable.

Addie wouldn't allow herself to become the subject. "I don't have an opinion."

"Oh, I bet you don't." She took another drag on her cigarette, forcefully blew out smoke. "When Robbie found me at the Irish World, I was just a kid. He told me later he was almost afraid to do me," her voice dropping, "'cause he might of broken my wee bones." She smiled, lifting her chin. It shone in her eyes how she felt about that man.

Addie wanted Katie to talk about prostitution, not her relationship with Jamieson. "And you came here because . . ."

"I came here because I was unhappy in Butte and it was costin' me too much. Robbie understood that. And I wanted to practice the art of love." She ran fingers through her red bob, patting down the back.

Any response Addie made to Katie's statement would sound like ridicule. She repeated deadpan, "The art of love."

"That house I was in offered only the basics." Katie moved a forefinger up and down. "Know what I mean?"

"I was married. I know what you mean."

"Well, it's not my style. I'm better than that." Having said what she came to say, her fire dwindled. She tapped a manicured nail. Over the years, she'd bitten her nails past the quick, halfway to the cuticle. They grew back without adhering to the nail bed, showing a lot of white. But they *had* grown back. "Yeah, if a girl's gonna use imagination to please a man, she's gotta have more time, and the man's gotta be willing to pay for it." Then she blurted, "If I said something the other night that made ya think Robbie was responsible for me going into the life, well, he wasn't. I'd been on the line about a year before I met him." She stood up. "Nice talkin' to ya." Pushing open the double doors to the hall, she gave Addie an inscrutable look before softly closing them behind her.

Addie remained seated. There was nothing feeble-minded about Katie or any of them. As for sin and damnation, she didn't believe in it much. But it would be easy to exploit these women as they searched for something better. Robert Jamieson had done that, to say nothing of Cousin Maud. And she'd be damned before she'd allow that man to inherit half of Jerome's legacy.

Chapter 36

Dressed for rough travel, his pack and mackinaw waiting at the back door, Jamieson took leave of Maud in her suite. He encountered Katie in a green kimono in the hall. Kept his voice low so Maud wouldn't overhear. "I'm leaving."

Katie placed a small hand on his chest. "You always do." She kissed him on the cheek, turned to mount the front staircase, stopping after a half-dozen steps. Gave him a playful salute. "So long, soldier." And ascended out of sight.

He headed through the dining room to seek out Mr. Moses in his room behind the kitchen and saw Addie. God, she was lovely. Wanting to hear her voice, he reached the kitchen door first and playfully braced a hand on the door frame, blocking her way. When the war ended, he'd come back to Spokane and maybe they'd get better acquainted. "Did you get the interviews you wanted?"

"Let me pass," she said, giving him a sidelong blue glare. "You are a panderer. You lured girls here." If her voice were an ice pick, he'd be dripping blood. "I said let me pass."

Stunned, it took him a moment to reply. "I'm no panderer. What did they tell you?"

"You take advantage of the economic weakness of girls like Katie for the profit of this parlor . . . maybe for your own profit, too."

She obviously viewed him as an integral part of this house, a pimp from the cellar of society, preying on downtrodden women. "I wanted to help Katie get out of the money hole she got herself into. I never made a penny off her." Seeing Addie's unwavering fierce eyes, his plea for understanding evaporated. If it was the gambling, drinking, whoring Mac she wanted, it was that Mac she'd get. "I'm no pimp, lady. You've got some nerve accusing me of wrongdoing with all the sneaking around you've done."

"What about Inga? Did you want to help her get out of the hole she was in and make her a better woman?"

"Don't stop there, Mrs. MacLean. How about Nancy? You never met Nancy. She's married now and living a good life. And Alice. Pretty Alice. She came to Maud's and now she has a tearoom downtown. How about all the women you never met that I lured here. All the 'lost souls' who've made good?"

"So you consider yourself a fine man. A Good Samaritan."

"Yeah, when the opportunity arises."

She stepped back. "I'll tell you what I think, Lieutenant. Maud is 'in the business,' but I don't think she's got a heart of gold. I think she's a practical woman. She makes the girls save, so when they lose their looks, she can push them out the door. When her customers with watch chains stretched across well-fed midriffs are looking for excitement and a fresh face, you provide her with it. They like girls from out-of-town, don't they? And you go far and wide to find them."

"Yeah, men like variety, but not from a sour woman who can't smile at a man."

She tried to pull his arm from the door jamb. Snapped, "Let me through. I have work to do."

He reacted by grabbing her shoulders and pressing his fingers into her flesh until they reached muscle. "You have work to do? How can you stand to feed women I've lured into white slavery?"

In a fury she kicked his shin and brought her arms up inside his, knocking his hands away, managing to squeeze past him into the kitchen. The door sighed behind her. Boot leather cushioned his shin, but he leaned against the wall to regain his composure. He wanted to charge into the kitchen, pick up Adelaide MacLean, carry her out the back door and dump her into a snowdrift. Then wash her face in snow.

Mr. Moses came out of his room in carpet slippers, a newspaper in one hand, reading glasses in the other. "The war will be over soon, Robert. Maybe, then, you can lead a normal life."

Giving the man an exasperated look, Jamieson folded his arms.

Mr. Moses continued. "Uh-huh. A normal life. What did I tell you when you first became a detective?"

Looking at the ceiling, he gusted, "Have all your adventures during your twenties."

"'Cause you'll be too old for adventure once you pass thirty. Seems the war's interfering with that. Here's another piece of advice. Don't get yourself killed before you come back to us. Everyone is trigger happy these days." He nodded toward the kitchen. "Dovey's waiting in there to say goodbye. Worries about you all the time, but she'll never let you see it."

They shook hands and when Jamieson pushed open the kitchen door, it was to the stinking odor of burning feathers. Dovey stood near the window looking out at snow speckled black from chimney smoke. Of course she'd heard their hot exchange.

He needn't say a word, just kiss Dovey goodbye and leave. But he couldn't resist the urge to shock the MacLean woman. *You think handing out Maud's card was damning, lady? Wait till I toss you this bombshell. It will astound you.*

"Well, I'm hittin' the road. A fella's gotta take care of ol' number one. I'm through with this man's army. Got word today charges were brought against me for assaulting some enlisted swine, and I've got better things to do than stand court-martial."

Addie stopped singeing pin feathers on two roasting chickens; dropped the burning twist of newspaper into a bucket of water. Her look of lingering anger merged with an expression he wouldn't name. "I guess you'll call it desertion, Mrs. MacLean." He was courting the devil, waiting for her reaction, and he got it.

Reaching into a pile of damp white feathers, she grabbed up a handful and came around the table. She flung them in his face. "This is for you! Coward! Deserter! Panderer of women! I hope I never see you again!"

He swiped some from his hair and face. "I wouldn't worry about that." Felt them sticking to his flushed neck.

When he bent to kiss a tearful, quiet Dovey, she put her arms around him. "Go with God, my boy." As she stepped back, she plucked a few pinfeathers from his neck. In the pantry he took up his pack and mackinaw and left as he'd arrived, through the back door.

Addie was shaken by her impetuousness, but didn't regret her actions.

Dovey appeared peculiarly calm. "You're a naïve young woman with a lot to learn. I'll finish the singeing. I think your work here is finished."

"Yes, Mrs. Blake, it is."

When she reached downtown, Addie didn't change streetcars to go on to her home. Lugging the large cookery book, she marched into the building housing the Pinkerton National Detective Agency, mounted the stairs and demanded of the receptionist, "I wish to see Mr. Gascom."

Taking in the shabby coat and hat, the girl said, "You'll need an appointment."

Addie's agitation reached new heights. "I'm Mrs. Jerome MacLean and Mr. Gascom is conducting an investigation my late husband commenced before his death." Garnering all the command of a society matron, she barked, "You tell Mr. Gascom I insist on seeing him." The receptionist stared. "Now!" The girl jumped up. A moment later, she held open the door to Gascom's office.

The agent rose. "Mrs. MacLean? I hardly recognize you."

"Mr. Gascom, I'm here to close the investigation. Immediately."

He stared at her attire. "If it's a matter of finances . . ."

"It's solely a matter of convenience, I assure you."

Back home, she glimpsed herself in the hall mirror while removing her hat. Her reflection appeared as worn out as her clothes.

Her tea cup rattled in its saucer. She calmed herself by petting Titus stretched out at her feet. The light in the room deepened. Rooms changed; people changed, some from life into death. Robert Jamieson had certainly changed, from an officer into a coward, but always a man who used women. He possessed the same birthmark as Jerome's old mother - that odd knuckle, out of line with the others. Neither Jerome nor Alonzo had it. Her word could offer it as evidence of his bloodline, but she'd be damned if she'd allow that deserter to inherit. She clutched a sofa pillow against her breasts. *You hateful man.*

Chapter 37

Dressed for winter travel and carrying packs, Jamieson, O'Neill and Krause separately entered the Union Gospel Mission to meet for one last meal; then it would be 'so long, Spokane, you cold-shoulder town.' Waiting at a corner table for the pre-lunch sermon, Jamieson eyed the wall clock and each small jerk of the minute hand.

Three soldiers carrying a large American flag burst through the door. Men stopped reading and playing checkers to stare at Uncle Sam's best as they poised on the threshold, searching the room. They wove among tables to intercept a cripple about to settle into a chair, a Scandinavian whose hip was smashed the previous year when a large limb fell from a tree he was sawing.

"Kiss your country's flag," the corporal commanded, holding up a fold of red and white stripes.

Surprised by unwanted attention, he pursed lips that never completely closed because of large projecting teeth.

"Jaysus," O'Neill muttered. "They best not be forcing that bloody rag on me like they're doin' to Beaver Sven."

The corporal bellowed, "You wiped your goddamn teeth on it." He kicked the crutch out from under Sven, who thudded to the floor.

"An' him with a flail limb. Feckin' bastards." Half-out of his chair when Jamieson gabbed his shoulder, O'Neill resettled himself. Crusty-looking men refocused on reading and games, hoping to avoid attention.

When he spotted the three at the corner table, the corporal lost interest in Beaver Sven, even toeing the crutch closer to the fallen man. "Over here." Wadding the flag's canton in his fist, he dragged the two soldiers attached to its fly behind him across the room to stand over Jamieson, O'Neill and Krause. Arms akimbo, flag pinioned against a hip, he demanded, "Why the hell ain't you men serving your country?"

Jamieson warily eyed O'Neill, who cocked his chin. "I love America sure," sounding agreeable enough, "but ye see I'm Irish an' I don't love England at all. Let her fight her own bloody war."

"You bastard," the corporal yelped, "that's seditious talk." He mustered all the authority of his uniform. "Show your registration card."

The two soldiers made a show of draping the flag over the corporal's shoulders before yanking O'Neill to his feet. He knocked off their hands and dug into a pocket, pulling out his orange card, flipping it at the corporal, who snatched it out of the air. "Used to carry it in me shoe, but sure if yer kind ain't always askin' after it."

The corporal tipped it to catch light from the windows across the room. "What's this crossed out with Ireland written over it?" He twiddled the dog-eared card in O'Neill's face. "You defacing United States government property?"

Old scars stood out white on the Irishman's seething face. "I don't belong to Great bloody Britain. I'm a citizen of the Republic of Ireland." He snarled at the two soldiers, "Keep yer feckin' hands off me, ye lousers."

Jamieson steeled himself for the ensuing brawl. "Aw, sit down," the corporal replied, dropping the card. Jamieson dragged O'Neill into his chair.

He turned to Krause. "What about you?"

Krause jumped up. "Yah, I kiss the bloody rag, sure." He grasped the edge of the flag and kissed it.

"Did you call my country's flag a bloody rag? Fuckin' Kraut. Show me your card."

"I am from Austria." Krause dug into his pants pocket and pulled out his card. "See. Says draft board status class number 5 Austrian. Yah, that me."

Eyes glued on Krause, the corporal ordered, "Go get the captain." A soldier started for the door, but it was unnecessary.

An officer in uniform jacket and jodhpurs strode in, riding crop in a gloved hand. Removing his campaign hat while crossing the room, his eyebrows puckered above steely blue eyes and a flaxen mustache. "What's going on here, men? Remove that flag from your corporal's shoulders."

The soldiers pulled it off and hastily folded it while the corporal gripped Krause by his mackinaw collar like a terrier a rat. "Captain, this man's an alien enemy. Claims he's Austrian, but sounds German to me." He stretched Krause's coat until the man's arms became useless.

The top button wedged against Krause's throat forced him to speak from the side of his mouth. "Ya, I speak German, but come from Salzburg, Austro-Hungarian Empire. I register with police like newspaper order." Another tug pressed the button into his windpipe. He choked out, "Vant to be citizen, but dey say wait 'til var over."

The corporal lowered his arm, but kept a firm hold. "Captain, he could be a spy. Want us to take him to the police station and have him checked out?" He gave the officer a sly glance. "Always make sure, you tell us, sir."

"Good idea, Corporal. Foster. Adams. Take this man to the station." Krause was led away. The officer narrowed his eyes at O'Neill. "What about him?"

"He's Irish, Captain. An Irish bum. Nothin' we can do about him."

"And this man?" He sneered at Jamieson, smacking his crop into a gloved palm as seen only at the cinema.

"On your feet when an officer addresses you." The corporal seized Jamieson by the arm, forcing him to his feet. "Another fuckin' alien, I'll betcha. Registration card."

While Jamieson was still in the act of withdrawing it from his pocket, the corporal plucked the orange card from his hand. "Robert James. Native born. What are you, a slacker? Why ain't you in your country's uniform?"

Jamieson recoiled from the corporal's thrust-out face; his breath was redolent of onions and bad teeth. Wired taut, he kept his voice agreeable. "Haven't been called up yet." From the corner of his eye he saw O'Neill palm a knife from inside his boot. This could be a disaster.

The captain withdrew a piece of paper from inside his jacket and studied it. Jamieson slid a foot, toeing for his haversack holding a couple of thin blankets and woodsman's clothes, caulked boots strapped to its outside. It would be a short sprint to the door.

The captain lifted hostile eyes. "I thought your name sounded familiar. Robert James, deserter."

"Hey, that's not me! That's some other guy!"

"The hell it is! Arrest this man, Corporal. The Irishman, too. Harboring a deserter."

Jamieson grabbed the haversack and swung it. Caulked boots hit the officer in the chest, sending him reeling into a couple of chairs, which slid out from under him. His fall unchecked, the back of his head hit a table's edge. His eyes went blank as he sprawled to the floor. Mouth agape, the corporal leaped to one side, protectively raising his hands.

Jamieson shouted a warning meant for the corporal. "Don't use your knife, Irish! They'll hang ya! Come on!" The corporal's eyes jerked toward O'Neill and he stumbled back until a table stopped his retreat.

O'Neill thrust the knife back into his boot, swept up his pack and cap. "We'll teach 'em a lesson first."

"No time!" Jamieson snagged his hat and rushed the door. Moments passed before O'Neill sauntered out, shaking his right hand, pack slung over a shoulder.

"I smashed that corporal's gob. 'Twas him caused the trouble." He gave Jamieson a lopsided grin of satisfaction. "An' I kicked the captain in the nuts. 'Twas him I caught spyin' on our Wobbly lawyer a while back. Nuts to him, aye?" Laughed at his own joke.

God damn! O'Neill recognized Dengel. "Nice work." Jamieson headed for the rail yards. "We'll jump a freight and head for St. Maries."

"Wait now. What about Krause?"

O'Neill's loyalty. He hadn't figured it into his scheme. "There's no time. I'm a wanted man and now they're after both of us. You punched a goddamn soldier. Same as hittin' a copper." They zigzagged toward the yards, peering over shoulders and around corners. No one followed.

"'Tis poor Krause satisfying their blood lust sure."

The police wouldn't hold Krause. He never said a word favoring the Kaiser or wanting Germany to win the war. He was following the letter of the law, even buying Liberty Bonds. How patriotic can a fellow get? "Go ahead, wait for Krause. You must have enjoyed jail more than I did. I'm headin' into the woods 'til this war's over."

At the tracks O'Neill turned around, elevated his maimed nose into the cold air like the palooka of scent dogs, then followed Jamieson as he hunted for an empty boxcar.

At the rough-hewn river town of St. Maries, they crawled from a freezing boxcar, hobbled on numb feet along a caulk-riddled boardwalk squeaking with cold, to the Skelton-Warren store near the riverfront. Houseboats on the St. Joe River sported floating blind pigs, brothels and gambling dens, all frozen in now. The temperature on a large thermometer hanging next to the store entrance hovered at ten degrees.

A bell over the door jangled when they entered. Next to the pot-bellied stove an old man with tobacco-stained whiskers opened his eyes and nodded, a self-appointed greeter. Dozing within the stove's warm radius, two lumberjacks balanced on overturned empty nail kegs.

Another lesson Sewell taught him. When seeking information from store loafers, purchase a few items, including some Red Man, and grizzled raconteurs, companions in habit, will welcome you. The lumberjacks, survivors of a night's bender, barely kept themselves from sliding onto the tobacco-stained floor. Jamieson made the purchases and sat down next to O'Neill, handing him a chew. One jack opened an eye to spit on the stove, generating a pleasant hiss. Only the old greeter, calling out to a customer by name, conscientiously hit a spittoon.

You're a stranger, Sewell had cautioned. Don't ask questions point-blank. Wait for the lowdown to come your way. Jamieson commented on the weather. The old-timer took up the subject. First one lumberjack and then the other eyed the caulked boots tied to their packs.

The old man asked, "Ya lookin' for work?"

Jamieson nodded. "Yep."

A lumberjack mumbled to O'Neill, "You look familiar."

"'Twas down at Fernwood I logged."

The old man shifted his wad. "Not much goin' on at Fernwood now. The sheriff hauled out a lot of Wobblies in the fall, stuck 'em in the stockade at the fairgrounds 'til November. Rest of the crew quit. Which was you?"

"After me time there. Heard there was work on Marble Creek."

Both jacks' eyes opened. One asked, "You ever work that drainage before?" When they shook their heads, he offered, "I'm not sayin' I'm afraid to work the Marble, but I sure as hell respect it. It's steeper'n a cow's face back in those mountains." Spat and closed his eyes.

The old man exhibited malicious interest. "There's men die up there. Don't recommend it unless ya got plenty of experience under your braces." He let fly a stream of juice. "Do ya?"

"Enough," Jamieson answered with a confidence he didn't feel. He spat at and into a cuspidor, the reverse of eyeing a baseball into a mitt.

The old man leaned forward. "I'm a sawmill man myself," offering himself, a prize of raddled flesh.

O'Neill asked, "Who's cuttin' timber up there?"

Eyes again shut, the other jack tipped up a bristled chin. "They all are. Rutledge, Blackwell, Herrick, MacLean . . ."

"MacLean's then. A fine place to work ye'd say?"

Why had O'Neill singled out MacLean's? The name sounded Irish, but had a Scottish spelling.

The old man thumbed over his shoulder. "I worked at MacLean's sawmill over yonder. Never been up to his camps. Don't think they's none of 'em good to work in. Show up, though, an' ya might get hired. Heard he needs more men. Take a freight to Marble Station, cross the Joe, then haul yourselves up the trail ten mile or so. That right, Ted?" He received a grunt of affirmation.

"Sure, 'tis a grand country ye have here," O'Neill offered as he and Jamieson hefted their packs and headed for the door. The old man nodded and lifted a hand. Missing all his fingers, he waggled the thumb in farewell.

Chapter 38
Marble Creek: December, 1917

"Tim-berrr downhill!"

Above the deep gorge through which Marble Creek descended toward the St. Joe River, the cry bounced off the canyon wall, echoing back. Skidders snaking horse teams along trails across the mountainside spotted its source and gave it a wide berth.

When he earlier approached the towering tree with his axe, Jamieson figured the tree's diameter to be about six feet, the lowest branches some thirty feet above his head. Finally, the white pine's top shivered as the seven-foot cross-cut's shark teeth bit through the enormous trunk. He and O'Neill yanked out the saw, tossed it into the snow and followed it, jumping from the spring boards they'd stood on. This monument to the passage of time was coming down.

They angled off to stand behind a nearby tree, balancing catlike, ready to leap if the sawn tree unexpectedly kicked back. It would take off a man's head if he stood behind its fall line. O'Neill crooked an elbow across his face to avoid flying splinters, but Jamieson braced a weary shoulder against rough bark to watch the cut slowly open. It was a wonder, this tree, having scraped the sky for a few hundred years. Now it groaned and creaked like timber spars on a storm-tossed ship, followed by a prolonged loud cracking as it slowly descended. Rooted at the top of a steep slope above the creek, its out-flung branches parted the air, creating an isolated maelstrom of swirling ice and snow. A loud whoosh and then it met the earth. Its top splintered and broke off. The ground vibrated through Jamieson's two pair of wool socks and rubber-soled boots as the tree bounced, then rose in a cloud of snow and needles before settling. *Horror vacui.* The Latin phrase came to mind as sunlight filled the gap where the tree once stood in the dark forest. Sparkling snow floated down to veil and shroud the fallen giant.

"Sure it keened itself down." O'Neill returned to the stump that would be taller than a man when the snow melted. He'd thrown off his mackinaw and rolled red checked sleeves up brawny arms, exposing black wool underwear. Retrieving the cross-cut, axes and steel wedges, he set them aside; picked up a maul and knocked out the spring boards. He squatted in denims stagged-off below his knees and cleaned the saw of its pitch with kerosene from an old whiskey bottle, its neck wired with a hook he'd jammed into the trunk.

Jamieson stood back, admiring his work. In his first tree-fall at the MacLean camp, each pull of the saw had enlarged his spirit, a David toppling a Goliath. He'd never stood up to a tree so huge. The ones in Michigan during college summers had been second or third growth. He pulled off his mittens to wipe sweaty hands on his shirt, shook his hat free of detritus, and raked wood bits from his glistening face. "I need some water before we move to the next one."

"'Tis somethin' stronger I'm thinking on." O'Neill stamped his feet. "How can a man be hotter 'n hell on this mountain everywhere but in his toes?"

A nearby voice cut in. "Only good thing about loggin' in winter is there ain't no ticks or mosquitoes." The swamper scrambled down the mountainside to cut off branches and knots from the felled tree while they moved to the next one.

Synchronizing their chopping, they made an opening for the saw. O'Neill hopped down from his spring board to retrieve the cross-cut. "Ah, do ye mind that! Here comes the master of the woods, an' no mistake."

Jamieson pulled a sweat-soaked bandanna from around his neck to mop his brow. Alonzo MacLean was picking his way down from a higher trail where horses in jangling harnesses trailed logs. The woods boss, Cruel Jimmy Kirby, was with him. No chopped-off Levi's for those two. They slid and goat-jumped among the trees in tall laced boots and tucked wool pants.

"Hey!" MacLean barked down to the axe-man moving in with a long pole, preparing to measure and mark cuts for Jamieson and O'Neill to later buck into lengths. "Don't mark this one into sixteen-foot lengths. I need 'em twenty-four foot. Special for the government. Ya hear me!"

The axe-man waved an arm. Satisfied, MacLean readjusted his beat-up hat and swung on Jamieson and O'Neill. "You two!" He sounded angry. Both men stepped away from the tree as MacLean closed in. Glaring at O'Neill, he demanded, "Is your axe sharp?"

Cocking his chin, bushy-browed eyes glared back at the taller MacLean. "What sign of a fool do ye see on me. If 'tis sharp enough to cut off a man's head, 'tis sharp enough to flay a tree."

MacLean spat, "I knowed who and what ya was when ya walked in this morning. Ya can't fool me. But I'm short of jacks and I see you two can do the job. Don't give me no trouble. No woods sabotage, understand? No filing chain links, no snapping weakened bunk-pins, no logs rolling the wrong way downhill. I'm wise to all that. An' don't go stirring up the men with your I.W.W. talk. Right here an' now I want ya to agree to my rules. I'll take a nod as your word."

Jamieson glanced at O'Neill. Six months earlier, all fire and fanaticism, he would have thrown down his axe and stomped out of the woods, but not before rising up like a prophet of the working man and taking the entire crew with him. What would he do now? The Irishman straightened over his axe and nodded. "Me hand to ye." He hefted the axe and returned to their tree. Jamieson released a lungful of white breath. O'Neill had to be his target, now following a different god of war, having switched from labor agitation to helping to raise holy hell in Ireland. Not a wild goose chase after all.

MacLean turned to Jamieson. "What about you?"

Jamieson gave a curt nod and turned to follow O'Neill, but MacLean would have the last word. "Then highball it back to pullin' that saw. And make sure you're fallin' those trees downhill. Don't matter if they break off. We're not takin' the tops." He climbed up the slope, followed by Cruel Jimmy, who'd stood with folded arms, never saying a word.

The corners of O'Neill's mouth were tight, his eyes humorless, but his self-control had been admirable. "A silver-haired divil he is. Heard he goes 'round askin' axe-men if their blades are sharp. One look down at yer axe and it's fired ye be. An' that hat." His mouth twisted. "Last summer he was stompin' it, that saddened with the men walkin' off the job at his mill. God's truth, I never thought I'd be workin' for that *mac soith.*" He spit, put a finger to the side of his nose and blew snot and wood dust into the snow. Jamieson didn't have to understand Gaelic to know what kind of a son he called MacLean.

Jamieson had taken MacLean's measure and, by God, he liked what he saw, especially the hawkish cast of frost-blue eyes.

Lunch arrived by pack mules toting milk cans in gunny sacks, insulated with stuffed hay, the cans filled with hot beef stew. Hearing the rattle of tin plates, cups, and spoons coming up the trail, lumberjacks converged from all directions. Jamieson and O'Neill gorged themselves on stew, baked beans, buttered bread, tea and doughnuts. Afterward, they sawed their downed trees into twenty-four-foot lengths. By mid-afternoon they were working in the blue shadow of the mountain, pausing to gulp cups of hot tea brewed from snow-melt in a large kettle set over a small fire.

Sometime during the day O'Neill's feet reached a comfort point. Sweat-sodden mittens grew heavy and slick. Quarter-inch-thick wool underwear wicked sweat from torsos, percolating it through wool shirts to evaporate in the dry mountain air. Stagged-off pants coated in paraffin did the opposite, repelling snow and trapping sweat, which ran from crotches down underwear-clad legs into wool socks. One day on the job and they stunk like the other jacks.

The woods resounded with thwacking axes, whining cross-cut saws, lumberjack calls and thudding timber. Logging horses snorted, obeying teamsters' low whistles. Harnesses creaked; trace chains rattled and clanged. Jamieson had never logged in winter. Some sounds were unfamiliar. Sledges piled with cut logs were skated by horses down iced tracks to landings above the Marble, accompanied by shouts for more sand to be thrown on steep sections to slow the wood runners. Muffled by deep snow, winter logging was quieter than remembered summers in Michigan. The Marble itself lay silent under a thick layer of ice.

Evening approached. Too dark to see anything but snow at their feet, they stopped sawing. Jamieson stretched out exhausted arms, sore shoulders and an aching back. In the valley below, a Milwaukee locomotive emitted a plaintive wail, the train's pulsings rising up to where he stood, kindling an urge to pack up and go. Like the men he'd ridden with, he had the heart of a hobo. The freight's staccato beat diminished until it blended with the wind sweeping the valley.

Shouldering their axes and carrying the saw between them, Jamieson and O'Neill fell in with some fifty men trailing back to camp behind twelve span of steaming, droop-headed horses. Except for cold-rouged cheeks and red plaid, the jacks appeared a gray army in the twilight, a long shadow moving through a dark forest.

The horses raised their heads as they neared camp and nickered, anticipating supper and rubdowns. It was a proper camp, all buildings constructed of logs. The horse barn was clustered with a blacksmith shop, sled shed and an office where the foreman, time-keeper, and MacLean, when he visited camp, slept. There was a commissary with items like chewing tobacco and socks a logger might need. The cookhouse dominated the camp, in the back of which the cooks and flunkies slept. A couple of privies stood near the long bunkhouse. Icicles, visible even in snowlight, hung thick from the low eaves of any heated structure.

A flunky had taken a hatchet to the bunkhouse icicles, dumping them into wash cauldrons attached to two heating stoves inside. Now that Jamieson was used to the cold, the bunkhouse felt overheated, but he longed to pry off his boots and flop down on the bunk he'd claimed that morning, bedbugs and lice be damned. Men were changing wet socks for dry before heading to the cookhouse. The camp was as regimented as a boarding school.

Chapter 39

Arms folded, O'Neill and Jamieson leaned against a log wall inside the cookhouse while lumberjacks crowded into their usual places at plank tables. Hanging kerosene lamps cast just enough light to identify the food they ate. A square steel stove crackled in the middle of the room, raising steam from the wool clothing of those seated nearby. The table nearest the door remained empty, claimed by the barn boss and teamsters, still rubbing down and feeding the horses. The blacksmith sat at one end, thick thighs encompassing the short bench, shoulders and arms bulging.

O'Neill jabbed Jamieson. "Strappin' lad, that smithy. Did ye know, Mac, I smithed in Ireland." He grinned at Jamieson's skeptical face. "'Tis so, though sure he must do the work of three of me."

Jamieson knew the drill. A young flunky pointed out what might be an empty place between two sets of wide shoulders on a long bench. He wedged in and loggers on either side shifted, grunting what passed for greetings. Across the table, but farther down, O'Neill slipped in with a genial grin, offering his hand to the two men immediate to him, who apparently recognized him from his evangelizing among them the summer before. No one spoke.

Men too old to be drafted and citizens of foreign countries crowded the tables. Americans in their prime were scarce and Jamieson received cursory looks. Silence was the rule during meals at camps in Michigan, and it was the same here. Notoriously short-tempered, when lumberjacks talked, they argued, and arguments flared like thumbed matches to become fist fights.

A flunky moved along behind them, pouring coffee while large hands vied for canned cream. Jamieson blew on his steaming mug. The rule was wolf it down and get out.

Along table centers flunkies slapped down platters of sliced ham and roast beef. They dealt out beans, mashed potatoes and bowls of gravy, canned peas, stewed tomatoes, freshly baked bread, butter by the pound, honey, and stewed prunes. Other than kitchen noises and the crackling of the wood stove, the only sounds were lumberjacks slurping coffee, chewing, scraping steel utensils against granite plates, and an occasional, "Pass the butter, if ya don't mind."

Jamieson was one big ache, in need of the aspirin and liniment in his pack. If he didn't gulp down his food and stand up soon, stiffening joints would challenge him to rise manfully from the bench. Tired unto death, he feared rigor mortis was setting in.

Across the table a young jack fixed on him while shoveling food into his mouth. Jamieson nodded once, then ignored him. O'Neill had pointed him out in the woods when a logger hailed him as "Giant Kid." About six foot six, he seemed intent on staring Jamieson down. *Goddamnit!* He didn't want to fight the camp tough. One punch to the belly and he'd lose his supper.

A pumpkin pie for each man finished off the meal. Jamieson got some down, crammed more into his mouth and pushed himself up. Once on his feet, he shoved his uneaten portion across the table as a peace offering to Giant Kid It was the best he could do.

Entering the bunkhouse ahead of the others, he stiff-legged it to O'Neill's bunk and searched his pack for letters and anything written. He found, instead, a metal hilt projecting from a long leather scabbard. Gripping it, he withdrew a bayonet halfway, but the door opened at the far end and he shoved it in and closed the pack. A couple of men entered and he nabbed a tin basin. All he had to do now was keep O'Neill in sight until he led him to the guns and their source. He'd pass on his intelligence and the Army would nip this gunrunning in the bud. He might still get to France before the war ended.

Jamieson filled his basin with steaming water from the wash cauldron's spigot and carried it to a long wooden trough on legs. Slivers of dirty soap stuck to its edge. He washed his face and neck and brushed his teeth. Once in his bunk he wouldn't move until morning.

The bunkhouse was sixty-feet long, but only sixteen-feet wide, the length of the green unpeeled logs used to construct it. Now shrunk and warped and slowly twisted, the logs allowed cat holes through which snow would drift come the next blizzard. Roughly barked, sooted and dusty, they also offered crannies and uneven corners as homes for spider webs and pests. Though better than none at all, the puncheon floor of smoothed halved logs had shrunk, too. Cold air seeped up between cracks as through chimney flues, competing with the fiercely burning barrel stoves set in sand boxes. A couple of hanging kerosene lamps each had the candlepower of a flaring parlor match. Nevertheless, it seemed appropriate for a lumberjack's abode to be built from the ancient forest in which he labored.

Jamieson washed the wool socks he'd worn that day. The stink of unwashed men was the inevitable accompaniment to all his jobs. The only place he'd smelled civilized since college was in a whorehouse.

Men tromped in, three of them joking and laughing with O'Neill. He brought them over.

"These men are fellow workers, Mac, keepin' their heads low 'til needed in the fight for universal rights. They led walkouts from camps last summer. Good men."

Jamieson wiped his wet right hand on his shirt before reaching out for meaty handshakes, acknowledging each man with a tired smile and a "Glad to meet ya, fellow worker." Secret handshakes would be next if Wobblies continued to be rounded up, jailed and deported. One was Scandinavian, another French-Canadian. The third man, Dakota Red, appeared to be native-born.

Men settled down to play cribbage or hearts. MacLean banned gambling, alcohol and smoking. It wasn't religion prompting his rules, but the need to tamp down hardened men's tendencies toward explosive violence and accidental fires. Jamieson and O'Neill reluctantly had checked their guns at the office when they arrived. A few men attempted to read old magazines in the dull light. Others, like Giant Kid, sprawled on deacon benches set against bunks made from halved logs and pegged legs.

After draping his socks on one of myriad wires crisscrossing the room above his head, Jamieson headed toward his bunk, intent on easing his aching back. Thin mattresses had been hauled up before snowfall, which beat the usual pest-infested straw all to hell.

Giant Kid stood up, blocking his way, a mad glint in his eyes. "I think I know you."

Jamieson took a painful defensive stance. Voice low, not wanting to challenge the tall logger, "Is that right?" If he had to fight this young giant, it might as well be now. Giant Kid had a hand in a pocket, fingers manipulating something metallic. The firewood bin was too far away to provide a ready weapon, but if he dove under the Kid's arm when it came out of his pocket with whatever he clutched, he might make the distance. This wasn't going to be pretty.

"Your name's Mac, I betcha."

He straightened. "Yeah. Who's askin'?"

"Here's that dollar I owe ya." Giant Kid flipped a silver dollar at Jamieson, who instinctively caught it. "And here's interest." The first dollar shifted under Jamieson's thumb as he caught the second. "Doncha know me?"

"You're beginning to look familiar." The man still wore his youth in the changing expressions on his face. Jamieson thrust out his hand. "Minnesota, right."

"You betcha. Minnesota Harv, that's me." He nearly crushed Jamieson's work-sore hand in his huge claw, and there was no better word for the kid's hand. His little finger was gone and the others were crooked. He still had the powerful grip needed to work the woods, but not to shoot a rifle at the Huns. Giant Kid addressed the watching men. "Hey, you guys, this is Mac. He saved my bacon in '13 when I come west in a boxcar. The brakey was shakin' us down an' I was broke."

"I see you got enough to eat." The kid laughed, an odd gulping sound. "Did you ever learn to fly fish?"

He boomed joyfully, "I sure did. Come summer I fish the creeks and river. Goddamn beautiful country out here."

The next morning came too early when Cruel Jimmy threw open the door and bawled, "Drop your cocks and grab your socks!"

Two smelly feet slipped over the upper bunk, almost in Jamieson's face. "And wasn't I thinkin' him the quiet kind," O'Neill muttered above.

Chapter 40

On the Marble

On January 1,1918, MacLean instituted the eight-hour work day. With tick mattresses, good grub and two hours less work a day, the men couldn't hold much against MacLean's Lumber, especially when other lumbermen were waiting for the federal government to make all this folderol official before conceding to Colonel Disque's demands to improve lumberjacks' living conditions.

"We still need a bathhouse," Dakota Red grumbled. "If the Ol' Man gives me an order, I won't be tearin' my guts loose to obey."

"A bathhouse would come in handy only if we get to go to town," said his sawing partner, who bunked below him. "I'm so used to your stink, Red, I'd think you'd gone missing if I couldn't smell ya."

Giant Kid carried a chair into the bunkhouse and demonstrated how he could jump flat-footed over its back. In a sour mood, Dakota Red called out, "How the hell did they shake you off the tit, Kid? Bang you against a door jamb?"

The Kid turned scarlet. "Ah, Red, you're just jealous." He wandered over to his bunk and flopped down.

Jamieson stuck like death-do-us-part to O'Neill, but the man seemed content in camp, cheerfully doing a full day's work for $3.50. Was he waiting for something? Maybe spring. Wanting another look in O'Neill's pack, at the first opportunity, he dug through it, only to discover the bayonet was missing. No letters, either. He searched O'Neill's blankets, felt around under the mattress, but sheath and bayonet had disappeared. It didn't matter. He'd seen them.

A week of bitter cold covered the Joe Country. As men moved to new stands of timber, trails had to be chopped through crusted snow and tamped down to avoid cutting the horses' fetlocks. Spiked shoes might keep a horse from slipping on icy slopes, but lumberjacks couldn't switch from rubber boots to caulked ones in this cold – the metal spikes would freeze their feet off. They floundered over what appeared to be hard snow, bruising their legs when they broke through the crust. No thermometer was allowed in camp in the hope of keeping down complaints while working in below-zero days. If a man didn't wipe his nose on his mackinaw sleeve, building up a silvery coating, he'd have two icicles down to his chin before he finished sawing and could snap them off. Earflaps on a wool cap shielded Jamieson's ears from frostbite, but beneath the beard he was growing, his cheeks were wind-burned. It was hard being cat-like on sub-zero days when trees were most dangerous and it was too cold to think.

One afternoon an ice-covered branch cracked overhead. O'Neill yelled, "Jump!"

Guessing wildly where it would fall, Jamieson dove off the spring board. A ten-foot chunk of pine crashed close by; a couple of smaller branches painfully swatted his back.

He crawled out and limped to the fire, dipped out a tin of hot tea and gulped it down. A shot of whiskey would have done more to calm him. Back on his springboard, he mused, "Sort a like playin' craps, ain't it?"

Balanced on the other side of the tree, the Irishman asked, "How's that, Mac?"

"It's the odds. Will the tree be an easy seven or snake eyes?" What he really thought was it would be even odds he'd become a casualty of the woods before accomplishing any intelligence work worthy of its name.

A real blizzard moved in with snow as hard as ice crystals, sharp enough to cut up a man's face. A day off with no pay. While wind sifted snow through log chinks, fifty-two lumberjacks lazed on bunks in black woolies and socked feet. Damp clothes hung haphazardly about the stifling room, while men played enough hearts and pinochle to make them see tricks in their sleep. Tobacco juice plinked into tin cans kept by their sides. When they spoke, it was to gossip about whores they'd known. They no longer smelled one another's feet, socks and unwashed bodies, except when a man blew back in from the privy, holding a mittened hand to his nose as he pushed through curtains of hanging clothes in search of his bunk.

Standing at a small frost-rimed window, an older man they called Disciple Paul droned from his Bible, proclaiming the end of the world. Only those verses he associated with the Second Coming interested him. "And I saw an angel come down from heaven, having the key of the bottomless pit and a great chain in his hand." He glanced up to see if he had an audience. "And he laid hold on the dragon, that old serpent, which is the Devil, and Satan, and bound him a thousand years." He scrubbed a hand against a glass pane, trying to remove the frost his breath had built up. "And when the thousand years are expired, Satan shall be loosed out of his prison . . ." He scratched at the frost with his fingernails, the last straw for a nearby jack.

"We got our own end-of-the-world shit right here." He called down the room. "Pickles!" The logger addressed was stretched out, staring at the bunk above. "Some here ain't heard what happened to you in the 1910 fire."

Men paused at card games; others hushed their patter. Wind rattled the window frame and snow sounding like sand hit the glass. Pickles didn't turn his head. "Ya know I hate to talk about it."

"Yeah, we know," the man persisted, "but it makes for a hell of a better bedtime story than Disciple Paul reading over us. Read to yourself now. It's Pickle's turn. August 20th, right?"

Pickles rolled onto an elbow. "I'll remember what happened to my dying day." He scratched his armpit through the wool.

"And it wasn't just one big fire, was it? Tell 'em that."

Pickles picked up the thread of the story honed through the years. If he hated reliving it in the telling, maybe he also felt obligated to the men who died. "There'd already been plenty of fires that summer, crews chasin' 'em every which way. But that day, August the twentieth, the wind come off the Palouse and into the Coeur d'Alenes strong enough to lift a man off his saddle. Someone said that later. Those tree-filled canyons might as well 'ave been chimneys. The fires went swoosh!" He sat up and swung out his legs, shoulders hunched to keep from knocking his head against the overhead bunk. Threw out his hands. "Swoosh!" More men turned to listen. He covered his ears. "And the roar, my God, them fires roared like they's alive!" Raised his eyes toward some distant point, maybe entering a story-teller's trance. "Conflagration. The word fire just don't describe what we seen." Repeated, "Con-fla-gra-tion. The wind picked up them little fires and spread them around the mountains like they's joinin' their red hands together." He chanted in a high voice, "Ring around the rosie . . . all fall down."

Pickles' delivery sent a chill though Jamieson. Men unfamiliar with the story pushed through hanging clothes to better hear. Those who knew it quieted out of respect.

"We couldn't breathe for the smoke. An' I thought I'd just combust in that heat. Wouldn't have taken flames to turn me into a pile of ash. The packers out of Wallace dumped supplies an' blankets for the firefighters, an' back they went, thinkin' they'd be safe in Wallace. But that fire took most of the town." Shoulders hunched, arms folded against his chest, he rocked. "Never so scared in all my life as I was that day. It was early afternoon, but smoke made it dark as night. End of the world dark. That's what Ed Pulaski called it later . . . end of the world dark. An' if it hadn't a been for Pulaski, it would a been the end of my world. And for a lot of men. He was the forest ranger in charge of our crew. We was workin' some eight miles south of Wallace in those mountains. Good God in heaven, I gotta pray now for them that didn't make it out." He stopped talking and bowed his head.

O'Neill stood leaning against the end of his and Jamieson's bunks, arms folded, head down.

When Pickles lifted his head, he seemed perplexed for a moment before picking up the story. "Pulaski, he yelled himself hoarse at us. 'Get blankets if you wanna live.' Couldn't hear what else he said 'cause of the roarin'. Noise somethin' awful. Wind blowin', fire roarin', trees crackin' and fallin' all around us." Pickles' eyes focused on what only he saw. "That Pulaski, he run an' we run after him, afraid of losin' him in the smoke." He fixed on a nearby jack. "Did I say it was dark as night out there?"

"Yeah."

Pickles took a shuddering breath. "An' right in front of me a tree falls on a man and kills him dead." Snapped a thumb and middle finger together. "Just like that he was with his maker. Let us pray." Again he bowed his head in silence, a hand covering his face.

Jamieson rose to stand next of O'Neill. "Jaysus," O'Neill murmured.

A moment later Pickles continued. "There was an old mine shaft Pulaski led us into. Just in time, too. Don't know how he found it. Guess he knowed those mountains good. Even in thick smoke he knowed where he was headin'. Swoosh! The fire come sweepin' along behind us. He yelled at us to lie face down." He stopped, swallowed audibly. "But, ya know, when death's comin' for ya, you wanna see him, not hide your face in the dirt. That was goddamn hard." A few nodded. "That tunnel, it filled with fire gas an' smoke, an' one man, he tried to run out. But he couldn't get past Pulaski. That ranger had his revolver in his fist. I can still hear him, so hoarse with smoke, he could hardly talk. 'I'll shoot the first man who tries to leave this tunnel.' Right then and there I flopped down. Figured he knew what he was doin'. He's the boss. Sometimes you have to let someone take charge of your life and hope the Lord is workin' through him." More nods, but not from all, lumberjacks being independent cusses. "It was so hot in that tunnel with embers blowin' in, the mine timbers caught fire. There was some water in the shaft and Pulaski hung his wet blanket over the entrance and pulled a couple more off some fellas. An' he fills his hat with water and splashes those burnin' timbers. We couldn't breathe, so how's he managin' to do that? I dunno. I heard prayin' an' cryin'. Maybe it was me. Smoky, hot as hell. We had our faces in the dirt and we all passed out. There was nothin' left to breathe. When we come to . . . well, most of us . . . we thought the boss was dead." Pickles peered around. "But he wasn't, ya know. We was unconscious all night. Couldn't stand up. Had a terrible thirst. You ever stick your mouth over a lamp chimney and breathed that hot flame when you was little?"

Swan Swanson, squatting nearby, answered, "Ya, by Gott, I do dat once."

Pickles nodded. "It was like we breathed that hot flame for hours. Our mouths an' throats was all burned and blistered and dried out inside. Outside there was a creek, but it was filled with ash. Couldn't drink it. We lost five men in that tunnel. Makes ya wonder why some lived and some didn't. I gotta pray some more."

The men silently waited. Disciple Paul had earlier put down his Bible. The story appeared ended and some turned away. Those who knew better shook their heads, waving them back.

"Pulaski, he was blinded when he put out the fires in the mine. Eventually he got his sight back, but that next day we had to get him out. We left that place staggerin' through hot ash, over burnin' logs, everything around us and under us smokin'. Sometimes we crawled on our hands and knees." He held up his hands, showing scarred palms. "We was only three miles from Wallace, but we didn't know it. Nothin' looked the same. Our shoes burned off and our feet got burned worse than our hands and faces. Clothes shredded, skin blackened by ash. Finally, we met a rescue party, but they wasn't in much better shape than us. When we dragged ourselves down to Place Creek, some ladies from Wallace was there with hot coffee and whiskey. Bless 'em, they thought we'd want that. Couldn't drink any of it. Our mouths was too damaged. First time I ever passed up free booze for cool water. We all spent time in the Wallace hospital. When Wallace burned, the fire never reached that hospital with those nursin' sisters. They left on a train just as the fire reached the other side of Wallace, but they come right back to take care of everyone afterwards. I'll never, never go near a forest fire again, so help me, Sweet Lord." Before rolling back into his bunk, he intoned, "I am the witness."

"Thought you wanted to be called Pickles," a lumberjack called from across the room, trying to break the tension.

A few days later, the reverend Dick Ferrell, the loggers' preacher, webbed into camp, toting his portable Victrola and a couple of records, his pack stuffed with Presbyterian mission pamphlets. He spent a day in the woods working with the jacks. Word passed around that he'd been a prizefighter before receiving his calling. During lunch he climbed on a stump and in a loud voice gave a rousing sermon on Christian manhood.

Disciple Paul sat enraptured, his stew growing cold on his tin plate. That evening Ferrell preached while they ate supper. Jamieson was bemused when he wound up the little Victrola and the thin strains of "Where is My Wandering Boy Tonight" filled the cookhouse. Older men and foreigners alike stopped eating to listen, weather-hardened faces staring down at their plates. Toward the end of the song Giant Kid covered his face with his big hands before digging into his dried apple pie. Ferrell passed around paper and pencils to anyone wanting to write a letter home, which he'd take with him in the morning.

Back in the bunkhouse, Dakota Red growled that religion was invented by the ruling class to keep the working class in subjugation, but Jamieson noted no one was listening.

Dreariness and irritability settled over the camp. If it wasn't Cruel Jimmy finding fault, it was MacLean popping up, yelling at pairs of sawyers, "You're aiming your tree to fall on a stump. Don't ya tell me different. You sure as hell are! You'll ruin that tree. Are you loggers or saboteurs?"

Jamieson became uneasy. He watched O'Neill, searching for a similar edginess in him, but he went about his work calmly, as though expecting to pass the entire season in the woods. Maybe it was exactly what he planned. What a shitty way to spend the war, scratching flea bites and cracking lice. He could be doing the same thing in the trenches of France.

A few weeks earlier a horse had collapsed and died and it bothered the men to have to plod past it on their way into the woods. The teamster piled snow over it, but the huge horse was dug out little by little, coyotes and other night scavengers gnawing at it, carrion birds pecking its flesh during the day. When the jacks approached, ravens called out deep resonant warnings and flew up into trees to await their passage. The sun warmed the horse's remains during the day, partially thawing them, which created a sickening stench. The men hurried past, averting their eyes from what had been a good old horse that trailed logs till its heart gave out. They all wished it buried, but the ground remained frozen. More white bones showed each day as rotting meat and red tendon strings turned the trodden snow around it pink and rose-colored, brown and nearly black.

Its eyes were consumed, but brown hide still covered the large skull, teeth projecting long and yellow. Unable to avert his eyes while trudging past, Jamieson imagined the tail, mane, and bones lying there for years until gradually covered by moss and pine needles. The leg bones were too large to be carried off to be gnawed at leisure. Only one animal would be able to carry off the leg bones of a huge draft horse. A grizzly. But they seldom came over the Bitterroots from Montana into Idaho nowadays.

Chapter 41
March, 1918

Working outdoors every day, a man senses subtle changes in the season. When lumberjacks cast aside their shirts, they revealed chest hair so thickened by winter, it bristled out the necks of black woolies. Beneath the snow, freshets trickled down mountainsides into the Marble's feeder creeks.

One balmy evening loggers slogged through slush and mud toward camp. A jack pointed, "There's Beaver Sven. Wonder what he's doin' back up here." Ahead, a crooked stick of a man was limping into camp on a crutch, mackinaw slung over his free arm.

"Who's he?" a companion asked.

"A branch come down last year an' broke his hip and leg to smithereens. How'd he get up here on that leg?"

Men passed Sven, some saying hello as he hobbled through the shadows. Coming abreast of him, Jamieson nodded and gave a low greeting, but the man looked straight ahead, grunting with exertion. He put his good leg forward, followed by the crutch, then dragged the cumbersome limb. Bucked teeth identified him as the man the corporal knocked down at the mission.

Jamieson deposited his axe and the cross-cut in the filing shack and turned to scan the trail for O'Neill, who'd stepped off to relieve himself. Beaver Sven dropped his coat in the mud in front of the office and leaned on his crutch.

"MacLean! Come out! I talk to you!"

MacLean emerged, bare-headed, jaw working a plug of tobacco. He stretched out his hand, but seeing Sven couldn't or wouldn't shake it, asked, "How's it going with you, Sven? Grub's about ready at the cookhouse. You're welcome to partake."

"I come for you."

Jamieson stopped mid-stride. The scene before him lay in blue shadow, but the man appeared to pull something from a pocket.

Still friendly, MacLean straightened. "Ya got a gun there, Sven? You got no cause to use it. Didn't I come visit you in the hospital? Can't see why you got a bone to gnaw with me."

The man moved a step closer, dropped his crutch and snapped a match alight with a thumbnail. He sparked the fuse on a stick of dynamite but, instead of tossing it, he stuck it sideways in his mouth, snugged behind those long front teeth. Propelling himself forward with his good leg, he clamped MacLean in a bear hug.

Acting on instinct rather than common sense, Jamieson ran toward the grappling men. He reached them the instant an axe flew from the shadows to sink into Sven's back, knocking him to his knees and sending MacLean sprawling. The dynamite clamped in Sven's teeth was short-fused. Jamieson had one chance. He jerked it from the slackened mouth and heaved it into the evening sky, using muscle memory from training with live French grenades. "Down!" he shouted, dropping to the ground, covering his head with his arms.

A soft "Jaysus" came from behind just before a loud explosion overhead sent down shock waves, followed by a gust of warmth and the odor of burnt powder. The blast's echo reverberated through Jamieson's skull. Rising to his knees, he sat back on his haunches,.

MacLean swore quietly from where he lay on the ground. Yellow lamplight from the open office door illuminated blood welling around the axe blade imbedded in Sven's back. MacLean crawled to him. "His spine's severed." Men poured out into the slush from log buildings. MacLean glared up at O'Neill. "This your axe?"

"Sure I niver seen that axe in me life. Mine lost itself in the woods. 'Tis why I'm late, searchin' for it."

MacLean took a ragged breath. "Goddamnit, Irish. You lose another good axe and I'll give you walking papers." He beckoned to Cruel Jimmy, who helped him to his feet. "Someone check to make sure Sven's really dead. If he is, I'll say words over him after supper."

The timekeeper stood shaking in the office doorway. "Shouldn't we carry him down to St. Maries?"

"Hell, no. I know everything there is to know about Sven Andersen. He just tried to kill me with a lighted stick of dynamite. Somebody out there saved my life, and Mac here tossed off that stick like he was fightin' the Hun." Turned to Jamieson, scrutinizing him with a new awareness. "Had military training, huh? Never mind. Much obliged." With that, MacLean stomped back into the office.

"'Tis the jack with the flail limb, Mac. The poor soul the soldiers assaulted up in Spokane."

"Yeah, it's him."

O'Neill turned away. "I'll be goin' for a walk with meself. Do some prayin'. If those feckin' soldiers hadn't humiliated him, maybe he wouldn't 'ave come back with revenge in his heart, addin' another sin on me head." He squished away.

Jamieson watched O'Neill's diminishing figure while allowing his mind to file the point off the prick of his conscience. This death was the unexpected consequence of what he'd pulled off in Spokane. The only amend he could make now was to help dig the man's grave.

The ground proved too frozen for a grave. After supper the men gathered and MacLean spoke of Beaver Sven's previous years working for MacLean's, concluding the accident must have deranged him. The lumberjacks recited the Lord's Prayer and the body was wrapped in a tarp, then carried into the meat house for safe-keeping until morning, bent so as to lay easily over a pack mule saddle after rigor mortis set in.

Chapter 42

In early April, Lieutenant Charles Dean of the Spruce Production Division of the U.S. Signal Corps, introduced the Loyal Legion of Loggers and Lumbermen into MacLean's camp.

Lumberjacks ate while watching the young officer proclaim the purpose of the 4L union. Over the sounds of knives and forks grating plates, he appeared to be fostering a rivalry. "We have one hundred per cent enrollment over on the coast. I know you men are as patriotic as those loggers." Absorbing his words, they stared at him. "I'm here to make sure you're getting proper wages for the eight-hour day Colonel Disque instituted for the timber industry on March first."

MacLean spoke from the head of his table. "I give 'em the eight-hour day on January one. You're kinda' late there."

"That's good, Mr. MacLean. Colonel Disque will be pleased to hear it." He'd repeated his speech in so many camps, he had it down pat. "I'm here to help settle potential trouble in the woods by making suggestions to improve your camp." MacLean scowled. "I'm encouraging you men to join the 4L and sign a pledge to put down sedition, disloyalty to your government, and pro-Germanism. And to devote your best energies to the production of lumber for this war." He looked around, making eye contact with a few loggers. "In signing this pledge, you agree not to strike, but to allow the 4L to settle any disagreements you men might have with management. It's working on the coast. I know I can count on you to make it work here." He reached into his knapsack and withdrew a handful of cards and short pencils. "This is the pledge you sign." He tried to hand them to MacLean, who waved him off to the camp foreman. A card and pencil were slapped down beside each logger. Then he brought forth a handful of shiny brass buttons the size of four-bit pieces. "Bring up the signed pledge to me and you'll get a 4L button to wear on your coat, announcing you're a loyal American." He raised his free hand. "And if you're not yet an American citizen, this button indicates you aren't pro-German and don't support I.W.W. agitators."

Dakota Red and three others stomped out.

Lieutenant Dean demanded, "I want those men fired."

MacLean answered, "They'll come 'round. Them's some of my best loggers. I'm short-handed and can't lose any more jacks."

Down the table O'Neill shared a scowl with Jamieson before going back to his meat and potatoes.

"Your cook and his crew have already signed up." He leaned into the kitchen. "Step out here, men."

Pork Grease Eddie strolled out carrying a cleaver, followed by the bull cook, Polite John, the pastry cook and two flunkies. "Sign up boys," Eddie called out. "I heard from over at the Rutledge camp that those who refused to sign were visited by the Idaho State Guard and hauled off to St. Maries. Don't let the boss down. He needs you out there in the woods."

Before leaving the cookhouse, one by one, lumberjacks squeaked forward in rubber boots to exchange signed cards for 4L buttons. When only a few men remained at the tables, Jamieson rose, curious to see the piece of brass.

When he handed his card to Dean, the officer looked at his name, then peered into his bearded face. Murmured, "Got a message for you." Jamieson took the button, tipping it toward the hanging lantern as though trying to make out its embossing. "Captain Dengel up in Spokane orders you to bring your man in. Said he'll personally get the information out of him."

Fisting the badge, Jamieson hissed, "I don't take orders from Dengel," and walked away. He paused at the door to watch the Irishman. *Goddamn it!* He wasn't going to speed up this case to please Dengel, or allow him to get his hands on O'Neill. One thing he knew about being a detective, you have to find the rhythm of the case and fall in with it. It takes patience to do it right. And you follow your hunch when there's nothing else.

O'Neill was the last to rise. Wearing a black look he started toward Jamieson and the door, then swung around and approached the lieutenant, handed him the card and snatched the button, shoving it into a pocket.

Backed by a sharp pin, the button bore a battleship on water with a spruce biplane flying overhead; tall timber on shore; a few logs felled in the foreground; a cross-cut saw and ax lying athwart; stamped with *U.S.* and *LLLL*. Jamieson almost missed the lettering around the bottom edge, *Authorized by the Secretary of War*. It was probably the only award he was going to get.

"Chuckie," as the men called Dean, made himself at home, sleeping in the commissary. The next day when the flunky brought lunch out to the woods, he announced, "He's been wandering around camp, writing stuff down. Pork Grease Eddie got mad when he inventoried the turnips and potatoes and asked a lot of questions. When I caught him in the bunkhouse, he said he was making the men's beds for them. Maybe he did, but he was snoopin', too." Dakota Red, the most ardent Wobbly, listened grim-faced.

O'Neill lightened the situation. "Are ye knowin' what those four "L's" stand for?" Before anyone thought up a good one, he answered, "Loyal Lovers of Ladies' Legs!" This inspired gruff laughter and more interpretations.

That evening Chuckie called an official meeting of the 4L. MacLean had left camp, but the timekeeper represented management. "Men, now with daylight longer, Uncle Sam wants you to put some extra hours on the flume after supper, getting those logs down to the creek so they'll be ready for the drive. What do you say . . . let's show some patriotism."

Dakota Red jumped up. "Instead of goin' back to the ten-hour day, I move we go to a six-hour day!"

The room erupted in affirmation.

Temporarily stunned into silence, Dean snarled, "Why you're all just a bunch of damn Wobblies," and walked out.

The next day he hiked down the Marble Creek tote trail and out of their lives. The entire camp breathed a sigh of relief.

*   *

"The Ol' Man wants to see you two back at camp pronto." The flunky who'd brought out lunch stood before Jamieson and O'Neill. They looked at each other, messaging, *What the hell did you do to get us in trouble?* "He says you don't have time to eat lunch. Here's some doughnuts." They dragged the flunky aside. "That's all I know," the boy said. "Honest to God. He come back into camp a bit ago an' first thing he says is, 'Take out the lunch an' tell Irish and Mac to get their asses in here pronto.'"

"Ah," O'Neill said, "'tis only ye thinkin' he doesn't want us to eat. He never said not to feed us."

"Let's go, Irish. If MacLean says, 'Come,' I guess we don't ask, 'How fast?' There'll be food in the cookhouse." He hefted his axe and a saw end, forcing O'Neill to pick up the other end and follow behind.

Standing in front of the office, MacLean shouted, "Why'd ya take so long?" He rose up and down on the balls of his feet as he talked. "Ya listen now. That goddamn Lieutenant Dean is bringin' Sheriff Roland and some state guardsmen up here from St. Maries. They'll be in camp any time now, lookin' for I.W.W., slackers and deserters. I want you two to grab your gear and get outta camp. Can't go down the trail, ya'll meet 'em comin' up."

"Roland can't come up here to arrest us," Jamieson disputed. "His authority stops just this side of St. Joe City at the Benewah County line. Marble Creek's in Shoshone County. He's got no authority to cross the county line and come up here."

His logic agitated MacLean more. He explained, one word at a time, "It don't matter whether it's legal or not. He's got the Idaho State Guard with him and they'll do the arrestin'. I know you must've walked away from the Army, son. You're a prime target." He turned to O'Neill. "And don't think I don't know what Roland did to you last summer after ya picketed my mill and got my men to strike. I don't forget a face. But I owe ya."

O'Neill's black eyes gleamed with dark humor.

"I want you two to head up the drainage. Hide for a few days before comin' back. Maybe wait for the drive to start at the end of April. Up to you. Here's your pay." He handed each man a mixture of gold, silver and paper. "Pork Grease made sandwiches for ya. An' there's some webs." He pointed at two pair of snowshoes leaning against the office wall. "Now git."

Jamieson had a hunch the sheriff and guard were coming on Dengel's orders -- but not for him. For O'Neill. He recalled Dengel bragging about chasing Villa on the border with

Pershing and the methods he used to obtain intelligence from captured Mexican guerrillas. If the captain got O'Neill in custody, he'd torture him. And the Irishman wouldn't reveal a thing. Damn it, he was going to conduct this mission his way, not Dengel's.

"We want our guns," Jamieson said. "And a rifle and ammunition."

MacLean frowned. "Don't go tryin' to hold off the guard if it finds ya."

"The rifle's for game. We don't know how long we'll be out there."

"That's all right then. Don't come in here with me. Ya might get trapped. I'll bring 'em out. Go get your gear."

Heading toward the bunkhouse, O'Neill said, "Dakota Red and the others, sure we should warn 'em."

"They may be Wobblies, but they're not deserters. And not one of 'em ever cold-cocked an army officer like you did. When you're a wanted man, you have time only to help yourself."

"'Twas you knocked him down. I but made certain his family line stopped with him."

Chapter 43

They strapped rolled blankets to their packs and tied on caulked boots yet to be worn. With MacLean's Winchester slung over his shoulder, Jamieson led O'Neill into the forest. Initially, hard-crusted snow made webs unnecessary, but the valley floor along the St. Joe River below was greening, hinting of spring. Weighed down by packs, they couldn't risk breaking through five-foot-deep snow.

O'Neill was less concerned than curious. "Where do ye figure to go, Mac?"

"I spent some time in these mountains. Might not have mentioned it. I know a cabin where we can stay a while." He readjusted his pack. "If you trust me to find it."

"No reason I shouldn't trust ye, Mac. Lead on."

Taking a circuitous, but safer route to Dovey's cabin, Jamieson led O'Neill deeper into the forested mountains of the vast Marble drainage. They crossed frozen feeder streams, slid down ravines, but more often climbed upward. He wanted to keep train whistles floating up from the valley to his right, but the terrain grew rougher. Following deer paths up ridges, Jamieson studied the vertical geography of thinner snow, picking where to place a snowshoe, avoiding rocks, pine cones and slick bones of long dead deer and elk. He seldom lifted his eyes when descending, fearful of breaking a leg. And still webs caught on lurking snags. With each fall, mackinaws sponged wet snow and grew heavier. Faces dripped with exertion. Sweat-soaked woolies and shirts steamed, vapor exiting at their necks. At a feeder creek O'Neill pulled the bayonet from his pack to sweep away snow and chop through ice. They drank water so cold it stopped their sweating.

"Nice weapon." Jamieson wiped a sleeve across his mouth and beard. Where had O'Neill stashed it? "Got the rifle it came off of?"

"No need for a rifle. 'Twould only weigh me down."

Jamieson held out a hand and, when O'Neill handed it over, its manufacture imprint sent a shock through him. Ross -- the rifles were coming down from Canada. He hoped his moment of clarity didn't show on his face. Some detective he was, webbing through Idaho wilderness, his prime suspect for company, only now discovering the core truth of his mission with no immediate way to tell his superiors. "How'd you come by it?"

"Ah, some fella I'm knowin' traded it for a few rounds of poteen at a blind pig. It had a useful look. Better'n a knife, but not so good as an axe." He took it back. "As for the rifle, have ye heard those Canucks tossed their guns by the wayside in France? Plugged up with mud they were. Why would I be wantin' a rifle like that?"

"I hadn't heard about that." *Who would want a rifle like that? Someone not fighting in muddy trenches, but in green fields and in streets. The Irish maybe.*

They trudged through towering trees that blocked out the sky, surmounted a low ridge only to see a sunless pewter sky. A cloud cover in the distance obscured Grandmother Mountain and Marble Mountain. The mental map Jamieson carried was failing him. They clawed over and crawled under felled timber lying criss-crossed and piled up; splintered branches reached out, snagging packs, gashing faces. Rocks, crags and rotting timber hindered Jamieson, confused him, turned him back. He was directionless.

Still he refused to admit he was lost. A man can't get lost in these mountains for long, with the Bitterroot Mountains and the Montana line east, the St. Joe Valley north. Instead of leading O'Neill in a straight course, though, he suspected he was zigzagging, or possibly walking in a circle. To his credit they hadn't come across their old snowshoe tracks.

When he stopped, O'Neill webbed up, still unconcerned. "Are we lost and damned, Mac, and soon to be served up cold to God?"

"We can't get lost here, Irish, but I'm sure as hell distracted."

Water bubbled under ice in a nearby clearing that would do for a camp. A spruce provided bottom twigs to kindle a fire. He was scraping snow from around it when O'Neill walked in with an armload of cut wood.

"I found a pile of wood sittin' in the middle of nowhere."

A half hour later the fire burned with a heart to it. Each man spread a blanket on fir boughs on either side of it, their heads near a boulder for greater warmth. Jamieson chambered a cartridge into the Winchester, which he placed within reach.

O'Neill asked, "Any food left in yer pack?"

"A couple of doughnuts." He propped himself on an elbow and tipped his haversack toward the fire, rummaging inside. A doughnut was in his hand when a quiet crunch of snow made him drop it to reach for the rifle. A shadow moved outside the fire's glow. He'd waited too long.

Chapter 44

A female voice cried out, "Dontcha move! I gotta a shotgun!"

Jamieson's hand froze mid-reach.

"I'll shoot ya. Both you'uns, hands up." She sounded resolute, but frightened. Young and dangerous.

Across the fire O'Neill was slowly sitting up with raised hands, making no move for the pistol inside his coat. Jamieson lifted his hands and carefully turned. A large-bore, double-barreled shotgun was aimed to include them both in its shot pattern. Wearing a long dark coat, face indistinct under a man's hat, she stepped closer. What would she do now? As though in answer, she emitted a high-pitched yodeling. Then, "Dontcha move now." Once more she rent the night, directing her strange cry up creek.

In a stomach-churning flash Jamieson knew this branch-creek girl's family ties. The chopped wood. The shotgun. They were camped too close to an illegal still. He'd led O'Neill beyond Dovey's cabin, up some arterial creek to the valley of the Holy Frights.

"Are you a Ranney?" If no one came, what then? Could they take her down? Talk her down?

"Who wants to know?"

"We're lost lumberjacks, not revenue men."

The shotgun swung level with his eyes. "Ya can't fool me. Ya come for my brothers for the Army. If they don't kill ya, I'll shoot ya dead myself. Be afeared, stranger." As an afterthought, "And repent."

The family was reputed to be quick-tempered with guns at the ready. The elder Ranney had killed a man. "Now miss, we're not lookin' for anyone. May God bear witness, we got lost." He glanced at O'Neill. Pleaded, "Irish, don't be so quiet over there."

A rich Irish lilt came from across the campfire. "Sure the man's tellin' the truth, before God on His throne. Wayfarers lost on a sea of snow, that we be."

When she focused on O'Neill, shifting the double barrels toward him, Jamieson considered flinging himself at her ankles. If she had time to shoot, O'Neill would be the immediate target.

Instead, he explained, "I was takin' my friend here to the Widow Blake's cabin. She's kin to me."

Her arms trembled and the gun bobbled. With two clicks she pulled back the hammers.

Damn it to hell! It hadn't been cocked. A day of blunders. Why did seeing a lantern approach fill him with relief? It shouldn't. "Your men are comin'."

She steadied the gun and listened. The swinging square of yellow light was accompanied by crunching of not two feet, or even four, but the peculiar arrhythmia of three feet.

The man carrying the lantern shouted, "What's goin' on ha're?" A taller dark shape crossed behind the girl, rifle aimed, ready to pick off whoever moved.

The girl's arms relaxed and she lowered the shotgun, appearing smaller inside the coat. "I caught 'em, Daddy!"

The lantern advanced. "What'd ya cotched, gal?" A stout staff in his other hand kept the old man upright. He carried no weapon.

"They's spyin' on me, watchin' me rustle the fire and do the cookin'."

A little knowledge was a dangerous thing. Jamieson didn't want to hear what she was doing in the woods. "Are you Mr. Ranney?"

"I am. Wha'r mought ya be headin', strangers, trespassin' on ma land?" His long white beard glowed beneath eyes shadowed by his hat.

"We got lost tryin' to find our way to the Widow Blake's cabin."

"Daddy, they's come for the boys, to take 'em to fight."

"The Widow Blake ain't home." He sounded resigned, as though he'd passed sentence on this one piece of evidence. "You'd a passed her place on your way up ha're."

This was critical. If the girl would kill to keep her brothers from being inducted into the Army, old Ranney would, too. He had to talk these transplanted southern mountain men out of a terminal situation. Hoping the old man wasn't going deaf, he explained slowly and loudly, "We come from the east where we're lumberjackin' on Marble Creek. We didn't go down to the valley floor to find the tote trail comin' up here, an' that's how we missed the Blake cabin." He grasped at a small finger of hope. "Had some trouble with the Army myself. Took to the woods to wait out the war. Both of us are just like your boys." Cocked his thumb at O'Neill. "He's from Ireland. Refuses to fight for England."

Ranney gripped the staff that could do duty as a head-cracking stave and lifted his face toward the heavens like an old time prophet awaiting a sign. A moment later, "You-uns come with us'n 'cause I ain't got the time to deal with ya out here." He nodded at the girl. "Ya done good, Tessa. Now git back to your business, gal." He directed himself to the tall shadow. "Romey, pick up that raffle-gun of their'n. Keerful now, strangers." Jamieson had lowered his arms. He arced them back up. "An' check 'em for pistols inside their coats an' knives inside their boots."

The younger man, most likely a son, inched forward and kicked the Winchester across crusted snow, his rifle aimed at Jamieson's chest. "Now toss yur pistols an' knives right here." He picked up the revolvers, dropping them into his coat pockets; thrust the knives behind his belt inside his coat and rousted them to their feet. They picked up packs and blankets and followed the elder Ranney, already thirty feet ahead, trailed by the girl.

She angled off and down into a small hollow by the creek. Jamieson averted his eyes from the squatty shed with its copper still over a low fire. O'Neill must have passed upwind from the still's smoke and she saw him steal her wood. A man with a wooden nose could smell it now. Moonshine.

Romey was following some paces back, toting the two rifles. Years before, Dovey had told Jamieson the Ranneys came from the southern mountains where men were easily riled, murderous at the slightest excuse. They were clan feuders, like those Hatfields and McCoys, who wouldn't fight face-to-face, but had no qualms shooting a man in the back.

Jamieson had a suicidal urge to push O'Neill out of the way and attack the trailing son, using his pack as a weapon. *That won't do, Agent Jamieson,* Sewell's voice echoed. *He won't be sightin', just pullin' the trigger. Kill you so fast, you'll barely register your own death.* No, Romey was too far back. Even if he overpowered him, what then? The night was overcast and he was lost and tired. A man didn't know the Marble drainage until he knew it at night, and he did not. O'Neill whistled softly behind him like a man out for a stroll. Jamieson increased his stride and caught up to the elder Ranney, his lantern, his wooden cudgel, and his quiet peg leg.

Chapter 45

They crested a hill, whiffed wood smoke, and saw yellow light gleaming through a window below. Dogs barked behind the cabin; braying mules added to the din. A woman threw open the door.

"You best hurry, Mister," she called out. "She's birthin'."

Ranney trod, off-gaited, into the chink-and-daub cabin, followed by the others.

O'Neill pulled off his hat. "Bless all here."

The woman stepped back, surprised by the intrusion, or maybe by O'Neill himself. Jamieson removed his hat. "Ma'am." Shadows grouped and divided as Ranney held up the lantern, then lowered it to a table. He ducked through a curtain into a lighted room, then came back out. "Not yet." He addressed Romey. "Give the man his raffle-gun."

Jamieson dropped his pack and, after a moment's hesitation, Romey handed over the Winchester, which Jamieson unchambered and leaned against a black bear pelt nailed to the wall.

The old man nodded. "Now the short gun." Romey removed the revolver. Jamieson took the proffered Colt, made a show of emptying its bullets, crossed to the rock fireplace and laid them on the mantel. O'Neill repeated the courtesy. Ranney's act of hospitality was balanced by their act of faith it would be honored. They had little choice in the matter.

Ranney nodded toward the fire. "Set yurselves." He tapped over the uneven floor to the curtained doorway. Flung over his shoulder, "I gotta attend a birthin'. The missus'll feed you-uns."

"Shove up to the fire," Romey invited, pointing his rifle barrel at a bench. He seated himself in a homemade chair, the gun across his lap. "Ma, h'it's likely these travelin' men air hungry." He spat into the fire. "Are ya? Are ya feelin' gant?"

"We are that," O'Neill answered. He swiveled, directing himself to the slightly stooped woman, "But 'tis certain we don't want to trouble ye, madam."

She mumbled, "H'it's no bother." Picked up an iron crook and lifted a stove cap, stoking the fire with more kindling. In a short time she served up fried corn pones and slices of hot salt pork on two chipped china plates.

Ranney trod back into the room, wiping his hands on a rag, announcing to his wife, "Three so far. I do believe she's fixin' to birth one more." He turned to Jamieson and O'Neill. "Ma bitch ba'ar dawg's throwin' pups. Best bitch I ever owned. Part Plott hound. A large cur showed up one day an' we took him huntin'. When I seed his joy at goin' for the ba'ar, I covered her with him." He warmed to his subject. "Them pups'll have the hound scent to run down the ba'ar and the cur courage to tree h'it." He studied them a moment. "What mought yur names be?"

"Malachi O'Neill." He rose to offer his hand. "But Irish I'm called. 'Tis a lumberjack I am sure enough."

"Osee Ranney," shaking his hand. "Ma boy Romey." The son reached over his rifle to briefly shake hands.

Jamieson rose. "Robert James. I go by Mac." He shook their hands. "I'm kin to the Widow Blake. We were goin' to hole up in her cabin for a few days. Thought I knew the way from Marble Creek, but winter played me a trick and I went off trail."

"Yup," Osee said, "The Marble's lesser creeks fan out like a turkey tail."

Firelight accentuated the sneer twisting Romey's lips within his beard. He pointed to his head beneath his hat. "Bet ya don't got the bump for direction and place. A ba'ar hunting man yu're not." The Ranney family apparently possessed the necessary phrenology bumps for the life they excelled at.

Jamieson nodded, gave a wry grin and kept his peace.

"You-uns come many an irk mile," Osee observed. His description of the day's trek couldn't have been more accurate. "Yu're welcome to rest here tonight." He pivoted the peg leg to pull a bottle of clear whiskey from a shelf; popped the cork with his teeth and took a drink, saying as he handed it to Jamieson, "Took the poison off'n the top for ya." Added solemnly, "Not sayin' h'it's killed anyone, mind."

Jamieson held the bottle to the firelight; tilted it and leveled it, observing the persistent rise of beads before taking a drink. Moonshine whiskey, limpid as water. Raw. Jamieson shivered, wiped his mouth and gasped, "That's good shine." It bloomed inside him like a small fire, warming his core.

O'Neill concentrated on the beads rising to the surface before taking a sip. With a studied look, he held up a forestalling hand and took a larger swallow before passing it to Romey. Momentarily unable to speak, his face showed his appreciation. Huskily, "It's murderin' strong poteen." Took a breath. "In Ireland we say, 'Strong drink when the sun is weak.'" The bottle returned to Ranney, who toasted the bitch and her new pups with another mouthful.

"H'it's pure double-distilled corn. Take another snort." And the bottle passed around again. Then Ranney excused himself to attend to his bitch.

A less-bearded youth entered to stare in surprise before setting his rifle aside. Introductions were made. Oakley. Another hand shaken.

Romey vacated his chair, which Oakley filled, and went out with his rifle, maybe to relieve his sister at the still. Sometime later Tessa came in, hung her hat and coat on a peg and stepped out of her boots. Grabbing a piece of corn pone, she surveyed Jamieson and O'Neill, then crouched before the fire, opening a shapeless knit sweater to its warmth. A mass of damp ringlets fell about her shoulders. When she rose and turned her back to the fire with legs parted, yellow flames outlined her from torso to knees, below which her wool skirt hung heavy and sodden.

Oakley was nodding off, chin on his chest. Jamieson and O'Neill rose when Mrs. Ranney approached the bench across from them. She nodded at their courtesy, spreading her hands in an almost queenly way as she seated herself. Gazing up at the girl, she scolded her for getting wet and cold.

A bit of a show-off, Tessa tossed her head. "I ain't sugar an' I ain't salt, an' I'm nobody's honey. I won't melt." Appearing suddenly flustered at having an audience, "Ain't that what you say, Mama?" She plopped down next to her mother, feet and knees apart, pulling up the wet skirt to warm her legs. Knitted wool socks bunched about her ankles.

Jamieson's eyes roamed from her socks up her bare legs, their hairs burnished in the fire's glow. Her knees were dappled red and white from kneeling in snow, pushing wood, one piece at a time, into the still's low fire. She reached down and scratched a shin -- new bites among old scars. "Little ole hatefuls." Aware of their eyes on her, she added, "Hate them bugs." Any bedbugs or lice the men carried on them would find friends here.

Jamieson asked Mrs. Ranney, "Do you have a barn where we can bed down, ma'am?"

"You-uns welcome to sleep here."

Quick as mice, Tessa's eyes darted from Jamieson's face to O'Neill's. "If ya don't have a rather 'bout it, you're welcome to that bed over thare." She pointed to what must be the connubial bed next to the log wall. "Daddy'll sleep in thare with his bitch an' Mama'll sleep with me in the cockloft," indicating the wooden ladder in the corner. The girl's pallet would be under the sloping raftered roof from which smoked hams, venison jerky, dried bear meat, and strings of dried apples hung. Extra hunting gear, too. This family had brought its mountain ways with them.

Jamieson rose." I'll go outside for a bit."

O'Neill jumped up to follow. Before they went back in, he whispered, "Ye're seemin' to know these people. Who might they be then?"

"I know about them. Homesteaders around here call them the "Holy Frights." Think they have crazy fits, hollering out hymns on the mountainside, wailing and babbling gibberish. Moonshiners from the south." Jamieson touched a furry hide hanging beside the door. "Bear hunters. Most figure Ranney was running from the law when he came here. We best mind our manners, especially around the women."

"'Twas my intent entirely."

Oakley dozed near the fire until Mrs. Ranney added wood, and then disappeared with Tessa up the ladder. His duty done of protecting his womenfolk, he picked up the lantern and went through a rough door next to the fireplace, into another storage room with beds.

Jamieson and O'Neill pulled off rubber boots and stagged denims, retaining their woolies and socks, and quickly crawled under the covers so their rank odor wouldn't offend the ladies in the loft. The feather mattress slid them helplessly into a trough down the middle where their bodies met. Silently they hauled themselves to opposite sides, clinging to the edges, strong back to strong back.

Before falling asleep, Jamieson searched his mind for more about the Holy Frights. When he was younger, Dovey divulged that Ranney had a reputation for violence. Stay away from that cabin up the valley, she warned as he prepared to go off hunting. They didn't welcome visitors. Later -- he was a Pinkerton by then -- from high on a ridge he glimpsed Ranney and his boys below, bear hunting with their dogs. The dogs gave tongue and the mountainsides echoed with their baying. The bear was treed and a sharp whistle called them back. One shot rang out. That evening Dovey caught him up to date. Talk was Ranney had been "hated out" of the Carolina mountains, not for killing a man in a fair fight with a knife, but for the resultant clan feud. His Scots-Irish pride and arrogance caused the near extermination of his extended family. He brought his latest wife and remaining sons to the St. Joe River Valley. To hunt "ba'ar" he told the store-keeper when he traded hides and corn liquor for provisions. He got $10.00 a bear pelt in bounty – or rather the store-keeper got that amount. Ranney simply traded it for what he needed, but kept the meat. Gossip wove the tales. Dovey added, "Nothin' lonely people love more than speculatin' about their neighbors. Guess I'm no different."

How Ranney lost the bottom half of his leg was general knowledge because it happened here while dressing out a black bear he treed and shot. The bear was only wounded, but stunned by the fall. It woke up and kicked the knife deep into Ranney's calf. Gangrene set in and his sons hauled him on a mule down the mountains to St. Joe City, where they traded whiskey to the captain of a steamboat for passage down the St. Joe to St. Maries. The doctor there, an Army surgeon in the Spanish-American War, took it off just below the knee. They paid him with more whiskey. It wasn't surprising Osee Ranney wanted to be left alone, especially with the war on, but he'd given hospitality on a cold spring night to two strangers. Jamieson snuggled under the quilts, glad the girl didn't shoot them.

While O'Neill snored, Jamieson awoke to Ranney's peg tapping from the curtained room to the door, coaxing the bitch outside. "Come on, Susie gal." She made loud snufflings and slaverings. Embers flared when the door swung open, but he saw only the bitch's rump and tail disappear outside. When it staggered back in and the fire flared again, its disfigured head and snout resembled no dog he'd ever seen. Ranney settled the bitch in the other room and returned to chunk up the fire. Eyes closed, Jamieson was chillingly aware of Ranney standing beside the bed before he limped back into the curtained room.

Chapter 46

Jamieson and O'Neill awoke to stove lids rattling as Ranney built the cook fire. They dressed and stepped outside to relieve themselves. Thirsty and wanting to rinse away the after-taste of moonshine, Jamieson eyed the water left in the bucket beside the stove. He hesitated, not wanting to put a hardship on the wife, but when she descended, she grabbed up the bucket, opened the door and tossed out the water; donned a coat and boots and left with the empty bucket.

Ranney was making up a bowl of corn mush with small bits of meat for the bitch. He must have seen Jamieson's look, for he declared, "That's dead water. Ya don't want none a that. She's gittin' fresh water for coffee and sech."

Light coming through a small window next to the door allowed him to study a large family portrait in a fancy frame. A younger Osee with a different wife, surrounded by four nearly grown sons, none of which he met the night before, and two little boys, which might or might not be Romey and Oakley. Below it books lined a shelf -- a large Bible, well-thumbed old school texts, and a partial set of encyclopedia, two of the volumes warped from water damage.

Tessa, dressed and yawning, climbed down the ladder. She offered, "Them's Mama's. She was a teacher afore she married Daddy." Early on, Dovey claimed the family was illiterate because they didn't send their children down the trail to the little schoolhouse. He realized they'd been schooled at home. "Mama said it liked to broke her heart when one of the crates opened up an' some of her books fell off the boat into the St. Joe. She jumped in, clothes an' all, but only saved two before the rest drowned. Wonder what I could'a learned from H an' M an' T."

After breakfast Jamieson and O'Neill sauntered to the privy, causing a ruckus among three chained hounds and some mules, whose high whinnies wound down to groans of aw-ah-aww. A matched pair of draft horses only stared, contentedly sunning broad backs.

"Holy shite!" O'Neill exclaimed from inside the privy. When he came out, buttoning his pants, a grin split his face. "Sure 'tis thrones for a lord 'n lady in there."

Inside wide strips of soft fur edged two holes. There'd be no frozen asses on frosted seats here. Making himself comfortable, Jamieson perused some shapely women in union suits in a catalog before ripping out the pages.

Nearby the Ranney boys were hewing logs into railroad ties. Romey stood atop his log, scoring jogs with a felling axe. Then with knees slightly bent and body loose, he swung a broad axe along one side, squaring it into tie shape. Without using plumb marks, he trued the cuts with his eye, straight and accurate.

As they approached, O'Neill paused to admire the hogs, and Jamieson cocked a thumb back at him. "Irish and I are sawyers. Lend us a cross-cut and we'll work off our breakfast."

"No need," Romey muttered. "Don't expect payment." His arms swung effortlessly, bark and wood chips flying, hewing the side flat and smooth without any slash marks. Coming to a knot, he simply added muscle to the swing to cut off the knot cleanly.

"Now that I know where I am, it'll take only an hour to get to the Widow Blake's cabin."

Oakley stepped off the log he was hewing to sharpen his blade, pointed his axe at the saw. "Obliged."

Coats and shirts discarded, Jamieson and O'Neill sawed finished ties into eight and a half foot lengths, occasionally pausing to help muscle up an especially long log the horses had dragged into the clearing, bracing it on branches partially lopped off at the small end.

A tie sold for five cents to the Milwaukee Road down at St. Joe City. Forty ties, what two strong men could cut in a day, would make them two dollars, delivered during the winter on a horse-drawn sled.

The Ranneys likely grew root vegetables in their short growing season, trading bear skins, whiskey and railroad ties for what they needed. As he sawed, Jamieson ticked off the provisions they'd need. Hundred pound sacks of grain for the mules and horses. Hay. Flour, sugar, coffee, corn meal, oatmeal, beans, rice, raisins, prunes. Canned cow because they had no cow or goats for milk and cheese. No need for butter with bear grease and hog lard on hand. Their biggest trades would be for corn mash and sugar. A self-sufficient family living outside the law.

At mid-morning Mrs. Ranney carried out a dipper and a bucket of refreshing water. Ranney accompanied her. "Your kin Miz Blake neighbored us'un. We'd be obliged for you-uns to stay to dinner. Chicken 'n dumplin's."

A short time later, she chopped off the heads of a couple of chickens, blood sprinkling snow around the chopping block. She tossed the heads and legs to the hounds.

The four men came in at noon. O'Neill was the first to compliment her chicken and dumplings. She replied, "Those chickens eats good, don't they. When they stops their layin', it's time to go chickenin'."

The talk turned to bear hunting.

Oakley said, "Pa, tell 'em about the ba'ar that got away."

"A few days ago we was out trainin' the dawgs. Bears is too runty in spring to hunt. One of them grizzlies come down early from h'its den. First one I seen. Killed one of ma dawgs. Huge and shaggy, white an' silvery from the head to that hump between h'its shoulders, the rest brown."

Jamieson's interest picked up. "I heard grizzlies were here before it settled up, but stay across the Bitterroots in Montana now. So I've heard."

"Heerd that, too. They stays high on peaks an' ridges. But not this ba'ar. See, I don't use no high-powered raffle-gun. 'The bullet'll go right through a ba'ar and kill a dawg. An' that's right huntin' for the black ba'ar." The low velocity rifle he shot at the grizzly had the effect of a bean shooter. "If'n I'd a aimed for the head between ear and eye where the skull's thin, maybe I'd a got h'it, but h'it come outta the mist like outta some Injun smoke tale 'round a campfire, making this loud 'hough! hough!' sound." He waved an arm. "First h'it weren't thare . . . and then h'it reared up outta the gray. Filled the whole sky. The teeth and jaws on h'it. Glory! What a sight!" Eyes wide, Ranney was seeing it again. "I couldn't get another shot off 'cause them dawgs went crazy afore I could call 'em off. I shouldn't 'ave confidenced 'em. H'it was a powerful fray. That ba'ar swung those claws an' broke Jock's back, a good dawg. An' what h'it done to my Susie in thare . . ." Waved a hand toward the curtain. "Hope to never see that ba'ar again. Don't wanna lose more dawgs."

Jamieson leaned back, nodding, savoring a chewy dumpling soaked in chicken gravy. "A good dog is worth a lot of bears."

O'Neill's eyes were bright with interest. "That bear, run off did it?"

"That ba'ar and me each had a rather 'bout h'it. H'it was hurt, but not a killin' wound. If'n I hadn't called off t'other dawgs, h'it would've killed 'em all. H'it charged some, but once the dawgs backed off, that ba'ar run into the mist, an' we went t'other way. If h'it's a travelin' ba'ar, I hope h'it's gone back over the mountains. Ba'ar track measured 'bout a foot. An' yit I figure it to be a sow ba'ar. Might've bin the same one killed those homesteaders a couple of years back. But don't ask me 'bout that 'cause I don't know what 'xactly happened."

Ranney shoved back his chair to light his pipe. He sat hunched over, white beard falling over his narrow chest, smoking with his arm resting on his knee. A few moments later, "Ya wanna to see the pups?"

Both men said they did.

"Susie's sufferin' pitiful. Soon I'll have to put her out of her misery. Now ya gotta be quiet."

The bitch Susie was a horrible sight. A claw had slashed across both eyes and forehead, ribbons of flesh swiped away, her eyes destroyed. Another claw had torn through her snout, leaving a deep oozing wound. The putrefying wounds stunk and she couldn't breathe through her nose.

"See," Ranney explained, "that grizzly's claws must've grown during the winter, a couple of 'em longer than the others. Susie jumped back, but not fast enough. A little closer an' that ba'ar would 'ave broke her neck."

The bitch should have been shot immediately, but Ranney wanted the pups she was carrying. He admitted it was a wonder she didn't throw them then and there with what she suffered. They were tiny, anyway. Ranney picked up two for inspection, but the men's eyes always went back to the suffering hound --

unseeing, unable to smell, drooling mouth agape with labored breathing, wounds festering.

Ranney spooned mush and meat bits into a sausage casing from a pig's bladder and showed them how he stuck it down her throat to squeeze out food and moisture. Dogs didn't chew, anyway. "Some gets in her windpipe an' she's gotta cough h'it up. Wished I had another bitch could nurse them little dawgs." He reached down and scratched the back of Susie's neck. "In a few days I'll see kin they suckle the sow out thare. If'n they kin, we'll eat the piggies so's the pups kin have the milk. Then I guess I'll have to let Susie go." He ran a hand down his white beard before limping back into the main cabin. "So's you'uns 'bout ready to take yur foots in yur hands and light out, huh?"

"Goin' down the trail," O'Neill said, "unless me partner here leads me astray again."

Ranney directed himself to Jamieson. "Did ya say ya had trouble with the Army?"

Could those penetrating old eyes tell when a man was lying? "It didn't agree with me, so I headed back to the woods." Half of it was true. He gave Ranney look for look. "I'm a marked man, but I'll take my chances. Yesterday morning we lit out of camp just ahead of the sheriff and some state militia lookin' for us. Well, mostly lookin' for me." He cocked his head toward O'Neill. "Ask Irish how he feels about the war?"

"Sure ye don't need to ask. We Irish won't fight for our suppressor, England, in any of its bloody wars. As I'm seeing it, America's not fightin' for herself, she's soldierin' for bloody England."

Ranney nodded. "Them's my sentiments. Ma forebears fought at King's Mountain against England for the freedom of Americans, an' my daddy fought to save the Union. So did a lot of mountain men. Them outlanders don't know that . . . thinks we's all Johnny Rebs, but ain't so. Some jest wanted to stay outta it 'till they was forced to fight for the grays. That was 'specially hard with England supportin' the Confederacy. My daddy was a Union loyalist. Went over the mountains into Tennessee and joined the 3rd North Carolina Mounted Infantry. I wouldn't raise a hand to help them lobsterback English win their war, an' neither will ma boys."

Jamieson nodded. These family feelings had passed from generation to generation, sustaining a hatred toward England. O'Neill smiled. Ranney must have warmed his Irish heart.

"The sheriff'll never git ma boys, not if they'd knowed these woods since yesterday. An' ain't this war gonna end soon, anyways?"

"Let's hope so," Jamieson said.

They webbed out with weapons and packs, the Ranney sons nowhere to be seen. But a short way down the trail a shot rang out, splintering a branch that fell at their feet. An exultation of whoops came from a nearby ridge.

"Jaysus Christ!" O'Neill exclaimed, swinging around, about to dive into a snow bank.

Jamieson gripped the Irishman's arm and hefted his rifle, pumping the Winchester above his head. "Just a parting shot. He hit what he aimed at."

O'Neill waved a farewell then. "Sure they wouldn't have wasted good food on us if they meant to kill us, I suppose."

Chapter 47

O'Neill broke the silence. "So, the woman who lives here is yer auntie?" They sprawled before Dovey's small cookstove, listening to the faint musketry of resinous burning wood. Heat eddied around them while they sipped moonshine purchased from Ranney.

"A sort of auntie." He tipped back on the only straight chair, legs stretched over a heaping box of wood stockpiled for Dovey's return in late spring.

O'Neill planted a stocking foot on either side of an old armless rocker, fashioned to accommodate wide skirts. Spellbound by the fire's glint through mica slits, he leaned back against a flattened velvet pillow and rocked gently, humming the Irish tune now familiar to Jamieson.

A pitchy knot snapped and popped and Jamieson recalled Dovey's pride in the elaborate nickel-plated iron stove she'd had hauled in pieces by pack mules up the tote trail. Good memories of times spent with her.

Moonshine might not make a man feel better about life, but it sure as hell makes him think it does. Sewell said that. *Here's to you, Billy.* Jamieson swallowed.

"What will I be callin' her?"

"Mrs. Blake. Dovinia Blake. Most call her Dovey. She didn't always live up here in the mountains. Did most of my rearing."

From the contents of lidded tins keeping mice from eating the comestibles, they made a sort of fried bread and smeared it with lard; pounded hard brown sugar to sprinkle on.

Jamieson was bone weary. With O'Neill in his sights, right here was the only place he had to be. And shouldn't the moonshine be loosening the man's tongue? "You've been around, Irish. Ever try mining?"

O'Neill scowled. "Don't get me started or I'll be spittin' me disgust, but for it being yer auntie's floor."

"That bad?"

"Bad? Ye'll ne'er get me down in a mine again. A week I labored in one. 'Twas night above an' always night below." His brogue became broader, "The divil himself dwells there. If not

directly beneath Butte, then close enough. 'Tis sure a' that I be."
Or maybe it was the whiskey on his tongue. O'Neill pinched
brows together, tipped his cup, and released an "a-a-a" of
satisfaction, a counterpoint to his flare-up. "More of this and
I'll be climbin' a tree backwards. I'm thinkin' a cigarette would
be a fine endin' to this evenin'."

Jamieson dug into his pack and produced a cigarette already
rolled and twisted in brown paper. "When are you gonna carry
your own makin's? From when I first met you, you've bummed
cigarettes off me."

O'Neill grinned as he reached for it. "'Tis often as not I've
not a penny." Head tipped back, he blew smoke toward the
rafters, reflective. The storyteller in him needed time.
Jamieson added more whiskey to his cup on the off-chance he'd
let slip some information.

"'Twas the damp down there. Ye know the ground ye'll be
buried in will be wet, so 'twas like that end place. Hearin'
drippin' water, smellin' burnt powder and bad air tha's sure to
kill a man. Darkness creepin' 'round, great black arms enfoldin'
ye, slowly smotherin' yer life away. Ye feel small, like a bug
crawlin' 'round a hole. I'd never felt a wee man afore." He
swiped a circle in the air with the cigarette. "Ye hear soft rock
siftin' down through rotten timbers, loose shelves of stone
ready to drop on ye. O, boyo, 'tis frail ye feel." O'Neill closed
his eyes. "Rats, they be down there, squeakin' 'round corners.
And the shift boss, as big a rat as ye'd ever hope to see, orderin'
'more rock in the box.'" He picked up his cup and took a
mouthful, savoring it as it slid down his throat. "But, above all,
'tis the carelessness of yer fellow man ye fear. 'Round the
corner an open trap door ye'll not be seein' in the dark. Maybe a
drunken engineer is missin' his signal, ready to hoist ye in a
bucket full of men into the shive wheel. I drew me pay at the
end of the week an' I never went back. At a bar afterwards the
miners I'd worked with told me I'd get used to it. 'Twas I
knowin' better. Not all Cork men are born moles."

"Is that when you got that bayonet?"

O'Neill glanced at his pack; ran fingers through sweat-
matted black hair. "'Twas years back the minin'. Got a thick of
friends in Butte, though. One of 'em give it me. Told ye I

traded poteen for it. 'Here boyo,' he says, "'tis what the Canadians flung away on the bloody battlefield, designed by an Englishman, wouldn't ye know." His face was bleary-eyed, but innocent.

There was something odd in O'Neill's last pronouncement. Even Jamieson's drink-fogged brain caught the way he said it. Where was the disgusted face and cutting edge whenever he mentioned the English? He was lying, concentrating on creating the story of how he got the bayonet, feelings having no part in the tale.

Jamieson slurred, "S'pose America shouldn't have helped Britain against Germany. Large German population here. But they shit on us, Irish, one humiliation after another. Can't take but so much an' not strike back." He couldn't say the letter "s" properly. Funny.

O'Neill flung out both arms, sloshed a few drops of liquor that hissed on the stove. "Jaysus Christ, Mac! 'Tis how the Irish feel about Britain! For centuries they piled humiliations on us. Can ye blame us for fightin' 'em now? I'm askin' ye, Mac, how do ye feel about Ireland wantin' her freedom?"

"Haven't given Ireland much thought. Been taken up with gettin' away from the Army and not havin' a fuckin' tree fall on me."

O'Neill whistled the tune he'd hummed for months. Jamieson always figured it was a love ditty. In a pleasant baritone, he broke into song.

> *The minstrel boy to the war is gone,*
> *In the ranks of death you'll find him;*
> *His father's sword he has girded on,*
> *And his wild harp slung behind him.*

O'Neill had hummed it while shaving on cold mornings and in the woods until weary with the day, even while he ate down table from Jamieson until getting an elbow in the ribs.

> *"Land of Song!" said the warrior bard,*
> *"Though all the world betrays thee,*
> *One sword, at least, thy rights shall guard,*

One faithful harp shall praise thee!"

He sang of the minstrel falling in battle, but tearing out the harp strings before dying.

Thy songs were made for the pure and free
They shall never sound in slavery!"

The words broke in his throat and he fell silent, eyes wet.
"Know any more?"
"I do, but 'tis the only song goes round an' round in me head."

The next morning they heated water for the wash tub, stripped and scrubbed themselves with pieces of lavender-scented soap they found in a tin, joking about smelling like fancy women. Wrapped in quilts, they emptied packs of soiled clothes, soaking those and what they wore, including socks, suspenders and union suits, in soft lye soap Dovey had made.
Jamieson marveled at how dirty the water was. "Gotta be the black woolies bleeding. Our clothes can't be that filthy."
"Sure the blessed Mrs. Ranney thought so. Nary a word, but her eyes were bright with wantin' to strip off our socks an' bury 'em in a snow bank."
The quilt slipped from Jamieson's shoulders when he reached for a stick of wood to feed the fire.
"Ye were shot some time then, Mac?"
"A couple of years ago."
"Any place I'd be knowin'?"
Refitting the quilt, he sat back, suddenly wanting to talk about Billy Sewell. "Seattle. I had this partner . . . killed when I was wounded. Good man. Getting on, but hadn't gone to fat. Still strong and straight."
"Would I be knowin' him?"
"Abilene Ed. Ever run into him?"
"Not that I remember. On the *Verona* was he?"
"No, killed before the *Verona*." He heard Billy caution, *This won't do, Agent Jamieson. Never reveal yourself.* O'Neill

could never be his friend. He was just the goat he was trailing toward a cache of guns. "A woman saved my life that night."

"Good nursin' she give ye?"

"I was being chased by the gunmen and ran right into her. Thought she was a whore, but she wasn't."

"So, an' how did this lady save yer life?"

"She walked out into the street and met those two killers head-on. I was pretty far gone, what with being shot. She told them I ran in the other direction and they believed her. Then she went for help."

"Luck was with ye."

"Yeah." Jamieson smiled, remembering Addie. "Guess we should think about supper." He stood up and felt his underwear -- still damp. His stagged-off pants were dry enough, though. "I'll cut more wood for the stove."

"An' I'll prepare the feast," O'Neill offered.

Jamieson came in with an armload of wood to the smell of more fried bread. But something wasn't right. He felt a prickling. Maybe it was the way O'Neill held himself, his crooked smile too wide. While they ate, the Irishman flexed his neck and shoulders as though an iron rod had wedged between his shoulder blades. And he wasn't meeting Jamieson's eyes, but concentrating on his sorry meal. After supper he passed on the moonshine.

"Feeling all right, Irish? Passing up shine?"

"Fine as a spring day, Mac."

"Guess we better hunt up some meat if we're gonna be good for the river drive. Tomorrow, I guess."

"Fine idea, Mac. Tomorrow then."

Chapter 48

They headed out to hunt down a limping buck they'd spotted on their way to the cabin. O'Neill pocketed in his mackinaw the hatchet used for chopping kindling. Jamieson webbed thirty feet before he raised a hand and stopped. "Forgot to look for extra cartridges for this rifle. Dovey must have taken her Winchester to a neighbor for safe-keeping, but there might be cartridges." O'Neill sat on a stump in the sun to wait.

Back inside, he searched the top shelf, found a tin of hardened honey and set it aside for later use. He pulled another tin down, but when he opened it, there were Dovey's photographs, the top one of him in uniform, a fatuous 'going to war' look on his mug. Had O'Neill rummaged around while he was out chopping wood and found it? He scrutinized the lid, then peered at the honey tin's dusty lid where his fingers left distinct prints. O'Neill had opened the honey tin, too. The photograph tin's lid was wiped clean. He held up his fingers, examining their tips and then the palm of his hand. Ran his fingers over the shelf and regarded them again. Had he wiped off the dust when he opened the tin? Or had O'Neill? He crumpled the photograph of the smarmy-faced officer, pried up the stove lid and dropped it in, watching it flare into a blackened wad. He flipped through the other photos. Most were from college -- in his football jersey and leather helmet; with some college friends; in cap and gown with Dovey and Maud. At the bottom lay one of Thea and him when they were small, standing in front of the big white house in Wallace. She'd been a pretty little girl. He snapped the tin shut and shoved it to the back of the shelf. This could be bad. He broke off his search for cartridges and went out.

Webbing ahead, breaking trail in wet snow, Jamieson felt O'Neill's eyes boring into the back of his head. He hadn't chambered the Winchester for safety reasons. Could he do it now without looking suspicious? You don't need a handgun on a deer hunt and he'd left his revolver in the cabin. But O'Neill was packing his.

His senses wired taut, he sorted through the implications of O'Neill's having seen that photo. Mac-the-deserter as an officer? How plausible was that? Would O'Neill recognize the Signal Corps insignia in the photograph and recall Captain Dengel wore the same at the mission? O'Neill had recognized Dengel. It wouldn't be a stretch for him to conclude Jamieson was the second officer spying on the I.W.W. lawyer that day. He focused on O'Neill behind him, recalling how swift and sure he'd hurled his axe into Beaver Sven, certain it wasn't the first time O'Neill killed a man.

They followed tracks up a side canyon to a small creek where a water hole had been pawed open, and he used this sighting of fresh prints to chamber the round. If O'Neill intended to kill him, wouldn't he have done it by now?

Ahead, beyond a windfall, a large blur of fur bounded up into the dark forest, powerful hind legs starting a small avalanche. Jamieson flung up a hand for O'Neill to stop.

Past the rotting log across the trail lay what was left of the buck, its carcass lying in a pool of blood and melted snow, slaughtered, skinned and eviscerated, its brisket torn from its chest. They'd surprised a feasting bear.

O'Neill leaned over the buck. "Jaysus!" he breathed. Its heart had been devoured; remnants of liver and lungs lay scattered in the snow. Widely-spaced tracks indicated the bear had rushed it. Jamieson raised the rifle, scanning the timbered slope.

Certain the creature was watching them, he whispered, "Think it was Ranney's grizzly? Tracks are too big for a black bear."

O'Neill refused to honor the predator with hushed tones. "How in hell would I be knowing that? I'm for scootin' back to the cabin."

O'Neill's threat to his person, real or imagined, receded before the grizzly's danger. But they needed meat.

"Shouldn't we be goin', Mac, or 'tis only me pookish imagination that it's watchin' us?"

"I want a haunch. It was a quick kill and the meat's still good. Help me flip him over." He hated having to lower the rifle to hoist its hind legs while O'Neill picked up the front ones. Steam rose from the pool of fresh blood.

Jamieson thrust the rifle into O'Neill's hands. "Keep watch." He squatted on his webs next to the carcass. "Hand me the . . ." Sunlight glinted off the descending hatchet blade. He jerked up an arm and flung himself backward into snow before seeing the proffered handle. "Damn bear's makin' me jumpy." Locating the joint, he hacked through a haunch while O'Neill rotated with the rifle, searching both sides of the canyon.

Jamieson dragged the severed haunch a short distance down the trail before he turned to spot O'Neill standing over the carcass. The forest was so quiet, he heard the patter as O'Neill urinated on it.

Carrying the rifle, the Irishman caught up, a smirk on his face. "'Tis a callin' card I left that dog-killin' bear. 'Twill not be finishin' its meal."

"Jesus Christ! It'll memorize your scent and follow us down to St. Joe City."

"Memorize me scent? Like some dog? Divil bless it then."

The haunch left a swath of blood on the trail.

O'Neill called out, "Here man! Trade places! I think I smelled that bear!" The dim trail lay empty behind them. "Sure 'twas only a whiff, but me hackles rose. Take the damn gun."
He seized the haunch and now Jamieson's webs cut diamonds into an intermittent trail of blood.

Uneasy, he frequently stopping to listen. If he actually heard the grizzly, it would be too late.

They strung the haunch in the tree where Dovey hung her kills and toted in more wood before it grew dark.

That evening Jamieson revealed he was an officer when he deserted. "About to be brought up on charges for assaulting an enlisted man."

"Is that so?" O'Neill sounded unimpressed. "In Ireland enlisted men expect to be beaten by their bloody officers. Made him unfit for duty as cannon fodder, did ye?"

"I was too drunk to remember. But I wasn't going back into a stinking jail." The odds were increasing that O'Neill would find him out before he revealed more about those rifles. Maybe he *should* arrest O'Neill and transport him to Spokane for Captain Dengel to work over. Dengel had bragged about jamming a grounding wire connected to a crank telephone magneto under a Mexican's fingernail. Laughed when he described turning the crank himself, watching the man convulse and scream while electricity burned into his finger. "When we wrapped it around his nuts, he shit himself." A Wobbly had died in detention in Spokane under Dengel's charge and Jamieson was damn sure he didn't want the Irishman's death on his conscience. They'd head down to St. Joe City where he'd telegraph the rifles' make to Colonel Disque and Major Gund. And leave Dengel off the distribution list.

Chapter 49
St. Joe City

A warming wind rattled the shrunken door of Dovey's cabin and rain drummed on its roof. The snow melted into rivulets. Signs of spring were in the air.

O'Neill snapped shut his jackknife. "The river drive will be startin' soon enough."

They cut down what was left of the venison and dragged it a short way into the forest. The following morning, wearing caulked boots carried since Spokane, they headed through rotting snow and mud to St. Joe City. Jamieson left some money and a note on Dovey's table. *Stayed a few days. I'm all right. Mac.*

It was nearing evening when they paused at St. Joe City's train depot to view a Prussian blot poster with a map of Europe and the Ottoman Empire delineated in red and gray, the red demarking those countries under the Kaiser's heel. Large letters proclaimed, "The World Cannot Live Half Slave, Half Free."

O'Neill's demeanor had changed since leaving the cabin. He seemed downright cheerful. "I'm partial to the poster sayin', 'If ye can't enlist, go find a recruit.' Means if a man don't feel up to it, he should send his sons to be sacrificed for bloody England."

Lumberjacks milled about in muddy streets, looking mean enough to eat each other raw.

"The drives haven't started."

The small town hugged the Milwaukee Road tracks beside the St. Joe River. Painted shacks fanned across enclosing hillsides like a handful of brightly-colored theater tickets. Loggers in various stages of inebriation advertised its only asset – it was still a wide-open town. Next to the Big Timber's doors lay a pile of four-by-nine shingles, intended to protect wood floors from caulked boots. Each man stomped nail-studded boots onto a pair and entered. Sawdust covered the floor to absorb tobacco spit, spilled drinks and blood. Sandwiches, coleslaw, sauerkraut, pickled pigs' feet – all free – accompanied over-priced whiskey and beer. Gaming tables were in back rooms and fancy women did business upstairs.

Like fledgling about to take wing, lumberjacks crowded the bar on shingles, drinking with cheerful intensity, winter months spent logging now forgotten. Piano music overlaid the hum of male voices, punctuated by female laughter. Powdered and scented girls descended through a haze of cigarette and cigar smoke, seldom remaining idle.

O'Neill took it all in. "Surrounded by the sweets of sin we be and, boyo, we only live once."

The bartender scraped bearded foam from their beer glasses with an ivory stick, unconcerned he was illegally selling alcohol in Idaho. They loaded up plates with food and found a table under which they kicked their packs. Jamieson slung the rifle on the back of his chair.

Giant Kid, standing shoulders taller than the rest, spotted them from the crowded bar and clomped over to bring them up to date on happenings at camp.

"Those soldiers arrested Dakota Red." Squatting beside their table, he raised his voice above the din. "The Ol' Man went to bat for him, but that Lieutenant Dean had found his I.W.W. pamphlets and took him away. And you know what? Word come back he's Canadian. Must be in the Canuck army now." They agreed it was a dirty shame a man no longer had the freedom of his convictions.

"The town seems packed to overflowin'," O'Neill observed.

"Well, sure. Down at St. Maries Wobblies rioted a couple of weeks back and the city council closed the card rooms and pool halls. They reopened 'em, but now they close at six p.m. sharp. Loggers down that way hop freights and come up here. Head back to their camps when their money's gone. There's fellas here from Clarkia and Fernwood up the St. Maries River."

"Lot of fights?"

"Oh, oodles. It's a scream."

Hearing his new lingo, Jamieson grinned, "You're spending time with the ladies, I see."

When Giant Kid wandered back to the bar, O'Neill's attention fastened over Jamieson's shoulder. "I'll be having a leg over that *rue*."

"What?"

"That red-haired woman."

He twisted to locate O'Neill's whore. Exuding a lusty sophistication, Katie was descending the stairs in a sashed black gown, her gaze roaming the room full of staring men. When her eyes met Jamieson's, they moved on without recognition. Comfortably anonymous behind his beard, he smiled. Her eyes swung back and her rosebud mouth opened in surprise. She stamped down the rest of the stairs and wove among the tables, fending off attempted embraces. He rose and she held out her hands. Before she could say the name forming on her lips, he blurted, "So, you recognized your old pal, Mac. I'll be damned if you don't have sharp eyes."

His name changed on her tongue, coming out a rough "Ro . . ac!" She said it right then. "Mac! How am I supposed to know you with a face full of fur? Were you looking for me?"

"I didn't know you were here."

"Oh." Her eyes sparkled. "Maud knows I'm here. I'm going by Kate now."

"Kate," he amended. A lumberjack left a nearby table and he pulled over the empty chair. "Can you sit?"

"I can do anything I want. This is my show." She plopped down, black silk skirts puffing out around her. "I've rented three rooms on the second floor. The two prettiest girls you see here work for me." She gave a throaty laugh. "I'm a madam. Whaddayaknow." She turned toward O'Neill with a beguiling smile. "I see you found a pal."

"My logging pard, Irish O'Neill."

O'Neill reached for the soft hand she offered. "Mistress Kate, 'tis a pleasure."

"Do you have a real name or did your folks just look around for inspiration?"

"Sure 'tis Malachi Brian Deaglan O'Neill, but me family call me Mally."

You never told me to call you that," but Jamieson was ignored.

"Pleased to meet you, Mally." If Katie did anything well, it was make men like her. "Will you join me in a cigarette?" Withdrawing one from a pocket in the folds of her gown, she handed it to him; removed another for herself. O'Neill half-rose, pushing back his chair, which snagged and tipped over.

Unmindful, he bent to light her cigarette, dark eyes roaming her face. She drew on it, holding his eyes. The match burned to his nails before he nipped it. Jamieson righted the fallen chair before O'Neill sat down.

"Got a cigarette for me?"

"Sure, Mac." She placed one on the table, her attention on O'Neill. Was she trying to make him jealous or had she developed an instant fascination for the Irishman?

Gesturing with her cigarette toward his grimy broken nails, she offered, "You're a working man, I see."

O'Neill flushed. "That I am. A lumberjack like the rest of these damned souls. But I'm a travellin' man, too, and as Saint Thomas a' Kempis, said, 'they who travel, seldom come home holy.'"

Katie threw back her head and laughed, the sultry temptress act forgotten. "My folks came from Ireland."

"And ye have the beauty of that blessed isle on yer face."

She chortled in the throaty way Jamieson liked when it was directed at him. "Are you propositioning me?"

"Were I cleaner, I would be delighted to proposition ye, but I'm badly in need of a bath, a shave an' a scalpin'."

"I have a gal who won't mind."

Jamieson ran a rough hand over his whiskered face before placing it on her shoulder. "He prefers a red-haired woman. Got that on good authority. We spent the last few weeks shacked up in the mountains, running from the law because I skipped out on Uncle Sam." He squeezed her shoulder.

"Yeah, I never understood why you run off like that."

"Irish here got implicated through no fault of his own. The law nearly got us at MacLean's logging camp and we had to hightail it into the woods." He gave her shoulder a small shake. "Come on, Kate, be a sport and show my partner a good time."

O'Neill protested, "Ah now, we'll talk no more of it."

She nodded. "We've got a bathtub upstairs. You go up and tell Roza you want a bath, soap and a razor, and bedroom number four. I'll be up in a half-hour." She added, "But house rules . . . money first." O'Neill pulled out a handful of coins and Katie fingered out two gold eagles. "This is for me." Then a quarter eagle. "And this is for the bath. Go on now. I bet there's a handsome fella under there."

O'Neill clopped across the room in his shingles and was stopped at the stairs by a bouncer, who made him remove his boots before going up.

Katie blew smoke toward Jamieson. "You could have been my gentleman tonight."

"I'm flat broke."

"It never stopped us before."

"There's a difference between your climbing into my bed and when I climb into yours."

She sighed and stubbed out her cigarette on the tabletop.

"This is important to me, Katie . . . Kate." His lips twitched. "God, I'll never get your new name straight. I want you to show him a good time."

"If I show you a good time, don't you think I do that for every fella I allow in my bed?"

Because he wanted her talents, he was sorry he'd irritated her. He put his lips to her ear. "I need this favor . . . bad. He's got information the government badly needs. I've trailed along with him for four months, logging on the Marble, laying low in Dovey's cabin, and he's as closed–mouthed as a trap. I want you to spring it. If I trust anyone, it's you." He caressed her arm.

"If you want me to fuck some murderin' German spy . . ."

"He's an Irish nationalist. There's a plan in Butte to smuggle rifles and ammunition to the coast to ship to Ireland. Find out if it's happened or when it will happen. By railroad probably. Which one? When? I'm involved in dangerous work and if I discover you breathed the word "gun" or "rifle" to him or mentioned me, anything to tip him off, I'll wring your lovely neck if those Butte miners don't kill me first."

He pulled back to look at her and she exhaled, low and incredulous, "Oh, my God."

"Katie . . . Kate . . . I need the information he has. Help me. Help your country. Do it for the red, white and blue."

She lisped, "All those pretty colors. Reddy and whitey and jolly blue. How can a girl say no?" Turning serious, she whispered in his ear, "Let me get this straight. First you said you were chasin' German spies. Then Mr. Moses lets slip you'd deserted the Army. You didn't desert, did you?" Tipped her head to one side.

"Now we both know. What do they say about two people sharing a secret?"

"I donno. Maybe it's like three on a match. One of 'em will die." She smiled. "Or maybe it brings a man and a woman closer." She leaned in and nipped his ear. Her perfume was intoxicating, but the whiskey on her breath indicated she might be, too, which made him uneasy.

He went up to the bar and came back with a pint of whiskey. "Take this with you. If you have to get him soused, do it."

She stood up and wrapped a hand around the bottle. "You could use a bath, too." Then she sauntered across the room without a backward glance, but plenty of smiles for the men she brushed past.

Jamieson picked up both packs and the Winchester, ditched his shingles at the door, and trudged through mud to the depot to telegram Colonel Disque and Major Gund in code. *Fishing not good along St. Joe. Stop. Consider Canada. Stop. Signed Ross Gunn.* He didn't much care if they figured it out. He'd continue to run the mission his way.

He returned to the blind pig, got himself another beer and sat down to wait for O'Neill.

*   *

O'Neill asked, "Should I go now?"

Katie stretched. "You can stay as long as I say."

"Ye're from where, Kate? Did ye say?"

"Butte, Montana."

"Sure 'twas me thinkin' a woman like ye was from Butte, where the Irish are strong an' proud an' still claim the green isle as their true home."

She replied cautiously, "I told you my mam and da came from Ireland."

"Would it be County Cork by chance? Ye have the look of a rebel about ye."

"My da was from Cork. Most Butte Irish came from Cork. Miners in Ireland first."

"'Tis true. Are ye an Irish patriot then, Kate?"

"I haven't thought about it." She lay back, her fingers caressing the back of his neck. "I don't like the bloody English, if that's what you're askin'."

'Tis a start," he answered, and buried his face in her red hair.

Chapter 50
Late April, 1918

Riding the plush. It didn't matter to Fats Gerard that it was an accommodation train, stopping at every depot where some fool stationmaster waved it down. It gave a man time to consider his future. Lolling back in the Milwaukee Road's tourist car, Gerard knew he had a future. He lifted his hip flask to his mouth. An occasional drink cleared those thoughts clanking about in his head like chains. He was doing all right now, though. Everything was going his way.

He ambled up the aisle to use the latrine. The Milwaukee was idling at St. Maries when he sauntered back, passing row after row of green chairbacks, bunched pillows protruding into the aisle while passengers dozed. A pretty woman sat alone next to a window. *Well, looky there.* But why the hell had she opened it?

The locomotive's hissing drifted in. And what was so pleasant about hog fuel odor from MacLean's sawmill? Burning sawdust and wood chip smoke made his eyes smart. Those lumbermen, they wanted it all - sawmills and real estate covered in timber to hell and gone. Not a drop of cream left for the deserving. She was nicely built, but her long legs stretched out with ankles crossed like she'd booked the facing seats, too. He took the aisle seat across from her and raised his bowler. "If the engine wasn't huffin' an' puffin', you'd hear the rigs at the mill chewin' away at those big logs."

She drew in her feet and turned a cold eye on him. It was too dim in the car to see their color. He dipped his chin and thick fingers touched his hat brim in a second salutation. *See these fingers? They've killed.* "Goin' far?"

"Not far." She turned toward the window and away from him.

He angled toward her. "Name's Gerard, Frank Gerard. Railroad detective." Undoing his overcoat's top button, he revealed the silver star on his tweed jacket's lapel. *Yeah, look at my star.* "One of my responsibilities is to keep an eye on ladies traveling alone. Make sure no one bothers them."

She replied drily, "You must enjoy your occupation."

Stuck-up broad. "It has its rewards."

"No one has bothered me. Please continue with your duties."

He rose and tipped his bowler. "Ma'am." *Fotze . . . cunt.*

He took a seat a few rows down, keeping her in view; fiddled with his badge, repinning it until he was satisfied with its display. He liked the feel of the star points' little round knobs. He watched the woman nod off.

He recalled the night a few years back when he saw a tramp dragging a kid through the Omaha yards. He'd pulled his knife and stabbed the man in the side, freeing the boy. "Come on, kid. Ya wanna go back home? I'll put ya on a safe freight. Where're ya from?" He'd put him on a boxcar heading east and returned to the tramp. Only it wasn't.

"Railway detective," the man gasped. "Takin' him to stationmaster. Gotta help me."

"S'that right? Should'a told me earlier," and cut the man's throat. While clawing for dough through the railroad dick's pockets, he'd felt the badge, sticky with blood. Ripped it from the detective's lapel and wiped it on the man's pants. He could use it. Those little knobs on its points, almost like a woman's hard nipples.

The woman was still asleep when the train stopped to take on water a few miles outside of St. Joe City. The conductor, obviously drunk, roused her and dragged down her valise. She followed him down the aisle. Gerard tipped his bowler and murmured, "Have yourself a nice jaunt."

Chapter 51

Shortly after Addie debarked from the tourist car and the train continued eastbound into the night, she realized her mistake. No, not her mistake, the conductor's mistake.

He shook the back of her seat. Mumbled, "Ma'am, you're my only fare for St. Joe City." When she boarded the train, he'd been talkative and jovial, confiding it was his first time conducting on this night train traveling west to east. It wasn't the *Olympian*, that grand train snaking from Tacoma all the way to Chicago, but he expected to be promoted to that schedule soon.

Now he fumbled open the observation platform door. Descending with valise and step box in hand, he carefully placed them on the ground, then unskillfully handed her down.

Befuddled with sleep, Addie alighted into the unexpected. Neither the depot nor St. Joe City itself materialized. In the past she'd arrived with Jerome by steamboat, never by train. It wasn't much of a town, but there had been electric lights.

The conductor, too, was mystified. "Well, son of a gun! Where's the station?" Breathing alcohol fumes, he reassured her, "Across the tracks and up a bit, I betcha. I shoulda set ya down on the other side. A lotta freight cars between us and the engine." His duty completed, he picked up the step box and winched himself up onto the platform. From the doorway he called down, "You'll be all right now, ma'am." More of an order than a query.

She replied from habit, "Yes, I'll be fine." *Whatever the circumstances, a lady shows a brave fac*e, she'd written in a column. *Hysterics belong on the stage.*

Spring came late in the Joe Country and the cold air cleared her head. Everything would soon fall into place. Even now the crate holding Titus was being unloaded from a baggage car farther ahead.

A brakeman up the tracks raised and lowered a lantern. Out of sight around a bend the engineer gave two short toots of the whistle.

No, this is all wrong! Addie picked up her Gladstone and strode toward the train's steps, but too late. Steel wheels squealed and the car lurched beyond her outstretched hand as the orange cars of the Milwaukee Road pulled away. The caboose clattered behind, its lantern receding into a red dot until it disappeared around the bend.

There was no depot across the tracks and no two-storied, hip-roofed hotel where steamboats docked. No town at all. It must lie ahead, its lights hidden by a bluff and those large pines silhouetted against the star-strewn sky.

Addie lugged her Gladstone up onto the tracks, fuming at the departed conductor. "You will never work on a train again if I have my way!" In shoes meant for train travel, not rough walking, she headed up starlit silvered rails pointing the way.

Except for those parallel gleaming rails, the tracks were black shadow on black. The cross ties didn't lie equidistant on the rail bed and, while trying to take one at a time, she stubbed a toe or crunched on cinders every third or fourth step. She'd gone only a few hundred feet when she heard dripping water plink from a wooden cistern that blocked a section of stars overhead. Of course! The engine had stopped to take on water. Stupid, stupid conductor!

The sounds of the river to her left eased her mind. She knew this river, though not from railroad tracks, or in the spring when it ran fast, swollen with debris. Those first few summers of her marriage, she and Jerome had traveled by steamboat up the lazy St. Joe to their summer cabin at Ferrell across from St. Joe City. Standing at the steamboat's railing, she'd watched trains rattle by and asked Jerome, stylish in white flannels and a Panama hat, "May we take the train next year? We'll reach the cabin sooner." He'd smoothed his beard. "Trains are for speed, dear girl. Boats are for pleasure. Nothing more pleasurable than an expedition across Lake Coeur d'Alene and up the St. Joe." Clever women agreed with their husbands, whose purpose in life was to protect them. Stupid women agreed with drunken conductors that they would be all right on their own.

Once past a stand of resinous evergreens, Addie glimpsed the lights of St. Joe City, but so distant, another forty-five minutes with the Gladstone bumping against her leg. She switched hands. Her shoes rubbed her heels through lisle stockings. If only she'd worn practical shoes but, having grown up on a farm in mud and dust, she loved her shoes -- street shoes, dance shoes, travel shoes. Vanity, thy name is woman.

* *

The week before, she'd picked up the ringing telephone's horn to hear, "I have a long-distance call for Mrs. Adelaide MacLean. Are you that party?"

After some back and forth between operators, the line crackled and a thin voice blared from miles away, "Addie, is that you?"

"Yes, Alonzo," she yelled back. "Is anything wrong?"

"What? Can you hear me?"

"Yes, I hear you."

"Will you come cook up at headquarters camp on Marble Creek? Pork Grease, he's doin' the drive. I fired the last man. Gol-darn drunk. Drank all the lemon extract. I need someone I trust. Are ya gettin' this?"

Well, doesn't the worm turn? He didn't want a woman butting into the lumber business, but now he needed her.

"Yes."

"What? Gol-darn connection."

"Yes. When do you want me to come?"

"Next week. We're about to start the drive. The ice is breaking up. Sooner if ya can."

"All right, I'll come."

* *

Three campfires glowed ahead between the tracks and the river, two in close proximity as the camaraderie of men would dictate, the third farther on. They were men who traveled, going where they pleased. She envied them their warmth. Stuffed with clothing intended to last until her trunk arrived, the leather bag's weight wearied her. And her feet hurt.

She was passing the two fires when a male voice exclaimed from below, "Fuck me, there's a woman on the tracks!" His silhouette angled away from the fire's glow. "Come 'ere gal!"

Realizing she was illuminated, she felt like a metal duck in a shooting gallery.

A thrown bottle broke on rocks. "Where is she?"

"Up on the tracks!"

Rough laughter and drunken jeers accompanied men scrambling up behind her. Her revolver lay buried in the Gladstone and so she ran, the bag thumping like an albatross against her leg. Quitting her hopeless attempt at escape, she squatted and jerked it open, dug through small clothes, willing the gun into her gloved hand. In a breathless squeak, she called out, "Stop! I have a gun!" A man hesitated down the tracks. Voice stronger, she yelled, "I mean it! I'll shoot!"

A drunken laugh. "I've heard that before, dolly. Come on down and have a drink. We're friendly."

A boyish voice slurred, "We sure are. Coochie, have some hoochie."

Her hand curled around the small revolver. "Don't you come near me!" Rising, she pointed the gun, but it was too late. A tramp grabbed her from behind, jerking her off-balance. She got off one wild shot before he knocked away the gun and pinned her arms to her sides. Her gloves inhibited her attempts to scratch his hands and face; she screamed in fright and rage as he dragged her down the embankment. Twisting and squirming, hoping he'd drop her like some feral varmint, she screamed louder, drumming heels against his shins and ankles. She lost a shoe.

He threw her down by a campfire. Men whooped and closed in.

"Let's see what we caught!" Her attacker rolled her toward the flames, revealing her face beneath a small hat that clung to unraveling hair. Instead of front teeth, a dark hole lay behind his wide grin. He yanked off her hat, its well-placed hatpins tearing loose her hair. "Thank you, Lord and Savior, this cock bucket ain't old!"

Squatting around her in a semi-circle, like boys about to torment a one-eyed pup, five grizzled drunks eyed their new diversion.

"Here, girlie, have a drink." He thrust a bottle at her. "Make ya soft and slick for me, though I won't mind if you're rough 'n dry."

Addie pushed herself to her knees, snatched the bottle by its neck and slammed it against what she thought was a rock, but it thudded against a chunk of charcoal. Ashes flew and whiskey gurgled.

The tramp grabbed it back. "Don't break it, cunt bitch!"

Like a cornered prey she reared back. Their eyes reflected firelight like wolves she'd seen in a framed print. They might kill her. They *would* kill her afterward.

"Unbutton your coat. Let's see what you got under there."

Addie remained frozen on her knees. A tramp drunkenly poked her with a long stick. "Lie down and spread your legs. Ya want my big bone or this stick rammed up your pooch." His one eye gleamed.

Toothless lisped, "Shut-up, ass-hole."

Low in the pecking order, the young tramp slurred, "Let's play poker for her."

An older one snickered, "Take too long. I'm ready now."

"We're all gonna have her. But who gets firsts?" Each man was restless for the show to begin.

The fire behind her burned low, crimson threading through chunks of charcoal, flames licking one moment, dying down the next.

The young tramp offered, "I got some dice."

Toothless snorted, "I get her first and ya'll gonna wait." As he made a grab for her, Addie knocked away his hand. He grabbed the bottle from his one-eyed pal and raised it.

She flung herself into the campfire and rolled to the opposite side, sending up a shower of sparks. The long wool coat protected her after a fashion. If she burned her shoeless foot, she didn't notice. Scrambling to her feet, she grabbed up a charred limb, directing its glowing tip at the men across the fire. Every nerve and muscle was in play to keep them at bay so she could live. They stumbled to their feet to encircle her, muttering and growling.

They would not touch her again. The glowing stick burst into flame as she swept it in a half-circle. Behind her the river's rushing water was loud and she backed toward it, preparing to turn and leap.

Chapter 52

A voice barked from the dark, "Get back or you're dead!" A gunshot followed.

Two tramps threw themselves down; the rest lurched drunkenly about.

The voice ordered, "Back! The next bullet's yours!" Those still standing retreated, darting fearful looks toward the shadows. "Irish, are any of these bastards Wobs you know?"

A second man holding a gun stepped into the low glow of the farther campfire and kicked up its flames. "Let's see yer faces." The rekindled fire failed to cast sufficient light and he pulled out a flashlight, beaming it from face to face. "Look at me," he commanded the one-eyed tramp. "I've seen ye afore, but ye're no I.W.W. All of yez sit down. Down! Or Christ himself will be the next face ye see." He kicked the legs out from under the nearest tramp, then swiftly retreated to cover them all. The others dropped and hugged their knees, the two on the ground crawling to join them.

His bearded face in ruddy profile, his revolver pointing at the tramps, the first man moved closer to Addie,

She swung the flaming brand in his direction.

"Ma'am, your coat's smoking."

The familiar timbre of a familiar voice. *Jerome? No, But like Jerome.* The charred brand burned through her glove and she dropped it. With trembling fingers, she unbuttoned her smoldering coat.

He pulled it from her shoulders and stamped on it. Steel caulks punctured cloth, but smothered singed fabric. "Was that your gun we heard, or one of theirs?"

She gasped a throaty, "Mine." Motioned toward the tracks. "Up there." Pushed a coil of hair off her face. "Do I know you?"

He glanced at her, then exclaimed softly, "Oh, hell!" Refocused his attention on his companion giving orders.

"Take off yer coats so I can see what ye're carryin'. Don't forget me partner has yez covered." Removing their outerwear was slow going. "Easy now. Pull that knife outta yer boot and toss it here or ye'll be the third man I've killed in me life." The gape-toothed tramp lobbed a knife across the space separating them. The Irishman dragged it in with a spiked boot, scooped it up and arced it toward the river.

Addie limped to Jamieson, reached out to steady herself, clutching his arm holding the revolver. Elevating it, he stepped behind her, encircling her within the crook of his left arm. She leaned against his shoulder and stuck out a stockinged foot. In a small and bewildered voice, she said, "I lost my shoe, Robbie."

Only his holding her fiercely against his side kept her upright as her knees buckled. "Don't faint on me. Bend over and get some blood into your head." When her faintness passed and she regained her feet, he hissed, "Which ones hurt you? Point them out."

Her shaking hand included every man across the fire.

"Which ones?"

"The man without teeth. Dragged me down here."

Jamieson lowered her to the ground, circled the fire and viciously kicked the tramp in the head, laying him out cold. In a raw fury, he barked, "Tie them up, Irish! We'll dump them in the river. This bastard's carcass, too."

Propped on an elbow, Addie witnessed Jamieson's attack with a rush of elation. Hearing his order and understanding his intent, the sensation dissolved.

A tramp gasped, "We never teched her! Ya ain't got no cause to throw us in the river! We'll drown! Lady! For the love of God, tell him we didn't do nothin'!"

The Irishman interrupted, "And what will I be tying 'em with?" He waved his gun at a tramp, who had risen to his knees in supplication. "Didn't I say sit down, ye pissin' rat! Each one of yez take off yer right shoe an' toss it here. Gentle now. First man hits me gets a bullet in his knee." As Jamieson returned to Addie, they hurried to comply, even pulling off the unconscious man's shoe. The Irishman hurled each shoe toward rushing water. "'Tis a great favor I've done ye blokes. Ye'll not be knockin' each other's brains out for a shoe as fits. As fer yer lives, I'm not wantin' to kill in cold blood, but I'll not be sayin' the same for me partner."

Jamieson holstered his gun inside his coat and lifted Addie to her feet.

"They didn't hurt me. Don't kill them."

Taking her by the shoulders, he studied her face in the dim light before calling out, "Irish, the lady lost her revolver up on the tracks! And her shoe!"

"Do I look like a bloody bloodhound?" But he shone his light toward the tracks and headed that way. Then he swung back. "Don't any of yez move while I'm up there."

Jamieson held her at arm's length, demanded, "Are you going to faint?"

"I never faint."

"Good." He picked up her coat and wrapped her in it. Tugged down his hat and then surprised her by slinging her over his shoulder like a blanketed pack. Pulling a flashlight from a coat pocket, he headed upriver. "And I hope you won't be sick all over me, either."

She hung down his back, head swinging from side to side, his earlier fury still vibrating through her. He possessed a primitive nature that had gotten him into trouble with the Army. Already outside the law, he'd just kicked a man unconscious. And yet, she had an insane urge to laugh. Instead, she huffed, "Do you have a horse?"

"What?" He shortened his stride.

She repeated from near his waist, "A horse? I can't walk without a shoe."

"No horse. No time to plan ahead, Mrs. MacLean." He strode on, carrying her easy.

Chapter 55

Lowering her to a log next to what she realized was the farther campfire, he straightened to look down at her with a baffled expression. "What are you doing out here in the middle of nowhere?"

"Could I have a drink of water? Something stronger if you have it."

He withdrew a pint bottle from a pocket and handed it to her. "Don't stint yourself."

She took a sip and then another; grimaced as the liquor burned her throat. "The conductor put me off the train out there." Waved toward nothing in particular, then lowered her gloved hand to peer at it.

"Why did he do that?"

But she was tipping her hand toward the fire he kicked up, studying the glove's burnt leather. On her first attempt to tug it off, she sharply inhaled and stopped. The leather was stuck to her palm. "The conductor was drunk. I didn't realize the engine had stopped for water. Apparently, he didn't either." She tipped up her chin to control its quiver. "I thought I could take care of myself. I really did."

He tossed driftwood on the fire, then squatted next to her, careful not to block its warmth. She trembled in realization of how helpless and terrified she'd been. He rested a hand on her arm as she continued. "I couldn't get the gun out of my Gladstone in time." Worked her way through the ordeal. "I shot it once. Did you hear? Is that why you came? Did I already ask that?" She looked at him. "Did you say?" Winding down, "I can't even remember what I've just told you."

"We heard the gunshot, but thought those tramps were only carrying on."

"I should have put it in my handbag when I got off the train. I lost that, too." She displayed her hand. "My glove's stuck to my palm. I think I burned it."

He picked up a canteen. "Cup your hand. Maybe the water will soften the leather. Otherwise, I'll have to cut the glove off." She cupped her hand and he dribbled water into her gloved palm. "Now listen to me, Mrs. McLean. This is important. I know you've been through a lot, but when my partner comes back, call me Mac. Mac James is how I'm known out here. Don't call me Robbie."

"Mac the Pinkerton?"

"No!" Under his breath, "Jesus Christ." Almost pleading, "If you tell anyone I was a Pinkerton, you're liable to get me killed. I'm just Mac. They don't like Pinkertons out here. Too much history."

"Not Lieutenant Jamieson, either, I guess." Her lips compressed with a hint of the old vehemence, "Since you're a deserter."

Quietly, not wanting to rile her, "You remember that right." She stuck out her unshod foot to exhibit her black lisle stocking torn and singed, her bare toes exposed. His hand curled under it and she winced. "Is your foot burnt, too? Am I going to have to pack you all the way into St. Joe City?" The flashlight's beam revealed bruised and bloodied toes.

She jerked it away. "No, I didn't burn my foot!" Wriggling off her glove, she allowed his light to play on it. Blood appeared where skin had come off her palm and there was blistering. "I didn't feel it burning until you showed up."

"You don't feel pain in a fight. And, lady, you were in one hell of a fight."

With a sour taste of suspicion, she asked, "How long did you watch?"

"My God! We weren't watching!" He rocked back on his heels. "I got there in time to see you roll through the fire. Thought your hair would catch and you'd flare up like a Roman candle." He brushed hair away from her face, fried strands breaking off in his fingers. "Irish was working his way to the other side, but I stepped in when I thought you were going to throw yourself in the river."

She closed her eyes and shivered. "They were going to hurt me."

"I know." He touched her arm. "We heard you scream. I thought it was a cougar at first."

"I didn't scream. I don't scream." The whiskey was calming her.

"Yes, you screamed. Thank God, you screamed or we wouldn't have come."

An Irishman's lilt came from the darkness behind her. "Like a banshee, ye screamed, madam." The newcomer moved into the firelight, dropping Addie's shoe and the Gladstone. "Even got yer wee pistol in me pocket."

Firelight played on the man's face and Addie smiled her gratitude, only to replace it with astonishment. "Mally?"

O'Neill peered at her, then stretched out a hand to touch her face. "Ah, Addie, me darlin'. By all that's holy, why were ye wanderin' about in the dark?" He pulled her up into his arms, kissing her cheek while she balanced on one foot.

"The conductor set me off at the water tank. Silly of me not to realize."

"'Tis safe now ye'll be," easing her back down. He held out his arms expansively, encompassing Addie and Jamieson. "Sure 'tis time I presented ye properly to me partner, Mac James, as he calls himself. An' this lady . . . this adventuress of the rails . . . me cousin twice removed, Mrs. Adelaide MacLean."

Addie looked up to see Jamieson's consternation become no expression at all. He simply said, "You're cousins. Small world, isn't it?" He lifted his battered hat. "I'm pleased to meet you, Mrs. MacLean. Glad we were able to be of assistance."

His formality stopped her from gushing that Mac was an old acquaintance. Why wouldn't he want Mally to know that? Standing behind O'Neill, he shook his head at her.

"Mac James is it? It's good to meet you, also. And thank you. Both of you." She busied herself with forcing her swollen foot into her shoe, giving her jittered mind time to understand why these two men were together. Partners, they called each other.

Jamieson squatted across the campfire, packing up, while Mally spoke of taking her to a hotel in St. Joe City.

"Why are you out here, Mally?"

"I've been cuttin' timber all winter with Mac. We're headin' back for the drive down Marble Creek." A sudden awareness. "Ah, Addie, is it ye're goin' to the MacLean camp to visit?"

"I'm going to cook at the main camp. After I pick up my dog at the depot, I'll cross the river to stay at the MacLean cabin in Ferrell. If we can rouse a boatman, you both can stay there tonight." Hopefully the place had been cleaned and provisioned by the Ferrell grocer and his wife in accordance with her telegram.

"That would be safer, Mrs. MacLean," Jamieson agreed. "Will your husband be coming to camp?"

Role playing. They did that before. "I'm a widow, Mr. James. Please call me Addie. May I call you Mac? With what happened tonight, our acquaintance seems of longer duration."

Jamieson smiled, though she did not. "You brought your dog?"

"Yes I did."

"A nice little dog, I bet."

"'Tis settled then." O'Neill rolled his blanket and hefted his pack. "Can ye walk, Addie?"

"I think so."

Jamieson carried her bag and the rifle, while O'Neill took her undamaged hand to steady her along the muddy path beside the river. The night was friendlier in their company.

They rescued a barking Titus from his crate at the station and awakened the ferryman, directing him to put them ashore near the MacLean cabin, last visited by Addie three years before.

An unclasped padlock hung from the door with its key inserted, and Jamieson insisted on entering first. Titus rushed in with him and while he swept the interior with his flashlight, the mastiff lumbered from wall to fireplace, chair to table, picking up old and new scents. The interior smelled of mouse. Jamieson lighted a kerosene lamp, bathing the room in a soft glow. Fresh provisions sat on the table.

"Are you hungry?" Addie asked. "I'll fry up some eggs."

"Ye must be all in, Addie," O'Neill sympathized. "And look at yer hand. Sit yerself. I'll fire up the stove and cook us all a meal."

Addie awoke toward morning. She bypassed the horror of the previous night to lie awash with guilt for having cheated Robert

Jamieson out of a quarter interest in the lumber company employing him. She'd done it deliberately with malice aforethought and now time had run out to name him as Jerome's heir. If she'd spoken up when she first saw that odd knuckle, if she'd demanded to know who his mother was - Maud or Dovey - and confronted her for corroborating details, would he have deserted? He saved her life and somehow she was going to have to make it up to him.

Chapter 54
Marble Creek: April, 1918

The packer warned, "Miz MacLean, ya gotta keep that big dog away from the mules. They hate dogs. They'll stomp him with their front hooves." He spat a stream of tobacco.

Titus was made to trail behind Addie, who sat astride a rented horse at the rear of a string of large pack mules. O'Neill and Jamieson had gone on a couple of days earlier, but she'd remained at the cabin until assured her burned hand was healing.

The Marble Creek tote trail ran above a torrent of deafening, rock-fanged whitewater. Wearing old boots retrieved from under the cabin's bed, she exulted in riding astride in jodhpurs, a loose white shirt and a shawl-collared sweater. A canvas fishing hat with a chin strap kept her mass of hair in place.

When she rode into camp, her eyes centered on the rusty saw blade hanging beside the cookhouse door, then shifted to Alonzo coming toward her in slouch hat and boots laced to his knees. She smiled into his upturned craggy face and pointed. "I suppose someone beats it with a big spoon at suppertime."

"Beats it with an iron poker. A saw is better'an a school bell." Pale blue eyes crinkled. "And it's good to see you, too. Hope ya had a fine ride." He helped her to stiffly dismount.

"I'm numb you-know-where," but rubbed the small of her back. "I stopped to chat with Pork Grease Eddie where he's set up camp at the river. He said he's feeding about twenty men there now."

"We been pushin' logs for a few days. The men will either hike back up here for chow or down to the river, whichever is closer. A few more weeks and we'll all be at that rag camp."

"I saw logs going down Marble Creek. They're huge."

"Those ain't all ours. I'm usin' my head this year, lettin' the Rutledge crew push our logs ahead of theirs when they open splash dams on a couple of feeder creeks they been loggin'. Sure makes 'em mad doin' our work for us." He expelled a rusty crow, as though he hadn't laughed in some time; jerked on one of his mustaches, more silver than she remembered. Once sandy, his eyebrows were now a bushy gray.

They chatted while cooks and flunkies unloaded boxes of foodstuff. A mule had carried her small trunk on one side, balanced by three bales of hay. "Ain't he the packer, though. Carries everything from eggs to dynamite."

Alonzo escorted her into the cavernous cookhouse. "I asked ya to come, Addie, because you cooked for harvest crews at your pa's. But this ain't the same. These men will eat the table clean and expect more. The camp serving the best meals gets the best jacks. An' I need the best. Got the world by the tail with a downhill pull and I mean to keep it that way." He patted her shoulder. "Since you're part-owner, I figured you'd run a smooth kitchen."

"Mama always says the day is wasted if you start work after sunrise."

"The men ain't allowed to talk while eatin', but when ya go outside, you'll hear cursin', some of it downright obscene. They won't mean to shock ya. All day they curse their saws and axes, the horses, an' the trees, too. They curse one another and spit tobacco everywhere."

He introduced the bull cook, Polite John, who wore a black derby, and then the rest of the staff. Not as many as she'd hoped. The large kitchen was *terra incognito* to her. She examined the ten-foot long sink and the two metal water barrels connected by lead pipes to fireboxes in the two ranges. "How much hot water do they hold?"

Polite John, a man about sixty, answered, "We get 100 gallons of boiling water three times a day an' keep the stoves burning from five a.m. 'til eight at night." When he grinned, a large scar drew his mouth up one side of his furrowed face. "I remember you, Miz MacLean, from when you come out to our other camp one time. Name's John Wheatley, but everyone calls me Polite." He pointed to the sanded stump for cutting up slabs of beef, mutton and pork. "My specialty's meat."

"I remember you, too." She recalled the jagged scar down his face, drooping an eyelid, but lifting his mouth. "Please continue preparing the meat. If I have a specialty, it's baking. Bread, cakes, pies and doughnuts."

"That's good," Alonzo broke in, "cause the pastry chef is with Pork Grease Eddie at the rag camp."

"I should do an inspection to see what supplies we have and what we'll need." She was feeling more excited than tired now, ready to tackle her job.

"You can do that later. I wanna show ya the loggin' train. That new little Shay locomotive is a beauty. I couldn't use it during the winter, but now with the snow mostly melted and no ice covering the tracks, she's everything I'd hoped for."

He was as excited as a boy, but he'd aged in those two years since she last saw him. His loose-skinned neck rose from a soft collar, a few whiskers the razor missed visible in creases beside his mustaches. Jerome had used gambling expressions when he talked about the business and she thought of them now - laying down his last bet; pushing his entire pile to the center of the table; rise or fall. With Jerome gone, she and Alonzo would rise or fall together.

Alonzo strode through melting snow along a muddy forest trail while Addie, sore from her ten-mile ride, gritted her teeth, but kept up. Titus padded along in front, alert to every new sight and smell.

"This will be the year it all comes together, Addie. Mark my words. You're gonna be well-off. Me, too."

They emerged from the shadows into a clearing, the sun so bright, she squinted. Stumpage covered steep hillsides. They entered a side draw where snow was deeper, and there was the Shay engine, crouching on its rails, grunting, hissing steam and spewing smoke. Chains rattled and clanged. A steam donkey, resembling a large metal teapot, winched a log into the air with a jammer, maneuvering it over a flatbed car already loaded high with cut timber. The top loaders controlled the log with cant hooks, slowly lowering it. Whoops and nickering drew Addie's eyes up a slope of rotting brown snow to where a man and a team of horses skidded a log down a muddy chute. The first log now settled, its chain was detached and spread on the ground. The team dragged its log across the chain and the rigging slinger released it. Without being urged, the horses headed back up the mountain for another log. The air was redolent of cut pine.

What she'd pictured as impenetrable stands of timber was a scene of carnage, stumps and slash littering mountainsides. And yet she felt pride of ownership. A bit of sadness, too, at the finality of timber grown two hundred years or more, escaping the big burn, and now being felled and sawed into logs. She reminded herself it would be used for houses, barracks, crates and airplanes America needed to win the war.

"The feeder pond and flume are about a mile east," Alonzo explained. "We laid tracks for the Shay to haul logs from here to there. We've been flumin' 'em down to the Marble, then drivin' 'em to the Joe." He spat tobacco juice. "Them toothpicks are gonna make us rich, Addie."

Gripping the mastiff's collar, Addie surveyed the scene. She recognized Jamieson and O'Neill below, planting cant hooks into the big log about to be yarded by the steam donkey. They appeared as small boys beside it. Them toothpicks.

"I better go down an' make sure they're doin' it right."

She turned back toward camp, Alonzo's yells echoing, "Lay 'em even an' pile 'em high!"

The next morning Addie rose at four. At 6:30 a flunky clanged the saw blade. Thirty men filed in, stepped over benches and spooned oatmeal mush with stewed prunes from large bowls. Addie and her staff followed up with platters of pancakes, bacon, ham, fried potatoes, and biscuits.

Thirty men tentatively examined the biscuits she'd made, checking the bottoms, then forking them open to peer at the insides before slathering on butter and jam.

Polite John watched from the kitchen. "They're gonna want more biscuits to take with 'em." He returned to frying up additional bacon, hash browns and scrambled eggs. Arms aching, Addie stirred more biscuit dough in a pail. It was fuel, not food. She peeked out and spotted Jamieson and O'Neill. Jamieson caught her eye, held up a biscuit and winked.

As though by mutual assent, a half hour after filing into the cookhouse, the loggers rose to make up sandwiches from platters of fresh bread, cheese and meat. They added cookies and more biscuits to tin pails, and stomped out the door.

Chapter 55

The wooden flume was damn steep. It came out of a spring-fed pond nearly a thousand feet above Marble Creek, sweeping from a high valley down mountainsides and curving canyons, ending behind a splash dam stretching one hundred fifty feet across the creek.

Jamieson and Giant Kid rolled the last log off the flat car to be decked beside the pond. The time-keeper was scaling, figuring each log's board feet before punching "McL" into its end with a three-pound stamping hammer. Out on the pond men trotted along logs in high-arched caulked boots with stacked heels, using pikes or peaveys for balance and control.

The gate was opened and the first log flew down the flume, wet sides catching sunlight, riding high water that splashed silver over wooden sides. Rolling and bobbing, it disappeared around a bend. As logs followed one another, MacLean shouted, "Space 'em! Space 'em, goddammit!" Balancing like a dancer, O'Neill leaped from one log to another; reached out his peavey to jam it into a log to slow it and keep it from entering the flume side by side with another giant.

"Faster! Faster now! Agh! Too much space!"

O'Neill gave the log a directional shove and down it went, back end angling skyward as it entered the flume.

MacLean jerked off his hat, waving it over his head. "They're jamming! Those damn logs are jamming!"

Balancing himself with his peavey, Jamieson leaped from log to log toward the jam. He'd practiced, searching for the young legs left in Michigan years before. O'Neill and a couple of Scandinavians ran along logs from different directions. Breaking the jam loose, they pointed the logs toward the spill. Jamieson separated two logs in a close horse race, slowed one so it trailed the other. During the next half-hour the pond emptied and the gate was closed. Not all the logs made it out, but the pond would refill overnight.

Soaked and exhilarated, the men hitched rides on clattering empty flats the Shay hauled toward camp.

"Where'd you learn to be so catty, Irish?"

They sat on a flat car, legs dangling. "I'll tell ye, boyo, I'm a natural whitewater man. Comin' across the Atlantic we hits a gale an' the old boat's bobbin' up 'n down. But me, I'm dancin' a jig below decks to entertain scared kiddies. When I come to the lumber camps and seen jacks rollin' trees down the river, I says, 'that's for me.' Didn't realize they had spikes in their boots. Makes it easier sure."

Jamieson grinned. "What a goddamn liar you are."

"Who's callin' Malachi O'Neill a liar?"

"I am. You knew damn well they wore caulked boots."

O'Neill flung an arm over Jamieson's shoulder. "Sure ye'd rather be doin' this than guidin' some dumb brute horse draggin' a log down a trail chute. Give me water on any day. 'Tis me natural element. Descended from a selkie I am."

"What's a selkie?"

His joke unappreciated, he yelped, "Ye lunkhead Yank. A selkie is a seal that becomes a woman by night, and that's when she'll bed a man." Black brows moved up and down. "Ask me cousin Addie about selkies some time. She's quite the teller of tales herself."

*   *

The men were curious to see Addie and her big dog. More than one logger squatting on a log, eating, had turned to see the mastiff drooling over his shoulder and taken to hands and knees, thinking it was a bear. In the cookhouse they craned their necks when Addie stepped from the kitchen.

One evening she saw a lumberjack pass the big heating stove and spit a stream of tobacco on it. The gob of brown saliva sputtered on hot metal.

"Just a minute there!" she called, crossing the pitted floor. "I polished that stove this morning while you were still sleeping."

The swarthy lumberjack stared. "What, lady?" He turned to a very tall young man. "What she say?"

Giant Kid mimicked a polishing motion. "She said she cleaned that stove this morning and she don't like you spittin' your tobaccy on it."

"Ah." Black eyes scowled at the floor, then over her head, refusing to meet her angry eyes. "Sorry. I spit no more." Recovering from his embarrassment, he flashed a smile and bowed. "I am Danko Popovic from Montenegro. This my partner, Giant Kid. We are best lumberjacks in whole world, Boss Lady."

She was tired. Her temper had flared like a Lucifer match and gone out as quickly. "Then I'm glad you choose to work here." She offered her hand, which Popovic, at first hesitant, grasped in hard fingers, bowing again.

Giant Kid stuck out a large hand with crooked fingers, the little one missing, and she shook it. "I admire to eat after ya," he said.

It was a compliment she hadn't heard said quite that way. "Where are you from?"

"Minnesota."

Other loggers lined up to shake her hand before heading out the door. Some told her how much they liked her biscuits and rolls, cookies and cakes. "Why, I saw ole Lenny over there slam a fist on one of your biscuits just to keep it from floatin' away."

Some grinned shyly and said nothing.

Afterward, she turned to find O'Neill and Jamieson standing behind her.

"'Tis everyone in camp has a moniker, Addie. Boss Ladys uits ye fine."

She smiled at her cousin, but not at the amused Jamieson, eyes crinkling at the corners. "So, you think his spitting on my stove was funny?"

He gave her a slow smile. "It's worked to your advantage, Boss Lady." With that, they wandered outside, leaving her and the flunkies to remove the supper's detritus from the long tables.

Chapter 56

Cruel Jimmy ordered Jamieson and O'Neill down to the Marble to pry logs off banks that had to be constantly patrolled. Jillpoked logs wedged askew among rocks would hold back more logs and create a jam. They bent their backs, prying with peaveys to roll them free. By afternoon they were working the downstream side of a huge jam. Sixteen- to twenty-four-foot logs stuck out at every compass point and then some. The culprits were a few bottom logs, hidden ends maybe caught on cedar stumps. Their visible ends stretched out like giant cat claws, clutching enough logs from the last run to clog the Marble's flow, but for an open section across the creek. Despite low water, the jam was under pressure. Logs creaked, grinding against one another, tightening the knot. They leaped from log to log below the center of the jam, picked and pried, searching out the key log that would set the rest free. If they could dislodge it, there'd be time to jump into the rock-strewn creek and wade ashore as the jam slowly broke up.

"Tighter'n a virgin."

"You ever have a virgin?"

"No."

"Then how would you know?"

Popovic balanced on a log downstream, watching up creek beyond the jam. Out-of-sight around a bend, the closed splash dam was building up a head of water. A half-hour before the sluice gates opened to release more logs, the creek would overflow; Popovic would see the small wave coming and shout a warning, and they'd get the hell out of there.

But no small wave came, only a flood. Popovic yelled, "Water!" and jumped up to his armpits in whitewater that tossed him on rocks from which he crawled to safety.

There was no escape for Jamieson and O'Neill balanced on protruding logs. They instinctively jammed in peaveys, expecting to be swept away in frothing water and logs. Their eyes met.

"Jaysus God!" O'Neill mouthed as water roared through the narrow opening beyond them. The logs they crouched on, butt ends hidden beneath the jam, rose with the flood. The jam would break apart, the logs released upstream crashing through.

Jamieson's impulse was to jump into swirling water and chance making it to shore, but O'Neill stood fast. The end would be the same. Death now or death in a moment. The jam shook as water and logs battered it. Jamieson's log shivered beneath his feet. "Fuck! She's goin'!" Downstream were canyon walls of granite to be crushed against. Logs, water and rock would be his end. Water running over and through the jam soaked them, and Jamieson saw his own fear and fatalism reflected on O'Neill's clenched face.

Hands numbed in a death grip on his peavey, knees flexed, Jamieson straddled the rising and grinding timber, expecting it to roll and hurl him to his death. Behind him flood and logs crashed through the narrow spillway at the far bank. Then their logs stopped rising and began to slowly lower as the flood dwindled and the last of the logs not caught behind the jam flowed downstream. Upstream the dam gates closed. The jam held fast, its Gordian knot of timber unsevered.

They clambered to the bank on unsteady legs, tossed down peaveys and lowered themselves against a large stump. O'Neill murmured in Gaelic. It sounded like a prayer and Jamieson bowed his head, but when he closed his eyes, the dizzying images of whitewater made his chest pound. Popovic stood silently beside them. O'Neill cleared his throat. "Are ye not a godly man, Mac? Ye yell His name all day long."

Jamieson opened his eyes on a beautiful world of blue sky, green trees and the cursed Marble flowing past. "Thought you were giving thanks for both of us."

O'Neill answered solemnly, "There now, I've added yer name." He looked at the logs sticking out like a porcupine's quills. "'Twill take dynamite to break up that jam."

Chapter 57
St. Maries, Idaho

Fats Gerard folded thick arms. "The feds are paying fifty dollars a head to bring in draft dodgers and deserters." He'd accosted Sheriff Buck Roland outside his office and they stood with heads lowered lest someone overhear. "We'll be doing American Protective League work, helping Uncle Sam and making money in the bargain."

His Pinkerton association dissolved, Gerard had found new identity by joining the clandestine American Protective League. Membership came with an eagle-mounted gold badge, identifying the bearer as an *Operative*, and the league as an *Auxiliary to the Department of Justice*. The league's secrecy appealed to him, but he was disappointed it was against rules to wear his badge outside his coat. He'd helped Sheriff Roland, another member, sweep through St. Maries' cheap boarding houses to pick up undesirables and a few alien enemies without proper registration.

"So, whatcha think, Sheriff? Round up some dodgers and make a few bucks?" He shot out his hand to snatch a horsefly circling the sheriff's head. "These buggers bite." Relieving it of a wing, he dropped it on the windowsill, where it buzzed in an aimless circle.

Roland studied the horsefly. "Sounds do-able."

"There're so many draft dodgers and alien enemies up in those logging camps, we'll fill the jail with 'em."

The horsefly fell off the window sill and Gerard stepped on it.

Fats watched each swipe of the straight razor in his mirror. Stared into his eyes as disgusting tears trickled down soaped cheeks. Wiped his face with a towel as the memory of the last time he cried rushed at him from behind.

He was twelve and had run away from Chicago. The train pulled into a freight yard and he slid open the boxcar door to escape the horror. The tramps who'd befriended him were drunk and snoring. When they'd stopped being his pals, they poured liquor down his throat. One jerked down his knickers, pulled his butt cheeks apart and rammed into him. He screamed in pain, thinking he was being split in two. "Squeals like a little girl, don't he," another laughed. "Think that plump little girl will squeal for me?" Blubbering, he begged them to stop, but each man took him. Later while they slept, he'd have stabbed each man if he'd had a knife. No one heard him groaning and whimpering as he lowered himself from the boxcar. Too damaged to run, he inched along the freight cars. Then he fingered the little box in his pocket. Shaking, he waddled another few yards, turned around and crept back. Cinders crunching at a distance frightened him, but the sound grew fainter. Gasworks illuminated the boxcar's open door and he squatted beneath it. He had to do this right. Mouse-like, he scratched at straw, terrified a tramp would grab his wrist before he could make a small heap. Satisfied with its size, he struck a match and set the straw aflame. He lit another and flicked it toward the corner where he'd suffered. Using all his strength he pushed the slider nearly shut, leaving a crack, like on the stove damper at home. As the *mudder* would say, "Da fire needs da hair for to burn, ya."

Bent over, pain shooting up his ass, he crossed empty tracks to scuttle along a line of freights. He turned, expecting to see the tramps come flying out. His legs weakened with failure when there were no flames. He was a pudgy helpless boy, unable to make a little fire. They would wake up and come searching for him. Snot slid into his mouth as he wept with renewed terror. When he looked again, the boxcar was alight, crackling flames chewing dry wood up its side. No shadows leaped out through the fire, but yard men were running up the tracks, shouting.

With effort he wormed beneath a freight car to watch workers trying to uncouple cars at either end of the burning freight. Within minutes they retreated from the heat, leaving three burning cars strung together, managing to uncouple and push other cars away.

He crawled out the other side of the freight and stumbled into the river, lost his footing on slick rocks and sat in cold water, where he stayed until his ass numbed. That night he learned railroads follow rivers.

Chapter 58

MacLean's rag camp sat at the confluence of Marble Creek and the St. Joe River, across from Marble Creek Station.

Jamieson, O'Neill and their drive crew trailed into camp wet and tired. They'd pushed the last contingent of logs down the Marble, keeping them moving with the aid of spill dams on feeder creeks until shoving them into the Joe.

The turbulent Marble had battered MacLean's logs, debarked and broom-ended them, and getting them into the river was still only half the work. The logs glided toward St. Joe City, mingling with Rutledge logs and those of outfits cutting farther up the Joe. There'd be more sweating and freezing in cold water before the crew finished pushing them to St. Joe City.

Thrumming with exhaustion, Jamieson leaned his peavey against a tree where he could locate it at dawn. He wanted only to bolt down a hot meal beside a fire, pull off soaked boots and socks and fall into a dreamless sleep.

He wearily watched MacLean riding up the river trail on a large buckskin, kicking up dust, followed at a distance by a man who must be Sheriff Roland and a third rider. What now? When he recognized the third rider, a cold hatred rose from the pit of his stomach.

Fats Gerard trailed behind, his shifting bulk appearing too large for the comfort of the little mare. Jamieson impulsively started toward him, but MacLean's buckskin swerved, brushing against him, forcing him off the trail and, in that moment, he reconsidered his recklessness. The attack on the *Verona* was past and he had a mission to complete. Their mutual hatred could wait.

He turned aside, bumping into O'Neill. "See the man riding in back, Irish?"

But O'Neill had other matters on his mind. He hooked Jamieson's arm and swung him toward the river. "Don't be lookin' at Sheriff Roland and gettin' his attention." He dragged Jamieson down to the river bank.

"I meant the other man. Name's Frank Gerard. Goes by Fats. Nearly killed me twice. The first time in Billings a few years back. Don't ever turn your back on him."

"The divil ye say!" O'Neill tugged down his hat. Once the sheriff rode past, he chewed thoughtfully on a blade of grass. "Did I ever tell ye, Mac, I never forget a face?" Turned dark eyes on Jamieson, who returned his look, heart thumping oddly in his chest.

"No, partner, I don't think you ever did." Like a cat that sets to licking itself when filled with uncertainty, he wanted to roll a cigarette, but didn't have the makings.

"That man Fats was on the *Verona*. Sure ye must remember?"

"Yeah. That's where he almost killed me the second time. His was the first shot fired."

O'Neill repeated, "The divil ye say?" His face became a study in changing emotion. "Do ye recall seein' him in the Seattle jail, Mac?"

"No, Irish, I never saw him there."

Suspicious of the sheriff's appearance, the river drivers squatted around the fire, eating supper in a sour mood. Jamieson sat back on his heels. With Gerard nearby, he wanted to be able to rise quickly. Hat still shadowing his face, O'Neill ate standing.

MacLean, the drive boss, the sheriff and Gerard stood pow-wowing down on the river bank. The Ol' Man sounded sore, occasional phrases floating up. ". . not gonna wreck my drive . . . don't give a goddamn . . . them's my boys."

A Finn wiped his mouth, observing, "When I hear Ol' Man talkin' 'bout his boys, I think he talkin' 'bout his nuts. But, by God, he talkin' 'bout us." Men chuckled, but looked grim.

MacLean led the others up the embankment.

"Men," he announced, "the sheriff and Mr. Gerard here are members of that American Protective League that's been instituted across the country. They're workin' for the government an' one of their duties is to check for draft registration cards and classification cards." The men's looks changed to consternation and anger.

A driver jumped up. "You ain't got no right to come up here an' hassle us, Sheriff. You ain't supposed to come across the county line. This is Shoshone County." He flung out an arm. "This county's sheriff is over those mountains in Wallace."

A bandy-legged driver rose. "Our cards are up at camp. Can't carry paper, workin' on water."

MacLean interrupted, "That's what I been tellin' 'em. They agreed they'll be satisfied with your names. If ya don't have your card, tell 'em where it's at. That goes for you foreign fellas, too."

Another driver shouted, "If you want our names, get 'em from the payroll clerk!"

The sheriff took a turn. "We're doing this to protect law-abiding men like yourselves. When the drive reaches St. Joe City, there could be trouble. Other outfits drivin' this river have I.W.W. and German sympathizers with them."

An older man quipped, "Ain't that supposed to mean the same thing?"

MacLean took charge. "Give 'em your names. When we drive into Benewah County, if there's trouble, the sheriff will know you're my men."

They had little choice but to obey. Tablet and pencil in hand, Gerard circumnavigated the fire, setting down each man's name. O'Neill moved in from the shadows and Jamieson rose to stand beside him.

"Malachi O'Neill from County Cork, Ireland. Exempt from serving in the British army. Me card is at camp." Gerard showed no recognition. The sheriff, however, glared at O'Neill, but said nothing.

With one word Gerard could ruin his covert assignment. Beard and lumberjack clothes protected him only from a distance. "Robert James." He pushed back his hat. "American. My card is up at camp." Baleful eyes met his over the tablet before Gerard scrawled his name and nationality.

Sheriff Roland gave him a once-over. "Why aren't you soldiering?"

"I was for a while. Medical discharge. Piles. Workin' in cold water helps. I'm shittin' better now." Voice flat, features bland, Jamieson maintained that thin line between fact and insolence, wanting Roland uncertain whether he'd been insulted.

The men crawled into two-man sleep tents and rolled into their blankets. In the middle of the night Jamieson awoke. O'Neill's blankets were flat. Maybe he was taking a piss. He crawled out, but didn't see him among the cooks and flunkies rustling up breakfast. He got a mug of coffee and walked to the bluff overlooking the river, where he squatted, making out two men a short way downriver. When Gerard hauled himself up from the bank, Jamieson retreated to hunker by the fire, watching him squirm into a tent. Jamieson was feigning sleep when O'Neill crawled back into their tent.

The next day, pushing logs down the Joe, he brooded over the image of O'Neill and Gerard conversing until every taste and color of inference had been extracted. Hours later, he remained baffled.

MacLean's river drivers spent the following day walking along the Joe, prying logs off banks and sand bars. Jamieson and O'Neill remained upriver pushing logs. When they tramped into the rag camp that had moved with the main contingent of men farther downriver, instead of finding the crew squatting around the fire or hunched on rocks and logs, eating, they spotted them bunched in a small meadow farther down the tote path.

Curiosity took them past the camp and down the narrow trail. Beyond a large knot of men, Jamieson glimpsed the red hair of a woman standing in a wagon bed. A few yards more and he identified her, but a moment passed before his tired brain figured out what she was up to.

"Goddamn," he breathed. "Katie's a bold one."

The red silk dress clung to her hips, its silk fringe drooping low off her chest. She braced the backs of her legs against the wagon seat as she mesmerized the men with smutty jokes like some lowlife vaudeville comedienne.

"Hey boys, you hear the one about the gal from a hot pillow joint in Spokane? She slaps down a couple of pints of moonshine on the counter and says to the clerk, 'I need some dough. I've gotta sell this . . ." Her kohled eyes sought those of lumberjacks standing below her. ". . or my ass."

The men whooped, slapping one another's backs. Supper was forgotten, the next day's log drive out of mind. Katie wasn't alone. Two girls in contrasting bright outfits posed behind her in the wagon bed. Three tents sat side by side beyond a pair of unharnessed mules grazing in the small meadow.

Resting her hand on the back of the wagon seat, Katie turned to indicate an olive-skinned girl, long dark hair curling down her back. "We're here for your pleasure, gents. We've got a bearded lady here. Show 'em, Zada." On cue the girl drew up her dress past her garters to show she wore nothing over the full thatch between her thighs. The dress slipped back down before the men could fully absorb the sight.

A man called out, "I want that bearded clam!"

Standing beside Jamieson, O'Neill breathed, "A furry Mary," and started forward for a better look. The men's roar and their own surge defeated him; he stepped back and folded his arms to watch.

A young flunky in front must have grabbed his wet crotch in embarrassment because Katie called out, "Hey, you rang the gong before paying." This brought hearty laughs from the men. "But, say, fellas . . . maybe you like 'em neat. Show the nice men what you've got, Jill." The other girl turned toward the men and slowly drew up her frock to show herself almost hairless. Although their eyes were glued to the right spot, once again a glimpse was all they got.

"I like that unbearded oyster," a man yelled out. Katie swished a hip at them to regain their attention. "So, we've got treasure boxes down here, gents." Sliding her hand down the front of her dress, she fluttered lacquered fingers over her sweet spot. "And we're here to let you fill 'em."

The lumberjacks cheered and stamped their feet, working themselves up. It was almost more joy than they could stand when Katie turned sideways and bent over, revealing pink silk stockings up to her garters, red silk tightening over her round rump, obvious to all that nothing lay between silk and skin.

Reaching into a wood crate behind the seat, she pulled out two pint bottles, swung around and held them up for the men to see.

The bottle tops were pasted with familiar green stamps -- Canadian whiskey bottled in bond. It was some time since the men had seen other than local hooch. Murmuring with desire, they pressed forward. Katie set one bottle on the wagon seat and broke the seal on the other; pulled the cork-rimmed glass stopper out with her teeth, drawing approving whistles. She removed the cork from her rouged mouth and slowly licked it before she tossed it into the multitude below.

When the grabbing and shoving subsided, a bearded jack held it up and kissed it before he dropped it into a shirt pocket. Smiling brightly, Katie held out the open bottle. "Any of you men care for some honest-to-goodness booze you can trust?" Male voices rumbled throatily in earnest need. "Well, we're settin' up a bar and serving real Canadian Club along with some lovin'. Any of you real men want some lovin?" Wolf whistles and hoots preceded obscene gestures. Silent men of the forest gave tongue to expressions seldom heard outside saloons and whorehouses, which didn't offend these good-for-what's-ailing-you women. Katie shouted, "Get ready for the party!" Each of her girls held out a hand for a man to lift her down, pay her, and accompany her into a tent. The two men nearest got first pleasure. Katie's driver, a gray old crag of a man, pulled down the wagon tail and poured whiskey into shot glasses. Any man with a dollar, silver or paper, got a shot. He deposited their tender into a money belt around his waist, and filled more glasses. Men were dropping to the ground to tug off boots, the only safe place to keep folding bills.

O'Neill raised shaggy brows at Jamieson, giving his black eyes a surprised look. "She's a show-stopper," he said in admiration. "The Ol' Man wouldn't be likin' this were he here." Jamieson stood impassive, mouth humorless, arms folded. "Well then," O'Neill added, "I'm for gettin' meself a drink."

He pushed his way up to the makeshift bar and put a silver dollar into Katie's hand. She grinned down at him and they exchanged some words before he downed the shot of whiskey. A few minutes later he wandered back, but didn't say anything until, looking up the river trail, he dug an elbow into Jamieson's side. "Speak of the divil an' ye see his tail. Here comes trouble certain."

Riding down the trail were Alonzo MacLean on that large buckskin and Fats Gerard trailing behind. They'd been upcreek at the main camp.

Jamieson took in the blissful Katie handing out drinks while MacLean's horse moved slowly through the crowd toward the wagon. Men nudged one another and murmured warnings, which caught Katie's attention. She straightened and looked at MacLean riding toward her; dropped her eyes to study the bottle in her hand, then picked up a shot glass and filled it.

Jamieson said to O'Neill, "This isn't going to be pretty."

"'Tis not MacLean's land she's camped on."

River drivers stepped aside, making way for the buckskin, then closed behind it. MacLean halted the horse opposite Katie to cast a menacing blue look on her. She tipped up her chin, smiled too widely and held out the shot of whiskey. MacLean's face turned an angry red. What he was about to say died behind his teeth when he saw one of his men exit a tent.

The partially-dressed whore invitingly held up the canvas flap and called out, "Who's next?" Giant Kid loitering nearby shot up a long arm and she beckoned him. "Duck on in here, big fella."

"Stop!" MacLean roared, spurring his mount through scattering men until he'd positioned it between the tents and the majority of his crew. "I won't have this going on here. You men get back to camp. Save it for St. Joe City." Giant Kid stood rooted, looking from the sweet-faced, chemise-clad girl to the Ol' Man a few feet away who, for once, towered over him. MacLean swiveled in his saddle to glare at Katie. "You and your gals clear out . . . the whiskey, too. I won't have this monkey business on my drive."

Katie thumped the bottle down on the wagon seat, slapped her hands against red silken hips and glared over the men's heads at MacLean. "It took us all day to get here!" She stamped a foot. "We're camping here with two cases of whiskey for thirsty men!"

"Don't leave," a driver bawled. "Not 'till I get my wick dipped."

MacLean didn't waste time swearing. He spat out each word. "Those tents . . . burn 'em down." The men stared, but no one moved.

Picking up an unopened bottle by its neck, Katie raised it like a club, a poor weapon for the distance between them. She yelled, "You can't do that!"

MacLean shouted back, "The hell I can't! You're not gonna get my boys drunk and give 'em the clap. I won't have it. No whore is gonna interfere with my drive." He glared at the men. "I said burn down those tents!" Turning in his saddle, he appeared to be searching for someone. Must have spotted the drive boss down the trail next to the cook tent, for he spurred his horse across the meadow, followed by Gerard.

While observing MacLean argue with the drive boss, who appeared to be trying to reason with him, Jamieson's attention shifted to Gerard, who'd pulled a piece of wood from the cook fire, waving its burning tip to get MacLean's attention. The Ol' Man jerked his head toward Katie's encampment.

O'Neill, also, was watching. "Sure didn't I said t'would be trouble? We can try an' stop 'em - fists aplenty here."

From where he stood at the edge of the crowd, Jamieson watched the hulking Gerard walking stiff and saddle sore toward the tents, the burning brand thrust ahead. Shifted his gaze toward a pale defiant Katie standing in the wagon bed. Fists balled at his sides, he shook his head. "No . . . two businesses competing for the same men. Bad timing on her part."

As Gerard advanced over uneven ground toward the tents, his stride limbered up; the ghost of a smile lay on his thin-lipped mouth. The bastard was enjoying this.

"You son-of-a-bitch!" Katie shrieked. Whiskey bottle still in her fist, she clambered down from the wagon, men's hands all over her to assist. "Stay away from my tents!" The open bottle on the wagon seat disappeared into the crowd.

Held back by a couple of river drivers, she leaned toward Gerard, brandishing the bottle, calling him every low-down name she knew. He reached the first tent and touched fire to the bottom corner. Only then did he turn silver eyes to stare her down. Nothing less than a gun would hinder him now. He disappeared behind the first tent to torch the next one.

The first tent's canvas appeared only singed, a small black spot growing larger; then it burst into flame. Tearing away hands holding her, Katie dropped the bottle and darted into the tent, emerging with a small white dog, which she thrust into the out-stretched hands of the girl who'd dashed from the smoking second tent, carrying most of her clothing in a bundle. Katie turned to go back into the tent, but a couple of men dragged her out of danger.

MacLean stomped among his men with smoldering eyes, daring anyone to interfere. "Put them women in that wagon and get 'em out of here."

The third girl managed to drag a case of whiskey out of the farthest tent, shrieking at anyone reaching down to help, finally sitting on the bottles to protect them. The elderly driver set her aside and managed to pick up the box, shoving it across the tailgate into the wagon.

Jamieson moved off a few paces to sit on a rock, back turned to the small inferno, not prepared to confront Gerard and ashamed to have Katie see him. As men pulled the wagon away from the burning tents, iron wheels protested, mules squealed, and harness jangled. Borne aloft by fire gasses, flakes of blackened canvas and bedding floated down. Gerard stood admiring his work, still fisting the burning brand. When Jamieson's turned his eyes back, he followed the cant of Gerard's head and saw he was watching Katie.

Unlacing and pulling off a caulked boot, from under its insole Jamieson retrieved a thin packet wrapped in a small piece of oilcloth. Out of this he drew two twenty dollar bills that had seen better days and handed them to O'Neill. "How about you go over and give these to Katie . . . Kate. It'll help her replace some of what she lost in the tents. She's a gambler and it might've been most everything she owned."

"Except the whiskey."

"Yeah, except the whiskey."

O'Neill approached the wagon where Katie sat beside the driver, clutching her little dog. The two girls crouched behind her. With the bedding gone, they had only the whiskey cases on which to sit.

Too far off to hear O'Neill, Jamieson watched him reach up and take her small hand, folding it around the bills. O'Neill cocked his chin over his shoulder and she looked across the meadow at Jamieson. Their eyes met and she raised her other hand in a forlorn little wave. The mules lurched off and the wagon jolted and bumped down the tote trail, which until now only pack mules had trod this far up the St. Joe. Katie might have broken new trail, but she'd picked the wrong lumberman to tangle with. Alonzo MacLean was a determined and desperate man. Jamieson studied MacLean standing at the edge of the meadow with folded arms, watching the wagon of whores leave before stomping back to camp.

Chapter 59
St. Joe City

Once past swiftwater, the logs carpeting the river floated easily until a spill dam up a creek released a head of water, sending a wave far down the river to wash logs up on banks and into muddy sloughs. Only muscle power refloated the round stuff.

The Ol' Man played mischief with the other lumber companies at Scott Slough, where logs had scattered into tall grass and mud. "You boys sit tight. Let them other outfits do the work." To get to their own logs, other crews first had to roll out MacLean's, some of the last logs pushed onto the Joe.

The MacLean crew grouped across the river, smoking and resting, calling out encouragement to men slogging in the mud. O'Neill, with his distinctive brogue, was especially creative in catcalls. Although they'd hoped for a free day, farther down the river many of MacLean's logs ran aground among cottonwoods on a shallow island, and they spent hours getting them back into the river.

A few days later they reached St. Joe City, their watering hole of choice. Tonight drivers of five lumber companies would claim the town, living up to their sobriquet of river pigs.

Jamieson looked for O'Neill, who'd been moving boomsticks around brails of logs, while others coupled them with short chains in preparation for a tugboat to tow the corralled logs to St. Maries, where they'd be sorted out. Where had he disappeared to? Maybe the Big Timber in search of Katie. He jammed his peavey into the river bank and leaned on it to rest his back. Wet from the waist down, standing in squishy boots, he wanted food more than a drink.

Sounds of celebration came from the rutted track called Grand Avenue. Why do the citizens of a dot on a railroad map give such a grandiose name to the muddy street passing through it? Maybe the Milwaukee platted it before plunking down the depot.

A knot of drivers passed him, then stopped to point upriver. He looked up to see the lumbering mastiff, Titus. Behind him Addie rode astride a bay mare and leading three mules. In a loose white shirt, jodhpurs and boots, and that old hat she favored, the woman looked comfortable on a horse. While she'd spent the day ambling along the river trail, he'd been balancing on numb feet, wrestling logs off sand bars, floating them back into the current. Handing off his peavey, he angled across the tracks. He'd better keep an eye out for her. She'd chosen the wrong day to come into town.

The locomotive drummed around a bend on its approach to the depot, whistle wailing and bell clanging. Long ears flattening, the mules panicked, bucking and jumping about. Bursts of steam drowned out their squeals. Addie had no loads to spill, but could she handle them? Too far off to offer help, Jamieson dug in his spikes and picked up his pace.

Addie lashed her crop across the lead jenny's nose. Shrieking steel wheels covered her yell, but the jenny stopped her antics. Once the animal fell in line, the two mules behind calmed down. Jamieson watched the tableaux of Titus, Addie and three mules parading down two blocks of false front buildings toward the livery stable. Carousing men scattered.

A shaggy-haired driver hooted, "Git a load of that dawg!" He rolled out of line outside a barber shop and clomped into the street. Prowling a few yards ahead of Addie's mare, Titus swung his head from side to side, eyes beneath wrinkled brow challenging all comers. "Is that fucker part bear?" The shaggy driver looked up, saw he addressed a woman, and went slack-jawed. He choked out., "Beg pardon, ma'am." Still, he captured the mare's bridle and forced Addie to stop, inciting the mules to complain loudly. More than a little drunk, he slurred, "What kinda dawg ya got?"

Addie kicked the mare and jerked the reins, trying to go forward. "The kind that will take off your leg if you don't let go." Hearing her, Titus swung around and released a loud growl, followed by ear-splitting barking as he rushed back. The drunk threw up both hands. When the mastiff gave a warning lunge, the man dropped them to his crotch. Afraid to turn his back, only his caulked boots kept him upright as he staggered back in retreat, bawling, "Call 'im off!"

"Don't look in his eyes," Addie called out, intent on dealing with the mules. "Walk away!"

The man reached the boardwalk amid hoots and laughter. With absurd bravado, he shouted, "I ain't afraid of that dawg. Where's my axe?"

Jamieson reached Addie's mare and then Titus did lunge, nearly knocking him down in slobbering friendliness. "Hey, you big brute." He grabbed his collar to avoid a hard snout doing injury and smiled up at Addie. "Long ride in, Boss Lady?"

She burst out, "Do all mules hate trains? Every train that passed made them crazy."

He reached up for the rope dallied around her saddle horn. "Go on. I'll bring them along." The jenny rolled her eyes as he snubbed up the line and seized her halter, but allowed him to lead her down the street. When the second mule jumped forward, trying to step on his boot heels, he understood the cause of Addie's difficulty. The rope line between mules was too long. After stabling the animals, the mules immediately started a racket, kicking stalls, squealing at whatever moved.

Jamieson carried Addie's saddlebags over a shoulder. She searched the knots of men. "Where's Mally?"

"Oh, he's around, probably getting supper." He grasped the mastiff's collar. "I'll take Titus into the butcher's and get him a bone. You go on to the mercantile. We'll catch up." Initially, Titus wanted to follow Addie, but when the shop door opened, the odor of raw meat decided him and he tried to rush in ahead of Jamieson. When they came out, the dog had a meaty sheep shank clamped between his jaws.

Jamieson slowed. Down the street Addie's and Dovey's grim-looking profiles were facing off in front of the mercantile. An apron-clad boy was tying knapsacks to Dovey's saddle, unmindful of the old mare's shifting weight until she stepped on his toes. He yelped and hobbled to the wooden steps, but the women paid him no mind.

Titus would have trotted up to Addie with his prize, but Jamieson kept him in tow. They approached behind her, close enough for him to hear some of what Dovey said.

". . . cuttin' over the property line into my trees . . . infringin' on my timber holdings . . ." Chin cocked, she glared up at Addie.

He couldn't hear Addie, only Dovey's retort. "You think comin' to cook for MacLean's would let me keep an eye on where the cuttin's going on? Isn't that the hen invited into the fox's lair. I spent fifteen years protectin' my holdings from the MacLeans. No thank you, Mrs. MacLean." She swung away and saw the boy examining his toes. "Get up, Henry. I need you to lead Prissy to the depot."

Maybe Addie had uttered Jamieson's name and it brought Dovey up short. Titus padded up to drop the mutton bone at Addie's feet, drool puddling the dust.

Dovey swung around on Addie, but then stopped short to stare. "Where did that brute come from?"

"This is Titus." Addie gestured toward the bearded Jamieson. "And this is . . ."

Jamieson interrupted, aware of drivers milling nearby, "Name's Mac. Mac James."

Dovey's eyes widened before her face closed up like a faded fan. "How do." She stuck out her small hard hand. "I'm Dovey Blake." A couple of heartbeats passed and then she said, "I'm gonna be cookin' for you men."

"That sure will be fine."

"I might bring a girl with me. Hard worker. You got room for another female up there?"

Recovering from her surprise, Addie gushed, "Yes we do, and I'll be glad for more help."

Dovey moved in on her then, ignoring the slobbering mound of dog. She cupped a hand to her mouth. "Are you two on speaking terms again?"

Addie glanced at Jamieson. "It seems we are."

"Tell her," he ordered.

"Mac saved my honor when I was attacked by some tramps."

"And probably your life."

"And probably my life," she amended. "He and my cousin, Mally."

Dovey looked at Jamieson. "Mrs. MacLean's cousin?"

"My logging partner. You'll meet him. Malachi O'Neill." He said it cheerfully, but narrowed his eyes, hoping to warn

Dovey off. She knew he was undercover, but that was all she knew.

Her eyelids fluttered. "Well now, ain't that somethin'." She turned to study her mare, still wearing a shaggy winter coat. "Well, I've talked long enough. Gotta put this mare in a boxcar so's I can get home. Big yeller moon coming up early . . . why I come for supplies today."

Chapter 60

Intending to stay across the river at the cabin, Addie purchased staples and more meat for Titus. Jamieson trailed along, carrying her saddlebags and purchases.

She asked, "Are you heading back to the rag camp tonight?"

"Thought I'd see the sights before rounding up your cousin to head back up the Marble. There are more logs to push down it."

The ferryman wasn't home, but his wife allowed them to borrow a boat.

"I'll pole you over."

"And I'll cook you some supper. You must be hungry."

"I'm feelin' a might gaunt, it's true."

It satisfied him to be alone with her, poling across the slow-moving current. He hoped he didn't smell rank, but only of river water and honest sweat. And wished he wasn't so tired. Bruised thighs, scraped knees and shins throbbed beneath paraffined denims. Addie sat in the bow studying the mass of logs, occasionally meeting his eyes. Titus sat between them, eyes fastened on his bone held captive between her boots.

He poled between brails anchored by boomsticks, alert for submerged logs or late-comers. The sounds of carousing drivers grew distant, replaced by water slapping booms in which corralled logs rubbed and scraped, yearning to break loose to join the current sliding past.

Jamieson accepted another mug of hot tea. "Glad to get the taste of the river out of my mouth." He was working on a second plate of fried eggs, bacon, bread and butter, hoping Addie wouldn't think him rude for eating most of her provisions. She of all people knew how much food a lumberjack had to consume. Lord help him if he added the sin of gluttony to her list of ticks against him.

"I don't know why I asked Dovey to come cook for us," she pondered, sipping her tea. "It was sort of spontaneous. I was surprised by her hostility toward MacLean Lumber. She accused us of cutting her trees. And then you came." She snapped her fingers. "And just like that she changed her mind. She must miss you."

How much should he tell her about the MacLean brothers' history? "Dovey has cause to be hostile. It's an old quarrel." He raked a hand through too-long hair, wishing he looked better. She was beautiful in lantern light, blue eyes luminous. "Have you heard about the Marble Creek timber war back in aught four and five, when the MacLean brothers hired thugs to jump homesteaders' claims?"

Her eyes widened, then narrowed, and she shook her head. "Are you accusing my husband and brother-in-law of committing unlawful acts? When timber was everywhere for the taking?"

Jamieson couldn't set her straight about much, but he could about the history of the Joe Country. "A couple of roughies were ambushed by unknown homesteaders. Common talk was the dead men were working for the MacLeans, scaring families off their claims. Dovey was using the Timber and Stone Act to prove up her quarter section and she wasn't going to let the MacLean brothers run her off." He almost added, *Can't you guess why?* Instead, he said, "Now she owns twice the amount of her original claim. A neighbor of hers . . . he taught me to hunt . . . well, they both did. He died a few years back and willed her his 160 acres, all of it covered with prime white pine. The Ol' Man must lick his chops whenever he gets near the Blake holding, but it's not for sale."

"But that was so long ago. Why would she still hold a grudge?"

"Some years back I was visiting her and here comes Alonzo MacLean up the trail, only I didn't know who it was then. She locked the door and made me crawl under the bed, and she was right behind me. She pulled the covers to the floor so he couldn't see us if he looked through the window. I was laughing myself sick under there, trying to be quiet, trying to keep my long legs curled up to my chest." He turned serious. "Dovey, though, she was close to being scared. And there isn't much that scares that woman."

"She's bound to run into Alonzo in camp."

"Yeah, I know. I was surprised she agreed to come."

"It's because of you."

He wiped yellow yolk from his plate with a last bite of bread. "Well, I don't know if I'm the reason. She might have taken pity on your being the only woman in camp. She liked you pretty well back at Maud's."

"Until I excoriated you in front of her," said with a hint of apology in her voice.

"Called me a coward to boot," he joked, ignoring the shadow of hurt her words had caused, knowing he'd brought it down on himself. He took in the tilt of her face in the light, the curve of her lips, the deep wells of her eyes.

And then she said his name. "Robert Jamieson."

Something was coming to ruin the moment and maybe his entire day.

"Robbie." While she hesitated, he pulled out his tools of artifice -- the poker face, the bland smile -- preparing himself. "What are you doing here?"

Did O'Neil put her up to this? He hedged, "You invited me for supper, remember?"

"I mean why are you working for MacLean's? Of all the places you could have run to when you deserted, why did you come here?"

He told her the truth. "I came with that cousin of yours. He chose where to look for work, as far away from the law as we could get. I hoped the Army wouldn't come snooping around."

"You're an experienced logger. Where did you learn to do that?"

"In Michigan during summers while I was at the university there."

"A college man. But you became a detective." She folded her hands, looking intently at him. "I know nothing about you."

"You know more than most."

She self-consciously lifted her hair. "You could have done anything with your life."

Her words made him uncomfortable. "Have you told O'Neill I was a Pinkerton?"

"No. He can be quite a talker. Might let it slip to the wrong person sometime. I wouldn't want to put you in danger. You have enough troubles."

"Darn right."

Robbie's face across the table mesmerized Addie. Despite being disheveled, it could have been Jerome's. Brown eyes instead of blue, but their color was insignificant in lamplight. He sounded like Jerome, that same timbre in his voice.

"Thank you for supper. As Irish would say, ye're a grand cook."

I cut you out of your inheritance. You should be driving logs for yourself, not for Alonzo and me. What have I done? I can't tell you, not here alone. I've seen your anger. You might hurt me. "I suppose you're going now."

"I should go hunt up Irish, though I expect he can take care of himself. I'm too bushed to raise Cain."

"If you want to bed down out here, I'll give you a couple of blankets and a pillow."

"Right now I wouldn't mind a place beside Titus." He gave her that slow smile. "Seriously, Addie, I wouldn't want to risk your reputation if someone saw me coming out the door in the morning."

"Well, if you do find Mally, bring him with you to pole me back across and I'll fix the two of you breakfast."

Chapter 61

Pushing aside an errant log, Jamieson poled back across, his way illuminated by a full moon and lights from a hotel and other buildings on the St. Joe City side.

He expected to find O'Neill at the Tall Timber and wanted to see Katie to discover if she'd learned anything. He suspected O'Neill had sought her out. Yelling and breaking glass came through the open door as he approached. Bad timing. He pulled his gloves from a back pocket, not wanting to tear up his hands in a fist fight while trying to get Irish out of there. Pushing through reeling bodies, crashing chairs, and general mayhem, he spotted O'Neill, his back against the bar, defending himself against two river pigs. A man's partner is supposed to protect his back, but now it would have to be his side. Jamieson had one advantage. He wasn't drunk.

Moving in on the larger assailant, he threw a hard right hook, landing it under his left ear. The driver turned from O'Neill, growling in Scandinavian, and Jamieson threw a straight left at his heart. Irritated, the man swung a solid punch; Jamieson backed off, drawing him away from O'Neill. He feinted toward the man's stomach and, when the driver dropped his hands, he hooked a right, making contact under his chin, knocking his head back. It rocked forward again and he clipped Jamieson above an ear, making his head ring. The man punched solidly and Jamieson reverted to his boxing days at school, moving in on him, throwing fast straight hits. The man tried for a head hold, but Jamieson pounded him hard in the gut. They backed off each other. When Jamieson moved in again, he hit the Scandinavian every place he found open until the man bent in the middle, wrapped his arms around himself and gasped, "Done!" Jamieson allowed him to stagger away.

Blood running from his nose, O'Neill and his assailant moved away from the bar. The driver, shorter than O'Neill, kicked up with both feet, driving his boots at O'Neill's face, trying to put the caulks to him, forgetting they were embedded in cedar shakes. They landed on O'Neill's chest, knocking him back against the bar, the driver thudding on his back in sawdust. Jamieson had seen French-Canadians in Michigan make those quick-as-lightning moves. O'Neill moved in to stomp him, but tripped on his own shakes and fell on top. It became an all-out fight then. The room quieted as tired and injured brawlers watched what seemed a fight to the death as first one man and then the other gained superiority, smashing bloodied knuckles into pulped faces. Unwieldy shakes prevented caulks from slashing and gouging, but didn't protect the men's shins from being bloodied.

Jamieson saw the barkeep rounding the bar with a baseball bat and yelled, "Look out! He's got a knife!"

They separated, dripping blood, chests heaving. Neither saw a knife in the other's fist, but they'd had enough.

Grabbing O'Neill's suspenders, Jamieson pulled him to his feet. Punch drunk, O'Neill shouted at the Frenchie, "To the divil with ye. I'll chew off yer balls next time we meet." Jamieson hauled him across the room, followed by some of MacLean's drivers.

The Canadian shouted, "You, Irishman, I'm cut out de tongue . . . me . . . next time."

Katie stood at the top of the stairs. As he dragged O'Neill to the door, he angled his chin up at her, a sort of signal. She shook her head and he took it to mean O'Neill hadn't told her anything relevant.

When he got O'Neill outside, his throbbing ear felt double its size; he fingered a cut under an eye, another on a cheekbone. "What the hell was that about?"

"How in hell would I be knowin' that?" O'Neill tipped up his face, gagging on blood running down his throat. He pulled his bandanna from around his throat to pinch his bleeding nose.

"You're comin' with me, Irish. Your cousin's at her cabin. I'll take you across so she can patch you up. She's invited us for breakfast."

Faces bruised and swollen, Jamieson and O'Neill sat in the open doorway of an eastbound freight. Most of the drive crew had ridden an earlier one back to Marble Creek Station, or would take a later one, depending on soberness. The two men had packed up Addie's mules and loaded them and the mare into a boxcar, while Addie traveled by coach.

Jamieson asked, "Did you see Kate last night?"

"Ah no, she was busy. Well now, I bought her a drink, but then she was busy."

Jamieson grunted, not quite believing him.

*   *

Two days later, on June 22, a tugboat hauled brails of logs the fourteen miles from St. Joe City to St. Maries and the MacLean Lumber Mill. MacLean oversaw men pushing the special twenty-four-foot logs from the river to the pond beside the mill, to be cut according to the schedule of dimensions prepared by the National Airplane Committee. They'd be kiln dried before being shipped to a factory where warplanes were being built. MacLean fretted over the days growing shorter. He left the mill in the capable hands of his manager and headed back to camp. He'd push the men to work faster.

Chapter 62
June, 1918

Katie had allowed O'Neill to cuddle her longer than normal before sending him down to the saloon and into that brawl.

He said, "I'm thinkin', Kate, ye're the type of woman likes a bit of adventure," and she agreed. He asked if she was ready to help Ireland and she said she was. Holding her against his chest, he whispered what he wanted her to do.

So, here she was, settled on the Milwaukee Road's fancy *Columbian,* carrying a secret message, regretting only that her destination was Butte, Montana.

In early evening she climbed the steep steps of St. Mary's church. A smoky haze making a bloody westering sun meant Butte's men were fully employed in mines and smelters. Inside, the church's familiarity made her ache. Stained glass figures of Christ, Mary and the saints spangled tall windows. Her fellow sinners waited for confession, the pine door at the center of the confessional ajar, the priest late. Kneeling in a back pew, she waited, too.

After blessing himself before the altar, Father Hannan hurried up a side aisle. Katie dropped her face in holy fear of being recognized. No one would mistake her for a miner's wife or daughter in her linen suit and pert little hat. O'Neill had warned, "Be cautious, lest someone be listenin'." No one loitering outside the maroon curtains, hoping to overhear a bit of gossip, was going to catch what she had to say. She would wait them out and go last.

Natural light faded. Votive candles flickered, silent prayers for the souls of miners – living and dead – and for soldiers in France – living and dead.

She didn't pray, knowing her words wouldn't pass through the door God closed on her years before. She was the last person to part the curtain and kneel in darkness with folded hands below the closed grill. Father Hannan's lilt was assisting an old woman through an Act of Contrition the "pur-r soul" couldn't properly remember. A moment later the panel behind the grill slid open and she knew he'd smoked a pipe after supper.

Like a child pushed out on stage to play a part, she murmured, "In the name of the Father and of the Son and of the Holy Ghost, amen." Without prompting from the wings, she continued, "Bless me, Father, for I have sinned." Stricken by her unintended words, she stopped short, and then whispered, "Father, I have a message for you. It's why I came."

"Go on."

"The bodies are to be shipped in coffins July ninth on the 11:45 morning freight from Butte. Destination St. Joe City. Himself will come to Butte to accompany the dearly departed." She trailed off with, "That's how he told me to say it."

"Ah, I see." Father Hannan whispered. "July ninth, 11:45 of the mornin'."

"Yes."

"Ah." A breath later, "As long as ye're here, are ye prepared to make a good confession?"

Her voice caught. "It won't do me no good, Father. I'm savin' my money and I'll be gettin' out of the life soon enough."

"I'm knowin' ye, aye?"

"Yes, Father."

"Brenda Sullivan?"

"Yes, Father." Of course he knew her. He had direct access to God -- and probably had spotted her before he entered the confessional.

"'Twas growin' up in Dublin Gulch put a crack in yer soul, Brenda. Ye hadn't the strength to mend it because ye were so young and unknowin'. 'Twasn't yer fault yer soul let in all that sin and wantonness. Not then. But afore Satan sinks his talons into ye for good, ye must mend your soul. 'Tis I'm not condemnin' ye, Brenda. I'm warnin' ye. Turn back for yer soul's sake."

He'd said much same that time he came to see her at the Irish World. Probably he repeated it to some fallen girl every few months. "Ah, Father, long-winded as ever. How are my brothers?"

Not a man easily offended, he replied, "As full of fire as ever. And Irish patriotism. Ye're an auntie three times."

"I'm glad for them." She prepared to rise.

"Well now, if ye're not ready to be absolved of yer sins, at least let me bless ye. Say an Act of Contrition now with me, Brenda."

She joined her husky voice with his and felt better for it. Someday she'd come back and confess to him. And wouldn't he be glad to know he saved a "pur-r soul" from going to hell.

Chapter 63

A wide straw hat shaded the Widow Blake's face when she rode into camp, knapsacks hanging down her mare's sides and a roll of quilts tied behind the saddle. A slip of a girl, blanket pack lashed to her back, led Dovey's Jersey cow and bawling calf. The Jersey's bell and full-voiced calf brought Addie and her staff out of the cookhouse.

"Well, here I am, in the camp of the enemy." Dovey hooked a thumb at the girl. "That's Tessa Ranney. Her ma and I thought it was time she got out in the world."

"Welcome, Tessa" Addie helped Dovey dismount. "There's a cot for you next to Mrs. Blake's."

Dovey stretched her back and rubbed her thigh. "I'm supposed to make sure she keeps some sense around the men."

Addie laughed. "You'll find them too old." She looked beyond the Jersey gently butting Tessa while the calf nursed. Alonzo had come out of his office.

Not certain Dovey would come, she'd asked Polite John and the flunkies to make sleeping arrangements, but cautioned them to keep it to themselves. Out of a new loyalty to her, they apparently had. Alonzo appeared welcoming, but puzzled. "Mrs. Blake, this is my brother-in-law, Alonzo MacLean." He tipped his hat and Dovey dipped her head, the straw brim shading her face. "These are Mrs. Dovinia Blake and Miss Tessa Ranney, my new kitchen help." When he frowned on hearing Dovey's name, Addie rushed on, "Since you decided to log all summer and Pork Grease Eddie has the rag camp on the river, I need more help."

Face still shadowed, Dovey made no bones about her hostility. "That's right, I'm the woman whose timber you been sniffin' around these past fifteen years."

Feathers ruffled, he snapped, "I wouldn't put it that way." His eyes fastened on Addie. "How, where . . ."

"How did we meet?" Dreading a scene, Addie feigned a confident smile. "I met Mrs. Blake last winter in Spokane and discovered she owned property in the area. When I bumped into her at St. Joe City a few days back, I asked if she'd cook for us and she graciously consented. Tessa will wait tables."

Never one to miss an opportunity, Alonzo turned friendly. "You got some fine white pine, Miz Blake. Maybe we can talk business while you're here."

"I doubt it."

A flunky took the cow's rope to lead her to the meadow.

Alonzo cleared his throat. "Brung your cow an' calf an' horse. Expectin' us to provide for them, too?"

"That was our agreement," Addie interjected, "in exchange for milk and cream."

Polite John took up the knapsacks and quilts. "Follow me, ladies. I'll show ya where you'll sleep."

Before following them in, Addie looked at Alonzo. He hadn't recognized Dovey. Had she been wrong about the woman's identity? Was she only a homesteader whose timber he coveted? As she watched him, a startled look passed over his face. He turned and stomped back toward his office. Later, while working in the kitchen, she saw him peer through the open screen door as he passed.

* *

The next day Alonzo accosted Dovey limping toward the cookhouse with a bucket of potatoes. Standing nearly toe to toe, they failed to see Addie inside the meat storage. She froze in the act of reaching for a filch of bacon. Alonzo was irate. "Ya think you're sitting in the pear tree, you and that timber of yours."

"I know I am." Addie didn't doubt Dovey could stand up to him.

"Your timber's past prime. Twenty per cent of it blue with rot."

"The rot's only in the outer part, just like in your trees. You must take me for a fool not to know I got a thousand board feet per saw tree. You're runnin' out of timber on your holdin's and payin' to cut on government land. You listen good, Alonzo MacLean. I've got plans for my timber that don't include you."

Through a chink between logs Addie saw Dovey set down the bucket and straighten with fists clenched. Alonzo's hands were flattened against his thighs. The proud and the proud.

Alonzo snapped, "My timber will last for years. You got no plans. No family line to inherit it now. Thea is in Wallace an' we both know what she's doin' there."

"You leave Thea out of this!"

"And that ain't her name anymore, neither, is it?"

"After what you did, don't you even talk about her."

"Last time I saw ya, you and Violet was tryin' to raise that little girl in a whorehouse. Why she went back to that town is more than I can figure."

Dovey reared back and slapped him. He staggered and made a fist, but she stood ramrod straight, daring him to hit her. Beet red, he stomped away.

The muslin-wrapped bacon still hung from a hook above Addie's head. *What little girl? Who's Thea?*

Chapter 64

The stoves had been stoked for the night and bread pans designed to hold five 3-pound loaves set to rise on their overhead shelves. Addie opened the kitchen door to let Titus out one last time. She was ready for sleep.

The dog poised in the doorway, inhaled the night, then rushed into it barking and snarling. Too late she realized the earlier faint clatter of tin cans hadn't been a logger tossing away tobacco tins. She snatched the reflector lantern from the wall and ran toward the sounds of fierce fighting at the dump. The bear roared as the snarling mastiff's jaws locked on a sensitive part. Heedless for her own safety, Addie raised the lantern high, moving closer until it illuminated the writhing and tumbling heap. When she screamed Titus's name, the jumbled bodies separated and the terrified bear broke free to disappear into the dark, Titus at its heels. Addie yelled, "Titus! Come! Titus! Come!"

Alonzo appeared in his union suit wielding a rifle as Titus emerged from the shadows. He didn't see well at night and she shrieked, "Don't shoot my dog!"

Barking loudly, Titus staggered into the ring of light, his flanks dark and wet, but looking self-satisfied. Lumberjacks in partial states of dress appeared.

While Addie calmed the dog, Alonzo ordered, "You men go back to bed."

She looked at the deep lacerations. "I'll need some help here . . . he's really gashed."

"A little blood can make a big showing," Alonzo muttered, peering at the dog's wounds, "but I guess he'll need some stitchin'. You'll have to hog tie him first, though. Wouldn't want those fangs in me."

O'Neill stepped forward. "I'll help ye, Addie."

"I'll help, too," Jamieson offered, coming out of the shadows.

She warned, "He's terrible when strangers try to handle him. H e's never been hurt before."

"We'll muzzle him with a leather strap," Jamieson said. "Once we get him into the kitchen, maybe we can lay him on the cutting block." He looked around. "Anyone got a leather belt in his pack?" This was the land of suspenders.

"I got one," a man offered. "I'll go get it."

Addie inserted herself back into the preparations. "Alonzo, I'll need some of that bottle of whiskey you've got cached away."

"You can't use good whiskey on that dog, or are ya just hopin' to get him drunk enough to pass out so's you can work on him?"

Exasperated, she snapped, "That's not funny."

Jamieson broke in. "Maybe soap and water will be enough. I know how it feels to have whiskey poured into a wound. I wouldn't wish it on a dog." He caught her look and hurried on. "Those slashes are bleeding pretty good . . . that's a plus. Bound to be some abscessing, but he's young and tough. It was probably a young black bear."

Titus flopped down to lick his wounds. The logger returned with his belt and Addie muzzled the dog before leading him into the kitchen. Grabbing up linen towels, she draped them over the large piece of sanded stump they used as a chopping block. O'Neill and Jamieson picked him up like a side of beef and laid him on it. While Alonzo held his head, soothing him, Jamieson and O'Neill tied his legs together with towels. Addie located the first aid kit, washed her hands and, with a bottle of iodine, sterilized a curved needle, silk thread, and some catgut she found. Hesitating to pour iodine into the wounds, she liberally doused them with hydrogen peroxide, then used a sterilized chicken feather to clean out detritus.

While Jamieson and O'Neill held the dog's haunches and shoulders, Addie knotted the catgut, gritted her teeth, pulled torn muscle together, and began sewing up a deep gash. Jamieson dabbed away blood with a clean dishtowel as she thrust the curved needle through the muscle a few times before tying it off. While Alonzo held his great head, Titus growled, snarled and whined; he curled black lips over large fangs, trying to open his jaws to snap the buckled belt that was keeping them safe. After she'd sutured the muscle, Addie threaded the needle with iodine-stained silk thread, knotted and anchored it to dog hide at one end of the wound. Taking quick stitches, she pulled the jagged tear together until reaching the farther end, where she tied it off. While the men held him fast, Titus struggled and kicked, protesting and threatening with every sound he knew and some he discovered.

"How did you learn to do this?" Admiration was in Jamieson's voice, but she couldn't pause to savor it.

"I helped Dad sew up the horses on the farm when they'd get cut."

Addie stood back to view her work. Titus quieted, whining softly as Alonzo stroked him, telling him what a good dog he was.

"How about rubbing some iodine into those smaller puncture wounds?" Jamieson suggested. "Might do some good."

Addie held up red-stained, trembling hands. In the flickering light she couldn't discern between the dog's blood and the iodine. "Will you do it?"

"Be glad to." There was more whining and moaning while Jamieson dabbed iodine into the wounds, but Titus was tired, too, and gave only token rejoinders to the stinging.

When it was done, Alonzo stepped back. "We all could use some coffee." The bull cook and flunkies had been up for some time, Polite John having kept surprisingly tight control of himself at seeing his chopping block tainted by a bloody dog. Dovey had rekindled the fires and transferred Addie's pans of rising dough to a sideboard. A large enamel coffee pot rumbled and gurgled, emitting a fragrant mist. Titus was lifted down and Addie removed his muzzle. He turned immediately to lick his wounds.

Alonzo poured himself a mug of coffee and studied the dog. "I'll have the blacksmith rig up an iron yoke to keep him from getting at them stitches." He looked over at Addie. "You done good there, Addie gal. You can sew me up any time."

Jamieson was the last to leave. Reinvigorated by the coffee, Addie walked out with him and they paused at the woodpile. Stars were growing faint in the east as the sky paled. Titus limped over to sniff around the dump.

Addie yawned and covered her mouth, took a deep breath of chilled air and shivered. Her cuffs were damp from washing her hands. "It's dawn already. I'd better start mixing biscuit dough if you're going to have some for breakfast." She didn't turn to go in, but continued standing beside him.

As though she expected a rejoinder, he said, "Soon be time to head back into the woods." Arms folded, he seemed in no hurry to go anywhere. He looked east and then about the camp. An outline of stables and bunkhouse was taking shape. Alonzo had lighted a lantern in the office, its glow coming through the window the only sign of life in camp.

She knew Jamieson would be tired all day; hoped he wouldn't make a mistake in judgment and get hurt. "I'm really sorry Titus and I kept you from getting your sleep." Standing beside her he appeared strong and capable, the type of man a woman could rely on in normal times. "I wouldn't have managed as well, you know, if you hadn't been there."

"Glad I could help. Sleep's not important. I don't expect the bear will come back, but you might have one of the flunkies bury those cans deeper." He was reminding her of her position at camp as an owner, maybe implying she was responsible for what happened to Titus. Instead of resentment, she felt grateful he was looking out for her interests. Turning toward him, she smiled. "I'll do that."

Her hand rested on the wood pile and he placed his over it. It was hard and dry and warm. She looked away, but allowed her hand to remain under his. How much did he resemble Jerome? She wasn't certain any longer. He'd been nice looking in uniform, but this thought brought home the gravity of his situation. A small lump rose in her throat. He was a wanted man. Those words placed him outside normal society and filled her with foreboding. She mustn't think about a possible future with him. She slipped her hand out from under his, immediately missing his touch. Took care not to use his real name. "Thank you, Mac. Thank you very much . . . for everything."

Their tired eyes met. "You're welcome, Mrs. MacLean."

Titus returned to lick Addie's hand at her side and then Jamieson's. All was forgiven.

There came a drift of wings overhead as a hawk circled overhead. They looked up and when it swooped farther down the ridge, the sound its wings made diverged from the breeze soughing through tall pine.

After breakfast Addie went to the stable to ask the barn boss if he had any Germ Killer solution. Her father swore by it for his horses. When she entered, the scent of horse manure and harness oil, hay and oats, made her homesick. A few heavy horses turned to nicker. The barn boss was currying, but stopped to bring her a bottle of antiseptic, and she stayed to admire the horses as men harnessed them for the day's work.

"I love these horses," the boss said. He went by Oats; she didn't know whether it was his last name or his moniker. He bore a logger's smallpox – a face scarred by another logger's caulked boots. It was hard to imagine this gentle man getting into violent brawls. In a low voice he shared an unpleasant secret. "Someday the big horses will be gone." Added emphatically, "Not in my lifetime. Maybe in fifty years." She nodded and reached out to stroke the soft white nose of a large chestnut. "You know, I seen a gasoline tractor pulling a plow. It's just like with them gasoline automobiles. Lots of people don't want buggy horses no more. I say, what would a farm be without its horses? Lonely, that's what. Same here in the woods. No horses trailing logs? Hard to imagine, ain't it?"

"It is," she agreed. She watched him harness up and bring out the matched pair of chestnuts before taking the medicine bottle back to the kitchen. She'd bring sugar lumps for the horses on her next visit.

* *

On this crisp summer morning the Marble's waters remained dark and chilled and in shadow.

Logs were rushing downstream from an open spill dam when Jamieson walked out on a partially banked log to hook a timber caught in rocks before it caused a jam. His log rolled, plunging him into water so cold, he lost his breath. Dragged downstream, he flailed to the surface and sucked in a wet breath before going under again. He kicked rocks, which meant he was close to shore, but the Marble's frothing waters tumbled him and its roar confused him. He knew he was drowning. His outstretched peavey caught on a submerged root, jerking his arm straight from his shoulder. Holding the peavey in a death grip, he was swept horizontal. Breaking the surface, he pawed blindly toward the rocky bank. A hand grabbed his wrist and jerked him upward. As he gagged for a breath, his sodden woolens pulled him back under. Again the hand dragged him to the surface. Jamieson's reddened eyes met O'Neill's above. He saw regret in them and felt the Irishman's hand relax before it gripped harder.

"I have ye! Hold onto yer peavey now!" Using every muscle in powerful shoulders and back, O'Neill yanked him clear of a passing log; slammed him against rocks that scraped his forehead and banged his jaw. Jamieson heaved up water before managing a painful breath.

O'Neill was braced with his peavey jammed into a cleft rock. It took all of Jamieson's willpower not to release his peavey to claw at O'Neill's arm with both hands, to trust the man wouldn't let go of his own volition.

The current slackened and his legs angled down, finding footing. The killing logs had flowed past, but the rocks were slick. One misstep and he'd fall back into deep water. O'Neill's thoughts shone plain on his face. "Ye'll try the divil's patience, Mac. Sure ye're tryin' mine." With gut-churning clarity Jamieson realized O'Neill knew about him. Fats Gerard.

Waterlogged and raw, he was able to stand as the creek lowered and the waters slowed. He sputtered, "Not catty like you." It set him coughing.

"Ye know damn well 'tisn't what I mean."

Descending the rocky bank, Addie appeared behind O'Neill.

In a strangled voice, Jamieson coughed out, "If you push me back in, should you do it in front of your cousin?"

O'Neill glanced over his shoulder, released Jamieson's wrist and lifted his hat to her. Addie shrieked, reaching out her free hand. The Irishman wrenched his peavey free and thrust it at Jamieson. He grabbed it, freed his own peavey and pointed it up for someone -- which cousin didn't matter – to land him.

Pulled up the bank, he dropped to hands and knees in water-logged wool, retching and coughing up creek water. He mentally examined his battered body before sitting up to dislodge a flake of bark from between cheek and gum and pick it off his tongue. His throat felt like he'd swallowed ground glass and his chest hurt. Addie crouched beside him with frightened eyes. O'Neill sat a few feet away. "Thanks," he croaked.

"Oh, Robbie, I thought you'd drowned."

Having said his name, she looked at O'Neill. Arms wrapped about his knees, staring at water deceptively shallow and placid again, the Irishman said, "This creek's gonna take one of us sure."

"Not today." Jamieson shivered despite the warm sun. He reached out to touch Addie's hair, as though to convince himself he remained among the living. She clutched his wet face and kissed him hard, then rose in one swift movement and headed up the ridge toward camp, missing the path and crashing through brush.

"Lost my damn hat," Jamieson said.

When they walked into camp and passed MacLean standing outside his office, the man barked, "That's what partners are for, lookin' out for each other."

Chapter 65
Spokane, Washington

A door stood open beyond the Army clerk's empty desk. The name stenciled backward on frosted glass read *Capt. J. H. Dengel*. Inside the office, sitting in profile behind his desk, was a poster image of a yellow-haired and mustached Prussian officer, flicking a riding crop at flies. Stepping back, Frank Gerard wiped his face and neck with a handkerchief, taking a moment to recover from the hike up the stairs. Then he strolled into Dengel's office.

"You Captain Dengel?"

The officer turned. "I am. What do you want?"

"Maybe I have somethin' *you'll* want."

"You think so?"

But Gerard was closing the door. Without invitation he dropped into the chair in front of Dengel's desk. "Name's Frank Gerard. Detective."

Facing the window again, Dengel tapped the crop on his boot. "What do you have that I would want?"

Gerard placed his derby on Dengel's desk and folded his arms, waiting.

Dengel swiveled his chair. "You were saying?"

"Any information I possess about happenings in Butte that would interest the Army should be reported to you, that right?"

"What would you have that would interest the Army?"

Show him a bone. "Information about Ross rifles comin' down from Canada, intended for an Irish uprising."

Expressionless, Dengel put down his crop, opened a tablet and picked up a pencil. "What do you know about Ross rifles?"

Let him sniff the bone. "Only what some hard rocker told me over a beer. I heard a name. O'Neill. Malachi O'Neill."

Maybe Dengel flinched. "Go on."

"I can produce the miner."

The Prussian put down his pencil, swung back toward the window and crossed his knees. "I'm listening."

"Mind if I help myself to one of your cigars?" He lit up and took a few puffs, enjoying the fine Cuban taste. "Before we get back to this miner, I understand you had an undercover officer turn rogue on you. Robert Jamieson."

The one eye Gerard saw in profile widened a fraction. "Lieutenant Germer in Butte has become a gossip."

Gerard stretched his mouth around the cigar. "I'm tryin' to help ya, Captain. I knew Jamieson when we was at the Seattle Pinkerton agency. Untrustworthy. I run into him recently down on the St. Joe River frontin' as a lumberjack." He paused to take a puff.

"And?"

"And I heard that when you ordered him to bring in O'Neill, he refused. I also heard you sent troops up to MacLean's camp for the Wobbly, an' the two of 'em run off. I knew O'Neill from when I infiltrated the I.W.W. in Seattle. Even odds those two are in cahoots now. Jamieson's easily influenced by a stronger mind. You must've run into his type."

Dengel's voice matched his Teutonic eyes. "You made a serious accusation against an officer of the United States Army. Sounds like treason to me."

Gerard dug out a shiny gold badge and palmed it on Dengel's desk. "I'm an official operative of the American Protective League. I've got authority to round up a trouble-making Wobbly named Malachi O'Neill and turn him over to the sheriff at St. Maries." He took another puff, rolled the cigar between his fingers, admiring its feel. *Now toss him a piece of raw liver.* "'Course, I could turn him over to you, instead."

"Doing your patriotic duty, I suppose. I suspect you want something in return. A reward?"

"What if O'Neill's confederate interfered with my citizen's arrest and got in my way. You wouldn't make a fuss, would you?"

Dengel turned to consider him. "Sounds like you want carte blanche."

"How's that?" *Over-educated prick.*

"No controls. I take it you have a bad history with my officer. Is that right?"

"I just want an understanding is all." *Now I'm gonna make you a good dog.* "This miner in Butte's not tellin' me a thing. Holdin' out for a payoff from the feds. If you come to Butte, I think he'll squeal. You come and we'll all sit down and have a nice chat." He tapped his cigar and a ring of ash dropped to the tile floor.

Chapter 66

After supper some lumberjacks gathered to enjoy the high summer evening. Mountain air was cooling the hot day and birds were chirping their evensong. Dovey emerged from the kitchen to sit on a stump. She and Jamieson exchanged smiles.

The talk between two seasoned loggers turned to bears. "Ain't no grizzlies this side of the Montana line. Ain't never been one seen in modern times. Brown bear, now . . . they's in these parts and rough to run into. Nothin' cute 'bout 'em."

"I'm gonna politely disagree with ya there. Heard tell there's a big 'un east of here, the same one that killed that homesteadin' couple a few years back." He caught Dovey's eye. "Was you about when that couple was killed by that grizzly, Miz Blake?"

"I was. That was the year we had a blizzard in early October before I headed to Spokane for the winter. It was terrible what happened. They had two little kids."

Men squatting in caulked boots or hunkered on logs, whittling, looked over.

"Tell us what you reckoned about it, Miz Blake."

She folded work-worn hands on her lap and sorted her thoughts. "The day after it happened, the seven-year-old girl come through snow to a neighbor, sayin' her folks hadn't come home. Seems her pa had forgotten his rifle when he went to saw wood and her ma set out with it. Makes you wonder why she thought she had to take it to him. Later on, the girl heard a shot. Then nothin'."

Jamieson knew the story and settled back to watch her listeners' faces.

Dovey continued. "Appears they heard a bear nosin' 'round the cabin the night before. An' the neighbor, Ted Young, found a large track under the eaves that the snow hadn't covered. He took the kids down to the Vincent family and got some neighbors together with guns and dogs. Tessa's pa and brothers come with their bear dogs if I got that right. But it'd been snowin' all day and any tracks were covered. It was hard to figure out what happened. It's still a mystery."

She looked at the men, brown eyes bright, enjoying herself. "If any of ya think you can figure it out, here's what they found. Mr. Kramer, he was hangin' down the trunk of the tree, legs wedged in the crotch of two big branches. His coat was ripped off and his body torn up. An arm and his head were missin', and his trunk was chewed on. They figured he was up the tree and had shot the bear, but not killed it. He'd wedged his legs in the tree hanging onto that gun, and couldn't get back up. The bear swiped away the gun and attacked him. Or maybe he just dropped the gun. You can bet the talk went on all winter and then some. In the spring before I come back to my place, the snow started melting and neighbors began snoopin' around and someone found a piece of what they thought was his skull. Doc Barker down at St. Maries said it was the top of his skull. It still had hair on it and there was a bullet hole in it. Doc called it an exit wound. We heard those words for months through the Joe Country. Exit wound. The bullet had come out of the top of his head." She paused, but not long enough to spoil the kicker. "So, people scratched their heads and set to arguin' about whether that bear shot Mr. Kramer."

The men looked stunned, then hooted and slapped their legs; a few looked out toward the camp perimeter. A lumberjack yelped, "You're joshin' us! I thought it really happened."

In genuine sorrow, Dovey said, "God's truth, it happened all right."

From where he sat, Jamieson asked, "What kind of tree was it?" He had a theory about the Kramers' deaths.

"Well, not sure I know. Would it make a difference?"

He grinned at her, keeping his thoughts to himself, and she gave him a well-worn narrow look.

"And the wife," a whittler broke in, snapping shut his jackknife, "what about her?"

"Well, just what they expected. Parts of her showed up some ways away. The bear must of dragged her a fair piece. They found the rifle at the foot of the tree weltering in blood. Mr. Kramer had a hound, but no one ever saw it again."

While the men speculated among themselves, Jamieson wandered off to sit on a rock near the kitchen door, hoping

Addie would come out to enjoy the evening. Titus rose from a large bone and lumbered over for a man-size caress. He still wore a spiked collar to keep him from chewing on his nearly healed wounds.

"How ya doin', big fella?"

Stroking the dog, he envisioned what occurred as though watching a movie reel, needing no dialogue at the bottom of the screen.

Kramer worked out at his woodlot with saw and axe while the hound went exploring. He heard snarling, then a yelp when the grizzly sent the dog flying with one killing blow. He looked around for his rifle and realized in a cold sweat that, in carrying a tool in each hand, he'd forgotten it. He ran toward the cabin through snow, slipped and fell, regained his feet in a panic. Maybe he glimpsed the bear. Mrs. Kramer carrying his rifle was following his tracks through the forest and they met halfway. They heard the grizzly. Well, maybe they didn't hear it. He and O'Neill never heard it, only sensed it paralleling them through the trees above. Kramer formed a plan he hoped he had time for. They would climb that nearby pine. Its lowest branches were high overhead and that was bad, but maybe also good. He had his wife bend down and he used her back as a springboard to boost himself into the tree. Arranging himself, he jammed his legs into a crotch that would hold him tight. With death yards away, you can't plan, can't even think straight. Mrs. Kramer was terrified at being left on the ground. After giving her husband a back up, she grabbed up the rifle and aimed into the dark woods where trees were so large, even a grizzly could shield behind one. She was too far down for him to grab her hand, so he intended to pull her up by the rifle as she walked up rough bark. Leaning down, he yelled for her to hand it up and she obeyed. Grabbing the barrel, he started pulling her up, but her finger had remained on the trigger. The bullet entered under his chin and came out the top of his head. Mrs. Kramer fell back with the rifle in her hands, staring up in horror at his dangling body. Maybe she dropped the rifle and fled, or maybe just lay there in shock until the bear came and dragged her away. Later it returned for Mr. Kramer - the parts of him it could reach. Only a grizzly would do that.

Where was O'Neill? He would have enjoyed that story. Since pulling Jamieson from the Marble, he'd become withdrawn, no longer joking with other jacks, barely speaking to him. And it wasn't because Addie had kissed him. He had Canadian rifles on his mind.

Titus disappeared around the cookhouse and Jamieson followed, expecting to find Addie. He spotted her long white apron among the trees and started toward her, but stopped when he saw O'Neill with her. He was beyond earshot, so he watched. Addie's face was lowered, listening to her earnest-looking cousin. When, finally, she looked up, she shook her head. O'Neill pointed east. East was Butte, the rest of America, and Ireland. Why had he thought she'd resist O'Neill's plans? They were kin and her mother was Irish. O'Neill continued talking, snaked his hand in a zigzag, then wriggled his fingers. Palm up, he rubbed a thumb and forefinger together. The first two gestures puzzled Jamieson, but the last was a universal sign for money and payoffs. Addie gripped his arm and again shook her head. He took her hand and put something in it, which she thrust into an apron pocket. They appeared ready to separate and Jamieson retreated. Damn it to hell! O'Neill had drawn her into his scheme and she went willingly.

Jamieson nursed a smoldering anger toward O'Neill. What part was he having Addie play in this dangerous game? If she left camp now, she'd be carrying O'Neill's message, but if he followed her, it would give the Irishman freedom to act. Maybe he intended to use Addie as a decoy. Jamieson doubted every thought going through his head. And he doubted himself.

*   *

Death swept down the Marble when it was least expected. O'Neill was drowning, pulled downstream through rapids while Jamieson and other men sprinted along the bank, catching a last glimpse of him as he disappeared around a bend, one arm upraised, grasping for a hold on a log end. Had he been able to hook his peavey into its bark underneath? If another log didn't crush him, water-filled boots, soaked wool and foaming whitewater would drag him under. Peavey in his fists,

Jamieson crashed through brush and clambered over decaying logs. *Shit! Shit!*

There was just a chance that a large boulder farther down the Marble would stop him. He'd claw at its rough surface, find purchase and cling with bloodied fingers, his face just above rushing water, but able to take a breath. The water's surge was subsiding; if trailing logs rushed past, they'd miss him. Wouldn't they?

Jamieson scrambled on hands and knees under cottonwood branches, losing another hat. The Marble widened past the bend where he last saw O'Neill. It was here where logs spaced out and slowed. He would find O'Neill clinging to that boulder, bruised but alive. He pushed through a large springy fir, inhaling its pungent Christmas scent.

The boulder squatted in the middle of the Marble, but there was no O'Neill, only a few logs wedged on nearby rocks. Although he knew it was pointless, he called out O'Neill's name. Stood for a moment, then dropped his peavey and sank to the ground, raised his knees and buried his face in folded arms.

Jamieson stood at MacLean's shoulder in the cookhouse, eyes fastened on Addie's face as Alonzo announced the appalling news. Polite John cursed and the flunkies groaned. Dovey moved to Addie's side and gripped her hand, then dragged over a stool. Addie sat in shocked disbelief as Jamieson, his throat tight, recounted what he witnessed.

In a ragged voice, MacLean added, "I got men combing both sides of the Marble. If he's there, they'll find him."

Dovey poured coffee, cooled it with cream, and urged Addie to swallow some, just to have her do something. She took a sip, regained some composure, then set down the mug. Fingers entwined, chin tucked, her lips moved in prayer. When she finished, she sat hollow-eyed.

Before MacLean left to check on the search's progress, he screwed up his craggy face. "Gotta tell ya, Addie, there've been times a jack's body hasn't been found 'til it floated down to the Joe, even farther to the sortin' gap outside St. Maries." Never adept at self-restraint, he added, "Sometimes we never find 'em.

God Almighty, I hate the Marble! Irish ain't the first good man it's took." He clumped outside.

Addie couldn't stop trembling and rose to go outside, maybe to seek the sun's warmth, although the kitchen was hotter. Dovey called after, "We'll handle the baking. You rest easy." She motioned Jamieson to follow.

Outside, he touched Addie's arm. "Will you be all right?"

"I don't know." Titus pushed his muzzle against her hip until she rested a hand on his head.

Jamieson raked fingers through his hair. Seeing Addie's distress made him feel worse, a twisted coldness below his heart, similar to when Sewell was killed. He liked that son-of-a-bitch rebel. Owed him his life. He wanted to hold Addie and comfort her, but feared she'd think he was taking advantage of her grief. O'Neill, God rest him, had complicated his mission. Where the hell were those rifles?

Before he left to join the search, he choked out, "I'm sorry I couldn't save him."

Addie didn't respond.

MacLean called off the search at nightfall.

That night Jamieson lay exhausted on his bunk, achingly aware of the empty one above. Hands laced behind his head, he obsessively relived O'Neill's death, unable to shake off its horror. The Irishman was catty. How did he lose his balance? The surge had passed its full strength, most big sticks already downstream, which was the reason they were rolling strays into the middle of the flood. A few minutes more and the Marble would have been low enough to walk across. O'Neill had worked his way down creek, some distance from Jamieson and the others. Maybe he stepped out on a swamped log to dislodge another jillpoked on the opposite bank and his log rolled, taking him unawares. He'd earlier seen O'Neill look upstream, maybe to see what kind of round stuff was coming through. They'd exchanged nods as Jamieson worked on a log flung up the rocky bank, so O'Neill knew how far from the crew he'd strayed. Cocky son-of-a-bitch. And then he was gone. Right at the spot where whitewater surged down and around that blind bend, trees and large rocks cutting off the view ahead. Which was why they couldn't see what became of him.

They knew the Marble. Push logs from point to point a couple of times and you've memorized its twists and turns - which was why he'd expected to find O'Neill at that boulder smack in the middle of the creek. It was fast water, deep water, but if a man made it that far, unless a log knocked him unconscious or he inhaled water or was tumbled against rocks, he could survive. O'Neill should have survived.

It was as though the Divine Finger touched his muddled mind and commanded, "See!" He didn't announce the revelation to the sleeping men. He rolled over and pounded a fist into his pillow.

* *

Jamieson said, "Addie, tell me about Irish. Your memories of him." They sat on a log a short way from the kitchen.

MacLean had held a short service earlier. Although the Ol' Man had been choked up and Addie had frequently wiped her eyes, without a body to bury, it seemed a sham, but maybe only to Jamieson. His gaze roamed the perimeter of trees and he thought of Huck Finn watching his own funeral. He still had to locate the rifles. If O'Neill had taken Addie into his confidence and if she were part of this conspiracy, she wouldn't tell him a damn thing.

"Oh, well, I really knew him only that one summer when he lived with us. In the autumn he went up to Spokane and never came back. Mam was awfully fond of him. He could be so funny, telling stories about Ireland and the family." Her voice caught. "I'm going to have to write my family. His, too." She patted his hand. "This is hard for you, too. You were his friend."

He took her hand. "Why did he come to America?"

"Because of English soldiers. I guess he was a hothead in his youth." She pressed her lips together.

While observing her every facial tick and intonation, he was careful not to turn it into an interrogation. "You hadn't seen him in nine years," he mused, "yet you recognized him after that run-in with those tramps."

"Ah, well." She patted his hand before gently removing hers. "I met him in Spokane last summer." Briefly she told him about Mrs. Sheehy-Skeffington's lecture. "He recognized me. I thought marriage and widowhood changed me, but . . ."

"You haven't changed a bit since I met you at the Independence Day parade in 1913."

"What?"

"I knew when I knocked those papers out of your hand last autumn I'd met you before. Remember? I asked if we'd met."

"Independence Day, 1913? That was a month before I married. How did we meet?"

"I was the bum who came up and asked to hold your parasol during the parade." *What the hell am I doing? It's the wrong time to bring this up.*

Addie shook her head. "I really don't remember."

"It's not important." Shrugged off his disappointment. "Irish mentioned he wanted to go back to Ireland to fight the English. Did he say anything to you?"

"He meant to go back, I guess."

"A few days ago I saw you two with your heads together behind the cookhouse."

"That was the last time I talked with him." Her eyes widened, those lovely blue eyes with dark rings, and in that instant she projected her thoughts on him. Then she squeezed them shut and stood up. "I have to start my baking." She was halfway to the kitchen door before Jamieson or Titus could react. He stood up. Then she was back, holding out a slip of paper. "He said if I ever needed to contact him, I should find this person." Jamieson looked at it and handed it back. There was hope in her voice. "I think he might still be alive."

That made two of them. He'd search for O'Neill in Butte, after seeing a woman in St. Joe City.

Chapter 67

A few days later, at MacLean's insistence that she was in need of a good rest, Addie left camp for the cabin at Ferrell, carrying O'Neill's effects. Jamieson rolled into St. Joe City a day later. He outfitted himself at the haberdasher and later emerged beardless from the barbershop after a shave and a bath. Tempted to toss his lumberjack woolens and caulked boots into the river, he thought better of it.

At the Big Timber he knocked down a whiskey and sent a message up to Kate, asking if she would see Mac, then ordered another shot.

Bathed, powdered and painted, Katie wore a black kimono embroidered with a multi-colored dragon over one breast, and not much else. But she was the one who said, "Well, don't you look pretty." She perched on the side of her bed and crossed her knees. He sat across from her and twirled his new hat on a finger while they studied each other. Except for the twitching foot with a satin mule hanging off her toes, she seemed pleased to see him. From a cushioned basket her small dog watched bright-eyed. "I'm sorry about Mally." She avoided his eyes, focused on his mouth and then his left ear. "I heard about it downstairs. Guess it was in the newspaper."

"Yeah." Weary of watching the jittering pink mule, he dropped his hat on a small table. "How many times did he come here?"

"Just a couple. He never told me anything."

"He didn't tell you anything about what?"

She pulled the black silk tighter across her thighs. "About what you wanted me to find out."

"And what was that, Katie?"

"Somethin' about guns. Only I wasn't supposed to say the word 'gun'." She narrowed green eyes at him, at least what he could see of them, wreathed by an abundance of kohl. "What are you up to, anyway?" She rolled on a hip, drawing up her legs.

He rested elbows on his knees, chin on his knuckles. "You know what I'm up to. I want the information Irish gave you." Why had he thought he could trust her?

"Robbie, what's got into you?" She flung out a hand in a theatrical gesture. "He didn't tell me anything. You'd be the first to know if he did."

"Why are you lying to me, Katie? You told O'Neill about me, didn't you?"

She appeared genuinely shocked. "I swear to God I never told him anything about you. Do you think I want you hurt or killed?" Her face screwed up. "But you didn't stop that bastard from burning down my tents with everything I owned."

He wasn't her damn pimp. "You got away with your girls and the whiskey . . . and I compensated you as much as I could."

"Oh. Was that from you?" She looked pensive. "I thought it came from Mally."

Had that bastard maneuvered her into his debt? "You're keeping something from me."

"You wanna drink?"

"I had two downstairs."

"My whiskey isn't watered." The bed creaked as she stood up.

He grabbed her and pulled her on his lap, imprisoning her wrists. Tipping his head back to see her reaction, he announced, "He isn't dead."

"How do you know?" But she didn't seem surprised.

"I don't know. But you do." He tightened his grip. "Tell me."

"Robbie . . . ow . . . you're hurtin' me."

In his younger days he thought he possessed a nobility of character, but he'd been fooling only himself. Now he snagged a handful of red hair and twisted it. "Katie, tell me what you know." Twisted harder. "I'll pull it out by the roots. By God I will if you don't come clean with me."

A small woman in the grasp of a powerful man, she made a half-hearted effort to free herself, then choked back sobs, which cued the mutt to leap from its basket and dash back and forth, yipping. Katie stopped struggling. Tears trickled down powdered cheeks and he knew why, but didn't care. He was hurting her. So what? She'd betrayed his mission.

"He asked me how I felt about the Irish cause. Stop, Robbie!"

Her sparsely clad, perfumed body still aroused him. He was just another cur drooling over evening leftovers. He loosened his fingers. "And what did you say?"

"I said I didn't like the English, either." She tugged at her pinioned hands and he released one, with which she flicked tears away from lower lashes, trying not to smear them.

"What else?"

"That's all. It didn't seem worth telling you." She tried to slip off his lap, but he held her fast, imprisoning both hands again, this time behind her back.

"He came back to you. You said a couple of times. He denied being with you the night he got into that fight. Is that when he asked you to help him?"

She spat, "He came back because I'm a good fuck."

Jamieson selected the same hank of hair, knowing her scalp must be tender there. "Did he ask you to help him?"

"No." Her soft body arched in his hard embrace. He was an instrument of medieval torture, slowly twisting her hair.

His voice remained low and calm. "He wanted someone to carry messages to Butte and you know Butte." A few tendrils tore away in his fingers. She shrieked, setting off the mutt again. Yipping, it ran in circles around the chair. He stopped, but only to quiet her screams.

She gasped. "Father Hannan. I carried a message to Father Hannan in Butte."

Releasing her hair, he slid his hand down to a bared shoulder. "What did it say?" Pressed his fingers into it; removed them to see white marks on pink flesh.

Defeated, she sobbed, "I don't know. I didn't open it." She hiccuped. "I rode the train over and back."

Believing her now, he pushed her off his lap onto the floor. She scooted to the bed and buried her face in the counterpane. The little dog scrambled to her side, whining and licking, and she curled an arm around it.

Slightly shaken, but triumphant, he unraveled a few red hairs threading his fingers. "You know he's alive, don't you?"

"I know nothing." The dog was licking tears dripping from her chin. "But if you hurt me again, I'll say anything you want." She turned her face away. "You want me to say he's alive, I'll say he's alive. And you won't know for sure until some kids fish his bones out of the river."

Jamieson reached for his hat and stood up, studying her crumpled figure. Despite the vestiges of artful makeup, she still resembled the waif he'd met five years earlier in Butte. He almost bent to lift her to her feet, but decided she didn't deserve it. He shouldn't have put a shred of trust in her. She betrayed him. It was her fault he had to coax out what she knew. Now a Butte priest was connected to the rifles. He had his hand on the door knob when she spoke.

"I thought you were different, but you're like every man who's paid for me. You think I was sweet on you?" She gave a brittle laugh. "You were as repugnant as the others."

She'd chosen O'Neill over him. His knuckles whitened around the doorknob. "That's a big word for you, Katie. You know what, kitten? No matter how hard you try, you'll always be an every-night-workingman's whore."

"Get out!" she shrieked.

Chapter 68

The sun had dropped over the mountains when Titus lifted his head and barked once, alerting Addie. Jamieson stood at the door of her cabin in a suit, doffing a new hat, clean-shaven and neatly barbered. Logging clothes and caulked boots poked from a partially-open portmanteau.

"Mind if I leave my bindle here while I'm gone?"

"You're leaving?" She recovered from her disappointment with a breezy, "No, I don't mind. Come in."

The way he smiled slowly into her eyes reminded her of Jerome.

Addie smiled back, then remembered the disorder of her clothing, her shirtwaist pulled from her skirt. "Just look at me. I found a tick on my back, but I can't get it off. I can only touch it." She shivered. "I hate ticks."

He removed his hat and coat, revealing a revolver in a shoulder holster. She couldn't think why it startled her; she'd seen him with a gun before and her own small revolver was tucked beneath her pillow. He slipped off the holster. "Come to the window. You'll have to remove your shirtwaist, unless you don't mind getting grease on it."

She unfastened the row of small buttons and slipped it off, exposing her low-cut chemise.

"There's the little bugger."

He reached for the lard can and dabbed in a finger. Having picked ticks off Titus, she envisioned the bloated gray body attached to her back. As he smothered it with grease, Addie shuddered.

He wiped his fingers on a dishtowel, then patted her bare shoulder. "Give it time." Fingering a tendril of her hair, he tucked it into place. She shivered under his touch. "Cold?"

"No." He wore almond astringent like Jerome had worn.

His fingertips moved up the back of her neck into her hair. "That make you shiver?"

"Yes." She lowered her chin, heart beating faster, willing him to kiss her where his touch lingered. His lips brushed the back of her neck and she stood silent in permission. He kissed her neck and shoulders, and then beneath her ear where her pulse beat. He turned her, and kissed her mouth. She cupped his cheek, a pale contrast to his tanned forehead and nose. As he held her closer, her hands moved over his hard back muscles. They explored each other with hands and mouths.

Her cheek pressed against his shoulder, she asked, "What about the tick?"

Not releasing her from his embrace, he plucked up the linen towel and removed the lard. "Came out clean." He kissed her back. "You smell like bacon. I love bacon." With her back against his chest and his arms around her, he murmured, "And I love you, Addie."

The timbre of his voice, it could have been a younger unbreakable Jerome. "I'm a widow, Robbie, not some girl you need to woo." She took his hand and drew him into the dim bedroom.

Before she could remove encumbering clothing, he swept her up and laid her on the bed. Hard hands shoved her skirt and petticoat to her waist. She felt his body heat as he knelt over her. Pulling the bow tie on her pantaloons, he drew them down her thighs and tossed them to the floor with her house slippers. The first time with Jerome, he'd held her before they made love. It wasn't what she wanted now. Ignoring her garters and stockings, Jamieson pushed open her thighs, grasped her hips and dragged her to him. Sliding his suspenders from his shoulders, he unbuttoned his fly and lowered himself on her. She raised her knees and guided him, their fingers touching until he thrust into her wet cleft. He would not be gentle and she was wild with need.

His plunging in and pulling out hurt at first. It had been so long. He pressed the breath from her, his own ragged breathing above her ear, hands entangled in her hair. The pain diminished to become a sweet numbing. Her hands moved down to pull up his shirt and undershirt. She pressed the small of his back to slow him. Murmured to him. This was not Jerome making love to her. He had been a gentleman, even in bed. She didn't care about any of that. Robbie was younger and larger, with the muscles of a laborer.

Hearts pounding against each other, breathing faster, this rough pleasure made her moan as she approached her climax.

She held him tightly, breathing, "Now," and he thrust wildly, releasing inside her with a gasp. She felt herself enveloped in . . . Later she found the right word. *Ecstasy.* They lay entangled in clothing and each other until their breathing quieted. She ran languid hands over him. The difference between father and son transcended age, but what was the harm of pretending this man was a younger Jerome. She'd make that up to Robbie, too.

"Is this what you wanted, Mrs. MacLean?" He raised himself on his elbows. She made out his eyes and smile in the dusk.

"I expect it was."

"Not a day when I didn't want you like this. Let me stay the night?"

"Yes." She would sleep beside him until morning light.

"I want us to lie naked together."

"I'll fetch a blanket from the trunk. Nights can be chilly."

"I don't think we'll need it."

She felt a vast happiness. Yet her half-Irish heart sensed it a precursor to what surely would be disappointment. Tonight summer sang within her and she resisted the urge to touch the place in her heart where it might hurt. Playfully, "I almost miss the timber beast."

In the soft night, that familiar voice, "If you want a timber beast, I'll oblige."

Awaking to the aroma of bacon frying, she lay quietly, remembering. They'd made love twice more, wonderful intimate explorations. She'd found the scars the bullet made on either side of his shoulder, indented places she touched and kissed. Because of that wound, their paths had crossed. She reached down a hand, but Titus was gone from the rug beside the bed. She flung back the covers.

"Get back to bed," he said, coming into the bedroom, holding a mug of hot tea. He was dressed, her long white apron wrapped around him, a well-heeled camp cook. "Breakfast in bed for all the early breakfasts you made for us."

"How lovely."

He watched her test the heat of the tea. "You are a beautiful woman, even with your hair a fright."

"I hoped I looked alluring." She dragged coppery tangles over a breast, desire returning to have his body against hers.

"You are alluring, and I'd crawl back in bed, but I have a train to catch." With Titus traipsing behind, he returned with two plates of bacon and eggs. "I fed you, you big tramp." He sat on the bed opposite her.

"Where are you going?" Would he come back?

He took a gulp of black tea. "Thought I'd take a run up to Spokane . . . see what's going on in the big city."

"Isn't that dangerous?"

He shrugged, eating quickly.

So conscious of him, she saw his face change, becoming unreadable. "Penny for your thoughts."

"All right." He set down his mug and plate. "Why did you lie to me about your cousin?" Reclining alongside her, he propped himself on an elbow, scrutinizing her from above.

"How did I lie to you?" She lifted her chin to meet his eyes.

"That day I saw you two together. What were you arguing about?"

"I don't recall an argument. Mally told me not to lose my heart to you, that you weren't what you seemed. I couldn't tell him I'd known you when you were a Pinkerton. I promised not to lose my heart." It was the truth, just not all of it.

"I saw you, Addie." He waited.

"I don't recall doing much talking. I was trying not to talk, afraid I'd let something about you slip out." She pulled the sheet over her breasts. "It's chilly in here."

He took a handful of her hair and gave a tug.

It shocked her. "How dare you raise your hand to me." She grasped her imprisoned hair and he opened his hand.

His voice was calm, almost sinister. "Addie, don't lie to me. I've watched you for so long, I can read your eyes."

She pressed her lips together to keep them from trembling. "I expect it's *you* who lied to me."

He ignored that. "Did O'Neill ask for your help with his plans for Ireland?"

"What plans?" And then she remembered Mrs. Sheehy-Skeffington's telling Mally there were men she wanted him to meet. Everything fell into place in bits and pieces. Mally was planning something. It was why Robbie had attached himself to him. Mally had said Robbie wasn't what he seemed. Why was he questioning her? What did he think she knew? If Mally were still alive, she had a duty to protect him. Warily, "I don't have to tell you anything, Robert Jamieson. Please get off my bed."

He obeyed. "You said at camp you believed he's alive. So do I. And I'll find him." He picked up their plates and carried them out, Titus lumbering after him.

Grabbing up a trade blanket, she pulled it crookedly over her shoulders, dragging an end into the main room to stand barefoot in front of the rock fireplace, the large open "V" at her breasts. Her chin held firmly, she adopted what she hoped was a contemptuous look. Titus thudded down next to her. "What happened last night won't happen again."

The lumberjack clothes were piled in a corner, the portmanteau in Jamieson's hand. His eyes swept over her without expression. "We both got what we wanted."

Humiliated, she grasped a fistful of the mastiff's neck. "Leave my house."

An unreadable look crossed his face. And then, "Addie, I didn't mean that. I'm sorry. Last night had nothing to do with this morning. I love you, but I've got unfinished business. O'Neill. This war. When it's over, you probably won't want anything to do with me. Do you know where he is?"

"If he's alive, I don't know where he is."

He came to her, slipped a hand inside the blanket, cupping a warm breast. Kissed her hungrily and she let him. Then he was gone.

Chapter 69

Everything now made sense to Addie. Robbie wasn't an army deserter. Although she didn't know what Mally was doing for Ireland's cause, she understood Jamieson was on her cousin's trail to try to stop it. If Mally was alive, she would protect him. That name he gave her -- Kate at the Big Timber.

With Titus in tow, she crossed the river, entered the railway station and approached the station master.

"I'm Adelaide MacLean of MacLean's Lumber. One of my lumberjacks took a train out this morning. I failed to give him all the pay due him. If I knew where he's headed, it might be the address I have and I can send it on to him."

"What did he look like?"

"Clean-shaven, wearing a suit. Tall. A nice-looking man."

He questioned the clerk behind a grill. "You sell a ticket to a clean-shaven man this morning? This lady wants to know where to."

The clerk screwed up his face. "Let me think on it."

"She's not some woman he jilted. He worked for her up at MacLean's camp and they owe him money."

"He bought a ticket to Butte."

Straightening her black straw, Addie entered the Big Timber's dim interior, Titus shouldering in with her. The scent of sawdust was overlaid with sour fumes of beer and whiskey. Murmurings ceased as surprised faces turned toward her. The bartender called out, "No ladies or dogs, ma'am. If that's what you got there."

"This is a business call. I have a message for a woman named Kate. Do you know her?"

"Go back out and head around back. Pull the bell. Might take a few minutes. Someone will come."

Wood crates and stacks of kegs stamped 'Root Beer' lined the deceptively long building. She pulled the bell. After what seemed a long time, she rang it again as a blowsy woman opened the door. "I have a message for Kate."

"You wait." Leaving the door ajar, the woman thumped back up narrow stairs. Ordering Titus to stay, Addie entered to peer up the dim passageway.

A woman in a black kimono appeared at the top. "What can we do for ya?"

Halfway up the stairs, Addie met the woman's unsurprised eyes and froze. Katie bent toward her, grasping the railing. "I'm not giving any more interviews."

"Katie?" She continued up to the landing. "What are you doing here? Are you Kate?"

"That's me. What are *you* going by these days?"

"Addie MacLean."

"Well, isn't it a small world. We both change our names and end up in this backwater. Roza said ya got a message for me."

"I'm looking for my cousin, Malachi O'Neill. You know him, don't you?"

"Your cousin, huh? Sure is a world of coincidence, ain't it. I hate to tell ya, but he drowned. I read it in the newspaper."

"I hoped you'd tell me he's alive. I believe he is. A few days before he fell into Marble Creek, he told me if I ever wanted to get word to him, I should come to you. Why would he tell me that?"

Katie leaned against the wall, arms folded. "I don't know."

"You knew Robbie was his logging partner."

"Not so loud." Katie waved a hand, giving off a flowery scent. "Yeah, I knew. So what?"

"Robbie thinks Mally is still alive. He left for Butte this morning to look for him. I just want to protect my cousin."

A look of concern crossed Katie's face. "Did you tell him anything about Robbie . . . about his past?"

Addie whispered, "Only that he was a deserter. Not that he was a Pinkerton."

"A goddamn Pinkerton! I suspected as much."

"He asked me not to tell Mally anything about him."

"Yeah, he told me the same thing. Crazy business, ain't it, trying to protect two men . . . maybe from each other."

Addie faltered, "If Mally is still alive."

"Yeah, if he's still alive. How can I reach you if I hear anything?"

She was nearly to the bottom when Katie called after her, "Hey, I never saw anything about us in the newspaper."

Addie turned back. "My editor wouldn't publish it. He said it wasn't righteous enough. The fallen women didn't suffer or mend their sinful ways." Katie's husky laughter trailed her out the door.

Chapter 70
Butte, Montana

On the train to Butte, Jamieson relived the previous night with Addie. He'd wanted her and he'd had her. It was good and would be good again, but he couldn't trust her. He loved her, but he shouldn't have said so. Until Addie, he'd been only with whores. Did loving a woman make it better? Maybe. He'd been fond of Katie and tried to look out for her, but look how she repaid him. He shouldn't have hurt her, though.

He'd telegraphed Major Gund in Portland the morning before and picked up his reply before boarding. *Wait for fishing party in Butte.*

Stepping off the train, he looked toward the "Richest Hill on Earth" and its massive black headframes silhouetted against the sky. It looked just as it was pictured on most postal cards of Butte. As a first impression the headframes trumped the distant thumping above midtown traffic and the stench of seven smokestacks at the Neversweat mine. He'd always enjoyed stopping in Butte. Its bustle attracted him, crowds of miners surging up through town heading to their shifts, ignoring traffic cops blowing whistles, nodding or calling out greetings to those coming off shift, trudging down. All day and night ore cars rumbled down from The Hill through Dublin Gulch and town center, out to smelters on the flats, gray ash and sulfurous smoke blowing back to entomb the city. But it was the only corpselike aspect of Butte. Alive and jittery with a cocaine high, the entire town seemed hooked on "snow." He took a jitney up a tilted street to a second-class hotel.

The next morning he caught a streetcar to the treeless bluff where the Montana School of Mines perched, and where federal troops - Company F of the 14th Infantry Regiment -- encamped near a clutch of buildings.

Passing soldiers with bayonet-mounted rifles at the camp's perimeter and seeing the "All Visitors" sign on a tent, he ducked in. "Master Sergeant, who's your officer in charge?"

"That would be Captain Bradley." The sergeant picked up a pencil to fill in another form. "State your business."

"I'll do that when I present myself."

"Name and affiliation or you won't get beyond this point."

"Lieutenant Robert Jamieson, Military Intelligence Division, attached to the Spruce Production Division, United States Army Signal Corps."

Looking up, the soldier replied with what might pass as regard, "Is he expecting you . . . sir?"

"I don't know. Let's see, shall we . . . Master Sergeant."

Bradley was signing papers in his tent. "Captain Bradley, I'm First Lieutenant Robert Jamieson of the Military Intelligence Division, MI-4, counter espionage. I'm here to make my presence known to you. And that's about all."

Bradley stood and shook hands. "Omar Bradley, Class of '15."

A West Pointer. He might have known, seeing how the young man held himself erect, like a goose quill was stuck up his ass. Matching his seriousness, he replied, "Michigan, Class of '09."

"I had an earlier visitor who told me to expect you. Major Gund is waiting to meet with you."

Bradley barked from the tent opening, "Corporal, go get Major Gund. Tell him his fishing partner's here."

Jamieson eyed the regimental flag behind Bradley's desk. "That a dragon?"

"'Golden Dragons.' The unit was in the Boxer Rebellion. Looks good, sounds good. Until something better comes along." With a hint of bitterness, "How about 'Stay-at-homes' or 'Peacekeepers of Butte?'" He added with a hint of a southern accent, "I'm still hoping to get to France. What about you?"

Jamieson shrugged, having offered more about himself than intended. He allowed the captain to fill the silent void.

"Didn't think I'd be playing policeman to a bunch of rowdy miners. Had to break up their St. Patrick's Day Parade." He offered Jamieson a cigarette. "Some men in my command are from here, Butte Irish patrolling their own town."

They filled the small tent with blue smoke. Maybe he'd stop rolling his own and fork out for made-up cigarettes.

"My career will be ruined if I don't get to France before it's all over . . . over there." Smiled wryly. "Have you heard that song?"

Jamieson shook his head. "No music where I've been."

Bradley sang, "Johnny get your gun, get your gun . . ."

"Oh, hell, sure I've heard that." The tent flap remained closed. Where the fuck was Gund?

When Major Gund finished briefing him, he filled his pipe. They sat in the tent Bradley's clerk had vacated.

Jamieson mused, "So Military Intelligence is using civilians as domestic spies?" It was new information, but he wasn't surprised. Mine owners had used them, lumber barons, too. Now it was the military.

Gund lit his pipe, thoughtfully drawing on it. "What's that? No, not spies. Paid operatives. Each one given a cipher. C-815 will meet us tonight. He's bringing in a miner who'll give us information for a price. We'll follow up on your priest tomorrow. Can't be everywhere all the time."

"So, this agent? Pinkerton? From another detective agency? Company stool pigeon?"

"I'm not authorized to say. I will tell you Captain Dengel received information that proved accurate. His informant claims to be with the American Protective League. Rather like an old-time vigilante group, but you'll agree the times call for unusual measures. They're doing great work ferreting out disloyal Americans - slackers, war resisters, German sympathizers. Agent C-815 seems to get around." Gund puffed, humming "Over There."

"Captain Bradley got to you, too."

"Played it on his Victrola for me. Did the honors for you, too, h-m-m? Let's go over this report. You wrote it on the train. I can tell by the little ink jogs." He puffed on his pipe. "You wrote that O'Neill appeared to drown in Marble Creek. How can a man drown in a creek?"

Jamieson described the Marble and its dangers.

"Did he drown or didn't he?"

"No body was found. I'm here because I have a hunch he's in Butte."

"Operating on hunches now, Lieutenant?" He grinned around the pipe clamped between his teeth. "Might be why I'm here, too. When you telegraphed the rifle's make, you baffled the cipher clerks for an entire hour." He snorted. "'Signed Ross Gunn'. That was good. We checked with the Canadian government and discovered it had filled an order of purchase from the Montana State Guard. Rifles and ammunition were delivered to the Guard's agents up in Regina in late spring. Paperwork proper, everything in order."

"Any Ross rifles at the arsenal in Helena?"

"No, and I didn't expect to find any. When the New York Guard purchased a large quantity, they were intended for training only. Not a weapon you'd want to bet your life on."

"But a damn fine sniper rifle."

"Exactly. You were on the right track, Lieutenant. Colonel Disque said to tell you 'good work'." He readjusted his spectacles. "Butte intelligence officers have been trying to sniff out those rifles. Not a single lead. Those Irish are a closed-mouthed lot, downright tribal. This miner coming in tonight is supposed to tell us something. German agents have got to be stirring these waters, providing money for the rifles and ammunition." He looked thoughtful. "Captain Dengel came over from Spokane last night." Jamieson caught a flicker of concern in Gund's otherwise inscrutable look. Anything involving Dengel wasn't good.

That night Jamieson and Gund entered the office Army Intelligence kept in downtown Butte. The officer in charge, Lieutenant Will Germer, was talkative.

"As Major Gund knows, Captain Dengel assigned me to Butte mainly to gather evidence of German spy activity here."

Dengel had yet to show and the only points of interest were wall maps – one of railroad lines converging on Butte, a city map, and a regional map of eastern Washington, northern Idaho, and western Montana.

"Where is Captain Dengel?" Gund asked.

"He's at supper." Reluctant to abandon the limelight, Germer continued, "The government suspected Irish miners would sabotage the mines to stop copper being produced for the war effort. That hasn't happened yet. I've got my informants. Cornishmen helping England and America. Major, when you sent word some Irish had acquired guns from Canada . . . whew! Instead of waiting for mine explosions, I'm expecting an armed uprising. Captain Bradley doesn't have enough soldiers to defend Butte."

Gund interrupted, "Hold on, Lieutenant, we don't expect the rifles to be used here. They're intended for Ireland. Thought you knew that."

"Yes, sir. But if you observed what goes on in Butte, you'd have more than one theory about those miners' intentions."

"That first shipment found in Ellensburg was by chance," Gund reminded Germer. "A fluke. It shows God's on our side."

They heard boots thudding up the stairs.

Chapter 71

Dengel flung open the door and surveyed the room. "Major Gund," he acknowledged. Blond mustache bristling, he gave Jamieson a scathing look. "So, you finally came out of the woods, Lieutenant. And without any meat to show for your hunt."

"Good to see you, too, Captain Dengel."

"I ordered you to bring O'Neill to me in Spokane and you disobeyed that order. Now he's lost to us. I could have you court-martialed and drummed out of the service for that."

"I answer to Major Gund, not to you." He should have hit Dengel harder back at the mission.

Gund looked pained. "It seems the chain of command has been modified. The captain here requested that Headquarters in San Francisco transfer you under his direct command and they complied. We couldn't reach you, and then it sort of slipped my mind."

Heavy footsteps labored up the stairs.

Gund and Jamieson slipped into the darkened inner office where the major took a straight-back chair. The door was left ajar and Jamieson leaned against a wall, out of range of a thin slant of light coming through. Dengel took the seat behind the desk and, at a ham-fisted knock, Germer opened the door.

Hunched in a chair, the man had the look of The Hill about him. The hands twisting his tweed cap were scabbed with copper sores from contact with seeping mine water. Even in street clothes, he carried the acrid after-odor of explosives.

Germer was greeting another man, whose muffled footsteps crossed the office like a burglar's, silver eyes probing the cracked-open door. He shook Dengel's hand. "Good to see ya again, Captain."

Fats Gerard. The old animosity tightened Jamieson's throat.

Lieutenant Germer seated himself beside Dengel. There being no seat for Gerard, he retreated to stand against the wall by the door, out of Jamieson's view.

Dengel addressed the miner. "I understand you have information for us."

The man motioned over his shoulder. "He said you'll pay two hundred for what I know."

"That's correct. Heard you had enough of the Mountain Con and you're moving on. That right?"

Jamieson was tightly coiled; with only the miner's profile in view, he was having difficulty interpreting the man's demeanor.

Germer encouraged, "Tell Captain Dengel why you don't want to mine anymore." As an aside, "You'll like this."

"Just got that feelin'."

"Tell him what you told me last week."

"It started when a new guy whistled while we was goin' down in the chippy."

Germer interpreted, "Bad luck whistling in the cage."

"That right?" Dengel slid matches across the desk. "Give our guest a cigarette, Lieutenant." Germer pulled a mashed packet from a breast pocket and handed one to the miner.

Lighting it, he inhaled and coughed. "The timbers talk to me. It's noisy down there, anyway, ya know. The other guys hear 'em, but not the same as me." He dragged on the cigarette.

The man had given himself Dutch courage, or Gerard had, his exhaled smoke mixed with fumes from a few boilermakers -- Sean O'Farrells they were called in Butte -- a shot of whiskey with a chaser of beer. "Guess I couldn't shut up about it. The guys on my shift said I jinxed the vein 'cause it run out where we was workin'. No one will work with me no more, not even my brother. I'm sick of goin' down there. That's what I told Mr. Gerard here, an' he says he could get me some cash so's I can start fresh."

Dengel nodded. "Tell us about the rifles."

Outside of Jamieson's view, Gerard said, "Tell 'em how you transported those guns from Canada."

"Right. I was along to help load and unload 'em."

Dengel leaned forward. "What kind of rifles?"

"Rosses."

"Ammunition?" The miner nodded. "Who was with you?"

He stiffened. "If I tell you that, I'm a dead man. Mr. Gerard here," half-turning to seek out Fats, "he said I don't have to rat."

"That's all right then." Dengel made these simple words sound deadly. "We just want the rifles. How many?"

"I'm not tellin' you more 'til I get my payment."

Dengel nodded. "Lieutenant."

Germer withdrew cash from a drawer. "A hundred dollars," pushing the short stack across. "Another hundred after you tell us the rest."

The miner pocketed it. "How many rifles? Not sure. Maybe four crates. Yeah, four crates."

Major Gund had given Dengel exact numbers from the Canadian Government, numbers larger than what the miner claimed.

"How much ammunition?"

"Bullets in crates. Two of those. Heavy buggers."

"Ten thousand rounds," Dengel translated. "Where are they now?"

"Now? I don't know nothin' 'bout that. They ain't in Butte. Swear on my old mother's head." An Irish expression O'Neill used.

"If not in Butte, where?"

"I don't know. I went along as a heavy lifter. Unloaded 'em a ways outside Butte. Heard they was sent on to the coast."

"How did they get from Butte to the coast?"

Sounding uncertain, "By train?"

"Which train?"

"The N.P. Butte to Seattle."

Jamieson didn't believe much of what the miner said, except that the rifles were Rosses from Canada.

Dengel prodded, "We want you to show us where the guns were hidden outside of Butte."

"I don't know as I can find exactly where. I was in the back of a closed delivery wagon. I can take you Sunday after mass, but I can't let no one see me with you."

"Lieutenant Germer will find us transportation." Then he asked the question Jamieson wanted the answer to. "You know an Irishman named Malachi O'Neill?"

The miner sat motionless a moment too long. "Can't say I ever knew that O'Neill. Mike O'Neill works at the Speculator. That who ya mean? How about the rest of my money?"

Germer withdrew a few bills. "This is all I've got. You'll get more when you show us where the rifles were hidden."

"That's not what we agreed. I'm riskin' my life comin' up here."

Gerard said from near the door, "Don't worry, Slugger. I'll make sure you get what's due ya."

Money still in his fist, Germer shoved a paper across the desk. "Sign here."

"I ain't signin' nothin'." He squinted at it. "Is this some kinda confession?"

"It's a receipt for the cash I gave you. I've got to account for all monies supplied by the American taxpayer. No one will see this unless some Army clerk accuses me of skimming."

The miner scratched out a signature, then stuck out a callused hand for the money.

Dengel offered, "Give us some names and you'll get another hundred."

"I'll think on that."

The miner left and Dengel addressed Gerard. "Thank you, C-815, for your assistance," and signalled for him to leave. Gerard made little noise going down the stairs that opened onto the street. The fucker was wearing gummed shoes.

When Jamieson and Gund came into the room, Dengel was fingering his mustache. He picked up the receipt. "What's this signature? Malachi O'Neill?"

Jamieson shook his head. "It wasn't O'Neill. You'd remember him from the Union Gospel Mission in Spokane, although he kicked you pretty hard."

Gund lit his pipe. "The miner played a little joke on us."

Jamieson's mind was elsewhere. "How did Frank Gerard get involved in this?"

With a hint of satisfaction, Dengel replied, "So, you know him, do you?"

"I've known him a long time and he's scum. He was a Pinkerton operative on the *Verona* and he fired the shot that started that bloody business."

"I never heard that."

"And you never will. He was a provocateur for the Everett mill interests and the agency covered it up."

Dengel said with finality, "We need him for this work."

Gund nodded, "I agree. Maybe passing yourself off as a lumberjack in Idaho was a waste of time. If a contingent of rifles managed to get through over the Northern Pacific, we can only hope we'll intercept the rest."

Jamieson turned to Gund. "Sir, I don't believe the guns have left Butte. He fed us a pack of lies to throw us off the scent. Gave us just enough valid information, hoping we'll believe the rest. If I can locate O'Neill . . . "

"If he's still alive. If he had anything to do with those rifles in the first place. The Army wasn't certain his presence in Ellensburg was connected to those old Springfields in that boxcar. We assumed they were intended for Ireland because of the rumors we picked up in Butte."

"O'Neill had a Ross bayonet in his pack. Where did it come from?"

"The Canadians verified the rifles were transferred in the spring. You said O'Neill had the bayonet last winter? That makes no sense."

Germer's boyish face flushed. "Sir, you sent that telegram a few weeks back to be on the lookout for Ross rifles. I may have mentioned its make to Agent C-815. Maybe he asked this miner if the make of the rifle was Ross, and that information inadvertently tipped them off. So telling us cost them nothing."

Jamieson added, "I suspect he was here to discover how much we know."

Dengel fumed, "I want that miner arrested. I'll take him to Spokane, get the names of the ring leaders out of him." He confronted Jamieson. "And I'm not finished with you, either, Lieutenant."

Gund addressed Jamieson. "If you can't locate O'Neill in the next few days, Lieutenant, it's my intention to have you transferred back to Portland. I'll decide what to do with your talents then."

Dengel contravened, "He's under my command."

Gund methodically tapped his pipe into a tin ashtray. "We'll see."

Jamieson wouldn't knuckle under to either man. It wasn't his style.

Chapter 72
Finlander Hall, Butte, Montana

He would hunt down O'Neill alone. Lieutenant Germer might be a good officer, but he was no detective, and he still had a soft spot on his head. Major Gund was a theoretician, and Dengel . . . he wouldn't even think about Dengel. Fats Gerard was stirring up slime in more than one mud hole. He remembered seeing O'Neill chumming with him at the rag camp. When he found O'Neill, he'd pound out of him all the answers he wanted.

Sorties of men wandered Butte's streets and alleyways at night, on their way somewhere -- or nowhere. Jamieson sauntered up North Wyoming past the two-story Finlander Hall, then past the boardinghouse Frank Little was dragged from and lynched. A spooky little piece of Butte.

He sensed he was being followed and decided to make something happen, hoping it would play to his advantage. The memory of Sewell's cautioning him not to make himself known when there was nothing to gain had grown thin. He was damn tired of seeing success receding before him. Sewell was a ghost, but he didn't think O'Neill was. He backtracked and entered Finlander Hall. Chatting men went silent; others lifted eyes from newspapers. He palmed his I.W.W. card. "I'm lookin' for a pal. Malachi O'Neill. Called Irish in Wobbly circles."

"Someone asked, "Which mine?"

"Not a miner. A lumberjack. Me, too, when we aren't organizing."

A thickset man pushed through a knot of miners. "Have a beer."

The bartender shoved it across polished mahogany and Jamieson wrapped a work-hardened hand around it, wanting the man to see it. He flattened the other on the bar.

"What's this O'Neill fella look like?"

Jamieson wiped foam from his mouth. "Bushy eyebrows, broken nose. Chipped teeth. From County Cork. Wouldn't draw a whore's glance, but I'm mighty fond of him."

"Haven't seen him. If he shows up, who should we say is lookin' for him?"

"Mac James. Partnered him in the Idaho timber."

"What makes you think he's here?" Maybe it was the cigar and cigarette smoke narrowing his eyes. Maybe not.

"Just a hunch. Figured if he came through Butte, he'd land here." He set down the empty glass. "Thanks for the beer. Guess I'll head back to Idaho. Maybe he's already there."

Outside he lit a cigarette under a streetlamp and stood smoking it before he sauntered up the sidewalk. How many times had he worked a case as a window man tailing someone? It was odd being on the receiving end. Two shadows crossed the street and a door opened. They strong-armed him, giving him a bum's rush into a dark hallway. A third man moved from behind the door and punched him over a kidney. When a drilling miner hits, something's going to give. A hard one to his stomach knocked the air out of his lungs and a fist slammed into his face. A cosh struck the back of his head, taking him to his knees.

They dropped a sack over his head and, through a fog of pain, he felt himself being dragged. In a back room they disarmed him and tied him to a chair.

"Forgot to gag him." The voice belonged to the mining canary who sang at Germer's office. The miner lifted the sack high enough to stuff a gag in his mouth. It tasted of salt. A snotty handkerchief.

The door opened. "Holy Christ in heaven!" It slammed, but he recognized the voice. Wanted to shout, "Irish, you fuckin' bastard!" Tried to spit out the rag, but someone tightened the sack around his neck, running tape around it over his mouth. *Goddamn.* He hurt bad.

Two men stomped out and he heard a muffled, "Fuckin' Pinkerton." But maybe not. His head was ringing. Heard, "Worse than Pinkerton, boyo. Army." Or maybe he didn't. The canary asked, "How do you know?" "'Tis I'm knowin' him well enough." Or maybe he was putting words in O'Neill's mouth. "Didn't suspect nothin'. Told 'em they already . . ." A mumble. ". . NP." And maybe he didn't hear, "Takin' 'em out in the mornin'." Maybe it was, "Take him out in the mornin'."

The canary came back in. "Leave him for the night. Let him piss his pants."

Being alone with a sack over his head gave Jamieson time to reflect. He should have positioned Lieutenant Germer down the block. After Sewell was murdered he'd developed a bad habit of relying on himself to get out of trouble. Billy had watched his back like a kindly uncle made of flint and gunpowder. Somewhere along the way he'd become knot-headed. Not asking for help can get a man killed. And those Butte Irish tied damn tight knots.

Chapter 73
Butte, Montana

Down the tracks from the Milwaukee freight depot, a cluster of men in somber suits, black silk covering their faces, transferred three pine coffins from Larry Duggan's mortuary truck to an express car.

A few days earlier O'Neill observed Father Hannan chide, "Ah, no, Brian, 'tis askin' too much to be usin' the glass hearse and matched blacks wavin' mournin' plumes."

To those watching from the platform the scarves were intended to give the appearance of men protecting themselves from the stench of corrupted flesh. Even Father Hannan was silk-swathed. He flicked his aspergillum on each coffin, sprinkling holy water and making the sign of the cross. Onlookers on the platform fanned the air to hurry the reek past, but were insufficiently offended to disperse.

"Mind out this one," Dennis Shea, the undertaker, cautioned as strong shoulders hoisted the last coffin. "He was a heavy bugger."

O'Neill and James Treanor followed the coffin into the car. The Sullivans handed in a basket of food and drink before cutting across the tracks.

Father Hannan pulled down his scarf and grimaced, "Will the paperwork bear scrutiny, Dennis?"

The damp spot widened across the silk covering Shea's mouth. "It will, Father."

With most of the foul air now restricted inside the freight car, a few curious souls came off the platform to approach the priest and undertaker. O'Neill drew back within the express and Shea turned to head for the truck, but Father Hannan stayed him with a hand on his arm and loud dulcet tones. "Duggan's Mortuary could have ignored the family's wishes and buried them here in Butte. Sure they're right ripe in this heat."

Shea lowered his scarf, answering in equal volume, "It's bad luck to go against a last request to be buried on home ground."

Those approaching stopped. The priest continued, "If that woman, bless her soul, had fed some of that jar of green beans to her chickens afore her family, the chickens would 'ave died and they be warned off. 'Tis a sad way to go."

Sprouting gray whiskers, a man in a shabby suit sidled up. "Who died?"

"A family named O'Toole. The pur-r man was to start at the mines today, livin' in a shack out on the flats."

"So it wasn't that Spanish Influenza they got back east we been readin' about?"

From the shadows inside the car O'Neill watched Shea study his shoes before looking up. "No, if it'd been that we'd have had to bury them here . . . and quickly, too." He looked beyond the man to the idlers keeping their distance. "I don't think we have to worry about that influenza coming to Butte. The air's so sulfurous, it'll kill it off any pestilence the minute it creeps over the divide and into the valley."

Whiskers nodded sagely and turned back to share these tidbits with the others. Father Hannan cranked the truck's engine for Shea before joining him in the cab. After a few explosive backfires, it pulled away.

To relieve themselves of some of the foul odor inside the express car, O'Neill and Treanor kept its door open until a brakeman came along, pinched his nose and bawled, "Let's go boys, she's time. Shut the damn door."

O'Neill rumbled it closed. The electric engine carried the flat bars of a pantograph to rub against overhead copper trolley wire, giving off its own sweet odor of ozone from high voltage electricity. No smoke from a coal-fired engine would slip through cracks to tamp down this stench until they crossed the Montana – Idaho line and changed back to a coal-fired engine. But they wouldn't wait that long.

They lowered their scarves, but immediately drew them up again. "Agh," Treanor gasped thickly, "pluggin' me nose don't help. I can taste it in the back a' me throat."

"For the cause, James."

Hunkered in a corner, Treanor lit a cigarette, tugged down the silk to inhale.

O'Neill eyed the small red glow. "Be havin' an extra? Tryin' to quit, but a cigarette might keep me from pukin' me breakfast." They blew cigarette smoke into stultifying air, but alleviated little of their misery.

An hour later the train rumbled into Deer Lodge. Jamming the door from inside, they braced for someone to attempt to open it. No one came, and the train pulled away, heading for Missoula.

"Now's the time." O'Neill shoved open the express car door and, donning gloves, they loosened the strappings and slid open each coffin lid. Raising a flurry of flies, they tossed three rotting goat carcasses out the open door.

Chapter 74

Shortly before noon the same day, Captain Bradley and Company F of the 14th Infantry Regiment assisted the local police in raiding Finlander Hall. They arrested some Wobblies, accusing them of organizing an imminent strike at the mines.

Going from room to room, a couple of cops found an unidentified man tied to a chair with a cotton bag over his head. They pulled off the tape and removed the sack. He'd worked out most of a gag. They asked his identity, but his reply was to demand they untie him so he could take a piss.

A cop shoved Jamieson, wrists manacled, out the front door and through a contingent of soldiers. Squinting, Jamieson spotted Bradley. His escort pushed him over to the captain. "We found him bound and gagged, but he won't tell us anything. I'm taking him down to the station."

Bradley asked, "What happened to your face?"

"Walked into a door." He'd seen himself in the small mirror in the toilet.

"He's one of ours," Bradley said. "I'll vouch for him."

The disappointed officer removed the cuffs and Jamieson pulled out his new pocket watch, but its face was smashed. "What time is it?"

"Ten after one."

"I have to get to the Milwaukee train depot." Seeing Lieutenant Germer exit the hall, Jamieson motioned to him.

Germer came over. Announced, crestfallen, "The rifles aren't here. I thought they'd be cached under the floorboards."

"They might have been," Jamieson said, "but it's unlikely they'd be so blatant about it. I'm guessing they're now on a train."

Captain Bradley looked mystified and then grim. Cut out of some Military Intelligence loop, he had to be content with a few sorry-looking Wobblies.

Germer asked, "What happened to your face?"

Jamieson would have commandeered a police car, but Germer protested he had to keep a low profile, so they haled a jitney.

At the freight depot, resplendently official in his uniform, Germer demanded to see all waybills. He handed the stack to Jamieson, who thumbed through them, looking for destination points and types of cargo, each yellow tissue a carbon copy in faint, nearly illegible, scratchings.

When Germer moved with him to a window for better lighting, Jamieson muttered, "How about a cup of coffee . . . black . . . and a doughnut. I haven't eaten since yesterday."

He gulped his coffee and consumed the doughnut held between blackened fingers. Then he handed the only paper he'd pulled to a hovering railway express agent. "What about this shipment of human remains to St. Joe City?"

"What about it?" The man had a face beloved of some Irish mother.

"Did you observe the coffins being loaded?"

"Saw 'em and smelled 'em. Already decomposing. Worse than shippin' hogs."

If Jamieson knew anything, it was railroad regulations. He considered the agent. "The morgue didn't embalm the bodies?"

"Of course they did. If they won't reach their destination within twenty-four hours of death, the bodies must be embalmed. The embalmer signed the paperwork. They died of food poisoning and no one found them for a few days."

"Who transported them here?"

"Duggan Mortuary."

"Anyone accompanying the bodies?"

"That's by regulation, too. Have to be escorted by a ticketed passenger. There were two escorts."

"Where's that train now?"

Ignoring the clock, the agent removed his gold watch and flipped it open. "Should be leaving Missoula about now."

"Next stop?"

"Next stop is Avery, Idaho, to change from electric back to a coal-fired engine."

Jamieson told Germer, "We'll interview the mortuary staff and look at their records." He again addressed the agent. "I'm sending a wire to the Benewah County sheriff for him meet the train at St. Joe City and open those coffins. The United States

Army believes they're filled with contraband rifles and ammunition."

Seemingly stunned, the agent sought Germer's verification. "Important stuff, huh? Wouldn't have guessed it by the stench."

Jamieson printed out the message for the telegram and had Germer sign it. "Makes it official Army business."

Germer adopted a superior look, which made his boyish face look sophomoric. "This train stops in Avery, right?"

"Yeah."

"Avery is in Shoshone County, right?"

"You should know, it's in your district."

"Why not wire the Shoshone County sheriff to open the coffins in Avery? Get into them sooner."

Jamieson's uncomfortable night didn't improve his disposition. "The sheriff can't reach Avery in time because there's a mountain range between Wallace and Avery and no railroad connecting them. Ever hear the expression 'No law south of Wallace?' Didn't think so. No law from the Montana line along the Milwaukee tracks until you reach St. Maries."

"Right. I should have known that." Added in his defense, "I'm from Pennsylvania."

"Yeah." Jamieson turned to glare at the telegrapher, who was sorting mail. When the man looked up, it was at the uniformed Germer. "What can I do ya?"

"Send this," Jamieson ordered. "Official Army business." He listened to the clicking key, remembering enough Morse code from a boyhood obsession to follow it.

"We want acknowledgement the message was received."

A few moments later he heard the incoming "X".

"Now we'll go check the receipts at Duggan Mortuary." Crossing the tiled floor to the exit, Jamieson asked, "What did you do about that Catholic priest?" When Germer gave him a blank look, Jamieson just shook his head.

After interviewing a nervous, but cooperative, Dennis Shea, and scrutinizing the paperwork on the O'Toole family, Jamieson returned to his hotel, shaved, bathed and slept for an hour. When he entered Germer's office, the lieutenant handed him a telegram. Sheriff Roland would meet the express freight at St. Joe City. Jamieson read it with a sense of accomplishment. His mission was to locate the rifles and he'd done that. And now he'd alerted the only civilian official with authority to search the train where the munitions would be unloaded.

He went to St. Mary's Church in search of Father Hannan. The rectory housekeeper said the good father had gone fishing for a few days. Just where, she wasn't certain, but could Father Slattery be of assistance? She'd be glad to ring him up.

Chapter 75

Deep in the night the coffins were off-loaded as way freight at Tank Creek, some miles east of St. Joe City. Their striped pockets padded with cash, the fireman, brakeman and engineer proceeded to take on water, ignoring the activity up the line. Had it been on the manifest, this unusual destination would have been a legal stop.

Treanor grumbled, "'Twould 'ave been a fine thing to send them to Tacoma right off."

"We can't be riskin' it. 'Tis how I planned it. A good thing, too, with that Army detective showin' up. He's likely got himself away by now. Sheriff Roland himself might be waitin' at St. Joe City and I'm not wantin' to meet him again in this world."

When the train pulled away, the Ranneys emerged from the trees carrying lanterns and leading a string of pack mules. Treanor and O'Neill opened the coffins, each one filled with rifles and ammunition. Told how many, Osee Ranney directed their transfer, evenly counted out, onto pieces of canvas manty. Experienced hands wrapped and lashed two bundles on each mule. The boxes of ammunition were roped on top.

"What about those coffins?"

"We'll float 'em down the river. If they're found, 'tis no concern of ours. We'll be done and gone."

Ranney handed O'Neill a lantern. "That old moon ain't givin' no light. These mules is kickers, so follow behind an' keep yur distance."

*　　*

O'Neill had offered Ranney a deal. "Ye'll be makin' money and be hurtin' the bloody English altogether. What do ye say?"

"Do ya reckon when this will happen?"

"Soon. We've trusted men workin' the Milwaukee from Butte to Avery to St. Maries. We'll unload the rifles at Tank Creek at night an' pack 'em up here. Hide 'em till the way is clear to the coast."

"Here?" Ranney shook his head. "It don't sound right. Revenuers and the Army, they're bound to come 'round soon. Can't be caught with stolen guns, too."

"Sure it's not stolen they be. Bought from the Canadian government with good American gold. I'll show ye where I'll be hidin' 'em."

The dogs and mules gave voice as O'Neill made for the hog pen. "Ye've a fine manure pile from these *muca*," pointing beyond the slumbering hogs. The ground was soggy with seepage.

"If you've a mind to do that, ya can bury those guns yurself."

"Can ye see the sheriff or Army diggin' under it?"

"They'll poke pitchforks in it lookin' for shine."

"They can poke all they want. I mean to move the manure pile to one side, bury the guns and ammunition, then put the manure back where it was."

Ranney closed his eyes and raised his face, seeking guidance beyond himself. A moment later, "Put 'er thare then." O'Neill seized his hand with relief.

"The missus'll make ya wash in the creek an' she won't be washin' yur stinkin' clothes." But he was smiling broadly within his flowing beard.

Comrades in purpose, they talked as they headed back to the cabin, followed by four frollicking puppies.

"They all survived then," O'Neill said."

"Yup. Gonna be some great dawgs." Osee reached down to scratch one. When he straightened, he asked, "An' our Tessa is doin' good at camp? Not no trouble for Miz Blake?"

*   *

The rifles and ammunition buried, O'Neill made his way to St. Joe City and Kate.

Inside her again, he didn't want to come out, moving gently over her like the rolling of a ship.

"Kate," he whispered afterward, "Since ye're a woman of adventuresome blood, will ye consider comin' to Ireland with me and joinin' the cause? 'Tis bound to be a grand time."

Chapter 76

July was hot and dry, the groundcover in the woods the color of burlap. Every footfall crackled. MacLean knew it was risky falling trees in this heat, using the steam donkey to hoist and move logs on cables, running the Shay engine up and down short tracks into the woods. Sparks. But there was a war on.

Supper over, some jacks sat on split logs or squatted, chewing tobacco and bullshitting, watching flickering heat lightning. Their intermittent murmurings carried on a warm breeze through MacLean's open office door. "That wind ain't nothing but a Chinook comin' from the southwest. Hot as hell this time of year. If a gust blows sparks off the donkey an' nobody sees 'em, it'll all be over." Then someone brought up the 1910 fire.

Sitting back in his chair, boots up on his desk, the talk tore open MacLean's old wound. Ancient timber that withstood centuries of fires had burned like matchsticks or was felled by fire winds. The reminder of what he lost that awful summer lay across the valley, crisscrossed and blackened on the mountainsides.

Disciple Paul began to preach. "The breath of Jehovah, like a stream of brimstone, doth kindle it." Paul's voice died away. Then a woeful, "Isaiah thirty." MacLean thumped down his boots to glare out the doorway. The Disciple rose and headed into the bunkhouse. Good riddance. More murmurings and then Disciple Paul intoned loudly, "But the fearful, and unbelieving, and the abominable, and murderers, and whoremongers, and sorcerers, and idolaters, and all liars, shall have their part in the lake which burneth with fire and brimstone . . . which is the second death." As the lumberjack breathed ominously, "Revelation twenty-one," MacLean roared out of his office.

"You shut that damn yap of yours before I put my spikes into your rear end. These men are jumpy enough without your caterwauling." Disciple Paul scowled, but MacLean scowled fiercer. The lumberjack plodded into the bunkhouse, reverently holding his Bible before him.

* *

When Jamieson came back to camp and slipped into his place at the table, he watched for Addie to step out to survey the room. When she did, his was the first place she looked. He smiled, but she turned back into the kitchen. After supper he stood outside the kitchen screen door until she flung it open and came out. She walked past him to the wood pile and he followed. He held out his arms and she loaded them with split wood.

"Did you find Mally? Is he alive?"

"He's alive."

"Oh, thank God! Where is he?"

"In Butte. Maybe not now." He longed to touch and kiss her, but the wood weighting down his arms made that impossible. "Tonight, after dark, I'm going to wash off in the flume pond above the Marble. You know where I mean? Will you meet me there?"

"I'll come."

"It's warmer than the creek. The pond will be filling, but it shouldn't be too deep."

He carried in the wood to find Dovey in the kitchen, arms folded. "Well, hello there, Mac. Wondered if you'd stop by to say hello now that you're back. You shaved that scruffy beard, I see."

"You're a saucy lady, Mrs. Blake. I've a mind to give you a smooch right on the cheek," which he did to the glee of Tessa and the flunkies. Polite John watched over his pipe, the only man in camp allowed to smoke.

He'd returned to camp for three reasons. The guns never arrived at St. Joe City, but he figured they must be nearby; he suspected Addie knew something; and he couldn't stay away from her.

The week before, he'd made a fast trip to Portland to apprise Major Gund of what transpired in Butte after the major's departure and to ask for more time to locate the rifles. That was granted, and he spent a couple of days watching the Big Timber, sitting in night shadows with a view of the back entrance, hoping to glimpse O'Neill. Maybe he dozed off and dreamed. In the dark a man whistled O'Neill's familiar tune. The sound receded around a corner, but when he roused himself, he couldn't find him.

He went in search of Katie, but was told she was away on a trip. He described O'Neill to the bartender, claiming they were supposed to meet up before heading into the woods, but the keep said he was never there. Jamieson hung around another day, then broke into Addie's cabin for his logging clothes and headed back to camp.

*   *

That night, Addie reached the outskirts of the camp before switching on her flashlight. The galumphing Titus, not in on the secrecy, ranged ahead, barking so loudly, she didn't hear pine needles crackle when Jamieson stepped from the shadows.

"Addie."

She yelped and turned the light on him. "Oh, you scared me." His arms encircled her and she found his mouth. When he released her, she said, "I brought a piece of soap and a towel."

"Then, let's go." He switched on his own light and, taking her hand, led her through the forest. When they emerged into the cut area where only slash remained, he paused to kiss her again, then stood behind her, holding her. "Look up, Addie." The spangled heavens spread out above them. "Living among tall timber, I'd forgotten how beautiful the night can be."

"When I was a girl, Mama and I would take a blanket into the wheat field after harvest and lie on our backs." She pulled his arms tighter around her.

"When I rode freights doing detective work, on hot summer nights I'd crawl on top and lie on my back as they rattled along. August was best with the sky full of shooting stars."

"That's when we went out, too. You and I were probably looking at the same sky." She turned in his arms and took his face in her hands.

"I missed you so much, Addie," he said, kissing her again.

"I won't be coy. I missed you, too."

Titus came back from his adventure.

When they reached the pond, they removed their clothes and Jamieson slipped into the water, but Addie stood hesitant on the bank. She leaned down toward him as he tried to coax her in, declaring the water, though thick with floating bark, nevertheless felt delightful.

Titus, ever playful, butted her from behind and she splashed in head-first. Jamieson raised a sputtering Addie to the surface and into his embrace. The dog jumped in to paddle about, biting at pieces of wood. Moving Addie close to the bank to find footing in the mud, he picked bark out of her hair and wiped detritus from her face. Then he ran his hands over her naked body and kissed her again. She relaxed against him, nuzzling his neck.

A short way back on the trail a girl's shrill laughter broke into their intimate world. Jamieson pulled Addie along the bank, but it was too late. Giant Kid and Tessa came on, holding hands behind a lantern. A moment later the four of them were staring at one another. Titus climbed up the bank with a piece of wood in his mouth and shook himself, making Tessa shriek.

Addie crouched close to the bank, water covering her shoulders. "Why are you sneaking off from camp this time of night, Tessa?"

Giant Kid spoke up. "We're tryin' to get clean, same as you two."

Deciding the best defense was attack, Addie continued, "Would your mother approve, Tessa?"

"We're not doin' nothin' Mama would shame me for. What are you'uns doin' here?"

"Come on in," Jamieson invited. "We all can use a bath. And then we'll walk back to camp together and keep this to ourselves. Won't we, Harv?"

"You betcha, Mac."

Early the next morning, MacLean marched into the kitchen, slamming the screen door behind him. "Whadda mean, we need supplies?"

Addie straightened from rolling biscuit dough. "I'm nearly out of eggs and anything fresh. I've waited all week for the packer. He's four days late. What happened to him?"

"How should I know? Maybe a mule kicked him."

"Then send a man with our mules down to Marble Creek Station for supplies."

"If I send a man for supplies, he'll head for the booze and won't come back till he sobers up and everything's spoiled. No one leaves camp unless he draws his pay."

Still cutting out biscuits, she said, "Then I'll go."

"You'll go? Who'll bake and run the kitchen? Every time you go off, things fall apart here. It's that Blake woman's fault."

Dovey limped into the kitchen. "She don't have to take orders from you, Maclean. She's part-owner and can do as she pleases. Don't worry your old head. I'll get it done in season."

Blue eyes blazed. "Who asked you? This is my camp and I decide who goes and who stays."

Addie ignored their open hostility. "I'll take the three mules, just as I did to St. Joe City, and have a list of supplies sent to the grocer in St. Maries. I'll spend the night at the hotel next to the depot."

Alonzo interrupted, "Ain't much of a hotel, more like a flophouse."

"And the next morning the train will pull into Marble Station with the supplies and I'll head back. I'll be gone two days."

"And just who's gonna load up your mules and throw a proper hitch? You're no packer. And that jenny likes to bloat in the mornin'. By noon she's got the pack slidin' off."

"She and I understand each other now. I'm sure I can find someone to pack the loads properly for me. And Mrs. Blake will do the baking."

Defeated, he glowered at them.

Chapter 77

It wasn't the Shay engine or steam donkey that started the fire, but a dry lightning strike on a giant pine. It simmered a day or two before flaring needles and cones fired dry tinder below. The forest ranger saw it from his lookout on Marble Mountain and rode down with firefighting equipment strapped to a pack mule. A slap of hot wind whirled in and, when he arrived, it was no longer a one-man job. The ranger rode through logging camps, calling out lumberjacks to fight the fire.

Ordered back to camp, Jamieson and the others smelled smoke as they walked in; the fire was heading their way. Men grabbed up extra blankets and heavier clothing, and pulled shovels and picks from a shed. Without the mules Addie had taken, logging horses were packed up.

Jamieson looked past stumpage and purple fireweed, hoping to see Addie coming up the trail, leading the pack string. He almost bumped into Pickles, bindle on his back, heading in the direction opposite from the one the jacks were taking toward the fire. "I ain't goin' up there," he announced, face white and slick with sweat.

"Pickles, now stop right there," Jamieson said. "If you don't go with the men, they'll lose heart. They'll think the fire is more dangerous than it is."

"It will be if the wind picks up."

"That's why every man is needed." Deciding he was wasting his breath, he snapped, "Go on then. Hope you don't get caught down there alone if it heads your way." He led a big horse around to the kitchen to load it with canned goods. Pickles watched him and then followed.

"All I found are canvas bags," Dovey announced. "You'll have to tie them together."

"Guess that'll work."

"I wish Addie was back."

"She'll see the smoke and turn back toward the river."

"Not if she's comin' up the old tote trail. It runs deep through the mountains. We can't see the fire from here, so we can't tell if it's grown much." She pointed. "Won't know 'til it crests that ridge."

He said to the woman who understood and loved him, "I'm worried about her."

"So am I, Robbie. Worried sick."

The ground fire spread fast, running up towering trees. An occasional stiff breeze carried it from treetop to treetop. Each crew was directed to a different area, ordered to clear fire lines to channel the ground fire away from old slash toward creeks and rocks. The MacLean crew worked a three-foot fire line, scraping away pine needles, debris and dirt down to mineral soil.

Suddenly two mules dashed through the smoky haze, eyes rolled back, packs in disarray, saddle trees askew. Seeing the men, the mules slowed and allowed themselves to be caught. No woman rode through the smoky haze behind them. A jack said, "Them's our mules all right."

Jamieson tugged the bandanna from his face and strode to the ranger sitting his horse. "Lend me your mount. I've got to find Mrs. MacLean."

"I can't let you burn up my horse." He jerked the reins, backing it away.

Jamieson grabbed the bridle, captured the reins beneath the horse's jaw, controlling it. "Lend me this horse or I'll chew your balls off and make you wish you had. Not a man here will stop me. I mean business."

The ranger called out to MacLean, who glanced up from where he stood calming the two mules. The Ol' Man looked from the ranger to Jamieson, then turned his back on them. The ranger had no choice but to dismount. "You're a damn fool."

"I'll send it back when I find Mrs. MacLean. I know horses are no good near fire."

"He'll try to head for the ranger station."

But Jamieson wasn't listening. He swung up into the saddle and made for the tote trail, mapping in his mind the lesser creeks emptying into the Marble that the trail crossed and ran beside. Addie would seek safety in a creek, wouldn't she? The last sanctuary is water and that's where he'd find her.

Never much of a trail, now smoked in and obscured, it was difficult to follow. Pulling up his bandanna, he nudged the horse on. A couple of miles farther through dense timber, a crack and whoosh rent the smoke-filled canyon as flames crested a timbered ridge and shot down toward him. Smoke cleared enough for him to see crown fires shooting into the sky and burning snags tumbling in a fountain of sparks. Sick fear filled his belly as smoke settled over him again. Thudding hooves and then a running horse nearly collided with his, swerving and disappearing up the tote trail. Addie's horse. The ranger's horse tried to rush after it, but Jamieson fought it.

Fires normally move slowly downhill, but this was a locomotive racing down the canyon, sucking life from the forest. He heard the desperate bray of a mule and then a bark. Titus! Through smoke and a scorching hot wind, he spotted Addie sitting in the middle of a rocky stream with Titus beside her. The jenny flailed on its side in the creek, heavy pack weighing it down as it struggled to regain its footing. Addie held its rope taut with one hand; the other covered her nose and mouth with the hem of her shirt.

Jamieson twisted the reins around the saddle horn, dismounted and slapped the horse's rump to send it back through smoke and blowing embers. He stumbled down the bank into the creek, spiked boots slipping on rocks as he avoided the jenny's hooves. He pulled out his knife and slashed the pack saddle's girth, releasing the its burden. Shouted to Addie, "Let go the rope! Give it a chance!" She opened her hand and the rope slipped through water as the animal struggled to its feet. Snorting and wheezing, it climbed the bank to disappear into the smoke.

He freed the canvas manty from around the crates as Addie gripped a corner, trying to draw it over her. Taking it from her, he pulled her to her feet. Tried to shout above the fire's roar, "Come on," but his words came out a throaty wheeze. Her eyes were swollen, nearly closed beneath her hat. Both were coughing, eyes raw and burning, as they dragged the manty through heavy smoke in search of deeper water. Flaming pine cones whirled into the creek, hissing and sizzling when they hit water. Titus splashed heavily behind, mouth agape, tongue lolling.

They couldn't have been in a worse spot. The fire had jumped the creek, forcing Jamieson to act fast. Fire-shrouded trees would consume their air. A hundred feet up the ridge, the top of a soaring pine cracked and broke off. It tumbled end over end, shearing off shorter snags, creating a rain of fire.

A rock jutted from the bank, maybe high enough to stick their heads under. The water wasn't deep enough, but time had run out. Their lungs were filling with smoke. Addie's knees buckled and he dragged her under the outcrop, scooped out mud and sand, trying to give her a pocket of air. Coughing and gasping for breath, she laid her face in curled arms. His own strength diminishing, Jamieson pushed down the wheezing mastiff to partly cover Addie, intending to use the dog for her protection and his own. He pulled half the wet manty over most of the dog and woman, scooped water with his hat, and poured it over her head. Then soaked his bandanna and laid it across the back of her neck before dragging the canvas completely over her.

As a last act, he splashed water on his head and jammed down his wet hat. He crawled under a flap of canvas and part of the dog, taking some of its weight off Addie. The mastiff's head was under the canvas, but outside the outcrop; it flopped heavily on their shoulders. Titus might drown if he lost consciousness and his head dropped between them, but it couldn't be helped. Whimpering, struggling for breath, the dog's hind legs kicked reflexively. They were getting smoked and they might run out of air, but they wouldn't burn up.

The water turned warm. The air was so hot, every breath drawn seemed their last. Trees exploded up creek. Burning cones plopped into nearby water, some dropping on the canvas, burning Jamieson's shoulder and back not covered by the dog. He couldn't knock them off without uncovering Addie. As oxygen burned away amid the hissing and snapping of doomed trees, a fire wind bore down. Titus stopped kicking, gave a long moan and was silent, a dead weight.

"Addie." His voice was weaker than a whisper.

She replied with a sobbing breath.

"Didn't desert Army."

"I know."

He lost consciousness.

Chapter 78

When Jamieson came to during the night, searing pain raced from his shoulder and back into his brain. Bits of smoldering debris had burned through the manty. He took in a shuddering breath, followed by a fit of coughing. The canvas had been pushed away, the mastiff's weight on him gone. Addie touched his cheek.

Too parched to speak, he squinted at her in the tawny light of a few scattered burning trees; lifted a wet gloved finger and touched his tongue. He craved water, but the creek tasted of charcoal, so he clawed out sand and gravel, hoping for something cleaner beneath. Lowered his mouth and swallowed, then retched.

She croaked beside him. "All right?"

When his heaving stopped, he managed, "You?"

A raw, "Yes . . . you?"

"Back's burnt. Dog?"

"Here."

Low whines and heavy breathing came from her other side.

He wheezed, "He's burnt, too. Don't drink water."

Pitch popped and crackled and ground smoke drifted over the creek.

Her guttural, "What now?"

He couldn't make saliva. His next word took effort. "Wait." He dozed then, escaping the torture of his burns.

Her murmuring raised his consciousness. " . . cheated you . . . inheritance."

He grunted that he heard.

Her voice could sand wood. ". . didn't deserve . . . deserter."

He managed, "Not important."

"Is . . . let time run out." A whispered, "Forgive me."

Throat so dry, deep in his ears he could hear himself trying to swallow. "Nothing . . . to forgive."

She rasped, "Marry me . . . make it up to you."

"Love you. Can't talk." Touched her wrist above her glove.

* *

Dawn came. Smoke wisped off smoldering logs of once sturdy forest giants. There was an occasional crash as another tree fell. A gunshot came from where the trail had been and Addie struggled to her feet. Almost blind from smoke and ash, she staggered across the debris-choked stream to where Alonzo and two men, blackened and ash-covered, picked their way through fallen trees.

Seeing her, Alonzo shambled forward until his arms went around her. "Thought I lost ya. God almighty, so glad you're alive." Blood-shot blue eyes looked into blood-shot blue eyes. He ran his knuckles down her grimy cheek.

Giant Kid and Popovic waded across the creek to help Jamieson to his feet. Titus dragged himself after them, his back raw and bloody where patches of hair and skin were burned.

"Addie, you want I should shoot your dog and put him out of his misery?"

She squinted numbly at Titus and then at Alonzo. Giant Kid handed her a canteen, but Alonzo stayed her hand.

"Don't gulp it. Sip a little at a time."

After she wet her mouth and throat, she managed, "Is he bad?"

"Hard to tell. He's sufferin'. We got the fire contained. Only place it was really bad was here. You got caught between two spot fires that merged on ya."

"I'm all right," she said. A little louder. "Mac is burnt."

"We'll take him to the hospital down at St. Maries."

Jamieson sat on the creek bank holding a canteen while Giant Kid peeled back his charred shirt. Pushing the Kid's hands away, he tried to stand, but then groaned and clutched the youth's wrist. Managed a guttural, "Not St. Maries. Sheriff . . . arrest me."

MacLean snapped, "Well, where in hell am I gonna get your burns treated? Addie, I know ya been through a lot, but has he come unhinged?"

"It was awful." She touched her swollen face. It felt like an attack of sun poisoning. Even blinking hurt.

"I know. Them two thought I was crazy to think ya survived."

Jamieson squawked, "Wallace."

"Ya wanna go to Wallace? Still gotta go to St. Maries. Put ya on a steamer there, transfer ya to a train at Harrison for Wallace. We'll take our chances with the sheriff at the hospital in St. Maries."

Jamieson took a drink. "Moon Pass."

MacLean sat on a rock, exhausted. "Son, that's crazy. You want us to take the train to Avery, hire horses and ride over Moon Pass to Wallace? The other side of the mountains? The time it'll take and the jostling, you'll go into shock with the pain."

"Take that chance. Nuns . . . Providence Hospital . . . good nurses."

Addie poured water in her hand and splashed it in her eyes. She looked at Alonzo, Giant Kid and Popovic, who'd fought fire all night, but were still on their feet. Gritty and dried out, they'd come searching for them. Why was Robbie so pig-headed about going to Wallace? She touched his arm and he gripped her hand, squeezing it until it hurt. It must be critical to him.

"Mac saved my life. If you can't take him to Wallace, I will. Those sisters at the hospital, they treated men burnt in the great fire, didn't they?"

"Most hospitals treat burns." Alonzo wiped his face with a blackened handkerchief, motioned for the canteen and took a drink. "If ya go, I'll go with ya." He untied a length of rope from around his waist, its purpose unknown, which he slipped through the mastiff's collar. "Giant Kid, you take the dog to camp an' tell the stableman to doctor him up. Have the timekeeper give ya a blank check and some cash. Saddle the horse and bridle two of the mules. Three blankets, food and water. And bring some honey for Mac's back. We ain't walkin' to Marble Station, even though it's downhill."

* *

At Providence Hospital a nurse tried to put a trembling Jamieson in a wheelchair. He refused and, teeth chattering,

walked the big-wheeled chair down the hall to keep himself
upright. "Don't want my back touching anything."

Standing at the reception desk, Addie and Alonzo watched
his efforts. They'd spent the previous night in Avery, then an
entire day riding the thirty miles from Avery over Moon Pass.
It was a hot day, but Jamieson complained of being cold.

Addie slumped onto a chair. "I didn't think he'd make it."
She still wore smoky jodhpurs, her scruffy ash-stained hat and
blackened linen shirt.

"I didn't think either of you would make it. I should've
taken ya both into St. Maries. I could've stood up to the
sheriff."

Addie had feared for Robbie the entire journey, mining raw
energy to get him to this destination on unpredictable hired
horses.

MacLean pulled a folded check from a pocket. Addressing
the nun behind the reception desk, he said, "Sister, if you'll
hand me a fountain pen, I'll sign this blank check for my man's
care. The hospital can fill it in when he's released. There's
insurance, too, through the MacLean Lumber Company." He
handed her the signed check. "Somethin' else. I understand
Sister Mary Jerome is nursing here. That so?" Told it was, he
nodded. "Tell her Alonzo MacLean will be pleased to say
hello. Maybe tomorrow. You can see we're in need of cleanin'
up and a good sleep."

*   *

Rapid footsteps came down the center of the men's ward and a
nun quietly moved a section of hinged screen surrounding
Jamieson's bed. "This patient is now assigned to me, nurse."

The young nurse washing Jamieson's arms and hands
straightened.

On his stomach, he painfully turned his head, meeting the
nun's concerned eyes. She held a tray containing a hypodermic
syringe.

The nurse protested, "Sister, I don't understand. You're
head of the women's ward. This man's back is burnt and
Doctor Daley prescribed morphine. Someone smeared honey

on him and that has to come off. There are bits of charred shirt stuck to the wounds. Dr. Daley ordered the burns dressed with silver nitrate. Did you bring it?"

The Sister of Providence set down the tray with authority. "As I said, nurse, Doctor Daley assigned this patient to me . . . at my request. I'm experienced with treating burns. Attend to the other men in your ward now, please."

The nurse gave Jamieson a word of encouragement before withdrawing.

Sister Mary Jerome contemplated him with piercing blue eyes, hands clasped beneath a long white apron covering her habit. Maybe she fingered the rope of beads hanging from her waist, praying over his unshaven face and matted hair, calling down healing spirits on crusted bloody burns that felt like bits of hell had landed on him.

He'd suffered on the trek over Moon Pass and was now worn small. A stubborn streak had clamped his jaw shut, not wanting Addie to observe his pain, but she saw his exhaustion and, taking his horse's reins, led it past blackened cedars, petrified in the 1910 fire, and then up rising switchbacks through sprouting green pine. Shivering, he clung to the saddle horn most of the ride. He was unable to stop the shaking now. Whispered hoarsely, "Hello, Sister. Couldn't lick my wounds, so I came for your healing touch."

She composed herself. "I was standing at a window and saw you come in." She picked up his chart; laid her hand on his forehead while reading it. "Tell me what happened . . . Mr. James."

"Forest fire. Spent a night in a creek. Night before last. Rode over Moon Pass today. Coming to you was the best idea I had."

She didn't smile, but if she had, her short upper lip would have revealed a slightly crooked front tooth. "You're trembling because you're in shock. I'll give you a shot of morphine before I dress your burns." She was matter-of-fact, what he expected. "You're in pain and you'll have some scarring, but I won't allow you to die." It was what he wanted to hear, that his survival was personal to her.

She gave him the shot in his bare rump and soon his apprehension lessened. As she held his hand, he began to drift.

Her voice was as soft as feathers, already receding, "And how are the mothers?"

"Mothers," he mumbled. Rings of fire were receding into pinpricks. He'd be all right now. Loving hands.

From far away, she whispered, "Robbie?"

"They're fine," he sighed.

Chapter 79
Holy Names Academy
Spokane, Washington: 1905

"Sister Superior says in order for me to enter the Sisters of Providence, I have to have proof my mother and father were married." In the school's parlor the girl faced the man with long sandy mustaches while a chaperoning sister pretended to read her Office.

Alonzo MacLean cleared his throat. "Well, that might be difficult." He'd received two letters, one within the other, which brought him out of his Idaho logging camp to Spokane. The first was from Sister Superior, in charge of the Catholic girls' school, the second from this girl.

"You are my uncle, Mr. MacLean?"

"That's right."

Smiling impishly, she revealed a slightly crooked front tooth. She took after the MacLeans, no doubt about it – blue eyes, taller than expected.

"Are you a rancher, Uncle MacLean?"

"I own a sawmill in Idaho. That's why I haven't been to see you. Seldom get over this way."

"You brought me to St. Joseph's Orphanage farther down this street. I remember."

He remembered, too. He'd found her playing behind a whorehouse in Wallace. When he saw her resemblance to Violet as a child and glimpsed her grimy hand, he knew who her mother was. Figured he knew the whole story. Pulled the girl to her bare feet and dragged her, protesting, through the back door, yelling, "Mary! You here, Mary?" The two women working in the kitchen turned in shock. The tall one and the short one. He wondered later why seeing them together surprised him. Freshly outraged, he bellowed, "Which one of you whores is this girl's ma?" They stood wide-eyed and he shook the terrified girl. "Who's your ma?" Sobbing, she flung herself against the shorter one. And Mary Smith wrapped her arms around the child, hushing her. "I won't let you raise this girl in a whorehouse!" Defiant, they ordered him out, but he shouted them down, threatening to get the law. The three of them exchanged harsh words and tears. Even love, he supposed, for they once had cared about one another. But he didn't relent; promised only not to tell Jerome, who wouldn't want to know, anyway, now that he was married to Gladys.

Sitting across from Thea, he remembered the frightened eleven-year-old girl he'd delivered into the care of the Franciscan Sisters at the orphanage.

"Figured it was for your own good." He was certain he'd saved her from the life of a whore.

"The sisters at the orphanage . . . here at school, too . . . told me my mother was not fit to rear me." She was matter-of-fact, but he wasn't so thick as to believe that what he'd told the nuns hadn't caused her problems.

MacLean ran his hat brim through his fingers. "I had to give 'em a reason so's they'd take ya, Thea."

She sat primly, her left hand covering her right. "I owe you a great deal." The winsome smile again. "I know you paid for my education here."

He nodded approvingly at her expression of gratitude. "Glad to help."

Within a month of his bringing Thea to the orphanage, she ran off to find her way back to Wallace. This time he returned with the sheriff. She came away docilely, and Mary and Violet appeared more disposed toward her going than the first time. Rather than take her back to Spokane himself, he hauled her over to the Sisters of Providence at the hospital. It was his last direct contact with her for nearly seven years. The nuns exacted her promise not to run off and had put her to work in the kitchen until two of them had business in Spokane and returned her to the orphanage. Those nuns must have impressed her with their intimate knowledge of suffering because here she was, wanting to become one.

"I'm eighteen and will be graduating next month."

"You sure grew up fast, a right smart-looking young lady."

"As I told you, I wish to enter the Order of the Sisters of Providence and become a nursing sister. I feel God is directing you to help me, Uncle MacLean." The rest came in a rush. "He wants you to provide proof my parents were married and I am not illegitimate." Her lower lip trembled.

God sure could play nasty tricks on people. Who would think his placing her in a Catholic orphanage and then this girls' school would make her want to become a nun? "Now, if it's nursing you want, your aunt and I will be more than happy to pay for your schooling. Won't that be enough?"

"I have an aunt, too? She never comes to see me."

His leg jumped beneath his hat. "Well, she doesn't know about you." He glanced at the nun in the corner.

"Am I a secret?"

The dread on her face brought a lump to his throat. "Well, that's hard to explain."

"It is my heart's desire, Uncle, to enter the order of the Sisters of Providence. If I cannot, I will have to return to my mother. Do you know where she is?"

The nun in the corner lowered her small reading glasses, peering over them at him, which stilled his twitchy legs.

"I don't know where she is. I'll see about getting proof that she was married to your father."

Within a week he returned with a sworn statement saying he himself had witnessed the marriage of Mary Smith and Jerome MacLean in 1886 in Murray, Idaho, officiated by a circuit-riding Presbyterian minister whose name he did not recall, the official paperwork destroyed in a house fire. He swore under God the marriage ceremony was official and religious. It satisfied the Sisters of Providence and Theodora MacLean was admitted as a postulant into the Order of the Sisters of Providence, her dowry paid by him, and entered into a course of nursing at Sacred Heart Hospital in Spokane, which fees he also covered.

Chapter 80

Alonzo and Addie returned to the hospital the following morning and asked to see Jamieson. They were directed to wait in a small room off the reception area. Addie stood at a tall window in a new suit and shoes, sickened at heart, certain Robbie had taken a downturn. Her tears were a good sign her body was rehydrated, but a poor sign for her spirits. The door opened and she turned to see a tall nun greet Alonzo and take his hands. Her stomach twisted, unable to make sense of the smile on the sister's face.

She blurted, "Is he dead?"

The nun, as tall as Addie, redirected cool blue eyes. "Mr. James? He's recovering nicely. Most of his burns are painful, but not life-threatening. The serious burns are small. Just now he's being bathed. If you return in an hour, you'll be able to see him."

Alonzo introduced Addie as his sister-in-law, the widow of the late Jerome MacLean. Sister Mary Jerome warmly shook her hand, appraising eyes alight, as though finding Addie of special interest.

"We'll be back," Alonzo said. "I can use a second breakfast."

"Mr. James told me about the forest fire you were in. I'm so glad neither of you was injured. A small miracle, we could call it."

At a nearby restaurant, Alonzo set into a stack of pancakes while Addie allowed her pot of tea to steep. He said after a couple of swallows, "I guess it's time to tell you about Sister Mary Jerome."

"She seems an interesting person." How would an occasional Presbyterian like Alonzo know a Catholic nun?

"Did you see her hand, Addie? She's got the same birth mark Mother had. Ain't it odd it skipped Jerome, Violet and me, but showed up on her hand? Did you see how that knuckle ain't flush with the others?"

In the act of pouring tea, Addie thunked down the pot before her cup was full, and wiped spilled tea from the table with her napkin. It allowed her time to absorb his words. "I didn't look at her hand." Was the nun Jerome's child? What about Robbie?

Aware of restaurant patrons nearby, she tried to keep her voice low, snapping hoarsely, "If you'd said something before I met her, I would have looked." Raised the half-full cup, then set it down to add cream. "After all this time are you telling me Sister Mary Jerome is the daughter of my husband and Mary Smith? And that you knew it all along?" The nun must know, too. Otherwise, why would she have taken Jerome for her religious name? Now she had blood in her eye. Hissed, "Why in God's name didn't you tell Jerome before he died and eased his mind? What kind of brother are you?"

Alonzo's mouth turned down and he flushed scarlet. "Ah, Addie." Eyes still bloodshot, they welled with unexpected tears, making them redder.

"At least you could have told me after Jerome died." Wanting to stick a fork in his hand, she ignored the tears trailing down his furrowed face. "You knew I was searching for Jerome's heir. You let the time expire and cut her out of her inheritance. Why did you do that, Alonzo?"

He wiped his eyes on his napkin and gulped his coffee, face working. "I was no better than a polliwog swimmin' in frog spit." His expression didn't explain anything. Tapping his toes, his knees jiggled the table. "I couldn't tell Jerome. And after he was gone, I didn't have the guts to tell you." Old anguish poured out. "I betrayed my brother, Addie. God forgive me. She isn't his daughter . . . she's my daughter."

His shame was so naked, Addie averted her eyes to the tea sloshing in her cup. She had an unwelcome urge to laugh.

"And how did that happen?"

"I got no excuse. Jerome, he left Mary alone a lot. Truth be told, he'd fallen out of love with her. A lot of that was Ma's doin'. She didn't like Mary. It was hurtin' Mary and I saw that. I just wanted to help her, but the more I was with her, the more I wanted to be with her. It just happened is all. I couldn't do nothin' 'cause I was already married."

What a family! Any righteous anger out of respect for Jerome's memory disappeared. Instead, her thoughts flew to Robbie and how she'd tried to replace Jerome with him, believing him Jerome's son. Yes, there was a resemblance -- his voice, his profile, his walk, but it was because he had MacLean blood in him. He was Maud's son then, not Dovey's. Seeing Dovey and Robbie together, she'd been so certain they were mother and son, she hadn't seriously considered the other possibility. Whoever his mother was, he wasn't Jerome's son and she hadn't cheated him out of an inheritance. This knowledge gave her dizzy relief. She'd spotted Robbie's recessed knuckle, but Alonzo never noticed. Robbie wore gloves when he worked. Why would Alonzo have looked at the man's hands, anyway? "You said Violet had a child, too."

"I said Violet was expectin'. When I found Sister . . . her name was Thea then . . . there was no other child at that whorehouse. Right here in Wallace. I put her in an orphanage in Spokane. You wanna see the house? It's on a corner a few blocks east of here."

She did want to see where Robbie spent his childhood, but when they walked east, it wasn't where Alonzo remembered. "Guess the forest fire took it when Wallace burned."

As they walked to the hospital, Addie decided she wasn't ready to tell Alonzo that Robbie was his nephew. The family had ostracized Violet, too.

"So you found your daughter." She couldn't help herself. "But what became of Mary Smith?"

"She and Violet was runnin' that house. Didn't keep up with 'em after that until . . ." He stopped and bent his face toward hers. "Hope this don't knock ya off your pins, but I recognized her when she come into camp." His voice still rusty from firefighting, it lacked the drama he obviously would have liked. "Dovey Blake is Mary Smith." He gave it time to sink in before asking, "How'd you come to know her?"

He'd asked the same question the day he recognized Dovey. Well, he'd kept vital information from her and she'd be damned if she'd tell him about her stay at Maud's and about his nephew. She'd talk to Robbie first.

She parried, "So the Widow Blake lived near MacLean's holdings all these years, trying to protect her timber from you and Jerome." Her dry voice cracked. "And you didn't know she was Mary Smith?"

He answered dismally, "That's about right."

"I know about that timber war back in 1904. You should be ashamed, having your men try to chase that little woman off her claim."

Chapter 81

A nurse in the men's ward led them to Jamieson's bed. Dovey was sitting next to him, holding his hand.

MacLean boomed, "What are you doing here?"

Eyes glittering with unshed tears, she snapped, "I guess I have a right to be here."

Addie grasped Alonzo's arm while she searched Jamieson's face. He smiled and she returned it with relief.

And then Sister Mary Jerome swooped down. "Please speak softly, Uncle MacLean. Be considerate of the other men. It's not visiting hours and you're allowed here only because you're family."

"I'm his employer, Sister, and I'm paying for his care. I guess I'm allowed to see how he's doin'."

Addie tugged at his arm, her eyes still on Jamieson and Dovey. Robbie, Dovey, Maud, Thea. She looked hard at Sister Mary Jerome. She did look like Maud and there was a good reason. He instincts told her she'd been right all along. Dovey was Robbie's mother. So that meant? She glanced up at MacLean, then looked back at Robbie. Dropping the older man's arm, she inched past him to bend over Jamieson. "How are you feeling?"

He rasped, "I've been better. Did you get some sleep?"

She nodded.

MacLean pointed at Dovey, addressing Sister Mary Jerome, "What's your mother doin' here?" He glared at Dovey. "Why ain't ya up at camp feedin' my men?"

"There's plenty of people feedin' your men. I'm here to look after my boy."

Sister Mary Jerome's clenched hands betrayed her calm exterior. "We'll all go down the hall, Uncle MacLean. I believe I owe you an explanation of my past misdeeds." She gave Jamieson an almost pleading look. "Do you want to be wheeled down with us, Mr. James?"

Cracked lips rasped, "I'll stay here, Sister. You sort everything out."

Baffled, Alonzo demanded, "Sort what out?"

Addie took pity on him. "Alonzo, look at Mac's knuckles." She lifted and displayed his hand. "Maybe now you'll understand part of it."

MacLean moved closer and leaned down. "Jesus Christ!"

"Please don't take the Lord's name in vain, Uncle MacLean. Follow me, everyone." The nun took MacLean's arm. "Please."

Addie still held Jamieson's hand. "You're going to miss some interesting revelations."

Dovey stood and pressed Addie into her chair. "Well I'm going to enjoy this," she said. She moved away to give them privacy.

His voice was a weak whisper. "I suppose you figured it out."

"Yes, I think I have." She bent closer to hear him.

He rubbed his thumb over her hand. "You can stop feeling guilty about me and that inheritance." She nodded, but her breath caught in a small sob. His eyes crinkled at the corners, bloodshot but unblinking. "I'm still drawing an officer's pay. So I want to know, are you going to break my heart . . . or marry me like you asked?"

"I'm going to marry you, of course." Straightening, she turned toward Dovey. "Does that meet with your approval?"

The woman smiled. "Peculiar as it sounds, it's what I've been hopin' for."

Addie's and Dovey's footsteps echoed down the hallway toward Sister Mary Jerome, waiting beside an open door. Addie leaned toward Dovey. "This morning Alonzo told me Sister Mary Jerome is your daughter . . . and his. He's been mistaken all these years, hasn't he? "

"Maybe you should be a detective," Dovey replied. "I had to set Robbie straight two years ago when he showed me a copy of the file the Spokane Pinkertons sent to his Seattle office."

The small room had only a large crucifix on its wall as ornament, but a dozen chairs -- a space intended for bereaved families. Alonzo sat with arms folded, appearing to have reached some conclusions of his own. He stood, a man in the company of three women, none his ally.

As befitted a MacLean, Sister Mary Jerome took charge, re-positioning her chair to face him. "Uncle MacLean, you are indeed my uncle. Your sister Violet is my mother." She rushed on before he could interrupt. "You thought I was Uncle Jerome's daughter, and I allowed you to believe it."

"You bilked me out of your education. Nursing school, too."

She stiffened and brushed back her veil. "It was you who took me away from them." Added contritely, "I'll pray for you and perhaps you'll spend less time in purgatory."

"I don't believe in purgatory. I'm Presbyterian." He swallowed. "I never thought you were Jerome's daughter." Voice rough. "I thought you were my daughter."

The nun's face flamed. "Is that what you thought?" She turned to Dovey. "Is that what you wanted him to think?"

Dovey sat tight-lipped, but she nodded.

Addie interjected, "She's still your kin, Alonzo. You should be proud to be her uncle."

"I never lied to you," Sister said. "You're the one who assumed Dovey was my mother."

"Ya didn't tell me the truth, neither."

Addie watched the exchange with mounting fascination. Neither Alonzo nor Thea had told the truth. Thea thought Alonzo believed she was Jerome's daughter; had even taken Jerome as her religious name to extend the lie. And all along Alonzo believed she was his and Dovey's daughter. Why did Alonzo and Dovey dislike each other so much now?

Dovey spoke up. "Now you listen to me, Alonzo MacLean. Violet and I had what is called a dilemma. We didn't want Thea reared in a whorehouse. After Violet took Robbie back to Michigan to boarding school, we knew we had to find a place for Thea. And then you barged in, thinkin' she was your daughter. It broke our hearts when you took her, but it was the best thing. When she run away from that orphanage and come back, we sat her down and told her she had to go back." Dovey turned to her niece. "You knew it was best, didn't you, Sister?"

"Yes." These new revelations must have brought up old regrets because the knuckles on her folded hands were white.

Puzzled, Addie asked, "Dovey, is this the first time you've seen Sister in years?"

"'Course not. We see Sister every winter when she comes to Spokane. Violet and I meet her at the restaurant in the Davenport Hotel. She usually brings Sister Amanda and we visit over lunch."

MacLean interrupted, "So Robbie is Mac down the hall?"

"That's right," Dovey answered. "When Robbie was born, I swore never to let you or your brother get your hands on him. You'd treat him no better than you treated me. Thinking Thea was your daughter threw you off Robbie's scent and gave Thea the education she deserved. Robbie is a university graduate and an army officer."

"He's a deserter."

"You fool man, he's working undercover for the Army."

"Then what's he doin' in my camp?"

Addie cautioned, "We aren't supposed to ask."

"Does he think I'm in cahoots with Germany, for the love of Christ?" He looked at his niece for censorship.

Addie felt she had to set him straight. "He's not after you, Alonzo. It's my cousin, Mally, he's been shadowing."

"O'Neill? The poor man drowned."

"No, he didn't drown, thank God. He faked it to elude Mac."

"By gad, that's good to know. O'Neill and Mac saved my life. People sure been keepin' a lot from me." MacLean picked his words carefully. "Heck, I always liked Mac . . . so what's his real name?"

Dovey answered, "Robert MacLean. I added Jamieson for his protection. It took a long time, but I gave you MacLeans your comeuppance for what you done to Violet and me. It was you MacLeans forced me back into whoring. You'd have let us and our unborn starve."

Addie was thinking, and what about Jerome? Unknowingly cuckolded by his brother, he didn't care one bit that he might have a child in need of his care. Only when death crept up on him did he attempt to set things right, burdening her with his secret, finding release in its telling so he could get on with his death.

Alonzo defended himself. "It was Mother run you two off."

"Pshaw!" Dovey exclaimed. "You're goin' to have to make way now, you ol' goat. I deeded Robbie my half-section of old growth timber. After Addie and he marry, they're goin' into the lumber business."

He stared at Addie. "You're gonna marry him?" She nodded. "I've had too many surprises for one day."

Sister Mary Jerome rose. "I have rounds to make. I'll pray for you all." MacLean stood and she took his hand in both of hers. "Sometimes I pretended you were my father, Uncle MacLean."

After she left, he said, "Guess I better go see Mac."

Dovey and Addie remained seated. The older woman appeared almost serene, no doubt visualizing the meeting between Alonzo and Robbie. The longer Dovey kept Robbie's identity secret, the more lustrous the secret must have become as she relished Alonzo's mistaking Thea for his daughter. But once a secret is revealed, it becomes dull as tarnished brass. Addie felt pity for the girl Thea, the living lie, ordered to fool Alonzo to protect Robbie's identity and gain an education for herself. And Robbie? Other than love, Addie wasn't certain what she felt.

Dovey turned to Addie. "You and me, we slept with the same man, thinking we was married to him."

After what had occurred, Addie still could be startled. "Wasn't I married to Jerome?"

"Guess that depends on the laws of the states we was married in. His mother claimed it was a pretend wedding, but later I found out Idaho allows common law marriage. Since we acted like husband and wife for a time, and he never sought a divorce, we was still married when he died."

"But you remarried a man named Blake."

"I never remarried. Dovinia Blake is my maiden name. I added the Mrs. for respectability. Don't worry about it, Addie. I'm not goin' after anything that's yours. We'll keep it our little secret that Jerome was a bigamist and you weren't legally married to him."

Having Dovey as her mother-in-law was going to be very interesting.

"You won't have any problem marrying Robbie. He's never been married."

In a small voice, Addie replied, "I'm so glad."

Chapter 82

Jamieson lay on his side. He'd passed on morphine that morning, wanting his wits about him when Addie visited. Dovey's arrival surprised him, though why should it? Now he waited to see if the Ol' Man still wanted to see him after being told the truth about Sister and him. He considered himself his own ancestor with no need of a father, but it was a half-truth. He'd sought out two father figures -- his football coach at Michigan and Billy Sewell. He didn't want anything from Alonzo MacLean other than an acknowledgement of their consanguinity.

Then MacLean was standing at the foot of his bed, swatting his hat against a pant leg. Jamieson tucked in his chin the better to see him. Always having been the observer, it was unnerving to see MacLean viewing him as more than an employee.

"You got her brown eyes."

"Yeah."

"M-m-m. You're bigger than Jerome."

Throat still aflame, "I'm not Jerome's son."

"I know that. I know now you're my son. Takes some gettin' used to." He moved up the side of the bed. "Is this a surprise to you, too, or did you know?"

"I was a Pinkerton detective before I accepted an Army commission. I knew I had MacLean blood." It was painful to speak, but he made the effort. "When the report came into our Seattle office about the search for Jerome MacLean's heir and I told my mother, she revealed who my father really was . . . is." His voice gave out.

"So, when ya saved my life when Beaver Sven tried to kill me, you knowed then?"

"Yeah."

"Would you have come runnin' if I wasn't your pa?"

Jamieson reached for the glass of water and took a sip. "I have a bad habit of running toward trouble."

MacLean nodded. "Wouldn't have wanted anyone but you goin' after Addie in that fire. Knew you'd save her if anyone could." He blinked a couple of times. "So you didn't desert the Army?"

"No."

"And you and Addie are gonna get married?"

"Yeah."

"When did all this happen? While you was lying in the creek during the fire?"

He swallowed more water. Not much above a whisper, he explained, "We've been acquainted a while. She saved my life in Seattle a couple of years back when I was shot. Been trying to pay her back ever since."

"Guess that's one I'll have to hear." He appeared to be thinking. "You know my history with your mother?"

"Yeah."

"Not something to be proud of. I know grudges can pass from one person to the next. Just wonderin' if she passed this one on to you. Think ya can acknowledge me as your pa?"

"Yeah, I think I can."

"That's good. Heard tell ya may be gettin' into the lumber business at the management end."

"When the war's over."

"Thought we might come to some arrangement."

"Probably."

"What should I call you now?"

"Mac. I'm still working undercover for the Army."

"So you was usin' my camp as a cover?"

"I worked damn hard for you."

"I know ya did. Got no complaints."

Jamieson took another sip of water, set the glass down and gestured so MacLean would bend closer. He whispered, "This Army mission is highly secret. Appreciate you keeping everything to yourself for now."

MacLean straightened. "Sure thing." He stood twisting his hat, then reached out and laid his hand on Jamieson's head. Set down his hat and took Jamieson's right hand in his free hand and pressed it. But it was the hand on his head that felt like a blessing. "Welcome to the family, son."

"Thank you." His voice cracked. "Think you can be nice to my mother?"

That took MacLean aback. "I'll try, but that woman's got no use for me."

"Can you blame her?"

"Not one bit."

As he turned to leave, Jamieson managed a hoarse, "See ya down the road."

Chapter 83
St. Maries, Idaho: July, 1918

"We're all members of the American Protective League . . ." With sudden violence, the speaker, a local banker, brought both fists down, startling his small audience, who watched in avid silence. A couple of rows back Gerard thumbed a tattoo on his derby. "We've got to do something, men . . . something important to help our government. What'll it be?" He looked them over, fastening briefly on Gerard, then rubbed the back of his neck as though giving his own question some thought. "You know those Ranney boys up in the mountains . . . you've heard about those boys avoiding the draft, refusing to serve their country." Pale aging faces of shopkeepers and hotel employees nodded. "Those boys are making money hand over fist bootlegging. Are we going to stand for that?" Gerard craned about for their reaction. Some lowered their eyes. *Ranney customers, no doubt.* A storekeeper stared back. *Yeah, he must buy in quantity.* Gerard had never seen the Ranney clan, but had picked up stories in blind pigs.

Sheriff Roland rose. "The Ranneys aren't the only bootleggers coming into Benewah County. My office is doing good work curtailing bootlegging. Any of you want to come along on a stakeout, I'll show you how it's done. Then if you've got an itch, you can go make some citizens' arrests. Get yourselves up an APL posse and go after the Ranneys." His sneer brought forth snickers. They knew the Ranney reputation for violence. "Their homestead is out of my jurisdiction or I'd have hauled them in long ago."

Gerard collared the sheriff afterwards and he agreed to take him along on a stakeout. A cattle car was attached to a freight train for the horses, while they rode the plush from St. Maries to St. Joe City. Gerard eyed the deputy guarding a hamper of food and decided he didn't count for much.

The train clicked along beside the river while Roland gave him the lowdown. "There's a bootlegger lives in Avery over in Shoshone County. Out of my jurisdiction, but that won't stop me. What he does is catch a freight to Saltese, the first stop over the line in Montana, and fills a pack sack with as much whiskey as he can carry. He rides up in the locomotive cab coming west and pays off the engineer and fireman with free liquor. Somewhere short of St. Joe City, the engineer slows way down and blasts the whistle like there's livestock on the track, and the bootlegger climbs down and hikes into St. Joe City. I caught him once before. Time to haul him in again."

They waited behind a blind a few yards off the trail running alongside the tracks, and over time saw four freights going west, but none slowed down.

Roland disappeared into the forest to relieve himself; a few moments later a bearded man riding a mule and leading two more came over the rise where they hunkered down.

"O my Lord," the deputy whispered, "that's Romey Ranney."

Gerard hissed, "How would you know?"

"I grew up around here, that's how." He drew his revolver. "He's a bootlegger *and* a draft dodger."

Gerard picked up the Ross rifle he'd carried since bringing the munitions down from Canada with the Sullivans. The deputy stepped from the blind out into the trail.

"Ho, there, Ranney." Voice low, not wanting to spook the mules. "Slide that rifle down."

Above a full black beard startled black eyes flashed, scrutinizing the deputy's face and metal star. "What're ya doin' way out here?"

"Waitin' for men like you. You heard me, let it drop."

Gerard hoisted his menacing bulk, drawing Romey's stare.

"I ain't lookin' for trouble. Are you'uns Shoshone County or Benewah County?"

"I'm Deputy Sheriff Capp of Benewah County and this man is a citizen. You're Romey Ranney and I'm arresting you for draft evasion and probably bootleggin'. Get off that mule."

Romey stayed put. "You've no call to arrest me . . . take some of the whiskey an' I'll be on my way. That's the deal Sheriff Roland made."

"We got no deal with you, Ranney."

"Thought ya might be a new one. Ya ain't the man the sheriff usually sends. If it's the guns ya got wind of, I ain't carryin' none of those."

"What guns?" Gerard moved forward, but not too close.

Realizing his blunder, Ranney's face contorted. He kicked the mule, leaned over its neck and disappeared over the rise the way he came, pack mules in tow. Not a shot was fired.

When Roland emerged and Capp told him about the encounter, he fumed, "A goddamn bootlegger and draft dodger. You should of shot him. Maybe it's time we go into those mountains and round them up. To hell with the county line."

On the train back Gerard ruminated on Ranney's words. "If it's the guns ya got wind of." The Sullivans had refused to tell him where they'd stashed the rifles. Had O'Neill transported them here and those Ranneys hid them? It sounded ludicrous, but you never know. Roland was just another crooked sheriff, paid off by bootleggers and shiners. With him in tow and a couple of Ranney mules, he could bring out those rifles to sell to that arms dealer in California. Stay on the right side of the law by promising a cut to the sheriff. Just the two of them, going to the Ranney place as private citizens and members of the American Protective League.

Alone with Sheriff Roland in his office, Gerard related what Ranney had blurted out about guns. Roland spoke of the express car at St. Joe City that was supposed to have been carrying rifles and ammunition the Army wanted confiscated.

"I wasted my time going up there. No guns . . . no coffins, either."

Rifles unsheathed, Gerard and the sheriff rode into the clearing past a corral where a couple of mules brayed, showing large yellow teeth. Chickens cackled and scattered. Gerard glimpsed what he thought was a woman scuttling into the brush behind the cabin, but wasn't sure.

"Hello the house," he called out. "We're lost." Next to the door a small window showed a blank eye. Four hound puppies crawled out from under the porch.

Roland said, "They must be out with their bear dogs."

It was what Gerard wanted. Dismounting, he crouched beside the door and lifted the latch, stepped aside and pushed it inward with his rifle barrel. A pot simmered on the stove. While Roland remained mounted, keeping watch, Gerard searched for the rifles -- under the bed, in the two attached rooms, up in the loft.

When he came out, Roland asked, "Find any whiskey?" Gerard shook his head. Roland stayed put. "I'll keep a lookout while you search for the guns. Holler if you uncover their hooch."

Gerard searched barn bins; climbed into the loft and stabbed a three-prong fork into fresh hay, but found no guns. Emerging dusty, wisps of hay clinging to his clothing, he had to remove his coat and celluloid collar to get at hay down his back. He searched the tool sheds behind the barn.

Irritation rising, he glared at a sow watching him with small mean eyes. Skirting the pig shed, he approached the manure pile, grabbed up a pitchfork and thrust it in, fully expecting to come up short against a metal carbine box, but the five tines sank to the hilt. Jabbing from different angles, he moved around the foul mess, a mixture of pig, horse and mule shit, dirty straw and clusters of blackened moldy hay. The rifles and ammunition had to be here, just the sort of place that bog hopper O'Neill would pick, thinking civilized men wouldn't give it a second look.

Removing his shoulder holster, Gerard unsnapped the revolver and dropped it within easy reach behind him. He forked manure left and right. Soggy with runoff, the ground sucked and squished at every step. Manure dropped on his boots; muck slid down the fork handle inside his cuffs. Sweating, he flung off his derby, not caring where it landed, and pulled out his handkerchief to mop his face. He saw Roland astride his horse, watching him. *Good for nothing bastard.* The stinking work was netting only the playful yaps of those goddamn puppies gamboling about his feet. He stabbed the fork into a pup and flung it screaming into the remains of the manure pile. Then turned in search of another puppy, but the death cry of the first scared them off. He dropped the fork and picked up his revolver, held it in a blistered hand and killed two more pups. The last one reached the porch and crawled underneath before he got off a third shot.

Strapping on his holster and gun, he retrieved his muck-covered derby and coat, and stomped over to mount his horse.

It shied and he punched it at the base of an ear. Turned to give Roland a menacing look before he mounted. The reek of shit went down the trail with them. A quarter-hour later he wanted to ride back to fire the cabin and outbuildings and shoot the livestock, but Roland was putting distance between himself and Gerard. He was tired, hot and thirsty, and wanted to get out of his stinking clothes. He hadn't located the rifles and not one goddamn drop of whiskey.

Chapter 84

Jamieson asked, "Did you marry me because I saved your life?" They lay on their bed in the cabin. When they made love, he claimed his back and shoulder felt better.

"Are we comparing scores again? I married you because you're a timber owner and marriage was the only way to get those trees into the MacLean holdings."

He chuckled. "You're an astute businesswoman, Adelaide." Raised himself to see more than the side of her face, coppery hair a tangle about her bare shoulders.

"Oh, Robbie," brushing her lips against his, "I love you."

Instead of returning the endearment, he asked, "Do you know that poem by Kipling. 'Something lost . . . go and find it?' I read it in college, but I can't remember the lines."

"It's called "The Explorer." I know some of it." She quoted, 'Something hidden . . . go and find it . . . go and look behind the ranges . . . something lost behind the ranges . . . lost and waiting for you . . . go!'"

He smiled. "Something hidden and lost, too. Remember more? Or just tell me what it's about."

"It's about an explorer who suffers privation, loses his horses in a blizzard, but locates a pass over the mountain ranges into new land with lots of timber and running rivers. The voice is really hounding him to go find it. At the end of the poem he realizes it was God whispering to him to find new lands to civilize. An English God, I suppose." She wrinkled her nose.

"Oh." Disappointed. "I thought it was about a man in search of himself."

"Well, it could be. I guess men with wanderlust can be in search of more than the end of the trail."

"M-m-m." He wrapped an arm around her, pulling her against his chest, his face in her hair. "I went looking and found you." Then he said what she wanted to hear. "I love you, Addie."

* *

A man said Addie's name outside the screened open window, drawing Jamieson up to the surface of consciousness, and then instantly awake.

"Addie, are ye there?"

Jamieson nudged her and she turned to him. "Sh-h-h." Put his fingers on her lips and whispered, "O'Neill is at the window."

"What?" she said.

The voice again. "Addie, come 'ere."

She heard him and stiffened. Jamieson held her shoulder, whispered one word. "Choose."

"Mally? I'm coming." She rounded the bed to the window. "I thought you were dead. Where have you been?"

"Sure I've heard that from ye afore."

"Do you want to come in?"

"'Tis too dangerous. I need ye to carry a message to Kate. Remember I told ye about Kate across the river?"

"I remember."

"Mac is huntin' me an' sure if her place isn't bein' watched. Nearly caught me there a while back. Ye're knowin' he's a dangerous man."

She put her mouth close to the screen. "Why is he hunting you, Mally?"

"Ah, nothin' personal. He's workin' for America an' I'm workin' for Ireland's freedom. If America wasn't allied to England, there'd be no problem atween us."

"I'm glad there's no grudge. When you disappeared and we thought you'd drowned . . ."

"Sure now I wouldn't 'ave killed the man, knowin' ye were sweet on him. So, will ye go to Kate? At the Tall Timber? Tell her Tank Creek. 'Tis all. She'll know the rest."

"Tank Creek," she whispered. "Yes, I'll tell her."

"Thank ye, Addie. God bless ye." And he was gone.

She stood at the window, then felt her way around the bed and back under the covers, but turned her back on Jamieson, burying her face in her pillow. He didn't try to comfort her.

In the morning, his first words were, "I want you to deliver that message to Katie."

"Wouldn't it be better if I didn't deliver it." She sat up and pushed hair from her eyes. "Then nothing will happen."

"I don't want 'nothing to happen.' Just deliver the message. Can I trust you to do that?"

She pulled up her knees under the covers, hugging them. "I feel I'm signing Mally's death warrant."

"Addie, don't be dramatic. I'm not interested in killing your cousin, or even arresting him unless I have to. My mission is to find the rifles and ammunition he's conspiring to transport to Ireland. He freighted them from Butte into the Joe Country, and now I know they'll be loaded on a train at Tank Creek. When I see it happen, I'll wire ahead for the authorities to remove them. Those are my orders. There, now you know everything. Feel better?" Watching her face, he added, "Guess you already knew most of that, didn't you?" O'Neill's hand gestures that evening behind the cookhouse, pointing east toward Butte, then zigzagging, indicating a train coming through the Bitterroots into the St. Joe Valley. He interpreted her lack of denial as an admission.

She asked, "How did Katie get mixed up in this?"

Now they both had something to hold back. "It just happened. She's Irish, too. Most everyone I know is Irish." He pushed himself up.

Addie changed his bandages. The burns were healing nicely. An hour later she crossed the river to St. Joe City, went to the Tall Timber and knocked until the door was opened. She mounted the stairs to deliver the message to a sleepy, tousle-headed Katie.

"Is that all he said? Just 'Tank Creek'?

"He said you'd know what to do."

"Yeah, I guess I do. But right now, I'm going back to sleep."

Addie bought some groceries, then stopped at the depot to inquire for any telegrams for Mac James. She signed for the yellow envelope the telegrapher produced. Back at the cabin she handed it to Jamieson and he tore it open. She read it over his elbow before he thrust it into a pocket. It relieved him of all military duties and ordered him to report to Captain Dengel in Spokane.

"I'm glad," she said, wrapping herself in an apron to begin frying bacon. When he went into the bedroom, she called out, "Maybe they'll accept your resignation. Then I'll have you all to myself. We can go up to camp and get Titus. I miss that big dog."

He came out and thumped down a haversack, into which he stuffed a moth-eaten, fleece-lined rubber blanket; Jerome had used both on fishing trips. "To hell with Dengel."

"Robbie, what are you doing?" She took his arm. "I'll go with you to Spokane." He shrugged off her hand and went back into the bedroom. "You aren't going after Mally now, are you? Not after that telegram?"

Emerging with his caulked boots, he dropped them and gripped her shoulders, muscles working along his jaw. "I'm a soldier, Addie. I might not look like one, and maybe I don't act like one. But I was assigned this mission by Colonel Disque, not by Dengel, and I'm going to accomplish it."

Addie pushed off his hands. "I read that telegram. The Army relieved you of your duties." She sank into a chair. "You don't have to hunt down Mally now." With no duty binding him, why would he do this? Couldn't he see he was bound to her now. His indifference cut deep.

"We're still at war and I'm going to do my best to stop this gunrunning." Hardened eyes held hers. "If you tell O'Neill, you'll be betraying your country during wartime. Don't you dare interfere with Army business."

She sat stunned, ignoring the boiling kettle. "I can't believe you're doing this."

He replied tight-lipped, "Believe it."

"But now Mally is your cousin, too . . . you don't hurt your kin."

"Damn it, Addie, he's working to weaken an American ally, and that helps Germany. I don't want to hurt him. I like him, but I'm going to stop him."

She pleaded in desperation, "He's helping Ireland free herself from Great Britain." Jumping up, she shoved him, sobbing, "I'm Irish, too, and we Irish stick together. If you go after Mally, don't come back here."

Turning away, he flattened his hands on the table. "You don't mean that." His arms trembled.

Suddenly she feared for him, knowing he hadn't recovered all his strength. She knew, too, she couldn't stop him.

Throwing up her hands, she exclaimed, "Why should I care! You'll probably kill each other! Go on! Do what you're going to do!" She was shaking as she sat down.

He slumped into his chair across from her. "Could I have something to eat first? I'm feeling a might gaunt."

Chapter 85
Tank Creek

Billy Sewell said he once worked a difficult operation the way he played a bad poker hand. Down to his last bet and not wanting to fold, he played what was left, a hunch. They were interrupted and he never finished his story to reveal the outcome of that operation. Well, to hell with Dengel and Gund . . . Disque, too. He knew what he was doing. O'Neill was out there and so were the rifles. Tank Creek was the rendezvous, but he didn't know the date or time.

The moon had been dark, but now was waxing. Maybe O'Neill and his cronies prearranged moving the munitions to the phases of the moon. The rifles must have been offloaded at Tank Creek, well short of where Sheriff Roland waited at the St. Joe City depot. O'Neill accomplished it during the dark of the moon. Why? Because it was unexpected? Or because they'd hidden them nearby? Now the Irishman would reload them for their transfer to the West Coast, using the same schedule out of Butte, the same crew he'd already paid off. Hell! Those munitions might be buried among the trees above the Tank Creek rail stop. Yeah. He'd finally gotten inside O'Neill's head.

Tank Creek lay close to the river, a short distance up the tracks from Marble Creek Station. During each twenty-four hours, six westbound trains stopped to take on water from a tank elevated on a wooden framework. Jamieson made a cold camp among trees and brush thirty yards above where the creek emptied into the St. Joe. He searched, but found no evidence of disturbed ground where rifles might be buried. As the gibbous moon waxed, he watched from behind brush. It wasn't his first stakeout, but he meant it to be his last.

From a homestead up the swiftwater, a dog keened at the full moon. The night was on the turn. The freight leaving Butte in late morning would be arriving soon. It had to be tonight or he was wrong in assuming he'd mastered O'Neill's way of thinking. He couldn't keep his mind off Addie. She was a proud woman but, when this was over, she'd take him back into her bed.

A lantern appeared from around a bend. Possibly a trainman checking for track damage, but when Jamieson raised his field glasses, he had no doubt it was O'Neill, cap pulled down, shoulders thrust forward, a man used to covering distance.

He stopped below Jamieson, looked up the tracks, then up at the brush and trees. Above the lantern's flame O'Neill's black eyes bored through the field glasses into Jamieson's. He cocked his head, listening, and Jamieson unnecessarily stilled his breathing. O'Neill turned back and signaled, lifting and lowering the lantern, all the while whistling that Irish tune, which merged with the river's tumbling melody.

A rhythmic clopping of iron shoes made Jamieson glass to the right, but the water tank blocked his view until a man led a string of heavily packed mules into the open, white beard reflecting moonlight. A stone dropped into Jamieson's gut. *Oh, shit . . . the Ranneys.* They had the rifles.

O'Neill beckoned Osee Ranney and his mules some distance up the tracks from the water tank. Romey brought up the rear.

A locomotive's headlight flashed peek-a-boo in the east as the train wove in and out along the curving mountain base that its tracks and the river hugged. It whistled, slowing, its powerful headlight sweeping over the Ranneys and their mules, which lurched awkwardly beneath heavy loads. Its bell clanging, steel wheels ground and shrieked to a stop beside the water tank. Steam shooting out drowned the mules' raucous brays as the engine settled down to a thirsty pant.

It was no boxcar to which Osee lead the mules. While the Ranneys unpacked two large bundles wrapped in dark oilskin, O'Neill tapped his revolver on the side of an oil tank car, and then mounted its steel ladder. Braced on top, he opened the cap. *You clever Irish bastard.* The Ranney son tossed up a length of tarred rope dangling from one end of the package. O'Neill caught it and hauled up the bundle. Anchoring the rope around the opening, he lowered what must be bound rifles into the tank and replaced the cover, unable to completely close it. Sure-footed, he leaped onto the next tank car, hauled up and dropped in another bundle. Six bundles of rifles went into six tank cars. Jumping onto another, he tapped it before going on to the next one. Satisfied with the sound he sought, maybe that of an empty tank, he hauled up three bundles of what could only be ammunition; tied their ropes together before lashing the end to the opening. He tossed in the ammunition to loud thunks as it swung against the tank's inner lining; shut the lid and a moment later was back on the ground.

A watching brakeman raised and lowered his lantern. The engineer gave three short toots, the brakeman climbed aboard, and the train pulled away. Already mounted, Romey led away the pack string while the elder Osee trailed behind. O'Neill picked up his lantern.

Jamieson had only to remember the numbers on the locomotive and one tank car, make a short trek to Marble Creek Station to send a telegram to Colonel Disque, and he'd complete his mission. The Army would do the rest. But he had too much invested in this case. Pain. Betrayal. Anger. He and O'Neill had played at deception too long, and he possessed a fierce desire to see O'Neill's face when he realized he'd lost.

Rising, he drew his revolver and shouted, "Hands up!" He emerged from the brush some distance from O'Neill and the Ranneys who, instead of hurrying away, pulled up. "I'm arresting you in the name of the United States Government!" The Ranney son pulled his Winchester from its scabbard, but Osee lifted a hand to stay him.

The familiar lilt floated up from the tracks. "That you, Mac?" O'Neill flipped up the lantern's metal top and blew out the flame.

"That's right, Irish. You picked a bright night for gunrunning."

"'Tis a grand night. Are ye alone then?"

"Do you think I'm fool enough to come down without soldiers covering me."

O'Neill laughed with genuine mirth. "Ah, Mac, 'tis certain I am ye always work alone. Come closer an' we'll parley."

"Toss down your revolver." When O'Neill's gun hit gravel, Jamieson addressed the mounted Ranneys. "Osee Ranney, the same goes for you and your son. Toss down your weapons."

The old man was visible in moonlight, but not so the son beyond the mules. Jamieson heard the distinct click of a bullet being chambered into the Winchester. "Pa, I see him clear."

O'Neill called out. "Wait now." Directed himself to Jamieson. "Sure ye're not arrestin' the Ranneys, Mac? 'Tis only packers they be, not even knowin' what's in them bundles. After they ride out, 'twill be only yer word they're involved. 'Tis certain ye'll be a dead man should ye try to take 'em in."

Osee called out, "That Dovey Blake's kin? I wouldn't feel right shootin' him. So, we're leavin', ya hear. You'uns work this out between yurselves. Put yur raffle gun down, Romey, and let's go."

Jamieson and O'Neill eyed each other until, glancing after them, Jamieson saw only moonlight glinting off rails. A rustle of brush came from the east, then ceased, leaving Jamieson and O'Neill with the river's flow and each other.

"Well then, Mac, come on over."

Revolver trained on him, Jamieson moved to within a few yards of O'Neill.

The Irishman's voice lost its playfulness. "Ye listen now, Mac, or whoever ye be. The dogs of war are reduced to whimperin' in Europe. A few more weeks an' the war will be over and ye'll have no reason for arrestin' me. I'm no threat to America. When did ye swear loyalty to Britain?"

"I'm completing a military mission. Find you, find the rifles."

"I'll be finishin' what I begun, Mac. I wouldn't murder a man to cover me own dirty tracks, but 'tisn't about me, boyo. 'Tis about Ireland. That bob-tailed God up there, sure He's not givin' a damn about the two of us." He took a few steps forward, hand outstretched. "Time's up, Mac. Yer gun there, give it here." Took two more steps.

The revolver weighed heavy in Jamieson's hand. "Stop, Irish. Don't make me shoot you." Why hadn't he expected O'Neill to do exactly this?

O'Neill came on, lop-sided smile visible below his cap.

If he shot him in the leg, he might hit an artery. If he only wounded him, he'd still lose Addie. "Fuck it." He threw down his revolver and lunged at O'Neill; aimed a right to his jaw, wanting to end it quickly. His fist missed the Irishman's face, not because it was less substantial in moonlight, but because O'Neill was catty. The shorter man ducked his head and came up under Jamieson's right arm, driving a shoulder into his armpit. Winded him and knocked him off-balance. Tender scarring tore open behind Jamieson's shoulder. He moved around O'Neill until he regained his breath. O'Neill's advantage was quick movement. Jamieson's longer reach was impeded by his wounded back and shoulder. He barreled into O'Neill and slammed him to the ground. Tried to hold him down, but O'Neill head-butted him, drawing first blood, and he painfully rolled off. Regaining their feet, O'Neill closed in, head down, punching Jamieson's stomach. He managed a right under O'Neill's jaw, staggering him, but the man remained on his feet. The muscles around the burns stopped hurting.

"That all ye've got, Mac? Ye toothless old dog." O'Neill powered into Jamieson, knocking him off his feet, leaping on top, smashing a fist into his face. He felt the sharp, numbing pain of his nose being broken and blood running down his throat. He hated the taste of his own blood. He rolled O'Neill off him, smashed a fist into his crooked nose, hearing the satisfying crunch of cartilage flattened against his face.

O'Neill bit his wrist, making him grunt, holding on like a chipped-toothed bull terrier. Jamieson smashed his free fist into the Irishman's face, splitting skin across his knuckles under his glove, but getting his hand back. He staggered to his feet, but O'Neill knocked his legs out from under him. They rolled and tumbled beside the railroad bed. He couldn't put the Irishman away. Another blow to his stomach and he lost interest in getting up; smelled his own blood and the creosote of railroad ties.

A boot to the back of his head laid him out, briefly paralyzing him, his face ground in gravel and cinders. When he painfully turned his head, Fats Gerard stood over him, unreal and ghostlike, his revolver shimmering in moonlight.

Chapter 86

"Put a bullet in him," Gerard growled. He holstered his revolver to pick up the lantern.

"Do it yerself." O'Neill sat near Jamieson, groggily looking about.

As though he had all the time in the world, Gerard raised and flipped the chimney; snapped a match alight, illuminating the immediate area. "I been wantin' to kill this fucker for years. You know what he is, Irish?"

O'Neill pulled himself to his feet, casting about for his revolver. "Ye told me a while back he was a Pinkerton."

"Yeah, but I didn't tell ya he's military now. Ain't it you who hates soldiers?" Gerard contemplated O'Neill from beneath heavy-lidded eyes. "I watched you load those rifles. Didn't take me long to nose out which crew you and your Irish pals paid off. I rode their schedule and kept my glims open." He sounded peevish. "Our deal's still on, ain't it? Sellin' the rifles to my arms dealer that supplies the Mexicans. Splittin' the jack?"

"For sure, Fats."

Through a swelling eye, Jamieson spotted his own revolver within reach and stretched for it. Gerard's boot stomped his wrist, making him gasp.

His weight pinning Jamieson's arm, Gerard set down the lantern. He reached into his coat and pulled out his revolver. Taunted, "I killed that fuck partner of yours. And guess who was with me."

A shot rang out and the revolver dropped from Gerard's hand. He clutched his arm, spinning toward O'Neill. "Ya shot me! Fuckin' son of a fuck."

From the gloom beyond the circle of light, O'Neill called out, "'Tis for the men on the *Verona*, Fats." There was a click as the hammer struck an empty chamber.

With both hands Jamieson reached for his revolver, but when he raised it to kill the man who'd murdered Billy Sewell, Gerard had disappeared into the brush at the base of the mountain. He shot twice, but from the ground his angle was all wrong. He heard Gerard crash heavily through brush and up among the trees.

Woozy from the kick to the back of his skull, he rose to his knees, then pushed himself to his feet. Raising the revolver, he steadied his battered gun hand with the bitten one, aimed slightly higher than the sound of Gerard's scrambling feet, and fired. The shot echoed in his ears, covering any grunt that might have come from the base of the mountain. *It was only a revolver, for Christ's sake!* No additional sounds came from the mountainside, but he wasn't going to crawl about up there to discover if he'd hit him.

O'Neill mocked, "A bullet bound for eternity."

He turned on the Irishman. "You let him get away."

"Me hand was shakin' an' the fault o' that lies wit' ye, brawlin' 'stead a standin' man to man in the squared circle. Feck ye for a divil! Didn't I save yer life wit' the only bullet in me gun?"

Jamieson was hurting - the torn scars on his back, the bitten wrist, his broken nose. He blew blood from each nostril. Said out of cut lips, "So Gerard wanted the rifles for himself."

"Ah, wasn't he the fly in the ointment. Never trustworthy, but havin' the connections to purchase the guns an' move 'em 'cross the border into Montana. But what to do with him then? A dilemma even the good Father couldn't solve with his prayin'."

"And the two of you planned to sell the guns to Mexico."

"So he thought. Long as I kept those rifles hidden, I knew he wouldn't be killin' me. That afeard of the bastard I was."

Jamieson picked up the lantern. "Let's go, Irish."

"What will ye be havin' a mind to do if I walk east on this track, instead of toward St. Joe City?"

"I'll be having a mind to shoot you."

They saw each other clearly in lantern light and under the full moon.

"So ye're ordered to bring me in dead or alive then?"

"I'm not ordered to bring you in at all, but that's my plan."

"Then why the feck do it?"

"It's my job."

"Ah, 'tis the difference atween us, Mac. It's I have a callin' to help Ireland. But you, 'tis only a job ye're doin.'"

"But I do it damn well." He was so fucking tired. "You dreamed the wrong dreams, Irish."

"The right dreams for certain. Do ye think twisted hemp is an object of secret terror for me?" He stepped over the first rail. "I'll be walkin' west as ye wish. 'Tis best ye join me. The next train comin' through is the Olympian and she'll not be stoppin' here."

Jamieson tramped behind O'Neill, who threw over his shoulder, "So, 'tis Sheriff Roland ye plan on givin' me to?"

"Not a good idea, is it?"

"The man hates me guts." Some little ways on, "Have ye seen Kate recently?"

"No."

"She's a grand woman. Loyal to the cause . . . 'an to friends."

"Did she tell you about me?"

"Not a word. Ye were no deserter, I knew, which meant ye weren't choppin' wood just for exercise. She wouldn't tell me anything, except what a swell fellow ye be. 'Twas Fats told me ye'd been a Pinkerton. But 'twas I figured ye'd been listenin' in on me lawyer in Spokane that day."

He had to ask. "Had you thought of killing me?"

"It crossed me mind. But killin' doesn't agree with me, Mac. The calluses have yet to thicken me soul."

"You could have let me drown that day in the Marble."

"Sure I nearly did."

"I saw it in your eyes."

"I knew Addie loved ye. I wouldn't hurt that woman, she bein' family."

"We're married now."

He swung around. "I wish ye both happiness."

The pulsing sound of a train approached from behind, as yet out of sight. Jamieson stumbled from the track to the right, wedging himself and the lantern against a blasted rock outcropping. "Irish, get off!" O'Neill kept walking down the center of the track. "It's not worth killing yourself!" The locomotive's headlight swept around a curve and then the train was thundering past, a blast of warm wind flattening him against the rocks, orange passenger cars visible even at night. It was a long train and when tail lights winked on the end baggage car and only an echo remained along the narrow cut, he climbed onto the tracks, expecting to see moonlight shining on parts of O'Neill strewn bloodily along the cross ties.

He thrust his gun into its holster and stumbled to where he last saw the man. Lowered the lantern, searching for blood. Walking along, head down, he looked for a lifeless mound on either side of the tracks. Listening, he straightened and raised the lantern. A steep and rocky incline to the left ended at the river.

"Irish," he called, "are you down there?" He listened for an answer, but why did he expect one?

Jamieson dragged himself to Marble Station and sent a telegram to Major Gund and Colonel Disque in Portland with the numbers of the locomotive and a tank car.

Three days later he watched a bundle of the *Spokesman-Review* being tossed from a baggage car onto the St. Joe City platform. The headline announced that rifles and ammunition were discovered when a train stopped in Spokane. A photograph showed Captain Dengel holding up a Ross rifle in oil-streaked hands.

Chapter 87

Case of Malachi O'Neill

1. Full name of person arrested: Malachi O'Neill.
2. Number of case (Bureau of Immigration file): 54379/18.
3. Date of warrant of arrest: September 1, 1918.
4. Charge upon which arrest was made: That he has been found in violation of the Immigration Act of February 5, 1917, in that he did advocate anarchy, or the overthrow by force or violence of the Government of the United States or of all forms of law, of the assassination of public officials, and that he was a person likely to become a public charge at the time of his entry into the United States.
5. Date and place of arrest: September 1, 1918; Seattle, Washington.
6. Disposition of case: Warrant of deportation to England at Government expense issued November 13, 1918. Transferred to Ellis Island for deportation. Writ of habeas corpus applied for and, in anticipation of adverse decision, alien was paroled on own recognizance.
7. A new warrant of arrest was issued by the Department of Labor, charging this alien with violation of the act of October 16, 1918, in that he was a member of, or affiliated with, an organization advocating the overthrow by force or violence of the Government of the United States, i.e., the Industrial Workers of the World.
8. Status of case at present: Pending.

In re Malachi O'Neill, age 30, native of Ireland or Irish race; subject of Great Britain; entered from Canada without inspection at Blaine, Wash., in 1909.

Malachi O'Neill was and is one of the most persistent and dangerous radical workers of the I.W.W. in the Pacific Northwest. He admits to being arrested and detained on November 4, 1916, in regard to the Everett shootings from the *Verona* and several other arrests because of his activities in connection with the organization to which he belongs. He has been a card-carrying member of the I.W.W. since 1909. He refuses to concede that he is a member of the I.W.W. at the present time, merely stating in answer to a question on that point, "It's for you to find out." He finally did admit that he had never taken any steps to renounce affiliation with the organization known as the Industrial Workers of the World. He appears to be a man of average intelligence and undoubtedly is familiar with the methods and aims of the I.W.W. There is no question but that he has supported the organization to the best of his ability and has assisted in spreading the doctrine of sabotage as set forth in its official books and pamphlets. He has no money, no property, or home ties, and is a typical member of the migratory herd which constitutes the majority of the membership of this order. He was accorded a hearing on the charge of advocating and teaching the unlawful destruction of property. His attorney caused to be inserted into the record certain excerpts and passages obtained from the I.W.W. official literature that it does not teach the unlawful destruction of property and that the word "sabotage" does not mean the unlawful destruction of property, but rather a slowdown of labor. A warrant for his deportation was issued by the Acting Secretary of Labor.

He was accordingly transferred from Seattle to New York for deportation to Great Britain with a party of deportees on November 25, 1918. Soon after his arrival at Ellis Island in New York he was paroled from custody on his own recognizance until his case would be finally disposed of because a writ of habeas corpus had been filed by his attorney in the Southern District Court of New York. Believing that the writ would be granted, a second warrant for his arrest was issued under the act of 16 October 1918, asserting that he was a member of an organization advocating the overthrow of the United States Government, namely, the I.W.W. However, at present his whereabouts are unknown. Please advise me what disposition you wish me to make of this outstanding warrant of deportation since this is an open case in my office files.

P. A. Baker, Superintendent

United States Department of Labor, Immigration Service

Office of Commissioner of Immigration

Ellis Island, New York Harbor, N.Y.

August 6, 1919

*   *

From Commissioner General of Immigration

Washington, D.C.

August 9, 1919

Answering your letter of 6th instant, No. 54379/18, you are advised that the warrant of deportation issued in the case of the alien, Malachi O'Neill, should be retained on file in your office, in the hope that he may eventually be located. Please bring the case to the bureau's attention about January 1, 1920.

 For the commissioner general

Exact copy signed by Alfred Hampton, assistant commissioner general

*   *

December 3, 1918

Dear Addie,
Here am I back in Cork, having come home a Yankee and in good health. If you see Kate, ask her for me if she'll come to Ireland to be my wife. If she won't marry me, ask her to come, anyway. There's much work to be done here. I'll send money for her fare if she'll write. Hope you are happy with Mac. He is a decent sort, but wrong-headed. Wishing you good health, I am,
Your loving cousin, Malachi O'Neill.

Chapter 88
Marble Creek

The sow grizzly normally denned above the timber line. Driven from a favorite cave by a heavier male and nursing a slashed haunch, she stalked down into timber, falling snow feathering the tips of her rough coat, until she arrived near a creek where she'd spent late summer eating berries. Under a windfall of dead cottonwoods, a bulwark against winter wind blasting down the canyon, she found a black bear curled in a den dug into a north-facing bluff and roused it with a roar of carrion breath, and then chased it away. After enlarging the den, she raked her claws along one of the rotting trunks, tearing out chunks of weathered bark, leaving paper-like brown pennants fluttering in the breeze. She looked at the whitening world, pushed herself into the den, curled up and drifted into hibernation.

* *

Spring was greening the St. Joe River Valley floor, but winter remained in the mountains where Jamieson was cruising timber on the land Dovey quitclaimed him. Following compass lines, he webbed over crusted snow, paced off distances and drew maps; noted diameters of tree butts and measured their heights in terms of log lengths. The previous summer's fire had burned onto his land but, nonetheless, he estimated over two million board feet of virgin white pine awaited the axe.

Loggers were felling timber a few miles below in a section adjacent to the MacLean holdings, the main camp expanded to accommodate more lumberjacks and a new cabin for Addie and him. She said, "Now that we're married, what's mine is yours and what's yours is mine. I'll keep the books so we'll know how much of our timber is being cut by the MacLean crews. Alonzo is honest, but he may cheat a little." MacLean himself was making big plans for the grandchild expected in early summer, talking about a MacLean lumbering dynasty.

Jamieson thought about the woman who belonged to him and wasn't on loan for the night; realized he'd soon be sharing her with an infant. Webbing along a lesser tributary creek of the Marble, he descended toward their confluence, trees throwing blue afternoon shadows on white snow. Both creek beds remained frozen with snow lying deep, but the air was softer, and he was a contented man. Tracks of martin, cottontail, bobcat, even cougar, led to breaks in creek ice. He took a deep breath of pure air, clearing his lungs of smoke from an earlier cigarette. Raised his field glasses to the crown of a huge white pine whose tip had broken off, stopping its growth. He hoped the heart wood wasn't dead. Webbing to the tree, he chunked his hatchet into the bark, marking it for felling.

Wings flapped overhead. He'd disturbed a large owl. Watching it as he snowshoed past the tree, he misstepped, turning a web into slumping snow at the tree's base. Thrown off-balance, he pitched into the well, simultaneously feeling a tug on his haversack as a rifle shot rang out from the middle distance. A sharp pain tore through his calf when another shot echoed up Marble Creek's canyon. In numb panic he rolled behind the trunk. His Winchester was at camp because softening snow put a drag on his webs. Too scared to curse his stupidity, he flattened himself, unbuttoned his coat and reached for his revolver, knowing it was a futile gesture. Blood from his leg pitted the snow red.

A voice shocked the quiet. "Are you dead yet? I'm gonna kill you this time."

He knew how close that son-of-a-bitch was downhill from where he lay bathed in the stinking sweat of fear. He was a wounded prey about to be turned over by a predator seeking the tender place between bone and yielding muscle into which to sink its teeth.

Think! But his only image was of Addie's body lying against his the previous night. *Don't let me die now, you heartless God.*

The Marble lay down a sunless slope of blue snow with a drop over a bank to the stream bed. If the snow held him up and he reached the Marble, maybe he could creep along the bank and get behind Gerard. Surprise him with one clean shot.

His leg screamed its uselessness as he unstrapped his snowshoes. Holstering his revolver, he shrugged out of his pack and pulled off his gloves. Using the tree trunk, he struggled onto his good leg and propelled himself out of the well, using hands, arms and one leg to drag himself through snow. Another rifle crack, but he was alive. Clawing and kicking, he rolled down crusted snow and fell painfully over a brush-covered bluff.

He was still above the Marble, but sanctuary appeared within reach - a deadfall of snow-covered cottonwoods lying diagonally against the bluff. On two arms and a leg, he plowed through a snow wall to sprawl under the deadfall, leaving an entry hole. The dark cavity in the bank offered more protection. Then he inhaled the sharp odor of bear.

Gerard's menacing bulk appeared on the bluff's crest thirty feet away, silhouetted against blue sky. The rifle's black bore swung toward the hole and Jamieson. A bullet sputted into frozen ground inches from where he lay.

The sound awakened the grizzly. Snuffling, it extended a huge hind leg with claws grown long, flexing them in his face. Already among the dead, only the pain of dying had yet to be visited upon him. From inside the hind leg, close to its belly, a cub squeaked. A flickering chance, but he snatched at it. Reaching into the fold of the sow's leg, he scooped up the cat-sized cub and heaved it as far as he could out from under the deadfall. He squirmed out the other side, dragging the bleeding leg, causing a mantle of snow to break loose.

Her cub's struggling cries brought the grizzly to full consciousness. Snarling and mumbling, she uncurled, poking out a black snout below small gummed eyes. Jamieson withdrew his revolver; craned his face over a shoulder to see her; tasted sour fear at the back of his throat, bracing for the crush of jaws on his leg. He aimed where he hoped the soft spot between eye and ear would appear, but the cub's squalls sent her crashing through ice-covered snags out the opposite side.

Up on the bank Gerard peered down at the cub. The grizzly lunged past it to sweep the rifle from his hands and crunch into a shoulder and arm. She dragged him toward the frozen Marble and he screamed all the way to the creek, pounding her shaggy head with his free fist.

Jamieson twisted around, crawled back through the windfall, and past the cub to the rifle. He used it to pull himself onto his good leg.

Gerard glimpsed him. "Shoot!" he gurgled. "It's killin' me! Fuck's sake, shoot!"

Jamieson struggled up the bluff, suppressing his own grunts and moans, ignoring Gerard's screams, intent on distancing himself from the bear. When she finished with Gerard, she'd remember the cub.

Floundering uphill, he broke through crusted snow. Using the rifle as a pick, he jammed it into snow and dragged himself from the hole. Forcing his wounded leg to cooperate, he thrust the rifle into crusted snow again and again, pulling himself along, creeping toward the pine and his snowshoes. Tying on his webs, he wrapped his bandanna around his calf, trying to staunch the bleeding.

For only an instant he considered finding a safe place from where he could release Fats from his agony with a single shot. Decided he wasn't worth the bullet. He cleared the chamber. *A goddamn Canadian Ross!* Tried using the rifle as a crutch, but it broke through snow. He managed to steady himself with it and made some distance.

Don't it frost ya, Fats. Gobbled up by a grizzly when you should be doing life for killing Billy. He thought he heard Billy Sewell chuckle. *Had yourself a real circus there, Agent Jamieson.*

During his painful retreat, he dragged himself up a rise from where he looked back to see part of Gerard – his trunk maybe - lying in blood on the frozen Marble, where in the full bloom of spring the ice would blacken and rot. If the grizzly didn't return, smaller animals would have their share of him.

You're going to be a seafarer, Fats, a fuckin' barnacle- back. Snow would melt and flood the Marble, flushing his cadaver past the MacLean camp and shooting it down foaming whitewater canyons. The Marble would slide what was left of his carcass into the St. Joe, which would head him west through rapids to the head of navigation above St. Joe City. There the river would slow, curl and snake down the narrow valley, maybe maroon parts of his skeleton on a sandbar before carrying them past the MacLean Lumber Mill at St. Maries. It would sweep his remains to the Milwaukee Road's long railroad bridge at Chatcolet, where the turnstile opened for steamboats and maybe for Fats. His bones would enter Lake Coeur d'Alene, moving north across the lake, unnoticed by steamboat passengers or tugboat masters hauling brails of logs. At the lake's far northwest end, remnants would be sucked into the Spokane River, pushed along by a sunken log. A couple of mill hands would spike the log to pull it ashore at one of the sawmills lining the river bank, maybe at Post Falls. But Gerard's bones would flow on, plunging over the falls and through the narrow canyon where birds nested in rock crevices high above the spray. Scraps of him would rush down the swollen river, from Idaho into Washington State, unseen by passengers on the Electric Interurban running within sight of the river; through a valley where vast apple orchards would have burst into pink bloom; into the heart of Spokane and over noisy Spokane Falls, adding its roar to the cacophony of whistles and bells, shrieking steam and steel wheels in the train yards. On and on to the great Columbia River. Faster now. The sun rising and setting only a few days before his shards passed though Portland and Astoria, and then out into the foggy gray Pacific. *So long, you murderin' son-of-a-bitch.*

He packed snow against the wound and retied the bandanna, but its tightness hurt worse, impeding his efforts to get back to Addie before nightfall, so he pulled it off. As shadows darkened and the temperature dropped, the rifle didn't sink so far into the snow and he felt he was making progress. At twilight he lost interest in the broken line of red trailing behind him. Addie was waiting.

And then Billy Sewell was walking beside him, throwing a shadow on the snow. "How you doin', Billy? You're lookin' fit."

Pretty good, 'cept for the hole in my chest.

"I'm sorry, Billy, runnin' away like that."

I was already dead.

"No. Don't think you were."

You couldn't see me. Black as a freight car in a tunnel out there. Nope, I was headed west.

"Thought you told me to run."

I did tell ya. Just like I'm tellin' ya now to put one damn foot in front of the other.

He dragged himself a few more steps. The snow was difficult to traverse and his webs wanted to trip him. "I've lost the trail."

Yup. I can see that.

"Maybe it's my time. That why you're here?"

Can't rightly say. What's that? Another bear?

Titus lumbered up to sniff Jamieson's wrist with a cold nose.

"That's our dog. We went through hell together, that dog, Addie and me."

Must have missed that.

Farther down a lantern bobbed through the forest, appearing then disappearing behind large trees. He stopped to watch it. Sank to his knees. Titus had disappeared. "Can't go on."

I'll see you down the tracks, Agent Jamieson.

Titus barked deep in his chest and, through the trees, the lantern seemed to come closer, but still so far away. It would be Addie's face above the bobbing yellow glow. The moon had risen and her silhouette was trailed by shadows above sweeping lights.

He was kneeling in the snow when they found him.

"We're going home now, Robbie," she said, as strong lumberjack arms raised him up.

Afterword

The events in this novel regarding the Industrial Workers of the World, the Wobblies, are factual, including the Everett Massacre of November 5, 1916; the northwest lumber strike of 1917; and the military raid on the I.W.W. hall in Spokane on August 19, 1917. By coincidence, that same evening Irish activist Hannah Sheehy-Skeffington appeared at the Red Men's Hall in Spokane to speak on the troubles in Ireland. Chapter 87 is an example of actual reports produced by the Labor Department's Immigration Bureau regarding the deportation of Wobblies. The I.W.W. remains active, organizing marginal and precarious workers and supporting their strikes for better pay.

Colonel Brice Disque headed the Spruce Production Division of the U.S. Army Signal Corps in Portland, Oregon, and worked to bring peace to the woods and get out the lumber, instituting the 8-hour day and better camp conditions for lumberjacks. Although most Signal Corps soldiers worked in the woods of western Washington and Oregon, his officers carried into far-flung logging camps the Loyal Legion of Loggers and Lumberman - the 4L - in an attempt to displace I.W.W. influence.

Captain Omar Bradley, later of World War II fame, and a five-star General of the Army, spent nearly a year during World War I in Butte, Montana, in charge of federal troops, there to protect the copper mines from strikes and sabotage. He graduated from West Point in the famous class of 1915 - the class the "stars fell on." Despite his time in Butte, where he interrupted the 1917 Saint Patrick's Day parade and later led a raid on Finlander Hall, he didn't mentioned being stationed there in either of his two memoirs.

Father Michael Hannan was the "miners' priest" in Butte, who went on maneuvers with the Irish Volunteers. He was from Limerick, Ireland, and his bones were returned home when he died.

The historic Marble Creek drainage, where 80,000 acres of virgin white pine were logged, is today a beautiful recreation area. You can visit its information center and drive up the forest service road to locate a steam donkey and the remains of spill dams. I was inspired to center my story on Marble Creek after reading excerpts of oral interviews of lumberjacks who logged the Marble, in *Swiftwater People* and *Hardships & Happy Times,* compiled by Bert and Marie Russell, originally self-published.

There was a timber war on the Marble in 1904 and men died.

The forest fire in the Marble Creek drainage in the summer of 1918 was worse than I portrayed. An entire logging camp was burned, its garbage-eating pigs escaped by jumping into the privy hole.

Philip Ahern headed the Pinkerton National Detective Agency in Seattle in 1916. In the 1920 Seattle census, he and his wife had two boarders. Maybe an agency head didn't make a robust salary.

Captain J. H. Dengel headed the Army intelligence office in Spokane during World War I and Lt. Will Germer was an Army intelligence officer in Butte, Montana, during the same period. A Wobbly did die in detention in Spokane under Dengel's command.

The Canadian Ross Rifle was a failure on the battlefields of France because it easily became clogged with mud and the bayonet fell off. But it was a good hunting and sharpshooter's rifle.

If you enjoyed this novel, please leave a review on Amazon Kindle. Thank you.

Karen Charbonneau lives and writes on 66 wooded acres in north Idaho her parents purchased in 1951. She is also the author of *The Wolf's Sun* and *A Devil Singing Small*, available on Amazon on Kindle and in paperback.

www.ingramcontent.com/pod-product-compliance
Lightning Source LLC
Chambersburg PA
CBHW060141260626
47160CB00001B/69